The International Goos

By the same author

The Lawnmower Celebrity

Ben Hatch

The International Gooseberry

An Orion Paperback Original

First published in Great Britain in 2001 by Orion
An imprint of Orion Books Ltd
Orion House, 5 Upper St Martin's Lane,
London WC2H 9EA

A CIP catalogue record for this book
is available from the British Library

ISBN 0 75284 385 0

Typeset at The Spartan Press Ltd, Lymington, Hants

Printed and bound by Clays Ltd, St Ives Plc

Thanks to: Liz Evans of the Stoke Mandeville Brain Rehabilitation Trust, my brother, Richard Hatch, Susan Lamb, John McCrae, Ian Preece, Helen Richardson, my girlfriend, Dinah Robinson, Peter Robinson, and all the reps.

26 November 2000

What I imagine travelling will do for me: I will come back energetic, suntanned and wise; I will meet beautiful women from all nations who will sleep with me, love me, comment favourably on my eccentricities and not be bothered that my hairline is receding and in profile from forehead to sideburns now looks like the coastline of South America. My Trailfinders round-the-world ticket is for a year, but more than likely I will extend it and be away for several years. I will live the life of a hobo, see and learn about the world and develop a Zen-like mien of quietude that will unsettle all but the truly honest. I will meet incredible characters with elaborate life histories who'll feel the compulsion to confide in me, give me food and shelter. I will be friend of rich man and poor man alike. I'll swap stories with down-and-outs, judges and kings and become a guru, a famous storytelling traveller who has lived through every natural disaster known to man. Then, finally, one day, maybe twenty years later, when everyone has forgotten me, I will turn up on the random doorsteps of former friends and family with a huge straggly beard and knapsack, and possibly a strange flute. My face will be grainy, I will be bald but beautiful, probably with a limp.

'Yes? Can I help you?'

I will say nothing and maybe they'll start to close the door, and suddenly there'll be a glimmer of recognition.

'Kit?' they'll say hesitantly and I'll nod slowly, closing my cloudy eyes. 'Kit, my God, it's Kit. Jane, Sophie, it's Kit. Kit, my God, we thought you were killed in that mudslide/volcano/earthquake/crazy shootout in Bogotà.'

I'll shamble into the house and be made a cup of tea, someone will take my knapsack, someone else will run a bath.

Everyone'll be chattering around me excitedly, children I've never met before but who have grown up on legends of me will tug at my frayed trousers but I will say nothing and cradle the tea in my hands like a Chinaman.

Hours later I will finally say, in a throaty, memory-laden whisper, 'It's been a long time. A long, long time.' And in that moment everybody will know and gasp at the realization that their own lives have been worthless compared to mine. 'A long, long time,' I will repeat as I hear them on the telephone spreading the word.

'He's back. Kit. He's back. He's here now. What? No. He's hardly said a word. Something about it being a long, long time.'

Either that or I'll hate it and come back for Christmas because I miss deep baths and bacon-flavoured Wheat Crunchies.

> Subject: < The cool traveller >
> To: Tom Farley Thomasfarley@hotmail.com >
> From: Kit Farley Kitfarley@yahoo.com >

Dear Tom, So, my elder more foolish brother, you all thought I'd bottle it, but here I am about to start backpacking round the world, sitting on the plane next to Carlos and Dominique writing on my laptop with a bad case of trapped wind because Dominique's mini-rucksack is taking up all my leg room and Carlos is snoring like a fat pig and I can't squeeze past him to go to the toilet to guff it all out. Accessories I possess for this trip: 50-litre Millets rucksack; Millets mosquito repellent; Millets bubble tent; Peter Jackson fleece (really Millets, they just call it Peter Jackson to make it sound more cool); luminous yellow Millets anorak; Millets sleeping bag, the cheap lining of which is already torn from my try out last night in the garden owing to my extra-long big toenail and its fibrous width (half an inch almost). I also have three pairs of tight pants to stop my balls aching (the mystery of my achy balls continues) and a pair of walking boots I borrowed from you without asking from the garage at Beech Road that are two sizes too small, and which are gradually rubbing my little toes into points.

I've just said goodbye to Lucy at Heathrow. Needless to say, she cried, 'Who am I going to talk to? Who am I going to laugh with? I can't bear it without you. We've only just got back together and now you're going away. Kit, don't do anything stupid, don't go down dangerous streets or anywhere that looks risky, don't drink and drive, don't take drugs, don't just eat peanuts – they'll give you kidney stones. Oh God, I can't stand it.'

In a moment of weakness I harked back to the conversation we'd had the night before, the one when Lucy had told me she'd already decided who was coming to her hen night if we ever got married. Then she gave me a card before we boarded, a picture of a cylindrical-pawed teddy bear, clutching a letterbox, a reminder for me to write. 'It explains all the shit,' she said. It didn't, of course, but was quite revealing and has made me angry. In it she said she hoped I now realized that dog-groomer she ran off with meant nothing to her. She said she was glad I accepted I was half to blame for everything. She said she loved me, would act like a nun the whole time I was away if that's what it took to pass my test. Then she ruined it and launched into a tirade of self-justification. I knew she wanted to get married and have children but I had stopped discussing the subject. I hadn't bothered to look for another job and I'd taken everything out on her over Danny. I didn't do the washing-up when she asked, I dropped clothes on the floor and never picked them up, I never hoovered, kept going to the doctor's with phantom illnesses she was expected to feel sorry for me over, and forced her to cook me meals, and when she didn't made her feel guilty by eating unhealthy 'party food' like Kit-Kats. I was half expecting her to mention the crusty poo stains I leave up the back of the toilet because eating too many peanuts influences the consistency of my shit!

It still fucks me off. You can bet it would've been my fault if I got off with someone else, and yet it's my fault when she does. Where do women get this logic from? You're a bastard if you cheat on them, but when they do the same to you, it means there's 'something wrong with our relationship. It wasn't about him, it was about me and you.' Bollocks!

That Roman Emperor Justinian, who came back from a year-long campaign to discover his wife had slept through the entire Garrison of Rome. She probably told him the same thing, she probably made out it was his fault for not paying her enough attention, for not complimenting her on her new woad make-up or something.

Right, this has gone on long enough – I'm going to wake up Carlos. I'm inflating like an airbed and must expunge this wind before it lowers the pressure of the cabin and the plane plummets into the ocean.

Kit Farley (brother and international-traveller, hobo and pal).

p.s. I have forgotten to bring a mallet so will have to bang the tent pegs in with your boots. Sorry.

> Subject: < hi from your father >
> To: Kit Farley Kitfarley@yahoo.com >
< From: Jon Farley Jonathan_farleyRBS@aol:com >

Dear Kit, Hope you got off safely. A whole year without having to lend you money: it's going to be very strange. I'm sorry I wasn't at the airport to see you off, and I have to say there was a feeling in the family you wouldn't go, and you don't want to hear this, but it does seem the height of craziness to leave Lucy behind after all you two have been through.

Travelling with a couple who've only recently got back together, and who you've said yourself have their own problems, is this wise? That said, have a good time and try not to be too daft.

Something important: Jane and I will be setting a date for our wedding very soon as you know and I was going to tell you boys at the weekend and I've asked told Tom so I might as well tell you now, too: I was hoping you'd both be my ushers. I am going to ask Ronnie, Jane's brother, to be best man to save having to choose between you. I hope you understand. I know what you two are like for fighting. It does mean you are going to have to get measured up somewhere for a suit. Can you arrange that?

A word of advice – I know what Lucy did seems unforgivable, but there is always another side to these things, Kit. Ponder that a little on your travels. I've always said she was a lovely girl – i.e. Extremely tolerant.

Love Dad x

p.s. I've put £100 credit on that WAP phone of yours. I expect you to use it to call home once in a while. Don't waste it all on surfing the Internet for porn.

Journal Entry 1

A bit about me and the family: Mum and Dad married two years before Sophie, my sister, was born. Tom arrived four years later, then Danny six years after that, and finally me thirteen months later in June 1974 – bred for parts, as the joke goes.

The first place we lived was a small terraced house in Leicester. I can't remember the name of the street, but we had a red door with a knocker I could never reach and there was an electricity sub-station at the bottom of the garden that used to hum all night. There was also a power line that went directly over our garden, which used to spark if a tennis ball hit it. That's about all I can remember about Leicester, although I was aware we were quite poor then because we didn't have a car. Dad worked in the Royal Bank of Scotland in the city-centre branch off Humberstone Gate and used to get there on a little moped he rode wearing a see-through mac that made him look like a beggar.

My memory of childhood is hazy because we moved all over the place after Leicester as a result of Dad's various promotions. The places we lived in after Leicester: Heston in Middlesex (1979–83), Beaconsfield in Buckinghamshire (1983–4) and finally Beech Road in Aston Clinton, also in Buckinghamshire, where Dad still lives now.

As really young kids in Leicester and Heston, Danny and I used to fight all the time. We fought over toys – he hated the fact I had more Lego than him, and I hated the fact his bike was brand new and had a rack on the back. He'd bite the heads off my 8th Army 1:32-scale soldiers and I'd retaliate by standing on his Subbuteo players. We fought over television programmes – *G-Force* versus *Grange Hill*; over what puddings we got for tea – Minty Angel Delight versus Neapolitan ice-cream; over our favourite Leeds United (Dad's team) footballers – for Danny Paul Madeley, the skilful one, for me Peter Lorimer, who had the hardest penalty kick in the League. We could even fight over whose turn it was to take the first scoop from a new pot of Marmite. Mum always bought huge family-size jars of Marmite that lasted for months and it was the greatest honour in our house to break that smooth black surface.

Danny was jealous of my arrival and this is what the rivalry stemmed from, I think. He had a schizophrenic attitude to me for a long time. His public face up to the age of about six was very different to his private one. Danny used to have great fits of generosity when Mum, Dad, Tom or Sophie was around, where for no apparent reason he would give me large quantities of his toys. He used to rock me in my cot; he loved me so much he stuck his favourite *Jungle Book* stickers on to my forehead. But when nobody was looking, Danny would take back all the toys he'd given me and some of my own, too, and instead of rocking me he'd pinch. Like the Romanian secret police Danny had undetectable ways of injuring me, too: bite marks on knees and elbows that could be attributed to falls in the concrete back garden; he manipulated my arms and legs like a balloon twister; and he practised his own form of martial arts based on using his chin like a rubber truncheon. Pinning me down on the living-room floor, he would bury it into tender, unbruisable areas of my body: 'I don't know why he's crying, Mum – perhaps he wants his bottle.'

Later there were mental tortures, too. He would cheat me out of toys in ludicrous swaps that once saw me give up my entire Jemima Puddleduck action figure set for a toilet roll he'd painted gold and claimed was the magic key to a Sherbet Dib-dab kingdom in the cupboard beneath the stairs. A cramped, dark and scary kingdom it proved to be when he locked me in there for an hour: 'I don't know where he is, Mum – perhaps he's hiding for a joke.'

He made me lick his armpits for 10p and then refused to pay up. He challenged me to competitions he had no intention of winning to make me do things he wouldn't dare.

'I bet you my Lego fire engine you don't go up to Dad and call him a dick-head?'

'I bet three Weebles-Wobbles I will.'

In 1979 I was five and Danny was six when we moved to The Croft in Heston. The Croft was a step up from Leicester and we lived down a cul-de-sac a couple of miles off the M4 in a semi that had big dormer windows with double glazing to protect us from the sound of aeroplanes landing at Heathrow. There was a wasps' nest in the garden, and a plastic climbing frame with a rubber tyre which we used to swing on like monkeys, but best of all, at the end of the road there was a huge, mysterious brick wall.

Everything about The Croft was typical suburbia apart from this wall. All the men down the road left for work at 8 a.m. in their suits. People drove Ford Granadas, dug water features and kept tortoises. Then there was the wall. I remember it as being ten or twelve feet high, but it was probably half that. It had shards of glass embedded in the top of it. We were never allowed to ride our bikes near it and were told never to try to climb it, which of course is what we always dreamed of doing because of the noises we could hear on the other side.

Most of The Croft is a blur. I was there until I was about eight or nine. We went around in canary-yellow Leeds away kits; we learned how to ride bikes without stabilizers; we started in school and Mum met us at the gate with a carrot, even though we'd have preferred a Finger of Fudge. I can remember getting stung after sticking a cane gardening pole down the wasps' nest, and I think it was there that I also hatched a caterpillar into a cabbage white butterfly and Danny grew a frog from a tadpole to upstage me.

But what I can remember most, was the first time Danny and I peered over the wall. It was a few months before we left that house and moved to Beaconsfield and it was both the most terrifying and most exciting thing I'd ever done. We shinned up some rubbish bags the binmen hadn't cleared away and it was like glancing into a whole new world, stumbling into a James Bond movie. At the end of our boring little road we discovered there was an army base – soldiers, jeeps, men in camouflage shouting and scrambling through nets. For a week we silently watched these soldiers and then something terrible happened. I climbed up as usual, Danny pushing me from behind. I got my arms over the wall to support myself and just as my head came up a line of soldiers directly in front of me, not more than 100 yards away, raised their rifles. I had no idea it was the 192 Heston Army Cadet Force drilling. I didn't know what a cadet or drilling was. I was terrified. It felt, to my eight-year-old brain, as though the Germans – because they were obviously Germans – had been waiting for us. I'd been warned not to look over the wall, and now I had and because of this I was going to be shot just like the French Resistance fighters in the films. And then, just as Danny popped his head up alongside me, they opened fire. Danny saw exactly the same sight, but while he remained draped over the wall transfixed I leapt to the ground in one go before they could reload and ran home crying. I didn't tell anybody what I'd done and hid under my bed, waiting for the Obergruppenfuhrer's gun butt rap on the door.

Danny was still there, half an hour later, when my conscience got the better of me and I went back to see if he was all right.

'They're blanks,' he told me contemptuously.

'I know,' I said, and made some excuse about getting back for *Chorlton and the Wheelies.*

In Beaconsfield we lived on a new estate in Station Road, but we were only there about a year and again I can't remember a lot of detail except our cat Boots was run over when following his brother Wellington across the main road, and that Danny was in tears for a week because for some reason he assumed Boots was his cat, even though he belonged to both of us.

There were three focuses of family life then, all competitive forums: Sunday lunch, summer holidays at Gran's and Christmas. Sunday lunches, especially as we got older, were all about being wittier than each other; the jokes and put-downs used to fly around. Christmas was about upstaging everyone by being the most generous and thoughtful. By Beaconsfield Tom and Sophie had stopped coming on summer holidays with us. Gran lived in Cornwall and the competition between Danny and me would begin the moment we climbed into the car with the pub sign game – the one where you're given points according to the amount of legs on the pub signs that pass on your side of the car. On Newquay beach Dad threw a sponge ball in the air as high as he could and we competed to catch it, stumbling among the rock pools and stones to keep our eye on it. We played tennis, snooker in the Newquay Snooker and Pool Club, and family games of Monopoly, mah-jong, Cluedo and cards. The games were never played for fun – this was a by-product – but to win, and your success dictated how happy you felt because of the piss-taking. 'So, Kit, I've won black Maria, knockout whist, I caught the ball four times more than you, won the pub game, found a starfish on the beach and beat you at tennis. All you've won is throwing the pebble and anyone can collect seaweed. He's not having a very good holiday, is he, Dad?'

Left to my own devices, I'm not that competitive. I have a sort of negative competitiveness, I think, that flares up when I'm around other competitive people. I only want to win to stop other people who really want to win winning. In this respect Danny was my spur. Danny's motivation was different. He needed bribery. There was never any point telling Danny what to do from about the age of seven upwards: you had to give him an incentive. He learned to tie his shoelaces up in Leicester because Dad bribed him with a Captain Scarlet car. He swam his first length in the Ludvig Guttman Sports Centre in Stoke Mandeville because of the promise of a Joe 90 lunar hopper. In a way we stayed the same throughout our lives: for me it was always all about keeping up with Danny; for Danny it was about rewards. It's something I never realized until recently.

27 November 2000

It's 6 p.m. and I'm sitting in my tent on our first night in America. We landed this morning, and, after a two-hour delay at Atlanta Airport, caught an internal flight to Charleston, South Carolina. Even though Charleston is in the opposite direction to where we're heading (Los Angeles), we've decided to start the trip from here so it'll be a truly coast-to-coast drive.

Except when we got here we discovered Charleston isn't actually right on the East Coast as it had appeared on the tiny map in the *Rough Guide.* Folly Beach, the nearest stretch of seafront, was eight miles away. No matter how much we tried to persuade her, Dominique couldn't be bothered to come with Carlos and myself in the taxi for the ceremonial picture of us bathing in the Atlantic, to go with one we'll take the other side of the continent in the Pacific.

'I will just take two pictures in California of me in this other ocean and nobody will know,' she said, in her declarative French way. 'And, anyway, I am hungry. On the plane they promise muffin, but there was no muffin.'

'You'll know and we'll know. Come on,' I said. 'It's like Neil Armstrong getting to the bottom rung of the capsule ladder on the Moon and saying, 'Ner, can't be arsed. I want a muffin.'

She wouldn't back down, though, and in the end Carlos and I went alone, took each other's picture in the water beneath the Morris Island lighthouse, and met back up with her in the city a couple of hours later for some sight-seeing.

A bit of history about my friends: Carlos is my oldest friend, we went to school together. Dominique is his French girlfriend, who he recently got back with. The reason I am travelling with them is threefold: (a) because they asked me; (b) because Dominique is attractive and I will enjoy the odd glimpses of her nude; and (c) because, although I will end up becoming a lone travelling guru with a mien of quietude that unsettles all but the truly honest, it would be good to find my feet first with a couple of mates.

Dominique and Carlos went out with each other, originally a couple of years ago, but split up when Dominique realized what everybody else already knew – Carlos was playing around behind her back. After initially forgiving him, in the end she ran off and married John the Aussie backpacker on the rebound, claiming she 'didn't feel safe'. She moved to Perth with him and didn't speak to Carlos for almost four months. Then, wallop, last year she suddenly phones Carlos up and announces she's coming back to him, she's made a terrible mistake, regrets everything, wants him back, is getting a divorce.

I accept all this but not Carlos's romantic interpretation of it all. It's what he wants to believe. Carlos is being a sap. All that garbled Gallic nonsense she gave him: 'I will convince you of our complicity in love. We can recreate the fairytale. We can be grown-ups in love, instead of children.'

Bullshit – she's just unhinged.

These are my early thoughts on Charleston. Charleston is apparently 'America's best-kept secret', home to the hospitality and culinary skills of the Old South. The place is as Olde Worlde as America gets and geriatrics from New York and Los Angeles wander around lifting up their gold-framed sunglasses to marvel at the ante-bellum, *Gone with the Wind* architecture, which isn't even as old as the Post Office in Beaconsfield. I wanted to visit the old naval shipyards in Charleston's harbour where they used to store Polaris nuclear weapons, but Dominique persuaded us to spend the afternoon in a boring flat-bottomed barge sniffing azaleas in Cypress Gardens because of a leaflet at the Visitor Center that went on about the reflection of nature's beauty mirrored in the inky-black waters (actually, they were full of McDonald's wrappers). Maybe I have a downer on the place because I fell for another lie in the Visitor Center bumf: 'Make sure you walk down every alleyway, take a different route everywhere you go, because every street in Charleston is an adventure.' So I did and almost got mugged on Market Street by a hobo who didn't like the way I was staring at him retrieving a Burger King chicken nugget with a coat-hanger from a dustbin near the Battery Building. 'You followin' me, man. I seen you before. You followin' me. One day I'm gerner fire, motherfucker.' Good old-fashioned Southern hospitality! Things Charleston is proud of: (1) the way it cooks shrimps; (2) the fact that it was the first city in America to pasteurize milk; and (3) there is no (3).

> Subject: < hi from your son >
> To: Jon Farley Jonathan_farleyRBS@aol.com >
> From: Kit Farley Kitfarley@hotmail.com >

Dear Dad, Don't worry about me. I'll be fine. And of course I'll be your usher. I can't wait for the wedding. Very tired from the flight and an encounter with a hobo who threatened to shoot me for gawping at him retrieving rubbish. I am not running away from everything as I know you all think. Travelling is something I've always wanted to do. It isn't all about shagging Bunac students.

Honest!

Love Kit x

p.s. By the way, thanks for the mobile and cash top up. I've already spent half of it surfing Analbabes! Only joking.

> Subject: < The cool traveller >
> To: Tom Farley Thomasfarley@hotmail.com >
> From: Kit Farley Kitfarley@yahoo.com >

Dear Tom, Why haven't you replied to my email? You've reprogrammed your computer at work so you can play Tetra in 3-D: don't pretend you've been busy. Even Dad has written to me and he is a far more important man than you. Get to it, dullard. I'm writing this in the Old Plantation campground, eight miles south of Charleston off Interstate 17. It's our first night in the tents and although nothing extraordinary has happened today, tomorrow we're buying the Cadillac to start the drive west to LA. This is where the fun starts.

The plan is to buy a really old one with leather seats, white-wall tyres and one of those horizontal speedos with the needle-thin dial that you always see creeping up to 100 m.p.h. in close-up just before a bad-ass mows someone down on the *Streets of San Francisco*.

I haven't emailed Lucy yet, although I have thought about

her a lot today, but I think this has more to do with the context. So far, being with Dominique and Carlos is not exactly as I imagined. For some reason the banter with Carlos that I've been envisaging hasn't materialized. Perhaps it's early days. I also sort of expected some flirting with Dominique, especially after our arm hairs interlocked tantalizingly on the flight on the shared armrest, although she may have been asleep.

For some reason, when Dominique and Carlos spoke today I felt slightly excluded. I don't know why but I found myself walking a few paces behind them everywhere we went: round the historic district, round the Civil War Museum. It made me feel like their moody kid and I don't know if it happened because I slowed down to let them walk side-by-side or if they speeded up on purpose. Occasionally one or other of them turned round to check on me, as if they thought I might have wandered into the road or had knelt down to eat dog poo or something. This exacerbated the feeling. What do they think about the fact I'm going to be with them for a whole year? Carlos, I think, is OK about it: he's a mate, he invited me, after all, and he'll need me around for light relief, to go for beers with. Dominique, I'm not so sure. I sense something in her, a displeasure. I hope I'm just being paranoid. Like earlier on when I suggested we went to JB Pivotts Shagworld Nightclub tonight she ruled it out. 'It doesn't mean there will be shagging. The state dance is called the Shag. Haven't you read the *Rough Guide*?'

'I know, I just thought it might be a laugh to send postcards saying we've been shagging.'

'I do not think so.'

A few other things, too:

Number one: Carlos got up to go to the toilet at the same moment as Dominique on the plane, and because I looked up at her at that precise moment and made a joke about the Mile High Club, she said to me, 'I do not know why you are looking like that, Kit. You are getting nothing.' What did she mean by this?

Number two: when we were filling in our US Immigration forms just before landing, Carlos made me feel funny. Along with all the 'Are you a convicted terrorist? Have you ever been indicted for crimes against humanity?' questions, there was one about bringing non-indigenous fruits into America. Carlos's joke that he didn't know whether to tick the box or not, 'because we are bringing in Kit – and he is going to be a bit of a gooseberry' didn't sound too much like a joke to me.

Number three: this evening before we went to bed Carlos said to me, 'I still can't believe you're here, Kit. I had a bet with Dominique the night before we set off that you'd bottle it. I thought there's *no way* he's going to leave Lucy. Not that I'm saying you shouldn't have come . . .'

Other important details – I have been bitten by three mosquitoes already. Three nasty white marks on the knuckles on my left forefinger which will probably become infected and maybe even give me West Nile encephalitis, for which there is no cure, and which has apparently made a comeback down the East Coast of America. This is concerning me.

Take care of yourselves and each other, Kit Farley.

p.s. Has Dad broken the news to you yet that you're not even an usher at his wedding? I think he's going to tell you at the weekend. Sorry about that. It's not that he wants you to think he doesn't love you, although he doesn't, it's just, well, you know what you're like around his important banking friends – all that brown-nosing. Still, I'm sure you'll be in the family photos.

It's much later. I've just woken up in the tent gripped by fear. What have I done? What will it be like? Have I been a fool? Have I thought it through? Dominique, Carlos and me meeting outlandishly odd people, having hairy experiences in a Cadillac. I can't see it. Yesterday on the plane I could. Now I can't. Does this explain Dominique's pinched little face, the chin she retracts that makes her neck look like an accordion, when I make a joke? Is she lowering my expectations? Am I going to be a gooseberry? And Lucy. I've just got back with her. Dad's right. A few months ago it was all I wanted in the world to have her beside me in bed again at night, our bottoms touching lightly in the reverse banana position. The smell of her in her radiographer pyjamas. Will Lucy run off with someone else, go back to the dog-groomer? Of course she will. All that nun bollocks. She's probably with him right now. What's the time in England? Morning. She'll be having breakfast in bed with him, shagging him, getting her hair brushed with a metal fucking flea-comb. Shit, now there's a mosquito in here. I just heard it dive-bombing me. Fuck off, you bastards.

Journal Entry 2

It was Beech Road in Aston Clinton where Danny and I really grew up. This is where we became what we've been ever since: best mates. A lot of older brothers are embarrassed by their younger siblings and try to exclude them. By the time we reached Beech Road, aged nine and ten, Danny was never like this. At Aston Clinton County Combined, and after school on the recreation ground, I always hung around with his older friends, and even though he could give me a Chinese burn whenever he wanted, he never allowed anyone else this privilege, and he always stuck up for me in fights and arguments over whether shots of mine had hit the inside of a jumper sleeve and therefore gone in off the post or had hit the jumper full-on and therefore been deflected back into open play.

By this stage it was harder to make friends than it had been in Heston and Beaconsfield. You're more self-conscious at this age, and gangs of local kids are harder to penetrate, no matter how many keepy-uppies you can do. Those two years before we started at The Grange, in Aylesbury, it seems as though it was just Danny and me. We played football in the goal Tom made for us in his workshop at the back of the garage, we played snooker on the miniature table Dad got us for Christmas that had balls the size of marbles you couldn't put backspin on. Another favourite activity was making dying speeches lying on the sitting-room floor after watching black-and-white war films (hand on heart, head propped up on a scatter cushion, a German bullet in the guts): 'They got me, Kit. I'm finished. Stay with me, Kit. It's all going misty. I love you, Kit. Goodbye, Kit. You can have my Tonker toys, Kit. And my Tony Meo pool cue. And my Subbuteo table. But Kit, I want Tom to have the Lego.'

'Fuck off, I'm having the Lego. Tom can have the cue.'

We didn't go to other kids' houses much – didn't really want to because neither of us liked baked beans, an extreme social drawback in those days – and instead we invented our own little games and our own little world. While everyone else was collecting Pannini football stickers we collected car brochures, for instance. For birthday treats Dad would try to persuade us to see *Disney on Ice* or the latest James Bond, but instead Danny and I forced him to drive us round car showrooms in Aylesbury and Princes Risborough so we could carry out sting operations on the brochure rack while Dad waited outside on double-yellows.

The other thing we were into was teddy bears. Dad never minded the brochures – they probably saved him a fortune in birthday presents – but he worried about the soft toys. Dad's quite old fashioned and I think he thought there was something slightly nancy about the whole thing, and maybe there was, although I was too young to see it.

We had about a hundred bears, which we collected from car-boot sales held every Sunday on the waste ground by World's End Nurseries and fêtes in surrounding villages we read about in the local paper and insisted Dad took us to. In a way, although it sounds sad, these bears were our mates. They were mostly mangy soft toys with ears hanging off, stuffing sticking out, eyes missing. One of them – Monkey – didn't even have a face, but each bear had its own identity, and its own living quarters in a warren of Tesco boxes made into the Animal Palace in the shed extension at the back of the house. They had individual accents, too, from Henrietta, the thick, posh, plastic poodle down to one-legged Big Ted, who spoke like Jack Regan from *The Sweeney* and always won gold in the long-jump at Animal Olympics. (Years later, on Danny's armed forces radio show he would often use fake voices for jingles and spoof phone calls – the animals were his training for this, I think.)

While the real Olympics comes round once every four years, Animal Olympics took place whenever we were bored, which was quite often. Long-jump: chucking bears down the hall; high-jump: chucking bears at the ceiling; and the toilet game: open the toilet lid, stand at the end of the hall fifteen feet away and take turns to lob the bears into the bowl until there's a winner (always a puppet because you could scrunch them up and throw them accurately like tennis balls).

They went everywhere with us in a special teddy sack, except for family holidays at Granny Cornwall's – a three-bear maximum then because of the Fiat's compact boot. We each had our favourites. Mine: Big Ears, a female puppet donkey. Danny's: Brown Bear, the King of the Animal Kingdom, a commonsensical bear-ruler who drove a customized Lego holder and wore a doll's blue dressing-gown round his shoulders like an ermine cape. If Dad was worried about me, and years later he told me that he had been, he must've been shitting himself about Danny – a year older, almost eleven, without a friend in the world not made of wool.

I can trace the symbolic end of our childhoods to one particular animal day in 1984. Even though we were pretty well-off by this point, Danny and I slept in the basement in the same bunk-beds we'd had since we were six. It was always damp down there, even with the dehumidifier on, and it used to get invaded with all kinds of bugs – earwigs, woodlice, centipedes and beetles – that Danny loved because he liked to experiment on them with his chemistry set in the hope of creating a super-insect, but which used to terrify me. This particular day when I opened the teddy bag I found a live maggot in Brown Bear's mouth. Dad, seeing his chance, decreed Brown Bear had to go for hygiene reasons. Danny had been learning about ancient Egypt in Mrs Mackay's general studies class and decided that if Brown Bear, King of Animals, was going to die, then, like an Egyptian pharaoh, all his subjects had to die with him. We burned them all in the metal bin at the end of the drive, all one hundred of them. Dad, probably very relieved, poked them into the flames with an old cricket stump. Throwing them one by one into the inferno, Danny and I gave them all dying speeches in their appropriate accents. The thrill of it: Arbuckle's belly going up like a torch; Dog's ears curling like a speeded-up leaf decaying on *Wildlife on One*; Big Ears and Brownie thrown in together, husband and wife.

The biggest fucking teddy day ever, until the next day when we both woke up sobbing like babies at what we'd done.

In a way this sums up another aspect of Danny – his selfishness. As a kid, and later as an adult, Danny was always selfish. We always did what he wanted: we played the sports he excelled at and the games he was best at and with the toys he preferred. 'Whatever my fair share is, I want more than it' was what he always used to joke at meal-times as he leant over to take extra potatoes. But Danny's selfishness, although infuriating, helped you know where you stood with him: he'd never do anything out of politeness, or because you wanted him to do it. He'd always have to want to do it, too. It made it special being with him because you knew he wanted to be with you rather than anyone else, and when he did anything for you, made you a drink of Ribena, or bought you anything with his own money, it always seemed extra special. 'Danny, I can't believe you bought me that Matchbox car.'

'Yeah, and you know how selfish I am.'

It was always exciting being with him because you never

knew when he'd have some mad idea. Danny had become a strange mixture by the age of eleven. On the one hand, he could be incredibly sensible, almost nerd-like. He used to collect stamps in Beech Road, for instance, and arranged them all with tweezers in leather-bound albums on special Hawid mounts. Danny could spend hours in our shared bedroom looking at his collection through a magnifying glass, trying to spot flaws and perforation anomalies that might make him a millionaire. On the other hand, every now and again he would have a wild, uncontainable day, a Danny freak day. These days used to frighten the life out of Mum and Dad, because he could do almost anything. 'Get your bike – today we're going to throw eggs at cars on the Wendover bypass.' Or 'Kit, I've made a mortar bomb out of your pogo stick and a French banger. I'm going to hide in the garden and fire a block of wood at you when you next come out of the house.'

He got the whack twice at Aston Clinton County Combined – once for jumping on the back of a Shetland pony in the school stables after watching *True Grit* and almost breaking the pony's back. And another time for trying to hang a member of the first year with a piece of electrical flex in the music room. Everyone always assumed Danny would grow out of this behaviour, but I suppose he never did.

I've brought three pictures with me in my wallet on this trip. One is of Lucy in the *Bucks Gazette* newsroom where we first met; the second is of the whole family together that last Christmas; and the third is of Danny and me, sat at the end of the back garden under the shade of the cherry tree, in front of the rose bushes at Beech Road. We have bowl haircuts and we're crouching in front of a wooden bench on which all the animals are laid out. Danny is holding up Brown Bear and I am holding up Big Ears. It's the one I like to focus on when I try to remember Danny the way he was before.

28 November 2000

I was right. I am a fucking gooseberry. We're at a campsite in Congaree Swamp, near Columbia, the state capital of South Carolina, after a 120-mile drive down I-26 and I-77.

> Subject: <thieving twat>
> To: Kit Farley Kitfarley@yahoo.com >
> From: Tom Farley Thomasfarley@hotmail.com >

Dear Kit, My younger, fatter, more ugly brother. No real news here except that I've broken into the garage in Beech Road where all your stuff is in storage and stolen £39.99 worth of your things to compensate for the boots you stole, you thieving little twat. And I sent you a reply yesterday but you must have deleted it by accident because you're a flid.

Tom.

p.s. How's it going? Have you discovered if the Kit-Kat is an international biscuit yet?

p.p.s. Thanks for saying I'll still be in the family photos, only Dad must have had a change of heart because it seems I am the main usher now – something about you being incredibly boring and stupid and not being loved in the family. Also during the service you're looking after the car park – apparently to make sure nobody's car gets broken into. Don't worry, though, I'll bring you out a chicken drumstick during the speeches.

> Subject: <where are Bunac students?>
> To: Tom Farley Thomasfarley@hotmail.com >
> From: Kit Farley Kitfarley@yahoo.com >

Dear Tom, I didn't delete your last message. You probably carelessly keyed in the wrong email address, which is why it didn't arrive. I don't mind – if you can't think of anything funny to say to me then that's fine, just bore me. You don't have to lie and make up ridiculous stories about messages going astray. I understand you're not as funny as me and that this causes you no end of bitterness. But that shouldn't stop us chatting amicably. Tell me what the latest standard base-rate mortgage is at your boring bank if you want. There's no pressure. Just be yourself.

Actually, it's going shit. I was right, I am a gooseberry. Our first day on the road and Dominique has been a nightmare. We haven't bought a Cadillac. She thought they were too expensive. We're in a hired fucking Mondeo. Not only that: she sat in the back while Carlos and I drove because statistically it's the safest place to sit in the event of a crash. She made Carlos drive at 58.2 m.p.h. because it was the most economical speed, and wouldn't allow the air-conditioning on because she said it wasted 13 per cent of your fuel.

I can't believe it. The whole reason for coming to America was the driving – foot flat-to-the-floor, sunroof open, elbow out of the window, music on full blast, haring down the interstate in a car too wide to be overtaken. And there we were pootling along like Uncle Fucking Buck, listening to Dominique's Deacon Blue album, hungry but unable to eat because Dominique didn't want to stop or we'd get to the campsite when it was too dark to put the tents up. Whoopee – another Philadelphia Light cheese baguette and some Cheet-os, and of course we've got to drink the warm water before we stop and buy some that's cool and refreshing. ('I do not mind the water like that. Cold water gives me aching teeth.')

We arrived here in Columbia at 3 p.m. and walked round Woodrow Wilson's boyhood home. Then the next blow. I thought we were going to spend the night in town, get a motel, have a few drinks, meet some rednecks and flirt with college girls from South Carolina University with Ys on their tight sweaters, but that's when Dominique came up with the idea of staying in this fucking swamp. I agreed to take a look at it, but when we arrived and I complained the city was ten miles away and that mosquitoes bit me more than anybody else and that it was an alcohol-free area and in bear country, Dominique said it was too late to drive back to town and look for somewhere else, we'd been in the car for hours, it was getting dark, and she needed a shower or she'd have a massive allergic reaction.

'A what?' I said.

'When Dominique gets hot her sweat pores close and her body overheats and if she doesn't get antibiotics she passes out, don't you, Dominique?' said Carlos.

Dominique fanned her face with the map. 'A gen-er-al infection,' she said proudly.

So now I have five mosquito bites on a part of my back that it's impossible to scratch even with a tent-pole extension to my arm, and my verruca's bled all over my sleeping bag, the lining of which has split so much because of my extra-sharp big toe nail that I wake up covered in acrylic cotton-like material that makes me look like I've got dandruff. This Millets roll-mat is ridiculous, too. It's so thin it's the equivalent of lying on a slice of processed cheese. I brought a pillowcase with me and have stuffed it with my clothes, but the zip from my fleece digs into my head however much I plump it. Calling it a pillow is like filling pastry with dog-shit and calling it a pie.

Tomorrow I am planning to empty Dominique's suncream bottle and fill it with axle grease. She'll heat up like a kettle and whistle steam through her fucking pores.

Kit.

p.s. The Kit-Kats don't taste the same here. The wrapping is shoddy – no silver paper and the red paper we get at home is just cheap red cellophane here, like you get on a Blue Riband biscuit. And the chocolate is milkier and less prestigious. America's shit.

p.p.s. Thanks for saying you'll bring me out a chicken drumstick, but it's weird because Dad's just told me he wants you to be head-waiter at the wedding after all your experience behind the bar in the Five Bells. Then, after this, at the reception apparently you're going to be giving Andy at the Rising Sun a hand with the sandwiches and you're the designated driver, so you won't be able to drink. And, of course, there's no room in Beech Road, so you'll have to find yourself a B&B. Actually, I've got an idea: as soon as Ronnie gets up to give his best man's speech, why don't we start heckling him, then cause a scene about Jane trying to take the place of our real mum? That should liven proceedings up.

p.p.p.s. What are you doing for Christmas? Are you going to Dad's? I'm still expecting a present from you, by the way. Send it post-restante and make it big enough to walk round.

> Subject: < it's a nightmare >
> From: Kit Farley Kitfarley@yahoo.com >
> To: Lucy Jones Lucyjones23@hotmail.com >

Dear Lucy, We're camping in a swamp and I'm sat cross-legged under the canvas like Buddha writing this on my laptop. I can't sleep because my verruca's itching, my trapped wind from the flight is still slowly releasing (I've farted thirty-six times today), my balls are aching because all my tight pairs of pants have mysteriously vanished, and I've got six mosquito bites that are already going red and blotchy like squashed tomatoes.

We picked up our car this morning. It was supposed to be the big moment: Jack Kerouac, *On the Road*, the whole beatnik-thing. We were going to be like Sal Paradise, Dean Moriarty and Ed Dunkel, travelling round the States. Rides on Boxcars, drinking moonshine with Minnesota oakies, driving at a crazy 100 m.p.h., smoking tea, getting high on life, and on the scenery and smells of the Deep South. Except Dominique made us hire a Mondeo and then ruled out most forms of overtaking because our indemnity insurance cover isn't comprehensive.

The scenery has been excellent – we passed a creek that had an alligator sign next to it! Cruised along historic Route 77 for a while, passed hundreds of scary-looking Baptist churches with sixty-foot wooden crosses on their lawns. But Dominique has undermined everything with her long face. She seems to get more out of a pecan pie than anything else. Carlos hasn't helped by deciding to go on a diet. It means he'll only drink Bud Light and, if that isn't available, a Diet Coke. It's not even 8 p.m. now and they're in their tent pretending to read their books, but probably having it off.

What have I done?

Love Kit x

Journal Entry 3

I don't recall Mum and Dad arguing much when I was growing up, although I was often aware of an atmosphere – Mum banging pan lids around in the kitchen, slamming cupboard doors after hushed-voice exchanges with Dad; Dad drinking too much, then snoring in front of the telly, arguing incomprehensibly in his sleep, sometimes scarily with his eyes wide open: 'I have to say that is outrageous'; 'I have to say I don't agree with that'; 'I have to say you're being very unfair, darling'.

For years I had no real idea they weren't getting along and that they were only 'staying together for the children'.

Mum left us after a family holiday – camping in Lochgilpead in Scotland. Mentally, I think she'd been gone for years. We'd burned the animals the year before: it was 1985; I was eleven and Danny was twelve. We were told about it on the last day of the holiday after playing golf. What happened before that day is a blur. We stayed in a log cabin somewhere fairly remote and I can remember trooping through bracken with jumpers round our waists, Danny and I practising our Black Adder and Baldrick impressions. And I remember we played that round of golf very early on the final morning and that Mum didn't come with us to hunt for lost balls as had been arranged the night before.

None of us had ever played golf before and, although we were all hopeless, Dad was by far the worst. We teed off in driving rain and all scuffed our first shots. This went on until the third hole when I became the first to lift the ball off the ground. By the sixth hole Danny could do this, too. Dad never managed to. Because of his competitiveness, we thought he was angry about this: Dad would rather die than lose to either of us at any sport and we thought it was funny, very Dad. 'He's *so* competitive,' Danny whispered to me after Dad called him a lucky bastard when his ball bounced out of a bunker and on to the green. 'He hates losing *so* much,' I said when he complained our trainers were better footwear for the muddy fairways than his slip-ons.

Dad must have topped more than a hundred strokes by the time we reached the seventeenth hole, and when he really lost it halfway down that fairway after taking twelve air shots in a row it wasn't that great a surprise. The force of his temper was. For the first four swings Dad kept his cool, realigned his feet, and took a practice swing before readdressing the ball. But as it went on – and the pairs of golfers backed up behind us – he became more and more ragged so that for the last six shots he was simply a whirling flesh and metal whish of frustration. Danny and I warned him to keep his head down and he told us to fuck off. We told him to keep cool or he'd fluff his shot and he threatened to take us home. His club just went round and round in a wide arc as he took swipe after swipe. Dad hit the ground before the ball. He hit the ground after the ball, jarring his back. He missed the ball altogether. Danny and I retrieved the divots and as Dad got angrier and angrier we had to try harder and harder not to look at each other.

What made it so funny, I think, was the fact that after every monumental swipe Dad would shoot a glance hopefully down the fairway, expecting to see the ball flying towards the green. No matter how many times he missed, he still expected this to happen. That we couldn't laugh just made it even funnier.

Dad's eleventh swing was so viciously powerful that it threw him to the ground, but he still wouldn't give up and moved more quickly than I'd ever seen him move before to get back to his feet, only to take an even more forceful running swish that caused him to slip on the wet ground and fall over again, caking more mud down his side. Danny and I could barely contain ourselves.

We eventually finished the round. Danny was too scared to declare himself the winner and in the car we didn't say a word the whole way back to the cabin. I remember actually having to stare out of the car window and make lists of things in my head to stop myself cracking up. This will be a good Sunday lunch story one day, I thought.

Mum was out when we got back and Dad went straight to the shower to get out of his dirty clothes. Danny and I went outside so we could finally release the pent-up laughter. One of my happiest memories was to become one of my saddest in the space of a few minutes, because when we went back inside Dad was sitting at the round table in the corner of the cabin in his dressing-gown. Instantly we knew there was something wrong. His fingers were behind his glasses, massaging his eyes. It was the first time I'd ever seen Dad cry.

Danny and I were both bewildered. We couldn't believe that Dad was so upset about being crap at golf. I remember feeling guilty we'd been laughing at him outside and we went up to him and put our arms round his shoulders. But when Danny said, 'You're quite a good putter, Dad,' I started to laugh. Danny couldn't suppress a snigger as well, but Dad didn't join in. He got up, brushing us off, poured himself a glass of water, and with his back to us at the sink, staring out across the bracken, he dropped his bombshell. I can remember it word for word. 'I am sorry about this morning. It's just that I have to tell you boys something and don't know how to do it. Don't be upset, because nothing is going to change, I promise you that.' Dad turned round to face us. 'Your mother is leaving us, boys,' he said, before turning back to the window to camouflage his tears.

I think Danny felt the loss the most, because although I'm the youngest, Danny was always Mum's unspoken favourite. Tom was most like Dad grown up, but I think in Danny she saw what Dad had been before. Mum used to protect Danny: she'd lie on his behalf, cover up his mini-thefts from Dad's sweetie jar of coppers at the bottom of his wardrobe, stick up for him after the various Danny-freak-day outrages. For the rest of us it was always 'no' with mum. 'Can I have an ice-cream?' 'No.' Can I go and play on the fields?' 'No.' Dad was the person I went to if I wanted something. The same with Sophie and Tom. Danny went to Mum.

Mum and Dad's divorce later that year was quite exciting and it wasn't until Jane emerged on the scene a couple of months later that things began to change. I remember feeling very grown up. It made Danny and me feel like adults, and we used to practise our nonchalance, jostling for position in front of our wardrobe mirror to try out different accents for the best effect: 'Me mum and dad are divorced'; 'Yeah, mine an' all – we're brothers, innit'; 'Just didn't get on, did they?'; 'They drifted apart, it 'appens, dunnit'; 'Ner, we ain't got a mum. She ran off'; 'They're dee-vorced'.

Dad relied pretty heavily on Danny and me around this time. Tom was out with girlfriends and Sophie was at university. Dad stopped telling us off, gave us unheard-of freedom, and suddenly confided in us like adults: 'Boys, should I get the drains fixed or wait until the summer?'

'I don't know, Dad – are they very bad?'

'Boys – this meat pie has been in the fridge for a week. Do you think it's still safe to eat?'

'I don't know, Dad, is it mouldy?'

Jane, like Dad originally, was from Lancashire, a no-nonsense woman who worked in the marketing department of Dad's bank. Dad had always been a typical dad: he fell asleep in front of the telly every night; he used to brag about how long he'd owned his suits; he watched *Grandstand* in old slippers with the toe-end flapping off; he drank and smoked too much. But he was always jolly and fun and had a great barrel laugh that he seemed to roll out especially for Danny and me. Pretty soon after he and Jane got together – about four months after Mum left – Dad began wearing Calvin Klein underwear.

'Look at these,' I remember Danny coming into the living room to say, 'they're . . . Dad's!'

Then one day that winter we came home from school to find him turning in front of the mirror in a collarless Armani suit. It doesn't seem much on the face of it, but underneath we knew somehow it implied more. It scared us – things were changing.

At first we used to laugh with each other about it. 'Dad – you look like a James Bond baddie. Look at Dad, Danny, doesn't he look like he's building a death ray?' Dad laughed, too, at first, but after a while, after he'd been seeing Jane for a while, he became defensive. He thought we were laughing at him. Sophie had to have a word with us. 'Sophie, have you heard? Dad's bought a pair of Morell's. He's turning into Tubbs out of *Miami Vice* now.'

Sophie: 'Kit, don't take the piss out of him. You know how sensitive he is. Just be happy for him. He'll calm down. He's in lurve.'

Before, our house was always full of MFI furniture and bodged DIY tables Tom had made after he left school and before he followed Dad into the bank, during the time he fancied himself as a carpenter. Old ashtrays we'd made in school pottery adorned the mantelpieces as well. These slowly began disappearing: first into drawers and then down the dump.

'Daaaad, where's my balsa-wood breadboard? You know, that one I made?'

'I threw it out, darling – it was falling to pieces.'

Dad was having a second adolescence, Sophie explained. He began buying antiques. He started going on foreign holidays instead of to Granny Cornwall's. New products began appearing in the fridge: fresh strawberries and expensive meringues.

He bought a brand-new car, got himself fit at the gym and lost all the weight he'd put on drinking at the bottom of the garden in the Dad-trap, the little benched corral by the rose bushes he had Tom build after Mum left. It was fun for a while. We enjoyed the profligacy, leaving lights on and desserts uneaten, but after a while the more weight Dad lost, the more he smartened himself up and the more he spent on the house, the less he seemed like our dad.

Jane never moved in. She kept her house in Little Chalfont, but she stayed over more and more. Danny started calling me Hansel and I called him Gretel and we wound each other up about how our evil stepmother was going to bake us in the oven: 'God, she hates you,' Danny would tell me.

'Yeah, but have you heard about the plan to send you to boarding school? I don't know why, mate, but she despises you.'

We were horrible to her face, too: immature and sullen. We ganged up. 'No, we don't watch *Coronation Street* in this house, do we, Dad? It's for northerners'; 'Do you mind not leaving those shoes there, Jane. Dad doesn't like mess. Take them upstairs or someone will trip over.'

I remember Danny saying something to me around this time. We must have been in the final year of Aston Clinton Combined. He said, 'Kit, you know something? You are my family, I still hate you and everything, but promise me you'll never change. Promise me we'll always be the same.' I said I hated him too and promised and made him promise the same thing and I never doubted for a moment it would be true.

29 November 2000

Things have got worse. We're on the outskirts of Atlanta, Georgia, and I'm sleeping in my tent on a grassy knoll outside the Super 8 motel Dominique and Carlos are sleeping in after our first row.

It started this morning and has been brewing all day. Dominique woke us up at seven-thirty this morning and we drove about sixty miles down I-20, after buying food from a Wall-Mart – cheese, bread and bananas, plus the *Weekly World* tabloid.

Dominique's reaction: 'How much is it?' And after I'd told her: 'All right I do not mind,' in a voice that obviously meant she did.

I read the headlines out in the queue – the seven secret prophecies of doom from the millennium papers. 'Nooo,' said Dominique huffily, because she'd expected gossip about movie stars.

Carlos drove while I read aloud and Dominique planned the night's stay at Flynn's Inn Camping Village in Augusta, which she earmarked for us on the Trip Trik route-planner. This is how our conversations went:

'Kuala Lumpur, Malaysia – a man shot another man to death, but the killer had an excuse: he thought the guy was a squirrel.'

'What shit!' says Dominique.

'Yeah, but funny shit.'

'Uhm, your sense of humour,' says Dominique and folds her arms.

'Cops say Harun Marat, forty-five, was climbing the tree to pick fruit when the idiot hunter shot him in the chest, killing him stone dead. Marat stood five-foot-seven and didn't remotely resemble a squirrel.' I burst out laughing and Carlos looks over.

'I can't believe you paid two dollars for that shit. We could have bought croissants.'

'What was that last bit?' says Carlos.

'Marat stood five-foot-seven and didn't remotely resemble a squirrel.'

Dominique, in her high-pitched voice of outrage: 'Croissants would have been lovely.'

We passed dozens more Baptist churches today with weird names – Later Rain Deliverance Church, U-Turn World Outreach Center, Abundant Life Foursquare Church, Hephzibah Baptists – crossed the Savannah River, and hicky highlight was when we drove into Georgia.

We spent the day sight-seeing in Augusta, looking round yet more Civil War museums, more boring gardens, but fell out when we couldn't find Flynn's Inn Camping Village in Peach Orchard Road and because the second campsite off the Gordon Highway was too dirty for Dominique.

'They will break into the fucking car. I am not staying at a drifter place. No. Look at these womans. They are animals.'

Eventually we arrived at this Super 8 motel and this is where the argument really started.

'Well, that is a cheap day fucked,' said Dominique, blaming me for the fact we were late setting off this afternoon because I spent so long looking for an anti-bear pepper spray in the Regency Shopping Mall in Augusta, even though the real trouble was her map reading.

The motel room was twenty dollars per person, and because I'd sneaked in without paying to reduce the shared cost, there was only one bed.

'We'll toss a coin for it,' said Carlos.

'Yes, but what happens if it's him and me on this bed? I don't sleep with him,' said Dominique, pointing at me.

'Great, I'm on the bed whatever,' said Carlos, trying to smooth things over.

'Right, so I'm on the floor, thanks a fucking lot,' I said.

I lay down on the hard, cockroachy floor by the door feeling like their draught excluder, listening to them talk in muffled whispers. ('It was your map reading that got us into this. Why were you rude to Kit?' 'I don't want his verruca. And he farts all the time and plays with his balls.')

To make a point, in the end I got up and pitched my tent out here in the woods round the back of the motel and will now probably get gored by a fucking grizzly. Dominique's comment when I mentioned this possibility: 'Just lie still and play dead. They will probably chew your foots for a while then fuck off back to the woods.' Thanks a lot.

> Subject: < moaning >
> To: Kit Farley Kitfarley@yahoo.com >
> From: Tom Farley Thomasfarley@hotmail.com >

Dear Kit, Who woke up on the wrong side of his roll-mat yesterday? And I did not key in the wrong address the other day. It's not my fault you keep erasing them accidentally, you berk. Check your mail properly – it was a very funny one, too. You owe me a message, except when I get it I'll just erase it without reading it and then we'll be quits.

And stop whingeing about travelling. You're on your way to Vegas and the Grand Canyon and I got up at 6 a.m. this morning and got ice up my sleeve trying to de-ice my car with a Marillion tape box. Don't pretend you thought you were going to be a beatnik, either. You've got a WAP phone and a laptop, for fuck's sake. Wherever I lay my hat, that's my home . . . providing they've got a socket to recharge my lithium battery!

Tom, who sleeps soundly on a thick mattress with three pillows.

p.s. Everyone is going to Dad's for Christmas. Then, of course, it's the wedding. Um, the wedding. Your attitude to Ronnie being the best man sums up exactly why Dad has decided to get married while you're away. He's probably implied he hasn't set a date yet. That's a lie. He doesn't want you there because he knows how you feel about Jane. It's ironic that being the youngest, most immature and ugliest member of our family, you took Mum and Dad's divorce worse than anyone, because . . . drum roll . . . you were actually adopted. Oh dear, hasn't he told you that, either? He was going to wait until after the wedding to break it to you. Don't worry, I'll still treat you the same and buy you a Christmas present, although naturally you won't be getting a share of the will. Soz.

> Subject: < missing you >
> To: Kit Farley Kitfarley@yahoo.com >
> From: Lucy Jones Lucyjones23@hotmail.com >

Dear Kit, Just got your message. Have you read my card? You didn't mention it. I hope it explains everything.

Yesterday I called up about coming out to see you in Australia or Thailand. To fly to Thailand return in January would cost £500 normally but if I go courier it's £379. I'm prepared to pay this to see my loved one so give me the go-ahead and I'll book it. Ring me.

I miss you. Lucy xx

p.s. I cried all the way home from the airport and then emptied the laundry basket all over the floor when I got in to make it seem as if you were still around. Be careful, messy fool. I'm thinking about what you said at the airport now about getting married and it's giving me a warm glow.

p.p.s. I read there's been an outbreak of West Nile encephalitis in New York. I expect you'll think you have that soon. You haven't!

> Subject: < Jack Kerouac >
> To: Lucy Jones Lucyjones23@hotmail.com >
> From: Kit Farley Kitfarley@yahoo.com >

Dear Lucy, I've read your card and am going to try to write a reply, although to be honest I am slightly annoyed that you still think I'm half to blame for everything, because right now I must admit I don't think I was.

I don't think this trip is going to be like I expected. I've been doing my best to change the mood. The blurb on the back of *On the Road* by Jack Kerouac: 'Riding the rails, hitching lifts, driving borrowed cars at a crazy hundred miles an hour. Wild parties, drink, drugs. Uncertainty, loneliness and dreams synthesized by jazz.' Carlos's reaction when I read this out: 'Kit, you hate jazz – you listen to David Hiskith on Magic FM and you're considering getting a mini-share direct-line ISA with Lucy when we get back. Get real and pass the Cheet-os.'

Dominique's still a nightmare. Did you know her sweat pores close and she has an allergic reaction if she gets too hot? And she refuses to leave the interstates as she's scared of being car-jacked, which means all we see of America is tarmac and huge billboards for Burger King, McDonald's and places to buy station wagons. There's a hidden agenda to this, too. I think Dominique just wants to get America over with so she can get to Australia. She is dying to get to Perth, where she wants to emigrate with Carlos after this trip because she used to live there with her Aussie husband and likes the climate. It's causing strains between her and Carlos because he wants to stay in England. It means she doesn't stop going on about Australia and is being very stroppy with me.

She hasn't a fucking clue how to map-read, either. The Trip Trik route-planners we got from the Charleston Triple A, the AA equivalent out here, are imprecise, but she fails to realize this time and time again. She sees a picture of a tent with 'Camping' written underneath it, and, in the absence of an arrow pointing to where the site is, believes that it's exactly where the writing occurs beneath the tent symbol. Never mind that it's in the middle of an area ten miles square, she always believes it's where the writing starts. 'Just because the writing's there, doesn't mean it's there,' I had to keep saying. 'It just means that's where the space was to write it. It could be anywhere between the highway and the ocean. You could hide Richmond in there and we wouldn't find it.'

Camping isn't quite what I imagined, either. In the Bill Bryson books he's always meeting wacky characters, but in reality, because everyone is so safety-conscious in this country, the only people who camp are poor bastards who can't afford a home and *live* on the campsites, which aren't really campsites but RV parks full of shiny metal trailers and huge fat people who'd be at home slapping love-rivals on *Jerry Springer*. Rolling up at an American campsite is like moving into a different slum council estate every night – there's already a community there, who you've got nothing in common with, and who resent tourists passing through and beating them to their toilet block in the morning.

My new tactic for not coming across as a gooseberry, by the way: in company I always sidle up as close to Dominique as possible so everyone thinks Carlos is the gooseberry. Carlos has noticed this, I think, and keeps ruining it by putting his arm round Dominique and calling her ''Un', short for Honey, something I have never known him call her before. This is annoying me a lot.

Kit King-Gooseberry-of-the-Fruit-Bowl Farley.

Journal Entry 4

I'd failed my 12-plus the summer Mum left and instead of going to Aylesbury Grammar like Dad had planned that autumn, I went to The Grange Secondary School in Aylesbury. There was always a bit of suspicion in Dad's eyes that I'd mucked up the exam on purpose, because this is where Danny went, too. He enroled at the same time as me because the year before he'd been put down a year at Aston Clinton County Combined on account of his reading problems.

It was at The Grange where we met Carlos. Carlos is half Spanish on his mother's side and he'd arrived in the country for the last year of primary school from Madrid. With his jet-black hair, his tan and the way he mispronounced Js as Hs (Hames Bond 007 was always my favourite) he was seen as a bit of an oddity in the middle of Aylesbury. We'd seen him around school in his funny shoes and called him Manuel behind his back like everyone else. Then, in the second week of school he kicked Danny up the arse.

'Did you just kick me, Manuel?'

'Yes.'

'Why?'

'I have no reason. Shall we play football?'

And that's how we all became friends – a boot up the bum with Carlos's cloggy Spanish slip-ons that flew off like missiles every time he volleyed the ball during 21-and-up. In a way he's been kicking us up the arse ever since. We did what everyone else in school did for the first few terms: we swapped stickers at break-times, played split at lunchtime, had ink fights in lessons, crawled into each other's booth in the language lab to fool Mr Trudeau, our French teacher, and the rest of the time we either talked about or played football. Danny was impressed with Carlos's ability to do a Cruyff turn and I remember feeling tremendously proud I had a new friend who'd been to the Bernabeu Stadium. It was Danny and I who became Carlos's unofficial English teachers at school that year and me who stopped him running away from school when he didn't understand *pi*. I think it is what cemented our friendship.

'Shep-air-d's pie?'

'No, *pi*. It's a maths symbol about circles, Carlos.'

'App-ill pie?'

'No, it's not a pie, Carlos. Remember *beta* last week?'

'Beet-ah-root.'

'No, it's not food. Why do you always think everything's food? Carlos, where are you going? Mr Ayres, Mr Ayres, Carlos is running away again.'

There was no real jealousy between Danny and me about Carlos suddenly muscling in on our two-man band, because in a way he understood the score. Basically we were the brothers and he was that foreigner called Manuel.

In the third year we started learning Italian in Mrs Granley's class and joined in with the school obsession of adding Os to the end of random words, the best of which was always 'It's three-thirty. Time to go homo.' Occasionally, in a cocky mood Carlos would use this joky cloak to try to drive a wedge between Danny and me. '*Uno friendos*?' he would ask Danny or me when he'd bonded with either of us over a bag of Flumps or felt on a high from discovering an extra blue bag of salt in his Smith's do-it-yourself crisps. '*No, due*,' we'd always say sternly, wagging a finger at him, and Carlos would never complain and just vibrate his fat bottom lip in a mock show of sorrow.

By the fourth year the three of us had become the focus of a small gang. It wasn't an ordinary gang, and probably owed a fair bit to the deformed teddy bears, thinking about it. Our gang was more like the playground equivalent of the film *Kelly's Heroes* – a sort of dumping ground for the school's outcasts. Simon was deaf in one ear, the result of someone throwing a French banger at him at the last school he was bullied at. Roger's parents were religious, and, worse, he was never allowed to watch *The Professionals.* Robert had been born premature with jaundice and was so woefully under-developed even at the age of sixteen that he had no discernible pubic hair and still had the spaghetti-thin body of a ten-year-old. Paul Lamb's father had died. Finally, there was Fraser Dobb, or Raise yer Knob, as he became nicknamed for reputedly once getting an erection in the boys' showers.

For some reason we never managed to penetrate any of the

cool groups in school. Carlos was Spanish. He still had a slight accent and every time he became within clawing distance of acceptance they'd rerun *Fawlty Towers* on BBC2 and he'd be back to square one. Danny was going through a terribly self-conscious puberty in the fourth year that finished him off. He went red whenever anybody mentioned virginity, child abuse or homosexuality.

My status was probably irreparably damaged in the third year when I contracted a rare muscle disorder called Guilhelm Barry syndrome that caused all my limbs to go flaccid and meant for three weeks Danny had to push me round school in a wheelchair. Every time I was late for anything from then on someone could be relied on to pipe up: 'He's got a puncture, miss.'

For most of the last years of school, despite not being particularly swotty, and often actual troublemakers, our gang was treated with contempt by our peers, the years below us and sometimes the teachers. None of this was helped by Simon Skeleton, the supposed school wit, who, noticing we were all short and flawed in some way, nicknamed us Snow White and the Seven Dwarfs (Danny, because of his pale skin, was accorded the questionable honour of being Snow White).

Not that it ever really bothered us. In our minds at least, I think, we thought we were so different, so completely anti-cool, we were almost cool. That's how we justified it, anyway.

Colin Hare started smoking so that became officially cool. In response we took 1p lollies to school in old fag packets and sucked them clandestinely behind the bike sheds, going on about how great they were with coffee.

We didn't work particularly hard, but we were the sort of New Romantics of schoolwork and took great pride in the appearance of our exercise books. We underlined headings in red with a ruler, carried top-of-the-range Oxford stationery sets, frowned on biros and wrote with expensive fountain pens from Fox's office supplies. We had our hair combed into ridiculous side-partings so matted together with hairspray you could probably have snapped them off and used them as frisbees. And while everybody else carried their books in Head bags scrawled with Tippex graffiti, we had attaché cases that for some reason we never used the handles of, but which we hugged to our chests like they contained uncut diamonds.

To compensate for our collective ostracism we had our own topsy-turvy code of ethics, too, and were very strict on any affectation of coolness among members of our group. Roger was almost excommunicated for expressing an interest in Lloyd Cole and wearing mittens with the fingertips missing. Another pariah, Alex Rose, who suffered from psoriasis, infiltrated our group for a term but was banished when he started imitating the way Bruce, the captain of the football team, rolled up his shirtsleeves.

It wasn't that we were goody-goodies. Just like at primary school, Danny managed to get himself the whack twice – once for hiding in the steepled beams of the biology room and making *ribbet* noises during the dissection of a frog, and once (Carlos and I received it this time as well) for persistently following the nervous supply teacher Mrs Gerrard around the school at lunchtimes in a thin crocodile formation.

'Please stop following me, boys.'

'No, Mrs Gerrard, we're heading for the engineering block, too.'

'I don't understand why you are doing this.'

'Doing what, Mrs Gerrard?'

For some reason, getting into trouble never did for our reputations what it seemed to do for other people's. Because we weren't smoking, because we didn't sit on the steps of the geography block looking moody while trying to stick our hands up the skirts of second years, it just confirmed in everyone's eyes the major crime of secondary school: 'They're *sooo* immature.'

We were always into something. Danny's enthusiasms could be almost anything: from obsessions with gory horror films to following the tenets of various religions. After watching *Flesh for Dracula*, in the summer of the fifth form Danny had a fantasy about the ecstasy of biting the throat of a really beautiful girl, and Carlos and I had to wear thick clothes for several weeks even when it was really hot in case he tried to bite us. The next week he'd go to the opposite extreme and become a vegetarian.

I look back on school as a golden era. We all did pretty well – none of us was a high-flyer, but we weren't in the dunce sets either, but more important than that, I don't think a day went by without a belly-laugh, a real laugh, one of those laughs that make your eyes water and hurt your stomach and give you an incredible adrenalin rush afterwards, and which you only really have with this intensity as a teenager because you've got your whole life ahead of you and you feel for the first time that you've got real friends. Blocking up the oil heaters in the maths huts with dozens of chairs and watching Phil the caretaker through the keyhole sighing as he has to remove them. The day Colin Hare spat in Danny's eye on the playing fields and Danny walked all the way to the headmaster's office, across the entire school, with his head tilted back to protect the sticky evidence to get Colin the whack. 'Bad news, Mr Anthony,' pointing at it, 'Colin Hare's just flobbed in my eye.'

Hundreds of big laughs.

30 November 2000

Today we drove 133 miles down I–20, and now we're in Stone Mountain National Park, sixteen miles east of Atlanta off Highway 78, and we're getting ready to go out.

Funnily enough, it was Carlos and Dominique who argued today, when we were trying to find the World of Coca-Cola in Atlanta (full of lard-arse Americans who stampeded into the free tasting room when the security rope was let up, and then puked all over the toilet seats after overfacing themselves on

Sunkist). Dominique was up to her old tricks again. She couldn't work out where Martin Luther King Jr Drive was, and Carlos ended up driving down a one-way street the wrong way, nearly crashing when his cap fell off and doing a U-turn across three lanes of traffic. Dominique exacerbated the situation by throwing the map over her shoulder and putting her trainers on as if she was going to get out of the car and storm off. Then she sulkily said that she wished that during Carlos's emergency stop she hadn't had her seatbelt on, so her head would have smashed into the front seat: 'I would have looked at you with the blood trickling down my face and I would have said, "Are you satisfied now?" You are not a civilized man, Carlos.'

I was almost disappointed when Carlos bought her a blueberry doughnut outside the Turner Broadcasting Building to make up because I was enjoying being the middleman for a change.

Carlos's weight is an obsession for both him and Dominique, and the holiday joke has become that Carlos and I are trying to make each other fatter. We had a competition to see who was least sweaty when we climbed Stone Mountain this afternoon, and at the World of Coca-Cola Carlos kept trying to get me to drink cups of fizzy orange, claiming they were new diet-variety Fantas. The weight thing's good because it allows us all to join in. Carlos and I can have a laugh and be competitive, which we enjoy, and Dominique is pleased because Carlos is slimming down from his bulky pre-holiday thirteen stones. Perhaps this is the answer.

> Subject: < letter? >
> To: Kit Farley Kitfarley@yahoo.com >
> From: Lucy Jones Lucyjones23@hotmail.com >

Dear Kit, Please don't say that you don't really think you were half to blame for us splitting up. You know how much that annoys me. Can't we just forget it? I'm missing you terribly and have been investigating flights to Thailand and Australia again. Courier flights are a no, no. They've all gone.

You are missing me, aren't you? I'm not being a fool, waiting for you? Is it any better?

Love Lucy xxx

p.s. Where's my letter?

> Subject: < Re: letter? >
> To: Lucy Jones Lucyjones23@hotmail.com >
> From: Kit Farley Kitfarley@yahoo.com >

Dear Lucy, We arrived in Atlanta this afternoon, and we're now in Stone Mountain National Park, camping next to an artificial lake near a granite mountain that looks like a Christmas pudding. It's been better today and this park is quite serene. I've seen a heron and a raccoon. Apparently, in the lake behind us there are kingfishers.

All around us there are little concrete areas to make bonfires in and there are a few families cooking sausages, although they're not very friendly. They try not to meet your eye as you walk to the comfort station. There isn't a camping muck-in mentality. Americans prefer Winnebagos so they can be locked behind a door at night. This country is paranoid about crime. Everything is drive-thru so you don't have to stop and get out of your car and risk a mugging – drive-thru cinemas, restaurants, banks, even laundromats. And the only time anybody is friendly is when they're behind a counter, telling you to have a nice day. Any time it's unstructured and random, like if you smile at people on the street or let them through at road junctions, they just ignore you in case you're a nutter jammed up with drugs, ready to snap. We're about to go out and I've been wishing I was with you instead – we'd have listened to hickey radio stations advertising ways to shoot chipmunks; we'd have watched the shopping channel into the night in motels and made jokes about the Cartesian steak-knife set; we'd have had a laugh, given each other quizzes en route – 'Who built the George Washington Bridge we saw yesterday? How many states have we been through so far? What nasal infection did the hitcher we picked up in Reno say he'd got?'

I'm still upset about your card, but I'm trying not to think about it.

I'll try to send a letter when I get a chance. Carlos's driving is too jerky for me to write one in the passenger seat. And by the time we get to campsites it's dark.

Love Kit.

> Subject: < American wankers >
> To: Tom Farley Thomasfarley@hotmail.com >
> From: Kit Farley Kitfarley@yahoo.com >

Dear Tom, Americans show off about everything and I am beginning to hate them. The Civil War tableau on Stone Mountain, next to where we're camping right now near Atlanta, Georgia, is the largest high-relief sculpture of its kind in the world. And the mountain itself is the largest exposed solid granite edifice in the world. By this token I am the world's funniest ex-TV reviewer with black hair who is five feet nine inches tall and has a sharp big toenail that is gradually gouging a hole in his older brother's £39.99 walking boots.

Another thing about American towns: they are all deserted after 6 p.m. and when the Americans do go out it's to soulless chain restaurants like Arby's off the major freeways. It's the equivalent of Londoners spending a night in the Little Chef at the Gateway service station off the M1. I think this could be why we're not meeting anybody.

We've just got back from an evening out in Atlanta in one such Arby's and the big news is: I've discovered Dominique takes Prozac every other day (something Carlos neglected to tell me before we set off). It's a relief to know it's not me who's to blame for the bad atmosphere, and it also explains why she gets extremely overexcited about the quality of the Caesar salads she's eaten, and other times is a bitch from hell who gets in a strop all day because someone (OK, me) misread the price of a melon and thought it said 29c, but actually said 29c a pound and the melon cost five dollars.

This evening was awful. Carlos stroked Dominique's lower leg all night like he was linseeding a cricket bat, kept telling me he and Dominique were like 'one person' and at one point told me this holiday had made him realize that we weren't that alike any more. He said he didn't mind going with the flow, whereas I needed more stimulation.

'You are more hyper,' said Dominique.

'I don't think you're as good a traveller as me,' said Carlos.

Bollocks. I'm a fantastic traveller. At least I have proper skin pores and can map-read.

Kit.

p.s. It's funny how you seem to superimpose your own frailties on other people. I've been meaning to talk to you about your real dad for years. I am afraid it's Andy, the landlord from the Rising Sun. I expect you've always wondered down the years why you were so thin and scrawny compared to the rest of us. I gather Dad has only just found this out, though, and is talking about pulling strings in the banking world and taking away the job he got you at HSBC. Blood being thicker than water, and all that. I expect he'll calm down in the end and, like I say, I'll try to have a word with him, but I wouldn't go for your Moss Bros fitting just yet.

Journal Entry 5

The downside of being a dwarf and getting 'hi-ho-hi-ho-off-to-work-they-go' sung at us in school was that later, in the sixth form, when these things matter, it was difficult to find a girlfriend. Carlos had a couple of skirmishes at the school disco – even then he had the upper hand where women were concerned – but apart from my liaison with Emily Matthews (a forty-second kiss standing on a copy of the Good News Bible in the library after school in the fifth year), Carlos, Danny and I spent most of the final years of school mooning hopelessly after Nikki Aldridge.

We were obsessed with Nikki Aldridge at The Grange in a way that still makes me sad. The innocence of it. The total infatuation. The complete absence of cynicism. Nikki had perfectly even white teeth, wore very short pin-stripe skirts and laughed quietly, almost silently, like the idling of a very powerful machine, and was all of our first loves.

We memorized Nikki's games timetable so we could ogle her playing netball. We went to Aylesbury town centre on Saturday mornings, got Dad to drive us down, on the off-chance of bumping into her coming out of Etam. I even changed my A level options to be in the same classes as her.

The highlight of my last year in school was sitting next to Nikki in geography and trying to make her laugh. In history Danny, Carlos and I all tried to make her laugh. Carlos used to smile, stare a lot and pretend to know less about Charles V than he did for comic effect. Danny's tactic was to fall off his chair: he used to make sure he got the one with the broken back and waited for a dramatic moment in the lesson to plummet to the floor. Nikki liked that, particularly if he banged his head. I was more subtle. Nikki thought failure was almost as amusing as physical injury. Nothing made her laugh more than a really bad mark for an essay. I used to get a lot of very bad marks in both geography and history.

I had the advantage that I did geography with her and Danny and Carlos didn't. This produced some golden opportunities for taunting them: 'She wrote the lyrics to a Smiths song on my folder.' Danny had the advantage that four years previously, in the second form, Nikki had asked him through her friend Susie Spatan to go to a party with her. He was too shy to agree to go: 'She still has a thing for me.

She's only sitting next to you in geography as a way of getting close to me.' And she'd given Carlos a peppermint once in the dinner queue. He used to talk this up ridiculously, even though Danny always maintained the whole thing had been a trick and that he'd seen Nikki deliberately drop the peppermint on the floor beforehand.

The more we talked about Nikki the more we loved her and the more we loved her the more we loved each other and ourselves for being sharp and deep enough to fall for someone as fantastically overlooked as Nikki. After school at each other's house we'd ask: 'Would you cut off a toe to be Nikki's boyfriend?'

'All my toes.'

'What about a leg?'

'A whole leg?'

'No, half a leg. Of course a whole leg.'

'Maybe.'

'Fuck, you're fickle. You don't deserve her.'

I tried to ask Nikki out three times on the phone in the lower sixth but bottled it every time. Carlos sent her an anonymous Valentine's card with a Spanish greeting to identify himself that she never responded to. And the closest Danny got to asking her out was the time he hid in the branches of a horse-chestnut tree on her route home from school. He'd taken the day off school to be there at the correct time and thought it such a great plan he never told Carlos and me about it in case we copied him. The first time he just let her walk past without jumping. The second time she never came past at all – she had violin practice. His third attempt at chatting Nikki up became a running joke for years. 'Hi, fancy seeing you here,' he said as casually as you can pulling twigs and leaves from your jumper after leaping six feet from a tree.

'Yes,' she said walking on, 'you're usually up there, aren't you?'

Maybe your feelings for girls you've fancied and never said anything to are a bit like plutonium. You can bury them as deep as you like but bring them to the surface however many years later and they can still fuck you up. Maybe this explains what happened later.

Our other major concern towards the end of school was what we were going to do afterwards. It was assumed we'd all go on to further education. Tom and Sophie had been to university, so it was expected we'd follow their lead. The major problem was how the three of us were going to end up at the same one. In the end we aimed low to cover ourselves if one of us didn't get the grades. I was predicted three Bs, and Dad couldn't quite understand why I'd applied to Thames Valley, where the entry requirement was about one E. 'Can't you visit each other at the weekends? Isn't it time you boys spread your wings a bit, Kit? Come on, have you even looked at that prospectus for Edinburgh?'

In the end I managed to hoodwink Jane, always the softest touch in her desire to out-mum our real mum, and she convinced Dad it was a vocational decision. So off we all went.

'Dwarves on tour,' we called it. Danny got T-shirts printed. But again, and hardly surprisingly, we never fitted in. At Thames Valley it was quite embarrassing: Carlos, Danny and I were not only at the same university, we did the same course (BA in sport, health and fitness management) and even shared a room at Mrs Arnold's on Darwin Road. I'm sure everybody thought we were gay. 'Right, so you all know each other from home. And you're doing the same course and live in the same house and, shit, you share a room. Right, see you round, I'd better just check in with a few independent, normal people over here.' Only one person ever came to our room: a guy called Paul Foster, who Carlos got talking to about Freshers' Week at the bus stop outside the Co-op on about the third day. Paul Foster had no idea about our history and living arrangements. The fact that both Danny and I had the same poster of Stan Laurel over our beds freaked him out before we'd even started on the really scary similarities, and he couldn't have been out of that house any faster if there'd been a gas leak.

For a while we tried slagging each other whenever we met somebody new to give a little chink of daylight to any would-be new mate, but in the end the Stepford Wives facts couldn't be avoided and we were given a wide berth. We never made a single new friend the whole time we were there because we did everything together – played the same sports, skipped the same lectures, and all gave up after eight weeks of the first term because we were clearly too immature, hadn't gone to any lectures, exams were approaching, and we'd had official warning letters from the dean about coming to tutorials in our pyjamas (event nine in that year's Carlos–Farley Challenge, the giant competition we've been having every year since we were twelve, and which pretty much dominated the Thames Valley experience).

'You're not allowed to take your pyjamas off for one month, starting tomorrow.'

'Are we allowed to wear our normal clothes on top?'

'Only for one day. You have to decide which day. That'll be your joker.'

'I am going to do it when I have to give my talk on performance pyschology. I don't think it would be a good idea to wear pyjamas for that. It's assessed.'

Danny left first after landing himself a job back home at Muswell's wine bar in Aylesbury, then Carlos quit. I hung on for a week by myself for decency's sake, had a few interviews with the student advice team, then succumbed too. We tried to convince Dad the course was shit. What would we be fit for? Running a leisure centre? His reaction: 'I told you so', mixed in with 'Couldn't you at least have given up on the same bloody day? That's two weekends of ferrying your stuff to and from bloody Ealing. I do have my own life, you know.'

For the next year we lived back at home and Carlos and I temped in London, while Danny started doing a radio show at Stoke Mandeville Hospital and began dreaming up the ridiculous get-rich schemes that would infuriate Dad for the next four years.

The following year I went to Leicester University to study journalism, Carlos found himself at Plymouth University and Danny, who had a place at Brighton, declined it at the last minute because he couldn't be bothered to study any more and didn't want to give up his radio show.

It's strange, but although we were the ones supposedly furthering ourselves at college, increasing our future job prospects, Carlos and I were both jealous of Danny around this time. His great enthusiasm was no longer cannibalism or religion; instead he wanted to become incredibly wealthy. If anyone else had stated this ambition, it wouldn't have meant much, but as it was Danny it did, because to both Carlos and me it seemed inevitable that, with Danny's energy and force of personality, one of his business ideas would eventually come off. It never happened, of course, but Danny's schemes of that time are still legends in the family. Every time I came home there'd be a new one that he and Dad would be rowing about.

'Come on, Dad, get your bank to give me a loan. I'm going to charter a yacht and take people for cruises round the Greek islands. Martin knows someone in Kefalonia. You can make a packet.'

'But, Danny, you don't know how to sail, chartering yachts costs a fortune, and you're only nineteen.'

'You don't understand – leisure's the future.'

'Dad, guess what, I'm going to buy a big house and knock it down and build a bigger house on the same piece of land.'

'So, Danny, you're going to spend thousands of pounds on a big house and the first thing you're going to do is knock it down and make it worthless.'

'You don't understand – it's the land.'

'I'm going to set up a business making biodegradable golf tees. George on the leather stall in Aylesbury Underground Market knows someone who works in a lab and they'll help with the testing.'

'But golf tees only cost about 1p – you'd have to sell millions to make any money. And don't people pick up their tees? Please get a proper job and stop dreaming, son.'

'You don't understand – the environment's the future.'

'Pigeons are a big problem in London, right? It costs companies thousands to clear up their mess. What you do is market this powerful glue, which they can put on the window ledges. When they fly away – *voila!* – it takes their legs off. No pigeons.'

'But then you'll have all these dead, rotting pigeons everywhere.'

'Fucking hell, why are you always *so* negative?'

When I came back from Leicester three years later it felt like Danny had lived through ten. His enthusiasms were as irrational and contradictory as ever. During my first term at Leicester he once walked all the way to London from Aston Clinton to sit outside the Japanese Embassy waving a protest placard after watching a Channel Four documentary about whaling. Then two months later he was wearing a whalebone necklace to emphasize his summer tan. 'Yeah, but this is from a dead whale. It's recycling, isn't it?' He had another spate of vegetarianism that year after watching pictures of seal clubbing, but then caved in and had a peppercorn steak when Dad took us out for a meal at the Enderby Harvester and there was nothing but lasagne for him on the menu. 'I'm only eating it so I'll be sick to show you how your body can become accustomed to eating just vegetables.' He became a Hindu after watching a documentary about the Ganges, but jacked it in when he read about a famous guru who was supposed to have stood on one leg so long in quiet reflection that birds made nests in his hair: 'If you stand on one leg for that long, you'd get thrombosis.'

By comparison, my three years at university were a bit of a non-event, and what I can remember most is a feeling of extreme naivety. It was Tom who drove me up, all my stuff crammed into the back of Dad's Sierra. In the car park outside Tapworth Hall he gave me three things – a packet of condoms, £10 to get pissed on and some advice: 'Make sure you stick at it this time and don't wear your Wake Up with Wogan T-shirt – people will think you're a tit.'

And he was right – they did. Even after a year out I wasn't ready for further education. The first person I spoke to at Leicester was a third year I mistook for a first year in the dining room. I asked him some excruciating question about his A level results. 'I'm sorry,' he said, 'I can't do this,' and he moved away and sat somewhere else, leaving me alone with my meatloaf. Everyone seemed a lot more grown up than me: they knew how and where to go to do their washing, they had credit cards, a knowingness about indie music, girlfriends, cars, pot plants, posters of Che Guevara, kettles and views about current affairs and politics. This amazed me, and I stumbled around making terrible mistakes: somebody came back to my room for toast and found my 'Ghostbusters' single, a rumour spread that I liked Garfield, and I got drunk at the freshers' three-legged race and repeated what Dad was always saying – that it was good for the country that Thatcher had broken the unions. At the first gig I went to, 'Trips and Es,' said the pusher and I thought he'd said, 'Chips and peas.'

In the end I fell back on Carlos and Danny, who would come up to Leicester and stay with me at weekends. We'd go to nightclubs and have curries on the Belgrave Road and Danny would outline his plans to retire at thirty-five. The next week we'd visit Carlos in Plymouth. Then it was home to get my washing done by Jane. I remember Sophie giving me some advice around this time: 'At university you make friends who'll be friends for the rest of your life. Why don't you give them a chance – stay up there one weekend, get into it? Join a few societies.'

But neither Carlos nor I ever really did, because we knew if anything happened to any of us the others would be there. We knew who our real friends were and always would be. Carlos's broken leg in the second year at Plymouth: Danny and I took a week off to visit him in hospital – we were both there. Danny's sackings back in Aylesbury: we bailed him out and I reasoned with Dad – we were there.

So university was uneventful. I watched a lot of *Neighbours*, lost my virginity, ate a lot of chicken tikka masala, photocopied a lot of people's lecture notes, and graduated with a disappointing Desmond, as in 2:2.

In the three years we were away Danny had no serious girlfriends, failed to set up six businesses, tried three religions and got through five jobs, including three months as a Dan-Air air steward, which ended when the company went into liquidation, partly assisted by Danny, who'd somehow managed to contrive forty-six consecutive bogus sick days for ailments ranging from an in-growing toenail to yellow fever.

When Carlos and I came back home I remember there was never any doubt what we were going to do. We were just going to carry on from where we had left off. Carlos, Danny and I moved in together. This is the time I most like to think about when I remember Danny the way he used to be. It's when he became my best friend again.

1 December 2000

Another day heading west along I-20. It's been our biggest driving day yet – 438 miles.

It's amazing how the radio stations reflect the different states. In South Carolina they were all about hunting – people breaking off mid-sentence to discuss the latest raccoon trap. In

Georgia it was bigoted evangelists like Rod Parsley highlighting the ten-step path to a shame-free life, castigating homosexuals and the black magic of Harry Potter. Today through Alabama it was redneck-talk about drinking beer, gambling and Dixieland. We're now in the Vicksburgh Battlefield Kampground, Mississippi, where it's the delta blues and hang-dog black guys strumming on their porches and singing about people getting drownded in de riber.

I'm starting to tire of this same road we've been on for days. After a few hours it starts to hurt your right ankle pressing the accelerator, so you use cruise control, but this gets so boring that you end up playing little games to stay awake. I get obsessed when I am in cruise control about not breaking out of it, which can be quite dangerous when you come up behind somebody, because if you're only doing a couple of m.p.h. more than them it takes ages to overtake. It's a question of bottle: do you press the accelerator or try to squeeze through the little gap between the car you're overtaking and the truck on the other side of the road? Carlos plays the same sorts of games. He's had several near misses and Dominique has shouted at him three times today.

Camping is starting to wear me down, too. I'm sick of packing the tent away and the daily struggle to get it back in the tiny tubular bag. Dominique never seems to have any problem, and even though Carlos gets up late they're always packed up and ready to go before me. Whenever I finish first – always when Carlos is packing away the tent – I offer to help him. I pull up tent pegs. They never do. It's the first taste of the isolation for the day. I am bent double, sweating through the task, they are obliviously discussing the route using the Rand McNally USA map. I am never consulted on where we might be heading or for how long, and the decision is presented to me as de facto after I have shut away my stuff in the boot.

'What about staying the night in Vicksburgh?'

And what am I to do? I don't know the road, it would take

ten minutes to study it and they are already excited about their plans. 'I don't mind. Whatever.'

And to cap it all off I've just had a row with Lucy. I said I missed her, she said she missed me and I started telling her what a nightmare I was having, but then she asked why I hadn't called her on my mobile and wanted to know if she could take £20 out of my Halifax account to pay for half the collect call.

I said no: 'I'm skint. I'm living off a handful of peanuts and a sliver of cheese a day. I can't afford it,' and we got into an argument about what we were going to do when I get back because we won't be able to afford a house.

'It doesn't sound like much fun. Are you enjoying yourself?' she said at one point.

'Yes, it's fantastic. We go to bed at eight o'clock because Dominique's tired, I have fifteen mosquito bites on my body that are red and inflamed and make me look like Mr fucking Blobby. It's like being on holiday with my parents and my toenail is slowly shredding my sleeping bag. I'm having the time of my life.'

'Why don't you come back for Christmas?' said Lucy. 'This is stupid.'

I said I couldn't do that, and then she started talking about getting married and how she'd told all her friends about what I'd said at the airport and also about how she'd had a dream about having a green-eyed baby with my colour hair. I knew she was trying to make me feel better but I only mentioned marriage fleetingly at the airport because I was paranoid she'd run off with that dog-groomer again if I didn't and now I feel like I'm being railroaded. And I wish she'd stop talking about children. What sort of incentive is this to come home?

> Subject: < News? >
> To: Jon Farley Jonathan_farleyRBS@aol.com >
> From: Kit Farley Kitfarley@yahoo.com >

Dear Dad, It's now 9 p.m. and we're getting ready to go to the Riverboat casino floating in the foul-smelling Mississippi River in Vicksburgh wharf if Dominique calms down and stops moaning. I expect Tom's told you what a nightmare she is. She's not happy with the facilities here, of course – an open-air shower, she doesn't approve of. Plus there are two young blokes playing Bob Dylan music in front of a campfire with a bottle of Jack Daniels right next to us. 'Drifters,' said Dominique, even though they are clearly just high school kids having fun.

Another example: we noticed the tents had got damp between leaving them there this afternoon and coming back after a historic tour of the city. 'Probably piss,' said Dominique, even though it was just early evening dew.

And at lunchtime, when we stopped for a picnic in Birmingham and saw a beautiful bright yellow hummingbird hovering over us: 'Probably shit on our heads,' she said.

She is so much harder than she used to be. Whether it's her divorce, the fact she doesn't like America and wants to be back in Australia, or my presence, I have no idea, but I'm starting to think it's me.

On the historic tour we stopped at McCraven Residence. It's some general from the Civil War's house. I needed the toilet as soon as we arrived and Carlos and Dominique took the opportunity to split from me. This is something they've started doing whenever we stop anywhere. 'Catch us up,' said Carlos, they shot off to be alone, and I never saw them until it was all over. At the end of it Carlos asked if I'd had the audio tour and when I said no he said: 'You had to have the tour.' He's started getting quite annoying about this sort of thing, pretending he's getting more out of it than me. He's like it with food, too. In the supermarket he doesn't have bread and cheese – he has to have something more exotic and fat free, and goes off to buy sardines, and rare pâtés. He eats them in his gourmet style as if it's poached marlin with great sweeping gestures: 'You've got to try it, Kit – I'm going to educate your palate. Go on, have a bite. I'll wean you off cheese, peanuts and Kit-Kats.'

In England I always assumed it was Carlos who was the boss of their relationship. But it's the other way around. If she gets in a mood now, he gets in a sympathetic one, too. I then end up getting sucked into their orbit and get in one myself.

Tonight Dominique said the highlight of her holiday so far was the Caesar salad in Charleston. This is what I'm up against. Although it was a close thing between that and one she had in Columbia.

It's weird, but I keep pointing out beautiful scenery like you used to do to us as kids to try to counteract all this. It's greeted with the same disinterest.

'Look at that sunset, everyone – that huge sun melting into the brown earth with the silhouette of Tuscaloosa behind us and the sky turning coral pink. It's beautiful, isn't it?'

'Uhm – I wonder if the campsite will have soft toilet paper.

'Can you just shut your window a little, Kit? Could you turn it down a bit? Can we have the air-con off – it's fucking freezing in the back? Can you get the water out when we stop? This is a fifty-five zone, isn't it? Slow down – I am not getting a ticket. Have you got that fifty cents you owe me, Kit? Can I just have the map? I feel sick, stop driving so jerkily. Can we stop for a post office? And I want to get a croissant.'

End of today's outrages.

Kit Farley (pissed off and far away in a tent with faulty insect-proof netting).

p.s. If my ticket was structured differently, I think I'd probably think about flying home for Christmas, what Lucy wants me to do. Not that I'm hinting you should pay for it.

p.p.s. Have you got a date yet for the wedding? I haven't had a chance to get myself measured up yet. Sorry.

> Subject: < erase this and you never get another >
> To: Tom Farley Thomasfarley@hotmail.com >
> From: Kit Farley Kitfarley@yahoo.com >

Dear Tom, I had my first argument with Lucy today. Just as I start to miss her and think things will work out, she lets me down again. It's reminded me why I decided to go away in the first place. And to make matters worse she is now expecting us to get married when I get back and has started going on about kids.

What made you propose to Suzie? Can you remember? Were you suddenly struck by a bright light or were you just panicky about your hair falling out and the realization you'd never find anyone else who'd have you? For some reason I've got this terrible dread about it all. Images of me sitting on the sofa ten years from now with a morphine-stare on my face watching *Peak Practice* with the *Radio Times* on my lap, slippers on my feet, jumbo cords on my legs and a mild thrill in my belly because *NYPD Blue* is coming on later.

It doesn't seem fair somehow: Lucy runs off and shags a few people, including a fucking dog-groomer, and then she expects me to take her back without a word because she's suddenly decided she wants a kid with someone safe. I'm not even allowed to complain about it. Occasionally along the roadside in the more progressive states we've passed through there are these small Adult Centers with no windows that must be brothels. There are always station wagons outside with cardboard in the windows so their owners don't have to sit in a boiling car when they come out after their hand relief. Occasionally I have an urge to go to one just to get Lucy back. Can you imagine it? 'Dominique, I'm really sorry, I'll be very quick because I know you want to get to the campsite before it's dark, but while you and Carlos are having that salad I'll just nip in for a hand-job.'

This is the crux of the matter: Lucy's biological clock has ticked to midnight and now she has a zombiefied need to bear a child. I've always told Lucy that one day I'd like children. The truth is I'm not sure I even like them that much. When you sit down to a meal the conversation stops immediately when there's a kid around and all anyone does is watch them shovel food into their mouths. Even if Jesus was the other side of the table spilling the beans about his resurrection, or the devil was outlining just what it took to go to hell, you wouldn't be able to concentrate because you'd be checking to see how the kid was getting on with that tablespoonful of chocolate cake. I don't think I'm ready for this, and although Lucy plays it down I know if we got married this is what she'd want next.

And what about my own biological clock, ticking down and demanding a Ferrari Testarossa by the time I'm thirty? I don't go on about it and gravitate towards girls who I think could help provide one. I never dragged Lucy off to car showrooms, like she forced me to spend time with her friends and sisters with their babies. 'Look at that weeny steering-wheel and brake horsepower, Lucy. Promise you're not stringing me along. Promise me you do want a supercar one day.'

UNFAIR.

> Subject: < berk >
> To: Kit Farley Kitfarley@yahoo.com >
> From: Tom Farley Thomasfarley@hotmail.com >

Dear Kit, I asked Suzie because I loved her and it felt right and I never regretted it for one moment. My hair is not falling out. I have a high, aristocratic hairline, so fuck off or I'll stop emailing and you'll fall to pieces.

Seriously, I don't really know what to say about Lucy. Perhaps it would have been better to have stayed at home and sorted it all out before you left. Think of it from her perspective. You've gone off for a year and left her. She's bound to expect some commitment.

Tom.

p.s. Special gloves-off message because you sound down: I'm going to miss you this Christmas, you whingeing little berk. I opened the first door of my advent calendar yesterday. Do you realize this is the first Christmas we won't be together?

> Subject: < letter? >
> To: Kit Farley Kitfarley@yahoo.com >
> From: Lucy Jones Lucyjones23@hotmail.com >

Dear Kit, Feeling funny after the phone call. Did I sense you cooling about what you said at the airport? I only brought it up because I need something to look forward to, and just because I tell you about a baby in my dream doesn't necessarily mean I want one. Not right away. We can wait a year or two. And anyway, you want them, too. Don't you?

Other concerns: I know this is boring but I'm very worried about where we're going to live when you get back. The sixth-month lease on this house runs out in January and I won't have the three grand deposit to buy a house. The last thing I want is us being homeless or having to live in some crappy flat because you won't be able to help with the rent.

I hope you're having a good time because if you're not this separation is ludicrous. Why don't you come home for Christmas? It will be cheaper than me flying out to see you.

Lucy xx

p.s. When are you calling next? Please try not to make it collect next time. I really am broke and I don't see why I should subsidize your holiday.

Journal Entry 6

A pebble-dashed semi-detached house, two miles outside Aylesbury: 76 Tring Road. Carlos, Danny and I lived there for two years. It hadn't been decorated since the 1960s. The carpets had swirly brown patterns and were so threadbare they scratched in bare feet. We had an electricity meter that took £5 cards that were always running out in the winter, and there was no sofa, just four tiny chairs the landlord got from a clearance auction at a primary school and kept promising to change but never did. But it had a pub over the road (the Plough), fast-food at the Parton Road shops and a Blockbuster video shop, so we didn't give a shit.

We didn't exactly make the house any more comfortable: we never dusted or vacuumed in the whole two years we were there. The fridge never contained anything but I Can't Believe It's Not Butter and cans of Breaker lager, and the only time we used the cooker was when Danny needed a light from the gas ring. The kitchen always stank from the stagnant washing-up water and was regularly invaded by great brown slugs as big as socks which came through an air vent under the kitchen cabinets and left glistening trails over left-out Sunblest. The bath had a Plimsoll line of dirt, and we used a long-stemmed vase for an ashtray to save on having to empty it.

Although I'd been to university, I'd never really lived the whole student experience. Apart from Thames Valley, it was the first time away from home for Danny, and Carlos had been in halls throughout his three years at Plymouth. It felt like our chance to cut loose and we turned the place into such a cesspit that Carlos's various girlfriends had to be directed to his bedroom in the loft through the second-floor fire escape in case the mess put them off. Jane cried the only time she visited because she thought the squalor was giving us bad breath. Danny and I once caught a mystery virus from the germs that caused us to lose all control of our limbs in the middle of the night. I still don't know what it was, but I can remember us both jerking into Carlos's room and throwing ourselves on his Arsenal FC duvet: 'Carlos, Carlos, where have we been in the house that you haven't? You've got to call the doctor – we've got Parkinson's disease.'

Yet I remember loving every minute of it. We took

perverse delight in the horror and pity our squalor inspired in others. It was our private joke that we were consciously making our lives more miserable than they already were. There was a house rule that the telly was never allowed to be switched off. It ran twenty-four hours a day, and, because of a faulty volume setting, often turned itself up in the middle of the night so we were woken to the sound of the Job Finder announcer booming about a great new opening in the Birmingham Bovis factory. Then it became a house rule that we were never allowed in the kitchen. It was blocked up with the tiny school chairs and we ate on the floor from paper plates with plastic cutlery. Then we decided we were never allowed to throw away rubbish. The telly had to be raised on a plinth above the takeaway wrappers and the house became infested with mice, little brown ones that came out in the middle of the night to stare at you when you used the toilet and squeaked and fought under the floorboards.

When we first moved in I was working at the Unwins wine shop in Parton Road, doing occasional unpaid work experience on various local papers – the *Bucks Free Press*, the *Bucks Gazette*, the *Bucks Examiner*, the *Thame Gazette* – trying to get into journalism. Carlos was working in London at the same fruit-packing firm his dad was a director of and before Danny got his job as an armed forces DJ at BFBS in Chalfont he was working as a grade-one tea-boy at the HSBC in Aylesbury Market Square, while doing his show at Stoke Mandeville Hospital on Saturdays.

Our drifting and shit jobs never worried us because we had each other, a little world of our own, having competitions to score impossibly angled goals through the coffee-table legs using the uneven contours of the living-room floor and prising slugs up off the carpet with the fish slice and dumping them on the A41 outside our house to be splattered by the traffic.

We had lofty pretensions, too (all the more lofty because

we never did anything about them). The dream was that one day we'd commit the perfect bank robbery and get out of Aylesbury and live cool London lives in Camden, going to theatres, art galleries and trendy pubs with stripped-pine floors that served drinks in half-pint vases. Or else it would to be Brixton or Peckham to become part of the local culture – get into drugs, wear leather jackets and Ben Sherman shirts, know the owner of the local greasy spoon and greengrocer and have cool friends with nicknames like Manny, Muff, Stroller and Bigman. Danny read books by black former drug dealer Stephen Thompson, and would resentfully read out extracts from interviews with him in the *Observer* review section as we sat in the Plough Beefeater on Tring Road listening to a smug London band take the piss out of the locals between records: 'Do you have electricity here? . . . Any sheep shaggers in tonight?'

'What the fuck are we doing in the provinces? Listen to this. Thompson was suspended from Hackney Downs Comp after smoking a spliff in front of teachers. The teacher ordered him to leave the lesson and Thompson said, "Make me," and when the teacher tried to, Thompson and Big Man beat him up. Fucking hell, what was the closest we got to this sort of behaviour? Miss Redding sending me out of a music lesson for continuing to play the glockenspiel when she'd told everyone to be quiet. You did privately tell me afterwards, Kit, that Miss Redding was out of order because Tim Walton had continued playing the triangle as well, but it's hardly wading in for me like Big Man did for Thompson. Let's move to Hackney and take on the Yardies. Let's become drug addicts. I need a better name, one word that sums me up. Something like Narrow.'

'What about Twat?'

Danny was going to become a Radio 1 DJ, a cool one with a gravelly voice who used the word 'nuff' a lot. I was going to get a job on a local paper and eventually end up on a national as a quirky columnist. Carlos's ambition was slightly different. His hands are too big for his arms, his ears are too big for his head, his lips are too big for his mouth, and his head's too big for his shoulders – a combination of his unusual parentage, possibly (half Spanish, half English) – and at school it made him look like one of those Happy Family characters made from the wrong body parts – farmer's legs, postman's midriff, baker's head. Yet somehow, against all the odds and rules of symmetry, during his three years at university his physical defects had managed to cancel each other out so that in Tring Road there was a certain off-the-wall attractiveness about him that he'd just started to become aware of. Carlos's ambition was to become a 'a ladies' man'.

'Shall we get a vid?' That was the weekday routine, and when it wasn't Danny's action-adventures, it was Carlos's Richard Gere movies, which he watched like they were Videorama educational aids. 'Freeze-frame,' he used to shout. 'Look at that slimy cunt,' he'd shout admiringly at Gere's wheedling mug, and he'd then play the tape backwards and forwards trying to copy it. 'Kit, Danny,' he would then say for days afterwards, turning his face slowly to look at us as if the new expression was balanced on his head and might fall off, 'you're the most beautiful women I've ever seen. I want to know *everything* about you. Good? Or too creepy? What about if I narrow my eyes?'

Carlos's nationality had been a drawback in school, but in Tring Road it became an asset. Combined with his ugly-beautiful appearance, it made him seem slightly exotic and he always had girlfriends then, unlike Danny and me. A pull-up ladder led to his huge bedroom in the loft, which he spent the first four months turning into a lounge-lizard's lair. He installed light dimmers, painted the walls mauve, and bought a powerful Bang & Olufson stereo system. The joke was he could remove a girl's pants simply through the vibration of the bass during a *Moon Safari* track. He two-timed most of them, three-timed some.

I saw a couple of girls on and off in Tring Road, but in the two years there, apart from Wendy towards the end, Danny just had a single one-night stand. But relationships, like work, weren't that important. Or at least that's how it seemed.

On Friday nights we had a routine, which varied only slightly the whole time we were there. We'd start in the Plough for a Beefeater two-meals-for-£5 special, get a cab into town, drink and play pool in the Bell, where we'd usually end up discussing Danny's ridiculous plan to drug the tea at the HSBC on Wednesday morning when the cash float arrived and escape to Bolivia with £100,000. We'd then have chips and curry sauce at Sun Hong's in Kingsbury Square, take the piss out of the naff china dragons in the Hadleigh crystal shop and then go to the Gate nightclub in the basement of the Hobgoblin, where Danny would try out his latest anti-chat-up lines. He had a new one each week. We used to think they were hilarious, but maybe they weren't funny at all; maybe they just seemed that way at the time. They were always based on Danny making a provocative, off-putting statement. Carlos and I would chat to a couple of girls and Danny would wander over and then announce something ridiculous: 'Hi, I'm a potato,' he'd say. If he was ignored the girls were boring. If they joined in and said, 'Have you got any tubers?' or 'Are you a King Edward?' they were OK and we'd try to get them back to our house, where Carlos would attempt to have sex with the prettier one before they discovered the mouse droppings.

A lot of people, friends from university, family, say they didn't like me much around this time, and of course, looking back on it, I was a wanker. We all were. But we were wankers together; that was the important thing. What's the quote, 'man can make a heaven of hell, and a hell of heaven'? In a way that's what we did: we made a heaven of the place.

We used to have this theory then that everything could be funny. Everything had the potential to be funny. War, famine, disease, everything. Unhappiness was all perception and nothing bad could ever happen to you if you could laugh about it and have people to laugh at it with you. All that had to happen for everything to be funny was to breed out all the people with no sense of humour – that vast group of people who laughed at *Last of the Summer Wine.*

We really believed it. It was the answer to everything. Danny even researched it. There are four distinct phases of human evolution from Homo habilis, the first real non-monkey human, to modern upright man. They are all marked more by social differences than physiological ones. Homo habilis used fire, Homo erectus tools, Neanderthals buried their dead, Homo sapiens farmed. Why should evolution stop? It must still be happening. So what characteristic would mark the next great leap? It seemed obvious – makes fire, makes tools, buries dead, farms . . . *makes jokes.* This was the difference between modern man and his ancestors. The only real snag is that you'd expect the gene for humour to triumph through natural selection because it's such a likeable human attribute. People with a good sense of humour should be in charge. A sense of humour is the most valued characteristic in modern society – it's what people claim to look for in personal ads – GSOH. Nobody says, 'I am 28, tall, dark and handsome and have a total inability to see the funny side of life.'

The reason why people with a sense of humour haven't triumphed is because intelligence and humour are so closely related they're often difficult to distinguish. The cleverer a person is, the funnier they tend to be, but only up to a point. Beyond this point they aren't funny at all. Beyond this point they tend to be cold-hearted geniuses who spend all day inventing things, or devising new mathematical theorems for the rate that gases expand. Very clever people are freaks, it's a disability, an autistic form of intelligence, an intelligence with something crucial removed that can't accommodate paradoxes.

This is what we thought. Geniuses don't run the world because: (a) they tend to die childless; and (b) they don't have very good senses of humour and are probably very difficult to get along with.

'Hey, Newton, do you want to hear this really funny thing that happened to me today?'

'No thank you, I am redefining the nature of the refraction of light through a prism.'

'Suit yourself, egghead.'

The other reason a sense of humour hasn't triumphed is because what people without a sense of humour tend to have instead is a sense of self-importance. This sense of self-importance is directly proportional to how much you're laughed at. If you can't laugh at misfortune the only way to cope with it is to blame others for your misfortune – hence people without a sense of humour are often vicious. Also, it's difficult for people without a sense of humour to be likeable. Why would anybody want to be with people who can't make them laugh? To cope with this, people with no sense of humour become cloyingly nice, pretend to have a sense of humour by repeating *Fast Show* jokes, or lust for power so everybody at least has to pretend to like them. It makes them very ambitious, so they tend to be the ones in very good jobs, including ones in the arts, where they can crush humour and insist on having programmes on the telly that star Les Dennis. Almost all of the world's problems, from poverty to war and disease, are caused by people with no sense of humour.

Doing-things-for-the-memory nights were the big thing at the time. They happened about once a month, always at Danny's insistence. The idea was to leave the house and do something different, something outlandish and weird, that we'd remember when we were old. It didn't matter what it was. There were no parameters. It could be anything, so long as it was different and didn't involve ending up in the Gate claiming to be spuds. One night we slept rough on Wolmer beach in Kent where the Romans landed in 55 BC. We wanted to feel the echoes of history but ended up cold and tired watching three fishermen angling for pelting.

Another Friday we all took a week off work and hitched down to Dover, persuaded a guy in a pig lorry to let us hide in the back of his vehicle and sneaked into France without passports. We threw our credit cards off the ferry to avoid temptation and tried to see how far south we could get on five pounds, hitching, hiding in toilets on SNCF trains and still smelling of slurry.

At my sister Sophie's fiancé's stag night we pretended to be monkeys in a Soho restaurant and got so into the role I remember we couldn't stop hooting and climbing things for two hours and ended up alienating ourselves from everyone else so much that I was almost stripped of my usher role. 'What's wrong with Sophie's brothers and Carlos – they're chewing each other's hair.'

When we couldn't think of anything else we picked up and terrified hitchers at Staples Corner on the M1. Danny would drive my Fiesta in his serial-killer leather gloves and Carlos would sit mutely in the passenger seat shredding a bin bag with a roll of masking tape in his lap trying to look jittery and lethal. I would be hunched up in the boot with a sock in my mouth for authenticity, ready a few miles into the journey to start the muffled cries for help.

Looking back on it, I suppose we were making up for school and our lacklustre time at university. At the back of my mind I was aware it wouldn't last, that things would have to change. A couple of times it went to the brink – Carlos would apply for a decent sales job in London, I'd have an interview at a newspaper in another part of the country. But the end came quite unexpectedly.

2 December 2000

Today we drove another 400 miles down I-20, through Louisiana and into Texas, and we're now in Cedar Hill State Park, ten miles south-west of Dallas off Route 67. I finally had a word with Carlos this afternoon when Dominique was shopping in Shreveport, where we stopped for lunch. This is what he said: 'Dominique thinks you're niggling her. She thinks you're taking the piss out of her for being sensible. She knows she's very sensible and is sensitive about it. You have to know one thing about Dominique – she likes to feel safe. I'm not going to leave her alone at campsites. America is a dangerous place. You two have got to sort it out because I'm sick of being the middleman. You don't see what happens when you're not there. Dominique and I have been arguing about you from day one. She thinks I stick up for you too much. She wants to know why she's the one who checks us into campsites, sorts out directions and does everything. And for God's sake stop going on about West Nile encephalitis. There are 350 million people in America and there've been two cases. You're not going to catch it and it's winding Dominique up.'

I said the trouble was that Dominique and I had different priorities: I wanted to have more of a laugh and she was more interested in there being soft toilet paper at the campsites. Carlos said I was making out Dominique was really boring. That's when I made the mistake of saying, 'Carlos, is it the Prozac? When does she take it next? And why is she taking it, anyway? Do you think she's gone a bit nutty?'

Carlos said the Prozac worked on a three-day cycle and had nothing to do with it. He didn't say it nicely either. 'I'm serious. It's you, Kit. She's getting really pissed off about the bugs thing. Do you know, I was actually quite relieved the other day when I finally got bitten just so you'd shut up. And stop shitting her up about the bears, as well. You know what she's like. We're standing in a car park in a major fucking city. Look at you. Do you really need to be carrying that anti-bear pepper spray?'

That was earlier. It's 1 a.m. now and we've just got back from the Texan Steak House. Carlos and I went alone at Dominique's insistence, and she only joined us for a drink afterwards when Carlos went to pick her up from the campsite. The restaurant was two miles off the freeway we came in on this evening and was done up like a Wild West saloon. There was a wooden balcony round the perimeter that looked like you could break off pieces and smash people over the head. The staff said, 'Howdy,' everyone was in ten-gallon hats and my bumbag felt like a gun-belt when I unhooked it and put it on the table. Afterwards Carlos and I found it impossible to stop flexing our fingers at our sides as if we were loosening them for a quick-draw gunfight.

A 72-ounce steak was free if you could eat it, a shrimp salad and a baked potato in under an hour, and the bar was inscribed with the names of people who'd achieved it: Robert Ormond, age 30, weight 234 pounds, nine minutes (the world record). They'd all made comments: 'Right, where's dessert?' 'I'm going to puke.' 'This is nancy food where I'm from.'

The cowboy theme bonded me and Carlos and at one point he clapped me on the back and told me in an American drawl not to worry, things were going to get better, it was just America. He was sorry I felt excluded. Then he announced he was coming off his diet for the night. 'It's gerner set me back three days and Dominique's not going to be happy, and I can see you're mighty pleased about that, Kit, but I'm starvin'.'

There was a buzz in the restaurant, Carlos's picture was taken, but in the end he failed miserably. He didn't eat half of the steak and blamed the pressure of the attention and the fact that his stomach had shrunk from all the calorie-counting.

After he'd come back to the restaurant with Dominique, because of the stuffed grizzly head in the corner of the room, we talked about what we'd do in the event of a bear attack. 'Not again,' said Carlos, but he was laughing this time.

The evening seemed a success. I thought we'd cracked it at last, and then on the way back to the campsite Carlos took a wrong turning on Route 63 and we were completely lost for an hour, and ended up at the main gate so late the park was shut and we had to the call the park ranger out to let us in. It's amazing – one mistake and Dominique panics. She started fretting about a suspicious gap-toothed man in a station wagon who kept passing us, and Carlos and her ended up having a huge row that splintered off into all sorts of other areas: Australia, their relationship, why Carlos had broken his diet, Dominique's husband, who it turns out she called when we were in the restaurant. It went on back at the tents and was so bad Carlos ended up sleeping in the back seat of the car.

This is the bit that really got me. 'See what happens when you go on about bears the whole time,' he said, ridiculously blaming me when I went over to see if he was all right. 'It's what I'm on about, Kit. You can be really thoughtless.'

I've been lying here thinking about it: I've come to the conclusion that I am being used as the whipping-boy for Dominique and Carlos's problems. Carlos says they've been arguing about me, but I don't believe it. I think they're really arguing because Carlos doesn't want to emigrate to Australia and Dominique doesn't like living in England. It's creating friction, and because they can't accept the honeymoon period is over, they cast about for someone to blame for the bad atmosphere. Hey presto, who's that in the passenger seat scratching his mosie bite? Kit. Let's blame him.

> Subject: <letter?>
> To: Kit Farley Kitfarley@yahoo.com >
> From: Lucy Jones Lucyjones23@hotmail.com >

Dear Kit, Monday morning and no email from you. You know that's a cardinal sin – I'm upset. Are you punishing me by not writing? I'm sorry about that phone call if that's what it is – I'd just paid Lorraine my deposit and I panicked about money.

Lucy xxxxx

p.s. Have you written me that letter yet? And why haven't you answered any of my concerns about money? Why don't I feel like I am your priority? Feeling low.

> Subject: < bears >
> To: Lucy Jones Lucyjones23@hotmail.com >
> From: Kit Farley Kitfarley@yahoo.com >

Dear Lucy, I *am* a bit upset, actually. Your phone call reminded me of all the shit. I know I wasn't exactly the British Standards Approved boyfriend with a kite mark on his arse, but I still just can't believe you left me because I didn't help you clear up the house and dropped peanuts down the plug-hole. Your card upset me, too, if you must know. I'm not having a go at you, so don't get on your high horse. I've got plenty of time to think out here and I just want to understand it all, but it feels to me as if you're not facing up to what really happened and this doesn't help me get my head round it because it worries me it might happen again.

And, by the way, every time you mention money it feels like you're pressuring me. I can't believe you wanted to take money out of my account to pay for me speaking to you! Can't you see how that sounds? And stop going on about babies.

Kit.

p.s. I've phoned Qantas and brought my flight from LA to Sydney forward a week. We're making good time and I don't fancy hanging around with Dominique and Carlos any longer than I have to. It also means I will be in Australia for Christmas, if that helps with your arranging. The funny thing was Dominique then brought her flight forward a few days because she hates America, and there were no seats left for Carlos, who will now be stuck in LA for five days by himself. It serves him right.

> Subject: < my son >
> To: Kit Farley Kitfarley@yahoo.com >
> From: Jon Farley Jonathan_farleyRBS@aol.com >

Dear Kit, You sounded down in your last email.

Don't let this couple spoil this opportunity. Make sure you see and do everything. Take it from me, you will never get another chance. I may have some big news soon. I will keep you posted. In the meantime can I please have your measurements for the suit? Thinking about you, my lovely lad.

Dad x

p.s. If you are serious about coming home for Christmas it would be wonderful. Let me know your plans, and if it's a question of money, don't worry, we can add the air fare to your current debt. We'd all love you to be here.

Journal Entry 7

Wendy was Danny's only ever girlfriend in Tring Road. She was working as an occupational therapist at Stoke Mandeville Hospital, and he got to know her when he was doing his show there: she'd come into his booth to request Billy Bragg numbers. Wendy was insanely good-looking: model-length legs, long blond hair, a body to die for, beautiful, clear green eyes and a fizzy laugh that showed off her sexily crooked white teeth. She was also incredibly intelligent – four As at A level and a place at Oxford she'd turned down to go to Leeds because, although born in Surbiton, she felt she had a natural affinity with the gritty north. In many ways Wendy was a female equivalent of Danny: good-looking, veering from shy to outrageously frank and slightly strange in a vulnerable but lovable way. Her dad had died when she was seven. She'd never got on with her step-dad, had lost all contact with her mum and her brother had leukaemia. Wendy was needy, highly strung and, until she knew you well, would speak in a put-on doctor's voice that she used to camouflage her diffidence. Whenever she called the house we'd all have to reciprocate and wait for the right moment to speak normally.

'Hello, it's Dr Wendy. Is Dr Danny there?'

'Hello, Dr Wendy, Dr Danny is out of the surgery at the moment. If you'd like to call back. [Normal voice breaking in] Hi, Wendy, yeah, Danny's out. How's it going? Are you coming over?'

'Kit, can we carry on being doctors?'

'OK, Dr Wendy, I'll tell my secretary you called and when Danny's finished consulting I'll get him to call you back.'

'Thanks, Dr Kit. Sorry, I feel a bit nervous today.'

Wendy was a real one-off, and was so unreal it took me a while to accept she wasn't secretly taking the piss out of all of us in some unfathomable way that only she understood. Her real passion was for rescuing things – people, animals, the environment, the whole world: 'my Florence Nightingale thing', she called it. She gave away half of her income to good causes, had spent two years after university doing Voluntary Service Overseas and claimed to have carried around a fatal dosage of paracetamol in her bag for the entire three terms of Margaret Thatcher. The mice explosion in our house that second spring was partly down to her because she'd had a fit at the spring-traps we'd laid, and refused to come round again until we replaced them with the humane ones that the mice treated as buffet trolleys.

The theory is women go out with men who are roughly as good-looking as they are. Wendy wasn't like this, before Danny, anyway. Her boyfriends had all been extremely ugly. And not only ugly, but losers. One of them, whom she always referred to as Mush, because he trimmed mushrooms at a local farm before they were sold on to supermarkets, had had an ear torn off during the miners' strike and kept a false clip-on one in a jar by the bed. Another, known as 'Brick', was a shy, bald, forty-five-year-old hod-carrier whose wife had left him and who'd been in prison for GBH. Wendy was by turns openly contemptuous and ridiculously reverent of these people. 'I know he was hideous, but he put me on a pedestal and he had such a hard life I just wanted to bring some sunshine into it. He's such a good person, too. He goes to the Ashridge recycling plant *every week*.'

Danny was a friend of Wendy's before he was her boyfriend, and I think he was partly an experiment for her. He was a good-looking vegetarian then, and I think she decided it was time to take the advice of her gaggle of mostly lesbian friends at the Ceroc club she went to at Aylesbury Civic Centre, who were always asking her, 'What are you doing with that ugly loser, Wendy? You deserve someone attractive. Why don't you find someone who'll look after *you* for a change?'

Wendy joined us on our Friday nights around March time in the second year in the house and was often great company. When in a cocky mood she took the piss out of us mercilessly – Carlos over his schmooze den in the loft, Danny for his ridiculous theories, and me for my hypochondria. We liked having her around because she was so good-looking, tidied up, and was quite flirty if you said the right things about Brazilian logging.

But she could be wearing in large doses. She was very introspective and had a theory about the distribution of beans, a metaphor for confidence, that dominated her everyday life. After she dropped the doctor voices a couple of months down the line, every time she came round she used to ask, 'How many beans have you got today?' Then, 'My boss told me off today for taking Arnold Peake to the multi-gym so I'm down to about two. You look smart in that jumper, though, Kit. There, I've given you a bean. Now I've only got one left. Say something nice to me. I want a bean back, please.'

She'd never been on a plane because of their harmful emissions, didn't read a paper because she thought they were corrupting, and was always psychoanalysing, trying to look for good in us that wasn't there. 'Tell me, is this mess a rebellion against the capitalist chaos of the world? If it is, then good for you.'

'Wendy, we're just too lazy to get the Goblin out.'

A disappointed 'Oh' from Wendy, then her sexy laugh, because she could see how ridiculous she was.

Probably Wendy's biggest drawback, though, was that she had a way of morphing every guy she met into a victim. Because she liked sensitive, flawed men, you'd always find yourself talking up your minor problems to her, and sometimes, if you weren't careful, you could come to believe they were as bad as you made out. This is maybe part of what happened to Danny. After a few hours with Wendy we'd often have the following type of conversation with him.

'Boys, turn down *Baywatch* a minute. I'm being serious now – do *you* think I am emotionally retarded?'

'Danny!'

Pause.

'Shit, she's done it a-fucking-gain.'

Danny didn't see much of Wendy to begin with because of her other commitments, which suited Danny, I think, and the rest of us. She spent most of her evenings at her Ceroc club, or doing her Lady of the Lamp bit at the homes of the disabled men she cared for during the day, and whom she ultimately seemed to make far worse, because they'd often fall hopelessly in love with her. 'That poor, poor man. Three pages that love letter was and every word typed on that special keyboard he has to press with a knitting needle in his mouth. It's given me so many beans, sometimes I think I ought to give something back. Would you mind if I let him have a quick grope, Danny? You've got me the rest of the time. All right, what if I just let him accidentally-on-purpose rub against me?'

Wendy provided an injection of seriousness into Danny's life and Danny provided the exact opposite service for her. She taught him about left-wing politics and do-good religions; he taught her to take the piss out of herself. None of us ever really thought it was going to be any more than this between them because we all agreed the bottom line was Wendy was an absolutely gorgeous mate, but would be an absolutely *nightmare* girlfriend.

It was on our European holiday that Danny really fell for her, I think. It was a major turning point for the three of us because it was when Dominique first truly came on the scene as well. That three-week holiday in Europe in Carlos's dad's Renault Espace was the pinnacle of the Tring Road era, but the beginning of the end of it, too.

The summer of 1998. A year and a half into the house. Danny had his big DJ break at BFBS (British Forces Broadcasting Services) and was beginning to get serious about work. I'd had a couple of interviews at the *Bucks Gazette* and it looked like I was about to be offered a job in journalism at last. Meanwhile, Carlos's parents had announced they were thinking about moving back to Spain and Carlos was thinking about joining them there. 'It's Tring Road's stag night, we've got to go for it': that was the gist of the build-up.

We hardly knew Dominique then, and she didn't really figure in the preparations, although I think Carlos always had one eye on getting her back to his loft. She'd met Carlos at his dad's fruit-packing place, where she was temping as a secretary while she decided what to do with her life, and was only supposed to cadge a lift to Paris, but ended up staying the whole three weeks.

I'm still not absolutely sure what made the holiday so special – maybe that we all knew it was the end of living like students and the start of something worse: proper work. At the time, though, we assumed it was special because of Wendy and Dominique.

We took the ferry from Dover to Calais, travelled north up to Amsterdam, then south through France and Germany, eventually winding up at the boot tip of Italy, where we turned round and came back. The reason I'm vague about the route is that for the whole three weeks I don't remember once looking at a map. Where we were going just didn't seem that important. The days were spent driving aimlessly, playing games that Wendy devised as a way of giving Carlos and me a chance to impress Dominique (part of Wendy's Florence Nightingale thing was that she was a tireless matchmaker). 'Dominique, if you had to be stranded on a desert island, who would you like it to be with? . . . OK, but if you couldn't have Mel Gibson, and say it was down to, I don't know, one of the men in this car, say, discounting Danny, he's mine, who would it be?'

By then we'd more or less stopped doing-things-for-the-memory, but the presence of Wendy and Dominique somehow turned the clock back, and it was this that dominated the evenings. 'Tonight we'll pretend to be tramps and sleep in the doorway of the Rome Tourist Board. Belts off, everyone – we'll hold our trousers up with guy ropes. Pour that Steinlager over my jacket, Kit, we have to smell right.'

Digging up potatoes in a field alongside the Frankfurt–Munich autobahn because we were hungry but not allowed to spend money on food for twenty-four hours – another memory. However much you wash the spuds, however much you peel them with the penknife, they still taste exactly like soil. Dominique: 'No, I am not eating dirt. I am only eating food that grows above this ground,' but scoffing them anyway, because somehow the atmosphere made you.

Because Wendy didn't approve of anything illegal or thoughtless, it was always a balancing act between her stunts and Danny's. When we hot-wired a beach buggy in Cannes one night she took no part, became sulky for a few hours, and the next night demanded we perform some outrageous act of charity to compensate. We did runners from some restaurants, then at her insistence left extravagant tips in others. We stole petrol from petrol stations and then spent whole days driving around looking for pensioners to help cross roads to keep her happy. 'There's one. There's one. Quick. Pull over.

She's stepping off the kerb. Go and give her some beans, Danny.'

It was the same with the places we visited. A drunken night out in Paris would be followed by a tour of the Somme battlefield. If we spent a day at a funfair, the next morning we'd be off to Dachau. Often, much to Wendy's frustration, the sombre days provided the funniest moments of all. She wanted so much to educate Danny about the world and its inequities it often became impossible not to laugh, and I can remember a severe telling off she gave Danny walking up the staircase in Anne Frank's house after I stitched him up by whispering in his ear, 'It's no wonder they found her. She left the fucking door open.'

The opposite forces of Wendy and Danny, and the thrill of chasing after Dominique, gave the trip a context. In terms of the Dominique situation Carlos was the obvious front-runner, bearing in mind his loft track-record and the fact he'd invited her, but he didn't have it all his own way, and Dominique kept us both strung along for virtually the entire three weeks. Initially, in northern France, during the first few days when Dominique was umming and ahhing about going to see her parents in Paris, Carlos was in the lead. By Amsterdam, after Carlos blotted his copy book getting over-excited in the Banana Club, I took over. Then in Germany it was back to Carlos.

My high point was when Dominique almost stole a pedalo with me on Rimini beach, which came a week after she'd gone for a midnight beach walk with Carlos in Naples. It was competitive in one way, but in another it was just a bit of fun because everyone was so aware of what was going on and joked so openly about it. Wendy: 'Kit, this is not a bean, it's true – she's mad about you. You've got to say something. It's obvious – she doesn't go for laddy blokes like Carlos. This could be your chance for true happiness. I am only thinking of him, aren't I, Danny?' And then the next moment: 'Carlos, you don't go for a beach walk with somebody if there's nothing there. Imagine her in your loft. Come on. Do your Richard Gere thing tonight and see what happens.'

The toing and froing went on like this right until the night before we caught the ferry home when Dominique fell down a grassy slope outside the Filliers nightclub in Foujeurs and broke her wrist and it happened to be Carlos who was sober enough to drive her to the hospital.

When we were about seven at school, Danny and I used to play this game on our digital watches. It was when the stopwatch function was still a novelty. The game was a test of reaction speed. We'd try to halt the stopwatch bang on the year we were in, which would have been 1981: 19.81 seconds. It was almost impossible. Coming home from that trip, the huge tangerine sun setting behind us the whole drive home from Dover, Carlos and Dominique hand in hand on the back seat, Danny with his head on Wendy's shoulder, I remember Danny saying he wished he could do the same thing right then – that he could stop the clock and never get any older. I wish this now, too.

3 December 2000

It's the morning in Cedar Hill State Park and I've just woken up after a very scary experience. Last night the shadow of something large and four-legged passed my tent at around 3 a.m. Because of Carlos's outburst yesterday, I vowed not to say anything, but later in the camp shop when we were asking directions into Dallas I saw a poster on the wall with pictures of snakes on it. There was a skull and cross-bones on top of it so I asked the ranger if there was any wildlife we should be wary of in the park. It was a perfectly sensible question. Carlos raised his eyebrows contemptuously at Dominique. The woman in the green uniform said, 'Hell no, there's nothing here. Except a pair of roadrunners down by the lake.' Then she casually dropped in the fact that there'd been a mountain lion spotted the week before. It was seen carrying its cub across the interstate outside the main gate.

'A lion!' I said. I looked at Carlos. He was turning a rotunda of postcards pretending he hadn't heard and I had to ask: 'Do they bite?'

Carlos closed his eyes as if he already knew the answer and the woman said, 'Heck, no – they're more frightened of people than people are of them.'

'Something that looked bigger than a dog passed my tent last night,' I said seriously to Carlos on the way out. 'And it had a very muscly neck.'

Carlos said it was probably a dog, but when we exited the campground I saw a sign at the entrance – a picture of a dog with a line through it.

'Dogs are banned from the campsite – there's a thousand-dollar fine for bringing them in, Carlos.'

He said for fuck's sake, it was a dog. 'They've been trying to catch it for a week and it just walks past your tent? You heard what the woman said – they're more scared of you.'

'It was probably a golden retriever,' said Dominique. 'Or a coyote.'

'Don't say that, Dominique,' said Carlos. 'Now he's going to have to go back and ask if they bite as well.'

The worst thing is we're going sight-seeing today in Dallas and staying another night. I really fucking hope Carlos gets mauled.

> Subject: < Lions >
> To: Tom Farley Thomasfarley@hotmail.com >
> From: Kit Farley Kitfarley@yahoo.com >

Dear Tom, We visited the Ewing Southfork Ranch today on the outskirts of Dallas and then separated for the day as it's accepted I'm putting a strain on Dominique and Carlos's relationship. It was good to be away from them for a while in one way, but it wasn't the same seeing everything on my own.

The Southfork Ranch was a massive con. Only the outside of it was ever filmed. The indoor shots were done somewhere seven times as big. Never mind, Randy Watt, the billionaire owner, had recreated what the rooms of the house would have looked like if they had been occupied by members of the Ewing family. Bobby's had a porcelain cowboy boy at the foot of the bed and the bedstead was decorated with Texas longhorn horns. 'Babby lurved the ranch much more than JR evah did. He was much more into making deals and bein' awl slipper-ahy.'

After Dominique and Carlos had disappeared for their time alone I went to the SixthFloor JFK Museum set in the book depository building from where Kennedy was shot. The main activity was round the guest book. Lots of people put down their own theories about the assassination and praised Kennedy. Some were in tears. I added a joky comment pretending to be a shallow Finn on a biking holiday, which I thought would make Carlos and Dominique laugh when they came through the museum later.

'It was definitely the CIA, John Brooks, New Hampshire' . . . 'Oswald couldn't have acted alone, Kelly Smith, Mass' . . . 'The greatest of all Americans, who knows what he might have achieved, Paul Fitzpatrick, Oregon' . . . 'Hey, my name is Jons. I am from Finland on a biking holiday. This was fun.'

I'm normally good at being on my own, but by about 6 p.m. the city was deserted because Dallas is basically like some industrial estate where nobody lives, and it got scary walking round and having to keep crossing the huge four-lane streets every time I spotted a shambling hobo coming towards me.

The competition between Carlos and me over who is the best traveller continues. This evening, in Applebee's Bar and Grill, a few miles up Route 67, I found myself exaggerating all my conversations with strangers to turn them into significant experiences. 'I talked to this really interesting man at the

Conspiracy Museum when we were in Dallas. Oh, didn't you go there, Carlos? It's much better than the SixthFloor museum. He was right – it is interesting how they never show the Zapruder footage of the assassination. They reckon it's too graphic, but then they sell it in the museum shop. Pretty hypocritical, really. And then this woman I met gave me a list of places to visit on the West Coast. And apparently hotels in Vegas are half-price during the week and you get gambling tokens. Maybe we should avoid the weekend. Oh, and this woman I spoke to at the library said we should stop at Roswell, you know, the UFO place in New Mexico. There's a museum there about the aliens that landed. Another woman said Santa Monica and somebody else Monterey. So how did you two get on?'

'Oh, all right, we had nachos,' said Carlos.

What a shit traveller he is.

For the rest of the night Carlos lent proprietorially over Dominique, touching her leg every time he said anything, and I got bored so decided to scare them with what a Dallas cop had said to me when he directed me to the library. He'd told me he was giving me a 'heads up' not to walk about at night or down alleyways because the druggies would kill me for my bumbag as soon as look at me. 'Plenty of times he said he'd seen foreigners go home in body-bags. He also told me the reason why nobody camps in America,' I said. 'It's because everyone's frightened of being killed. People are always getting murdered in campsites, apparently.'

Carlos said the policeman had probably been trying to wind me up, but I could tell it had got to him because when we returned to the campsite he wouldn't go to the shower block on his own.

Apparently there is a mountain lion on the loose somewhere in the park feeding off small mammals and last night something large passed my tent, so I brought this up to add to the atmosphere. I said I'd read about them on the US Wildlife and Fisheries Service website. They were the classic predators whose preferred kill was a bite to the base of the skull to break your neck. In the end I wished I hadn't said anything because it started to scare me as well and now I can't sleep.

Kit.

p.s. I *can* see things from Lucy's perspective. You're wrong there. This is why I got back with her. But she can never see my point of view. This is the problem. Before I was too weak to press the point, I just wanted her back, but now I am outraged with what I put up with. I have decided not to ring to punish her.

> Subject: < annoyed >
> To: Kit Farley Kitfarley@yahoo.com >
> From: Lucy Jones Lucyjones23hotmail.com >

Dear Kit, I did not leave you because you dropped peanuts down the plug-hole. You're cleverly simplifying everything to make me feel bad. I'm sure it's what you want to believe, but it isn't true and you know it. They sound like small things individually but when you add them all together they become much more. You were taking me for granted. I like doing things for you because I love you – I enjoy the look on your face when you climb into a hot bath I've run you, the way you smack your lips when I've made peppercorn steak. I clear up your computer desk for you to make it nice, do your washing so you have clean clothes and don't smell. The fact you did nothing for me made me think you didn't love me. I was wrong: you did. I see that now. I used to think you were pulling the wool over my eyes when you said you couldn't notice dirt. I could almost imagine you laughing with Carlos about it. 'Guess what? I've convinced her I can't see dirt.'

In my family I'm considered irresponsible. But you're even less responsible than me. It's quite a strain, me having to be responsible for both of us, especially when you don't seem grateful. Doesn't the fact that I put up with it all show you how much I love you? No other girl would tolerate this. Sometimes I am ashamed of what I do for you. I don't tell people I do your ironing, washing and cooking because they'd laugh at me. Then when you phone collect it just seems like you're taking the piss.

Let's think ahead to the future. I've been speaking to my mum about weddings. It would be cheaper up north. What do you think? I'm not pressuring you, by the way, I just want to have something to look forward to. And you have to book some venues months in advance.

Lucy.

p.s. I've asked Sue to wangle me a press trip to Australia, although it probably won't be until the New Year and might end up being Thailand. It means I'll have no holiday left for the rest of the year – that's how much I love you. You'll have to let me know quite soon which you prefer, because it'll take a lot of arranging.

Journal Entry 8

Danny's break-up with Wendy came about a month after our European holiday. It was a couple of months before he moved to Germany with BFBS Radio, Carlos and Dominique moved to Spain and I started at the *Bucks Gazette* and met Lucy.

Danny's sex life was a bit of a mystery in Tring Road. He'd been out with girls for meals and so on, but they were always too young, too stupid, too thin, or too fat for him to take it any further. Before Wendy's arrival it had become accepted that Danny was just unlucky in this area. Although Danny never admitted it, certainly not to Wendy, the bottom line was that he just didn't really fancy her that much, but in true Danny style he had hundreds of theories about why this was. They ranged from the ridiculous ('Her hips are too high – she looks like a cartoon character who's been dropped out of a building') to the absurd ('I've been soiled by too many porn movies – I respect her too much to treat her like a sex object').

Danny came to see his relationship with Wendy as a beautiful sacrifice. In a perverse way he thought it showed how much he loved her. Being with Wendy meant a life without sexual fulfilment, but this was better than life without Wendy, and made him feel good about himself – he was somehow above sex.

Not many women would've put up with this situation, but Wendy was different: (a) because he never told her as it's not something you can really admit to over a romantic meal at the Five Bells. 'I love you so much, Wendy, I have to masturbate over images of other women getting fucked in porn movies; and (b) because the situation appealed to Wendy's natural martyrish instinct. As it obviously couldn't be her fault (Wendy was very aware of her beauty), it had to be his. They went to Relate, where, from what Danny told me, Wendy spent the whole time talking about *her* problems: her dad's death, her step-dad. It wasn't that he was sensitive about the lack of sex in his life either: he used to joke about it all the time. They both did.

'Oh God, *Nine and a Half Weeks* is on the telly tonight. I suppose I'm going to have to shag you later.'

'If you can still remember how to.'

It became a major event when they did have sex. Danny would announce it triumphantly to Carlos and me, in front of Wendy sometimes, like he'd just scored with a stranger. 'We did last it night,' he'd say, and expect us to clap him on the back. 'Yes,' Wendy would say. 'We're thinking of making it a regular thing.'

If you read any newspaper or magazine, watch any soap opera, film or drama, you're bombarded with the notion that sex and love are indivisible; that it's the ultimate display of affection. This used to wind up Danny because he came to think *not* having sex was the ultimate show of affection. 'Take it to extremes,' he would tell Carlos and me when we tried to tell him it wasn't going to work out. 'Who loves his girlfriend more? The man who only sees her because he enjoys having sex with her or the man who sees his girlfriend because he likes being with her and enjoys nutty views about aeroplane emissions? It's the second one, isn't it? Old men, who don't have sex any more with their wives, they must fancy younger girls. But they stay with their wife because of all the years and memories they've shared. Wendy and I are like that. When I'm old you'll both be jealous of me. When Wendy and I are pottering around having a laugh and you're with a girl you once fancied but don't any more, you'll feel like something's gone. I won't.'

'Yes, but you'll be sticking on *Naked Filth III* when she's out at the post office collecting her pension.' Big laugh from Danny.

While Wendy assumed there must be some tragic past that Danny was concealing everything was fine, but as it began to dawn on her that Danny simply wasn't that attracted to her, the situation became more difficult. As the more obvious avenues were gradually exhausted, Danny resorted to ridiculous excuses to escape sex, often using medical conditions he looked up in my *Symptoms* handbook. Initially Wendy was sympathetic: 'Poor Danny, you boys have got to give him some beans this week. It might be glandular fever.'

After a while Danny became a worse hypochondriac than me, convincing himself that he had all sorts of things. Once he dramatically announced that he'd gone for tests and probably had polycythmelia, which meant he produced too many blood cells. He started taking half an aspirin every day to thin his blood. 'Wendy's upset because it means we can't shag so much,' he told me one night without a hint of irony. 'But what can I do? Even a game of keepy-uppy could be fatal.' Then Wendy would tell Lucy or Dominique who would tell us, 'The tests came back negative. She saw the letter, but he still says he's got it. Wendy just wants to know why. She wants to help. The poor girl's going out of her mind.'

Occasionally Danny would have bouts of clarity and admit he was consciously avoiding sex. He told me that he often went two or three days without a bath so his knob smelled cheesy. Other times he claimed Wendy was overweight, even though she was like a stick. Once he told her she didn't hold his knob properly: 'She's too fucked up in the head to let herself go. All that shit over her dad. What can you do? She holds it with two fingers like Eric Bristow throwing darts.'

In true martyrish style Wendy eventually left Danny – to help him, she said, to set him free so he could find someone better. In reality I think she simply found a more deserving cause she could wave her lamp at.

I'll remember the day Danny moved out of Tring Road for the rest of my life. Sometimes I think your life is nothing but a series of big moments, like the points in a connect-the-dots picture that need to be linked up before they make any sense. But I knew that was a big dot at the time, and it's an even bigger dot now. Danny had been posted to a BFBS military base in Herford, Germany. It was a serious promotion because he was going to be doing a live breakfast show to a much bigger audience, instead of the prerecorded one he'd been doing in Chalfont. Maybe he'd have gone anyway, but the break-up with Wendy was certainly the final trigger, even though at the time he seemed to have taken this quite well, too well, we all thought at the time. He moved out of the house three days before his flight and Dad and Jane came to pick him up in their Land-Rover and take away his stuff. I ended up following their car for three miles down Aylesbury Road before they turned off for Aston Clinton. It was 29 December 1998.

Sometimes I do think Danny and I are almost telepathic because there was something in the way Danny stared after me when they turned for Beech Road that made me know instantly that this was a moment I'd never forget. I'm very good at moments. I never really think about anything until it happens. I can never predict how I'm going to feel about things before they happen. But when a moment occurs I always know instantly. Lucy cries at shock, irritation, driving incompetence and babies on the news with heart valves missing. The only times I cry are when I'm involved in big moments – when you know that things are going to be different for ever, when something's over, when the future suddenly seems unpredictable.

Beforehand, I think half of me was slightly glad we were all moving out. We'd sucked Tring Road dry, a new year was about to start. It was time to move on. Then it rushed in on me in the front seat of my yellow Fiesta – the whole two years that was coming to an end. Danny was wedged into the back seat of Dad's Land-Rover among the boxes, craning his neck and staring back at me; not grinning, not waving, not doing anything but staring. As Dad winked the indicator and the car started to turn the moment came on me so suddenly tears sprang into my eyes with the overwhelming realization that Danny and I would never live together again, never be as close again. That we'd drift apart and never be able to recapture these times and feelings.

Memories of Danny I won't forget: coming home late to hear the reassuring rat-a-tat of gunfire coming from the living room signifying Danny was watching another Steven Segal movie; the great slug culls we went on; the nights staying up playing three-card brag for tuppence; driving Danny to Stoke Mandeville to do his radio show in my Fiesta with the passenger-side door that wouldn't close, so he had to open his window and hug the door shut with his outstretched arm and once almost fell out on the Hen & Chickens roundabout when I took it in third; thinking up ideas for his show in the living room over a few beers; the three-quarter-sized cardboard cut-outs of Whoopi Goldberg and Bruce Willis we had in the front room behind the net curtains that first winter – a loyalty bonus from Blockbuster. The old lady Mrs Roberts from next door mistook them for home-alone children and reported us to the landlord: 'The poor things – they're so bored. They just stare out of the window all day. And that little boy – he must be freezing: he only wears a vest.'

4 December 2000

We're camping in the Bottomless Lakes State Park, twelve miles east of Roswell, New Mexico, off Highway 380, and I think I'm starting to realize something – Dominique isn't the major problem any more. It's Carlos. He just can't bear to be without her for more than a second and gets really edgy every time she emails her ex-husband John because he's so jealous and suspicious. Then he takes it out on me. Before we started this holiday, Carlos told me he'd tried to persuade Dominique not to come to America. He told me he was trying to get her to fly straight to Australia so we could do America by ourselves. Only this afternoon it came out that Dominique wanted to go to Australia first and that it was Carlos who persuaded her to come to the States. This and a big argument we had this morning about driving have made me start to question other things, too.

Today we drove non-stop for almost nine hours, finally leaving I-20 west of Abilene at Pescos, and took Route 285, the lonely highway, north through the Texas panhandle all the way to Roswell. The plains of Texas with their oil derricks disappeared and it became scrubland, tumbleweed, dirty brown earth and roads so empty you could go fifteen minutes without seeing another car. The skies seem huge now and the land is so flat you can see the sun melt into the earth at sunset like a giant fried egg. The radio stations which play Garth Brooks disappeared and were replaced by nutters in garages broadcasting on their own bandit frequencies, muttering about government cover-ups and conspiracy theories involving the military-industrial complex.

The driving row came just as we passed Carlsbad, and it's worrying me that there's more to come. All I said to Carlos was 'Which side of the road do you drive on, Carlos – the middle or the kerb?'

He went berserk: 'Just fuck off about my driving, will you –

you're the worst fucking driver I know and I never criticize you, so leave me alone. All holiday you've been saying my driving's jerky. When I drive anywhere with people from work we have a rule not to criticize anybody's driving. You do it all the time. Everyone I know thinks you're a shit driver, but I don't say anything, so shut up. You never know where you're going. I never fucking criticize you. So just keep your fucking nose out of it.'

He looked almost as shocked as I was by his outburst. I said I'd only been asking a simple question.

He said, 'You were going to have a go, though, weren't you? Whenever Dominique has a go at your driving you have a go at mine to make up for it.'

Then I said, 'I thought you two were one person, anyway, so what does it matter which one said it? And I wasn't the one who almost crashed three times the other day playing games with the cruise control.'

Carlos's nostrils flared, and Dominique told him to calm down. Carlos said it was no wonder he made mistakes. 'It's because nobody directs me – I have to do it myself. When you're driving we have to spoonfeed you. The other day you didn't even know whether we were travelling east or west of Vicksburgh and we'd been on the road all day. That just winds me up.'

'That's because when I get up you two have already worked out what we're doing. Anyway, when I say you're a bad driver I'm not talking about you getting flustered when you don't know the way and go up one-way streets the wrong way, mounting the kerb and nearly losing control because your cap fell off. I'm talking about the way you brake too late and come out of corners and overcorrect on the straight, which wakes me up and means I can't write to Lucy because I can't hold the pen still.'

Carlos said there were lots of things that I did that could annoy him, but he didn't let them.

'Like what?' I said.

'No, you don't want me getting into that.'

I said, 'Come on, like you wish you hadn't invited me? Is that what you mean?'

He didn't answer, but after about five minutes he said, 'Stop sulking, you sulky fucker,' and I said, 'You're the sulky fucker.' He looked over at me, swerved and nearly hit a car in the other lane, so I said, 'And you veer all the time.' Carlos said, 'Fuck off.'

Roswell is a tiny town miles from the nearest city and it's where aliens supposedly landed in 1947. It was my idea to come here and I had hoped the town would be tiny, with one bar and lots of goatee-bearded weirdos clutching creased photos of UFOs, whispering about the truth being out there, while clandestinely revealing puncture marks behind their ears (the tell-tale sign of alien abduction on the *X-Files*). But it's like any other American town. Arby's had a poster saying, 'Aliens Welcome' and there was a bridal shop that had an alien-looking dummy with almond eyes in a wedding dress in the window but that was it.

We visited the UFO museum, but it was done up like an infant school project, full of children's drawings of ET, so it looked like even the museum didn't really believe the stories. Carlos is now annoyed I dragged us out of our way and has started wondering about 'all those people you supposedly talked to in Dallas'.

This evening we had a beer in the Prime Rib Eye Steak and Seafood restaurant and, to restore some pride, I tried to get the barman talking about aliens, feeling like I had to justify the diversion. 'We're driving to Los Angeles and just read in a guide book', I raised my tone disbelievingly, 'that some aliens landed here once?' The guy looked at me as if I was nuts and Dominique made me laugh: 'Kit, it happened in 1947 – it is like somebody going to France and thinking every person will be talking about the war. "Excuse me, I have just been reading the guide book and I gather there was a war here fifty years ago." '

Then we went to a bar called Peppers in the basement of the

Bank of America and met a man called Ralph. We sat next to him at the bar for a while and I asked him about close encounters. He told me about being on I-40 heading for Albuquerque in his Corvette and being overtaken by a seven-foot-tall albino going 170 m.p.h. in a jet-black Zil. Carlos looked quite impressed for a moment, but then Ralph started going off the subject. He took a tell-tale pill from a little metal box and said the US military could microwave a flock of geese out of the sky with the touch of a button and that aliens had always been here among us – his daddy had told him and it said so in Genesis. 'I've sat in this bar with people I've never seen again,' he said. Perhaps they were just passing through, I wanted to say. 'I could be an alien, *you* could be an alien,' he said to Dominique, and Carlos decided we should go back to the campsite. Dominique is a pain, but she can be funny: 'I am not an alien. I am French,' she said as she put on her coat to go.

That was about an hour ago. Just now Carlos and I had a strange conversation on the picnic tables back at the state park and I'm wondering if there was a hidden subtext. He asked me about Lucy and I told him things were difficult because she couldn't face up to what she did. 'I know what you mean,' he said, 'Dominique and I have got to find a happy medium where we're both happy and feel safe. On our own we're fine. It's outside influences that upset us. The trouble is I can imagine me travelling on my own, but not you. I don't think you'd be able to cope.'

What does that mean?

And he was talking bollocks, anyway. They always argue when they're on their own. They're arguing now in their tent.

It's strange – back in England Carlos blamed Dominique for leaving him. Now he's blaming himself. 'If I hadn't fucked everything up and slept around, she would never have left. No way,' he says.

The other thing I've noticed is an Aussie twang creeping back into Dominique's voice as if in preparation for returning there. Her sentences go up in pitch at the end. Carlos hates this because the only person she can be copying is John the Aussie, who she calls every other day.

> Subject: < it was a dog, not a lion >
> To: Kit Farley Kitfarley@yahoo.com >
> From: Tom Farley Thomasfarley@hotmail.com >

Dear Kit, Email Dad. He's got some news.
Tom.

> Subject: < News? >
> To: Jon Farley Jonathan_farleyRBS@aol.com >
> From: Kit Farley Kitfarley@yahoo.com >

Dear Dad, Tom says you've got some news.
Kit.

> Subject: < Beech Road >
> To: Kit Farley Kitfarley@yahoo.com >
> From: Jon Farley Jonathan_farleyRBS@aol.com >

Dear Kit, Yes, I have. Kit, I've decided it is best that I move into Jane's flat and sell Beech Road. Big step, I know. But probably about time. I thought it would be a tough decision, but making it only took ten minutes. I think it's for the best – we're both getting older and it's smaller and there are too many bad associations here for us both to feel comfortable. I am putting it on the market after Christmas. It does mean it will be the last Christmas here – tempted? We also think the wedding will be some time in late Jan. – provided I ever see your measurements. Just an idea – why don't you come back for both?
Love Dad.

> Subject: Re: < Travelling and being cool >
> To: Tom Farley Thomasfarley@hotmail.com >
> From: Kit Farley Kitfarley@yahoo.com >

Tom, That is big news. What do you think about it, seriously? I must admit I'm a bit gutted. I don't know why.
Kit.

> Subject: Re: < ring me >
> To: Kit Farley Kitfarley@yahoo.com >
> From: Lucy Jones Lucyjones23@hotmail.com >

Dear Kit, Please try to phone me tomorrow. We've got to sort this out. I feel really shitty, like you're putting me further and further to the back of your mind. I've said I'm sorry. Why do you always have to punish me like this?
Lucy.

I woke Carlos up just now to break the news to him that I might be going home early and he tried not to appear relieved. Weirdly, Dominique almost looked disappointed, probably because she'll have no one around to share the petrol costs. I'm going to write my journal entry and then I'll ring Lucy and see what she says.

Journal Entry 9

The first thing Danny said to me about Lucy: 'Watch yourself, Kit.' I thought nothing of this at the time: 'Watch yourself, Kit' was what Danny always said. If I was driving somewhere long distance, doing anything slightly risky, 'Watch yourself, Kit.' It was one of those things we just said to each other.

I met Lucy on the *Bucks Gazette* about two months after Danny left for Germany. Maybe this meant I paid less attention to Danny than I should have done. Could I have visited him more that year? Probably.

The first time I met Lucy I didn't fancy her at all. She was just another face in the newsroom. And not a very pretty one – she had a tooth abscess that made her look like Babapapa. Her first words to me, her face swollen to the size of a beach ball, were: 'Sorry you've got the Wendover patch. I'm doing Risborough. And by the way, you're sitting at my terminal.' Steer clear of her, I thought.

The *Bucks Gazette* was a small weekly paper, so, as trainees, we got to do everything. I wrote news stories, did features and was given a patch to cover. This is what Lucy had been referring to when she said Wendover, and it was this that ultimately brought us together.

I loved everything about the job right from the start – the people, the competition to write the front page, the nutters in reception, my new home in the *Gazette* company flat on Walton Street. Everything, that is, apart from finding stories for my patch. How were you supposed to find a story? One afternoon was set aside each week for the task, and it wasn't just one story I needed, either: I had to fill a whole page.

Occasionally stories would magically materialize – a post office robbery, a fatal car accident – but normally there was nothing. No amount of ringing contacts (if you can the call the chairman of the Parish Council Street Lighting Committee and the playground organizer of the Wendover Aqua Tots contacts) or wandering the streets using the fabled 'eyes and ears journalism' could turn up anything. I used to sit there in Ye Olde Wendover Teashoppe on Tuesday afternoons with my head in my hands, a flapjack in front of me, watching pensioners going in and out of the antique shops exchanging cheery words with each other about the best-kept village competition and I'd wonder how the fuck I was supposed to turn the place into the hotbed of vice the editor demanded. There were no excuses for a slow week either and you'd get hauled into deputy editor Steve Pandy's office and given a warning. 'Sit down, Kit, and open your legs. I'm going to kick your balls.' Two warnings and you were relegated to keying-in the planning bulletin. Three warnings and you were out.

Lucy and I shared a work-station for a month, but didn't speak much. Then two incidents changed everything. The first was an evening in the Lobster Pot in Aylesbury Market Square when Lucy and I got drunk for the first time, and admitted we were guilty of what we'd been taught was the most heinous journalistic crime of all: we both made up quotes.

In a way this led to the second thing, because over time this changed our attitudes to the job. The afternoons in the districts became fun. Instead of trudging off separately to our one-horse towns we went together, usually stopping off at the pub on the way back to the office to compare notes. Pretty soon we realized the only way to gather the sort of news Pandy wanted was to make it up. It started with the fabricated quotes, moved on to invented people, and ended in totally fictitious stories. The first fabricated story was about a friend of Carlos's mum's best friend, who'd moved into a house in Little Hampden and was prepared to have his picture taken in his loft claiming it was haunted by a poltergeist which interfered with his septic tank. This was followed by the fertility stool in Monks Risborough which seven women had sat on and then mysteriously become pregnant. We had the phantom bugler of Aylesbury Vale Park who came out only at a full moon, the UFO corridor that was said (by us) to exist along the A413 and, most famously of all, the panther of Wendover Woods (and Risborough playing fields so Lucy could use the story on her page, too). It was this scam that led to our first kiss.

One lunchtime Pandy wandered over to our desk and asked if we'd seen a story on the front page of the *Mirror* about a big cat sighting on Bodmin Moor. 'Pity we haven't got one of those in our area,' he said. We got a pliant mate of Danny's from BFBS Chalfont to claim he'd seen the panther.

Then we discovered there was a football-shaped dent in his car. It was about the same size as we imagined a panther's head to be, so we added this to the story. Instead of just having seen the beast, it had now tried to attack him, headbutting his car in Lovers' Lane, where he'd been smooching with his girlfriend. We arranged for another sighting in Monks Risborough, getting a dodgy friend of a friend of Lucy's to claim he'd seen teeth marks in one of his dad's sheep that 'couldn't possibly have come from a dog'. Then we overcooked it. Lucy came into the office an hour before I was due to take the snapper round to Alan Poole's for the picture, and she slipped into my inside jacket pocket a clear plastic bag of black fur from her landlord's cat Smudge. Like a spy on a dead-letter drop she said out of the side of her mouth, a phrase both of us still laugh about now, 'Smudge is moulting – stick it in the dent.'

Things started to go wrong when I rang the RSPCA and Inspector Tom Holmes refused to be quoted. To get him to co-operate I told him about the fur and he got excited. Overexcited, because he called head office in Oxford and before we knew it the Chief Inspector for Southern England was on the phone after a fur sample. The police, who'd been informed of the incident by the RSPCA, wanted to seal off the area and send in marksmen. There was talk of scrambling a police helicopter. Lucy and I started to panic. The story was getting out of control. We knew we'd lose our jobs if Pandy found out what we'd done so I called the police and told them off the record I thought Alan Poole might be a nutter. But it was already too late because someone in Aylesbury nick had tipped off the nationals and next thing the newsroom was besieged with calls, asking for pictures and contact numbers for Alan Poole. They were talking of the Beast of Wendover.

I rang Alan Poole to tell him to get rid of the fur. I told him what was going on – leaving out that I'd told the police I suspected he was a nutter – but he still panicked. He was on housing benefit while working for BFBS in Chalfont and was worried this would come out when the national spotlight descended. So then I tried to get the story spiked. I told Pandy Poole was a nutter; he told me to imply this in the story. I had to ring Poole to tell him we were going to be implying he was a nutter; he started making threats. He was going to tell the whole story on his show the moment he saw the paper unless we kept his name out of it.

That night Lucy and I, unaware the story would be pulled to make way for news of a huge fire at the Aylesbury Nescafé factory, in a spirit of depressed abandonment at the Gate nightclub dropped two pills each. When we got up for a dance all I could say was, 'Lucy?' quickly followed by, 'I love you.' She laughed and said she loved me, too, so I said it again, more insistently this time.

I must have decided I could no longer communicate coherently so had to do it in another way. I don't know how long we kissed for, but the next thing I remember we were propped up against a lamppost outside the club. I woke up in bed with Lucy at her flat in Quarrendon.

Pretty soon Lucy and I were going out and there was something comfortable about her company then that made everything seem perfect. She was my first girlfriend who really became my friend, and within a few weeks I was out of the company flat and we'd moved in together, into a fairytale cottage on the outskirts of Aylesbury in the village of Whitchurch. It was so quaint you could half believe it was made of marzipan.

Being with Lucy was like being in another world, our own little world, a world that was only occasionally invaded by outside forces. It was fun and exciting in a totally different way to living with Carlos and Danny. We liked to look out for Allied Carpets ads and try to guess which of the members of staff talking to camera were the boss. We read the papers together on Sunday mornings in the Whitchurch Brasserie for hours at a stretch, often ending up covered in newsprint and looking like giant pandas. If we were on different shifts we talked in a weird muted voice in the mornings when one of us left the house earlier than the other. 'See you later . . . Be careful,' we'd say, without opening our mouths, but the other person always understood the words from the vibration of the lips.

Lucy couldn't watch any horror films, struggled with action and adventures, and I was never allowed to talk in disembodied voices or pretend to have turned into a monster, zombie, ghost or anything supernatural or possessed by evil. It was so bad, if I entered a room and Lucy had her back to me, I'd have to announce my presence slowly, otherwise she'd jump or lunge at me with whatever was in her hand.

Another habit of Lucy's: watching telly while curling hair round her little finger. This used to distract me if she was sitting next to me on the sofa and if we were alone when she did it I'd slap her hand, and without saying anything she'd change over and twiddle the hair on the other side of her head. For some reason this always reminded me of something you might see gorillas doing on *Wildlife on One*. I loved it.

I could talk to her about my writing and ambition to be a columnist one day in a way I couldn't with anybody else because they wouldn't be interested, or, more importantly, wouldn't indulge *my* interest. She was also great about my hypochondria. The fact that she dismissed every medical complaint I thought I had as nonsense made me start to believe it was nonsense, too, and it calmed me down. 'It's no wonder your balls ache, you keep rubbing them. I am not squeezing them again. There's nothing wrong with you.'

She was always applying for new jobs. There was never a time when she didn't have a CV in the post. And she was incredibly impressionable, something else we used to joke about and which also made me love her. She wanted to be a political researcher, a police press officer, a news reporter on the nationals, a lawyer, someone who renovates houses and a teacher.

'But I've always wanted to be a teacher.'

'You've never mentioned it once the whole time I've known you. At least shadow a teacher for a week before you resign.'

'Why should I when I know that's what I want to do?'

'Because a week ago you watched *Ally McBeal* and wanted to be a lawyer.'

'You're so unsupportive.'

After watching *Friends* she became Jennifer Aniston.

'You're talking like an American again, Luce.'

'I am *so* not.'

'You *so* are.'

If she read an article in *Cosmo* that implied we were incompatible because we slept in a reverse banana position she worried. She used to do a little temper jig when she was angry, dancing on the spot like someone squashing grapes. She always lost her keys, was always ten minutes late, and was obsessed with buying candles, tea trays and new handbags from DKNY.

With Carlos and Danny gone, we had our own Friday nights together and even though we never did anything outrageous I was never bored. We'd go to the small pub, the Cherry Tree, round the corner from the house, where the locals all got to know us and the barman allowed us the privilege of being one of the select few to throw logs on the fire. Normally we'd start talking generally about work-related incidents: an interesting person on a job, another reporter clashing with a member of authority, that kind of thing. After this it was Lucy and her quest for a better job on a magazine, and then usually my writing, because I was trying to get the editor to give me a TV column. After this we'd have a brief disagreement about something – women's rights, the definition of love – before finally we bonded again with a joky conversation about how we'd cope without having each other around.

'I would turn to drink.'

'Me, too. And I'd stay up late and smoke a lot.'

'Me, too. I'd probably become a mercenary and deliberately put myself in risky situations so I'd get shot and killed because my life would be worthless.'

'I know what you mean. I might become a lollipop lady on the A413. It's lethal down there.'

In the summer we had our dinner in the garden on the picnic table we bought together from B&Q and in the winter we turned the heating on full blast and liked to stare out of the window that looked on to Whitchurch High Street and relish the fact we were inside in the warm. We laughed together at least once a day, normally before bed during hugging and rolling: hugging and rolling was Lucy and I hugging each other very tightly and rolling backwards and forwards from one end of the bed to the other laughing loudly, while having ridiculous conversations about our lives and relationship.

'Would you still love me if I had no arms and legs and one eye where my nose should be?'

'Yes. But would you still love me if I had a tail?'

'Yes, if you swished it when you were happy.'

'But what if it was eight feet long and extremely powerful and I kept swishing things over with it like the polyanthus your sister gave you for your birthday?'

Once, during one of our Friday night debates, in the disagreement interlude, Lucy confessed that in idle moments when things were going particularly well between us she thought about stabbing me through the heart with a kitchen knife. 'I can't stop myself. I think, What is the worst thing I could do in any given moment? The thing that would destroy my life and make everybody hate me the most. But it's not as if I'd ever do it,' she said.

I tried to explain many times to Danny over the phone how I felt about Lucy, as you do when you're first in love: 'And she likes the same books. And guess what her favourite TV programme is? Yup, *NYPD Blue.* She bought me the soundtrack album by Mike Post for my birthday. She met Jane and

Dad last weekend for Sunday lunch and they got on brilliantly, and I'm seeing her parents next weekend in Birmingham. She's so funny, too. I didn't realize girls could be this much of a laugh.'

But 'Watch yourself, Kit' was all Danny would say. It never came across as jealousy. I just assumed he was still thinking about Wendy. I bumped into her occasionally in Aylesbury, she still phoned from time to time, and was in contact with Dominique. It became my job to keep Danny regularly informed about her. I'd get the information from Carlos, who'd got it from Dominique, and I'd pass it on to Danny – who she was seeing, had she mentioned him, did she get his letter, what did she say about it? This didn't seem that unusual. Wendy had been his first proper girlfriend, he'd moved to a different country and he was bound to want to stay in touch with his old world. Anyway, Wendy was still anxious to be friends with him, too, although they had regressed to talking in doctor voices.

When I asked about his current love life, Danny was very vague and would tell me about various girls he'd had flings with, then say he had to get up at 5 a.m. to do his show and it wasn't conducive to a relationship. Several times I tried to arrange to go over and see him, but most weekends either Lucy or I was on Sunday afternoon fête duty for the paper. Danny mentioned the Christadelphian religion he'd got into on the phone at one point, but that just seemed par for the course – another Danny fad.

Some people talk incessantly about their feelings and what's going on in their life. Danny rarely did. There was no such thing as an ordinary conversation with him. What have you been up to? How are you? These were questions Danny never asked nor was interested in hearing replies to, so I just assumed he was fine. Instead we talked about mad schemes, theories, ideas, like the one about the world being free from war, famine and disease if everyone had a great sense of humour. We are all computers was another one:

humans designed computers in their image, so likewise, Danny thought, we'd been designed by some alien computer race in *their* image. Each week I'd tell him about the bogus stories Lucy and I had dreamed up and he'd tell me his latest fantasy.

'I've been reading this book and space is infinite, right, Kit, so it stands to reason that everything is infinite, including me and you. We're alive on an infinite number of earths. Isn't that fucking amazing? On one earth I'm a movie star, on another I'm a professional footballer, on another I race Formula One cars. It's just unlucky I happen to be here in Herford with a bunch of Jerries. It means it doesn't matter if you die, because you won't even know it because all your souls are connected and at one with all the other infinite yous. When you dream, the reason it's all disconnected, I've worked it out, is because you're seeing the world through the eyes of all the other yous on all the other infinite Planet Earths. The bit of the brain the scientists can't work out what it's for, it's a fucking great filing system for all the experiences and memories of all the yous that exist in the space–time continuum. When you've got a problem your brain goes through all the situations that the similar yous are having and combs them for possible solutions to your own problem. That's why you have ideas in your sleep, that's why your dreams seem to echo your own life. That's why you need to sleep. It takes up so much brain capacity everything else has to shut down.'

Danny, Carlos and I used to smoke quite a lot of weed in Tring Road and normally about midway through the third joint Carlos and I would suddenly realize we were talking gibberish, but with Danny you could never tell when he was stoned because this is what he was like anyway. It meant I had no idea how bad things really were for him until we eventually went to see him in the summer of 1999.

5 December 2000

We're in El Paso now. It's been a day of empty roads heading south to Artesia on Route 285 retracing yesterday's steps, then west through the Sacramento Mountains and finally south on Route 54, running alongside the Jarilla Hills. El Paso is wedged between the Franklin Mountains and the Rio Grande. The Mexican border town of Ciudad Juarez is the other side of the river. The buildings are all pink and remind me of the *High Chaparral*, and the signs are in Spanish and English, and there is an air of danger about the place with roadblocks everywhere to trap Mexicans who have slipped through the border and are making a run for California.

We had another separation day today. I tried to make out I didn't mind when Carlos suggested it this afternoon, but I do. I can understand they want to be alone, but Carlos and I have hardly spent one moment together all holiday. Quite often Dominique will say at 8.30 p.m. that she doesn't mind going back to the campsite alone so that Carlos and I can go for a drink, but Carlos always has a headache, gets all mock-honourable about leaving her alone or like today says he's saving money because he's already shelled out for a pair of Roman sandals.

Because we aren't having a laugh in the evenings, I am determined to learn and experience things to get *something* out of the trip. But this causes problems. Carlos can't be bothered to do anything, Dominique has the attention span of a goldfish, so I end up feeling guilty for dragging them round museums, which I wasn't that concerned about in the first place, like the one at Roswell yesterday.

I think it's more isolating being with people who don't really want you there than it is being alone. It's been a week and a half and all the time I envisage it getting better, but it never does. Little things have started to grate, too: the way Carlos talks very quietly when he's in a bad mood. For some reason it makes his lips look huge, like tyre inner tubes. Dominique's passion for Caesar salad and pecan pie.

Today I walked round the El Paso Insights Science Museum and then went over the border into Mexico across the Sante Fe Bridge. It was teeming: women beggars with shawls holding out Styrofoam cups, kids in bare feet trying to sell beads, and there were lots of swarthy bandit-like people loafing about suspiciously. I had a taco in a boiling-hot street café, became concerned when a gang of youths started eyeing up my bumbag and ran back to the car. I met Carlos and Dominique unexpectedly there. They didn't look pleased to see me and I felt almost guilty, as if I'd engineered the whole thing to cling on to them. Carlos was stroppy.

'You all right, Carlos?' I said.

'Yeah, you all right?' he said threateningly.

On top of the big row with Lucy last night it's made me feel shit. It certainly wasn't my fault. I called collect again. I had no choice, what with my mobile credits running low, and how come I'm to blame for pay phones being so crap? To ring England you have to find a coin booth that works (most don't) and then ring the local operator to get hold of the international operator. Only they never tell you in the phone booth what the number for any of these local operators is and they're different for every state. Not only that, but when you finally get hold of them and get them to dial the number for you they want a ten-dollar connection fee, and seeing as the highest-value denomination coin is the fucking quarter you'd have to walk round with about a ton of silver in your pocket to get anywhere.

'Kit, what are you doing calling collect again?' she said before I had time to tell her about maybe coming home for Christmas.

I started explaining what a nightmare it was using the phones, and she said, 'It's seven dollars a minute. My rent's seven hundred quid. I can't afford it. We're going to have to find a better system or you'll have to stop calling so often. You're bleeding me dry.'

'I've only rung twice. Shall I stop ringing then?' I said.

There was a pause and Lucy said: 'That's not very nice.'

She asked why I didn't get a phonecard. I said I was calling from the middle of a forest, how was I supposed to get one, buy one off the fucking squirrels? Lucy said people were laughing at her.

'You're living in the most technically advanced country in the world and you can't work the phones. It does seem a bit stupid, and you know I'm saving for when you get back. Don't you want us to live together when you get back? I told you to get a phonecard.'

'Who's laughing at you?' I said. 'The fucking dog-groomer?' There was another pause and I said, sorry, I hadn't meant that.

'I've just paid for a new tax disc, the council bill was a hundred and twenty quid, I can't afford the garage bill for the car and how are we ever going to be able to afford to get married? I can't even pay for a rail season ticket. I have to buy one every week.'

'Well, maybe we shouldn't get married then,' I said.

There was a pause.

'Fine,' said Lucy. 'You've changed your mind. That really cheered me up at the airport. Right, it's all off. Forget it. Stupid Lucy getting carried away.'

I said I hadn't said it was all off, I just wanted it to happen naturally. She was making it seem like a chore: land, collect baggage, get married.

'All right, I'll never mention it again,' said Lucy. 'Never mind that it's a perfectly normal thing for people who've been going out together for almost two years to discuss. Never mind that you said you wanted to. Never mind it's what I've been looking forward to.'

I said she had left me and slept around. It wasn't quite as simple as that. We hadn't been going out *solidly* for two years.

'Great! Bring that up again – make me feel really shit. I've been looking forward to this call all day. I was going to tell you I'd arranged a flight to Thailand,' said Lucy.

I said we couldn't just sweep it under the carpet, we had split up and I was bound to have doubts. And anyway, I'd been planning to tell her some news myself: I might be coming home for Christmas because Dad was selling Beech Road and it would be the last Christmas there.

'Oh, great – now you've got doubts. I can't talk about this at work. Everyone's staring at me. My make-up's running, I'll have to go,' she said and hung up.

When I rang her back later (costing me almost twenty dollars) we had *another* row. This time it was all about Christmas and me coming home. I expected her to be pleased, but I should've realized she wants a winter tan. She said she'd spent the last three days sorting out a flight to Thailand. I told her I thought she wanted me back. But no, I was being selfish – Lucy hadn't had a proper summer holiday, she'd planned to get her hair cut specially at Vidal Sassoon to surprise me at Bangkok airport, she'd joined Weight-Watchers and had lost three pounds. She'd been half expecting me to propose in Thailand and now realized it was all bollocks.

'We might as well forget it. Shall we forget it?' she said. 'I've been such a fool. *Such* a fool.'

I didn't say anything.

'I'll take that as yes. You've really upset me, Kit,' she said and hung up, again.

> Subject: < Chicken soup >
> To: Kit Farley Kitfarley@yahoo.com >
> From: Tom Farley Thomasfarley@hotmail.com >

Kit, You sound funny about Beech Road. I know what you mean, but it does make sense. They're getting married. What's the point of having two houses? Dad practically lived at hers, anyway. It is sad when you think about all the memories, but we won't forget everything. I'll still be here to remind you of the time you threw that pan of Jane's disgusting chicken soup out of the back door and forgot to let go early enough and it swept a thick orange stain up the outside wall and wouldn't scrub off because of the pebble-dashing. And that you then blamed me for it, you twat. Come home for Christmas. Don't feel embarrassed and ashamed.

What are you doing there? I promise not to make jokes about the fact you said you were going away for a year to discover yourself and came back after a week because the Kit-Kat wasn't an international biscuit.

Tom.

> Subject: < can you read this? >
> To: Tom Farley Thomasfarley@hotmail.com >
> From: Kit Farley Kitfarley@yahoo.com >

Dear Tom, We're heading for Hueco Tanks State Park to camp the night, about thirty miles east of El Paso off Route 180, near the Tex–Mex border and this is in reduced point-size so Dominique can't lean over and see what I'm writing. The latest news is I'm not coming home. Had a big row with Lucy who's sorted out a flight to Thailand because she thinks I'll propose there. So no pressure there, then. I'm really fucked off about this, so don't rub it in any more. I want to come home and I can't. Let's just leave it at that.

I was right as well. I've been thinking about it for a few days – Carlos does want to get rid of me. Yesterday I mentioned I might be going home early and when I told him just now I wasn't any more he said if I wanted to meet Lucy in January I'd have to 'push on', but that he didn't want to 'rush Australia'. I knew what was coming: 'Maybe it will be best if we do our own thing in Australia, Kit.'

I *do* feel funny about Beech Road. I don't want to get all mushy, but all the memories are there and everything. Why couldn't Dad have waited until I got back? Why can't Jane move into Dad's?

Kit.

> Subject: < nightmare >
> To: Lucy Jones Lucyjones23@hotmail.com >
> From: Kit Farley Kitfarley@yahoo.com >

Dear Lucy, I tried to phone you earlier, although not to apologize. When I don't want to talk about getting married you have a go at me, yet when you won't talk about what you did to me, you have a go about that, too. You can't have it both ways. And all I want to do is be with my family for the last Christmas in Beech Road. We can even go to your parents' on Boxing Day if you want. You know I hate having to point these things out to you and I don't like rubbing your face in it, but sometimes you're so slow on the uptake I have to. You do know it will be almost a year to the day that it happened, and Danny is obviously going to be on my mind, yet you force me into an argument over it. This really pisses me off and makes me think you have no fucking idea how I think or feel. It also looks like I might be travelling alone soon. Carlos is being a cunt.

Kit.

> Subject: < still annoyed with you >
> To: Kit Farley Kitfarley@yahoo.com >
> From: Lucy Jones Lucyjones23@hotmail.com >

Dear Kit, I am sick of you expecting me to feel sorry for you. You chose to go travelling, remember. Stop taking everything out on me.

Lucy.

p.s. But don't hitch, please. You'll be kidnapped by a greasy trucker and kept as a gimp in a chest freezer.

Journal Entry 10

Danny always had a peculiar way of speaking to men. But then he spoke to women in exactly the same way. He seemed to flirt with everybody, men and women. It was different from Carlos's flirting, was never in a sexual or obvious way. It wasn't camp, either. It was just Danny. There were never silences when he was around, for instance. He couldn't stand them and always thought they were his fault. He had this tremendous nervous energy that's rare in good-looking people. Most good-looking people are too interested in looking pretty to talk. Danny never was because he never really believed he *was* attractive. He had no inner poise at all; I used to call it his scatter-gun approach. The first few minutes of any conversation with Danny was like watching an open-mic act at a comedy club. It used to make *me* nervous. You could never tell where he was going; he'd be heading down some embarrassing blind alley and just as you were thinking, Danny, shut up, man, you're dying on your arse, somehow he'd manage to turn it round with a self-effacing gag, which would make you feel so relieved you'd laugh more than if anybody else had said it.

He also had a wonderful way of describing things. He wasn't great with words so he used to draw everything or use objects to back up his point. It was like watching *Take Hart*: 'Your happiness is like an inflatable life-raft.' He'd move the salt cellar into the middle of the table. 'The older you get the more it gets punctured.' He'd pick up the salt cellar – his raft – and poke it with a fork. 'You mend these rips.' He'd lick a Rizla and stick it on the side of the salt cellar. 'But they never entirely reseal and always take in water.' He'd put the salt cellar in a beer puddle. 'People who end their lives do so because they have giant gashes that let in water, or have so many small leaks they can't plug that they sink.' He'd drop the salt cellar into his pint and laugh outrageously. 'Me and Wendy are over,' he'd say, 'and I am still bailing out from that one.' He'd pull the salt cellar out and grin broadly. 'Now you', he'd say, realizing he'd stretched the analogy too far again, and picking up the pepper pot, 'are a fucking pepper pot,' and we'd all crack up laughing.

He was also incredibly unguarded. He would tell anybody anything about himself without the slightest hesitation – well, anything except what was really important to him, I suppose. It used to amaze me. He'd trust perfect strangers with the sort of personal things I wouldn't tell best friends. We'd meet somebody for the first time, a friend of a friend or something, and you could guarantee by the end of the night Danny would be sat in the corner with them spouting off, telling them all about Mum and Dad's divorce, how he was occasionally worried he might be adopted, that he was worried his penis wasn't wide enough. Incredible things.

Danny was just a very engaging, open person who both men and women seemed to like because he seemed such a well-balanced fuck-up, I suppose.

I visited Danny once in Germany before that final Christmas. It was about seven months after his posting, the weekend of the big summer Shutzentest party in Herford, where all the local clubs and societies in the town take to the streets in lederhosen and oompah bands and beer tents take over the main square. It was supposed to be a sort of Tring Road reunion. Carlos was meant to be flying in from Spain with Dominique. But in the end they never made it because that was the weekend Dominique left him for the Aussie John.

Danny was still in touch with Wendy then and she came over with me on a platonic basis (although I think Danny was hoping for something more), because she thought Dominique was going to be there.

Danny's life in Germany was pretty sad, from what I could gather on that one overnighter, and I remember feeling shocked. His flat was in a large warden-monitored block with its own underground car park on Salzufulerstrasse, overlooking Herford's main square. It was huge but contained virtually no furniture and was as Spartan and soulless as a bedsit. Because of the irregular hours Danny worked doing the breakfast show and the fact that he hadn't bothered to learn German, he clearly didn't have much of a social life outside the radio station either, where everyone was a lot older and tended to be married with kids.

I don't know what I'd been expecting. A wild night, I suppose. Doing something for the memory. Maybe I should have gone alone, without Lucy.

I couldn't believe how different Danny seemed after just a few months. It was like he'd physically shrunk. He looked thinner, older, not his usual self, and he spent a long time trying to justify why he was there, something he'd never felt the need to do before on the phone. He got great overseas military allowances, his petrol was subsidized by the army, all the latest video releases were in the Naffie shop. He even bragged about his washing-machine, which he'd got for £200 cheaper than an equivalent model in the UK. When he said the job wasn't going that well, that he was having run-ins with colonels and majors for being too flippant on air, I didn't think anything of it. Danny always had run-ins with his bosses. It was what made his show so good. He didn't know where to draw the line, was always pushing at the fence. Like the National Cheese Week thing, when Danny ran this spoof campaign in Chalfont to send cheese to dairy-poor countries in the third world (Cheese and Caracas) and the radio station was inundated with smelly cheeses from all round the world that had to be returned at great expense.

That evening in Germany was strange. We had a few frothy beers at Danny's flat and watched the singing and dancing of the party below us in the main square ('German beer is so much better than English – there are no impurities'). And then we ate Thai at a place in town ('The Thai food here is the best in the world'). But we ended up getting into a ridiculous argument about evolution and religion.

Christadelphianism is basically a fundamentalist Christian faith. Its followers believe every single word of the Bible and in a creationist version of human history. Also, according to one pamphlet I read in Danny's flat, they think the world is going to end in 2013. There were books and pamphlets about Europe being the seven-headed beast of the apocalypse. (Already out of date, as I pointed out to Danny, because by then there were fifteen members. 'Ah, but you can't count countries like Luxembourg, can you?' he said.)

We'd talked about it on the phone a couple of times in a joky way and at the time I even imagined he'd left the pamphlets out on purpose to spark a debate. So he could get serious and intense in the way he always liked to after a drink.

The argument in the restaurant followed the same pattern as some of the phone calls, but this time it was even more personal. I was quite drunk, tired from the journey and annoyed because Danny wasn't living up to how I'd described him to Lucy. At one point I said he sounded insane and that Christadelphianism was just a barmy sect. 'At least Hinduism was mainstream. You'll be wearing purple robes next and talking about the Godhead. Don't tell us that's why God made you a DJ – so you'd have the communication skills to spread the message. You're not mentioning any of this on air, are you? Why do you always have to get obsessed with these things? We've come here for a laugh, Danny. I haven't seen you in ages. Can't we talk about something else? You'll be a Jehovah's Witness next week, anyway.'

Danny got unusually hurt by this, and didn't joke his way out of it like normal. At the time I thought it was perhaps because Wendy was there and he felt I was making a fool of him when he was out to impress. Now I realize he probably *was* talking about it on his show. Danny's voice rose in pitch and his jaw muscles clenched. Then he said, 'It's not a fucking sect. It's like any other Church.'

'Yeah, that happens to believe the world's going to end in 2013.'

'They don't know when the world's going to end. They never said they knew when,' said Danny defensively. But he hadn't got an answer to the next bit.

'So why is 2013 the pin number to your Switch card? Danny, I think you should learn German or something, you're spending too long in the flat. Come on, let's talk about something else. He knows it's bollocks really, Wendy.'

'Fuck off, Kit, you patronizing twat.'

The next thing we were on to was homosexuality. Wendy was campaigning for Stonewall about a free vote on lowering the age of consent for gay sex to sixteen and that's how it came up. Danny immediately switched his vehemence to this subject. 'That's ridiculous. It's unnatural. Sticking your willy up another man's arse. At sixteen!'

I was shocked by this. Wendy, who usually enjoyed these debates, asked why it was unnatural if both parties consented. Danny said, 'Of course it's unnatural. Does your new boyfriend stick it up your arsehole? No. And why is this?'

'Because I don't want him to, Danny.'

'OK, so answer me this, would it be natural to have sex with a hamster if it consented? Come on. No, I'm serious.'

'Danny, this is ridiculous,' I said.

'No, it's not. If a hamster could say yes, would you say this was right? Answer me. Would this be natural? If a hamster nodded and said yes?'

Wendy said, very patiently, 'Number one, a hamster would never be able to say yes because hamsters don't talk, Danny; and number two, if it said yes and it could be proved a hamster had a big enough brain to mean what it said then of course it would be OK. Why are you being like this?'

'I can't believe now you're saying it's OK to have sex with hamsters,' said Danny.

I laughed but Wendy became angry and upset and said she'd never heard Danny talk like this before. She said he sounded homophobic and wanted to know where it had all come from. 'I'm not fucking homophobic. I just think it's unnatural, that's all. Why can't I have my own views? You're the one who's advocating shagging pets. And *I'm* the one who's being outrageous?'

There was an embarrassing silence before we got on to Danny's old theory about how there were two different species of human on earth battling for supremacy – those with a sense of humour and those without one. 'And my aim is to make sure we are the ones who survive,' said Danny, after going through it all. I laughed at this because he was being more like his old self – and Wendy said teasingly, 'Oh, it's your species now? You're the boss of it, are you? Danny, I've heard this a million times and it's *boring*.'

Again, normally Danny would have laughed. Instead, he said, 'If people pretend to have senses of humour when they don't they are recognizing it's important to have one, which means people without one must be deficient, and under the rules of natural selection they will therefore die out. Why do you think people send jokes around on the Internet? Have you noticed you never get people with good senses of humour doing this? No,' said Danny and looked round triumphantly. 'Two–nil to me. Fucking hamsters is wrong and humourless people are today's great apes. Another Tiger beer, Kit? I think we're getting somewhere.'

After the waiter had left Wendy said, 'I only sent those Gary Glitter jokes, Danny, because someone sent them to me, if that's what you're on about. I wanted to give you some beans. You're being really flippy tonight. I don't know whether I like you any more.'

Towards the end of the night Danny grew very serious. We'd had about eight Tiger beers each by this stage and while Wendy and Lucy were talking he said to me that when he'd received his recent salary rise the first thing that had crossed his mind was something they'd said at the last Christadelphian meeting. Apparently, the leader of the Bible-study group had told Danny that if he ever turned up at a meeting and found nobody there he wasn't to worry, it just meant they'd been whisked away by Jesus and the apocalypse was imminent. The leader had also said before this happened that there'd be 'a time of plenty'. I listened to Danny, who for a moment looked genuinely worried, and asked him whether he believed this. I didn't for a moment think he did. He clenched his jaw muscles again: 'The extra allowances I get for working in Germany amount to seven thousand quid a year,' he said.

Things worsened when we got back to his flat. Wendy went to bed in tears over something Danny said and when Lucy went in to comfort her Danny leant across the rail of his balcony to tell me: 'Wendy asked whether I was gay tonight. When you two were getting ready she wanted to know why we never had sex when we were going out. Can you fucking believe that girl?'

It was a cue surely for me to say something, but then Lucy walked in. 'What are you doing out here, Danny? Go and speak to Wendy. She thinks you've been implying she's from an inferior species for sending you those jokes.'

We left very early the next morning because Wendy had to get back and there wasn't an opportunity to mention it again.

6 December 2000

> Subject: < mates and what they do to you >
> To: Tom FarleyThomasfarley@hotmail.com >
> From: Kit Farley Kitfarley@yahoo.com >

Dear Tom, We're still in El Paso. Big news: I was right – there was something brewing. Carlos has just more or less ordered me to leave them. The flash-point started with a row about what type of cheese we should have for our picnic lunch this afternoon. I refused to eat orange cheese slices ('How can you tell what a cheese tastes like from its colour?' Dominique said). Then she refused to eat mozzarella because of its consistency ('Yeah, so how can you tell what a cheese tastes like from its texture?' I said). It moved on to the bill for peanuts we've been running up, then Carlos and Dominique had a massive row when we stopped at the bank and she rang her ex-husband yet again, and it all concluded just now after Carlos dropped off Dominique at Lake Lea for a swim.

I was looking through the *Lonely Planet* to find somewhere cheap for us to eat that night and he came and sat next to me at the picnic table. 'Kit, you're probably going home soon anyway,' he said. His lips went all rubbery with guilt. 'I think we should go our separate ways. Don't you?'

'What do you mean?' I said. I thought perhaps he wanted to go out alone with Dominique for the evening to straighten out their earlier disagreement.

'In America. Now. Well, tomorrow,' he said. 'I think we should go our separate ways.'

He said the hairdresser at the Isleworth Chopshop had warned him it might be like this – that he'd probably end up losing a girlfriend and a mate, and the other day during the driving row he'd realized this was starting to happen. He and Dominique were arguing constantly. And now we were arguing, too. 'We'll drop you off at the nearest Greyhound station, there should be one here or in Tucson, and we'll buy out your share of the hire car. You can even have the Cheet-os. I'm sorry, mate. I have to make a decision. It's outside influences.'

Carlos stood up, walked round the table and put his arm round me aggressively. He rocked me up and down with gritted teeth and called me 'Kit-boy' and now he's at the lake breaking the news to Dominique. I feel absolutely shit.

Kit.

> Subject: < who needs mates like him, anyway? >
> To: Tom Farley Thomasfarley@hotmail.com >
> From: Kit Farley Kitfarley@yahoo.com >

Tom, It's an hour later and they're still not back from the lake. I've been thinking about it and it's almost like the way you try to chuck a girlfriend by making the relationship so unbearable she leaves you so you don't have to do it yourself. All the way across America Carlos has been promising that in the next city we'll go out. 'Atlanta, Kit-boy! Dallas, Kit-boy! . . . El Paso, Kit-boy.' It's not that he's worried about Dominique getting mugged: she can look after herself better than we can. Basically, he just doesn't want to be alone with me, and why's that? Because he thinks I've changed. But why have I changed? Because of Danny. So what sort of mate does that make him?

And anyway, it's Carlos who's changed. He doesn't laugh like he used to. Something's gone since he got back with Dominique. He's lost his sense of humour. We used to belly-laugh all the time and it was always about ourselves and what failures we were. He doesn't make jokes about any of this any more. If I remind him of a funny story about school or Tring Road he remembers it differently, or pretends to in front of Dominique. 'We were such prats in those days,' he says, and I think, Fuck off, no we weren't.

I will prove I am more of a traveller than they are. It's bollocks that I can't cope on my own. They will be home before Christmas. I will return years later bearded and jaded with friendship bracelets up to my elbow. 'What, this one, Carlos? This bracelet was given to me by Firewater. Yeah, I lived with the Iroquois on a reservation in Wyoming for three years and we got married and had a kid who's now a brave. Nice boy – should be riding bare-back by now.'

While I tell stories of beauty in the Rocky Mountains and being kidnapped by the Amish, Dominique will be regaling people about the toilet facilities in various campsites: 'The showers were very good and the toilet paper was so soft. I think it was the best campsite we have stayed in. Yes. Really.'

Fuck them.

I think I've inadvertently bonded Dominique and Carlos, not driven them apart. Without me as the common enemy they will fight among themselves like the Yugoslavs after the communists lost power. Carlos will come back alone, jobless, emotionally shattered and enormously fat, and will never forgive himself for not experiencing the deep and meaningful things I've been through.

My only problem is cowardice, though. I might just check into motels and cower in front of the television until my money runs out, paranoid about the slasher films. Four people were gunned down in a burger bar in California yesterday. I read about it in *USA Today*. A man was knifed to death in Maryland, and a tourist was shot at traffic lights in Florida.

And we'd planned to go to a rodeo – that's another thing I won't be able to do now.

Kit.

p.s. I've got a confession to make. You know that thing Danny had with playing cards? Well, you're going to think this is slightly strange but I've started doing it, too. It's weird but you *can* associate everyone's face with a playing card. At the start of this holiday I cut Lucy's card three times, which felt like a good omen, but I haven't cut it for days and it's worrying me now after our rows. Do you ever feel like Danny is communicating with you? When I cut the pack, this is when I can feel him. It sounds mental but I think of his face while I do it and I always seem to get the card I want. Nearly always, anyway. You should try it. It works with almost anyone. You, for instance, are the five of spades. Black hair, the colour of a spade, a five because you have a high forehead like the vertical line on the top of the number 5. And the curly bit of the number at the bottom is your mouth, which often gapes open idiotically.

Journal Entry 11

Danny wasn't supposed to be coming home for Christmas last year because he'd have to be back in Germany on Boxing Day to stand in for someone's show at BFBS in the afternoon. Danny liked to spend hours writing material, designing jingles and packages for every show he did, and he was nervous he wouldn't have enough preparation time if he came home. He'd recently got the audience figures, too, which hadn't been very good – the town of Hamlyn apparently found him patronizing, for some reason – but I persuaded him it'd be OK – we'd write some jokes together.

Because he made the decision to come home so late, and also, I think, because he'd just bought a brand-new convertible BMW, he decided to drive. The journey to Dad's is almost 500 miles and involved crossing four countries. Dad is always panicky around Christmastime when the nights grow darker earlier and he'd wanted to pay for Danny's flight, but Danny said it wasn't about money, he wanted to drive.

In the run-up to Christmas I didn't notice anything too odd. Most of the emails and phone calls I'd got from Danny since my visit were about his new show, abuse about Hamyln ('They think I talk down to them – they're from Hamyln, for fuck's sake, what do they expect? If they're not careful I'll buy a pipe and lure their fucking children away to the mountains') and, of course, the new car. He'd bought it a week after he'd learned Wendy had got engaged. I'd found this out through Carlos, who by then was back with Dominique in Spain, and I was the one who'd broken it to Danny, basically to stop him going on about her. I saw buying the car as a piece of retail therapy, and it had seemed to do the trick because he was insane about it. Danny always loved cars, right from when we were kids collecting brochures. He'd told me how fast it could go, he'd told me how much cheaper it was than the equivalent model in England, he'd told me about the electric retractable roof, he'd even called me once from his car phone to tell me about the global-positioning system. 'It's fucking amazing, Kit. To get home, all I have to do is key in the address of my flat and it tells me exactly where to go, what roads, where to turn. I feel like fucking Knight Rider. I keep expecting it to call me Michael in a camp voice.'

If anything, he seemed slightly better – he wasn't going on about Christadelphianism quite as much, although we'd both become wary about bringing it up after the German visit, so maybe that was a false impression. I knew he was still obsessed about Wendy. I thought maybe that was another reason why he was driving home: perhaps he was going to take the car round to hers to show it off.

He arrived late afternoon on Christmas Eve and we went straight out for a drink with Tom, and Lucy, who was staying with us over Christmas. Tom, Danny and I going out on Christmas Eve had become a tradition since we'd become old enough to drink. Every year we went to the same pub – the Brickies on Walton Street – on the off-chance of meeting old classmates from school and in the distant hope of bumping into Nikki Aldridge, whom we'd met there one year with her boyfriend.

Every year, though, Dad, Sophie, and Jane, who always stayed at Dad's over Christmas, would kick up a fuss. They'd always make out what we were doing was in some way a family sacrilege. The pattern was that first Dad would try to tempt us: a special bottle of port he'd been planning to open, or a family game of Monopoly? Some years he devised a Christmas quiz and would suddenly want us to compete at that. Eventually the tactic would switch to making us feel guilty, and finally to pretending they'd have a better time without us anyway. The three of them would get all pally, and Dad would say, 'Let them do what they want. Stuff 'em if they want to risk their necks on those icy roads. Paul [Sophie's husband], what's the film tonight?' And then, after being told this, 'Perfect,' even if it was something shit like *Herbie Goes Bananas.*

In the pub that night there was no trace of anybody from school, although there were lots of jokes about it: 'Christ, Nikki's just walked in' . . . 'My God, guess who that is at the bar smiling at me?' . . . 'Danny, you'll never guess who I bumped into outside the gents' and who was asking after the guy who hid in the tree.'

That night Danny and I laughed a lot in exactly the same start–stop way that everyone always commented on. It's a laugh I only do when I'm with Danny. It comes from nothing, lasts about three seconds, then stops abruptly, then starts almost immediately again like a car engine misfiring. At one point we all went outside to see Danny's car and he demonstrated putting the roof up and down. We persuaded him to take us all for a drive and Danny got deliberately lost down dirt roads in Haddenham so he could switch on the global-positioning system.

Then back in the pub Danny and I disappeared into a corner and tried to think of some funny ideas for his show. In Tring Road we'd always had a fantasy one day we'd do a show together: *Brothers' Breakfast*, it was going to be called – he'd do all the technical stuff and I'd be there as someone for him to bounce off. It was going to be a first on radio, two brothers on air niggling each other. For years I'd been storing up anecdotes I was going to embarrass him with on air. Like the time I caught him kissing our cousin's bottom in the attic of Beech Road when he was about eight and he tried to make out he was looking for a sticklebrick. They were the same stories I was going to use one day for my best man's speech at his wedding.

Before he went to Germany every evening in the pub would end up with us discussing this, but that night Danny didn't speak about it with the same enthusiasm. Then at closing Danny became sentimental because he'd drunk too much. In this mood Danny used to stare at me with his big brown moist eyes, his mouth would go down at both sides, and he'd hold his square chin slightly higher than normal like his head was a bucketful of water he didn't want to spill. He'd put his head on my shoulder and grip me round the waist with one arm, very tightly in a way that sometimes hurt because he liked to dig his fingers in to show how strong his hands were and how he could probably still have me in a fight. Then when Tom and Lucy were choosing some music on the juke-box, Danny said to me, 'You're still the closest person to me, Kit. We don't see enough of each other. Sometimes I worry that we're drifting apart. We're not, are we? We'll always look after each other, won't we? I'm sorry about that time you visited. I didn't put you off, did I? Does Lucy think I'm a nutter?'

After the final bell we left Danny's car in the car park, shared a taxi home and back at the house Tom and Lucy went to bed. The house had been decorated by Sophie's kids a few days before. There was tinsel everywhere, and the little nativity scene that Dad and Mum had made out of toilet rolls when we were kids was out of the loft. The kids had taken down the encyclopedias and set it up on the shelf. I thought it might be this and being home for the first time in ages that made Danny so nostalgic. We stayed up and chatted in the living room. Danny talked for a while about the radio station and maybe coming back to England if he could find a good job at a commercial station, without revealing how bad things really were in Germany.

Then we had an idea. So we didn't wake Sophie's kids, Danny crept up to the spare room, where he was staying the night, and I disappeared downstairs to the basement to mine and Danny's old bedroom, where I was sleeping with Lucy. We brought up our Christmas stockings that Dad had left at the end of our beds to feel the bulges and to chat about Christmases past and what freebies from the bank Dad would be fobbing us off with that year. Every year Dad raided the stationery cupboard at the bank and our stockings (warm-ups for the main Christmas tree presents in the afternoon) were always full of bank notepads, pens and diaries.

After we'd inspected all the presents Danny put on a tape of a recent show he'd done in Bosnia – they'd sent him there for a week and he'd broadcast from a tin shed to the peace-keeping troops. While I listened, Danny commented on his links ('God, that one was shit'), while going through lots of childhood memories. He seemed very rueful. 'Do you remember the year you wanted an air-rifle for Christmas because Carlos had one, and even though Dad said you weren't getting one, you were sure he was bluffing? You thought that umbrella in your stocking was a gun. That was quite a good year, 1990. What was I doing then? Was that the year we were mad on Nikki Aldridge?' . . . 'Kit, do you remember how we used to skive off school together? I'd be genuinely ill and you'd come into my room and ask me to put in a good word for you with Mum and I'd get round her by saying, "Mum, I think Kit's got it, too," and we'd spend all day playing ping-pong on the dining-room table with those bats Gran gave us for Christmas, using stacks of Ladybird books for the net.' . . . 'Kit, do you remember that little song we had as kids? What was it? "Kit and me are friends because of ninepo in the way." What the fuck was ninepo and why was it in the way? Do you remember?'

By the time I went to bed Danny had become quite maudlin about all kinds of things: he talked about Sophie's kids in a way that just stopped short of envy ('I don't think I'll ever have kids, you know'); he got bitter about Wendy's fiancé ('Probably turn out to be a bender') and his bosses at the radio station ('No fucking imagination'); about Carlos, who was already cheating on Dominique again, or so Danny imagined ('Why do women go for blokes like him?'). Then he said he felt slightly out of it and a bit of a tit because Sophie's husband was spending Christmas with us, Dad had Jane, I had Lucy, and he had no-one *again.*

It was around 3 a.m. – a couple of hours after we'd turned in – that I heard what I thought might have been a faint knock on my bedroom door. I must only have been half asleep because I woke up straight away. Beech Road is a very old house with a field out the back where horses graze in the summer. It was built in the eighteenth century, and the place used to scare us as kids because of the animals we could hear outside at night and the beams, which expanded and creaked when the heating went off. I couldn't work out if it was Danny still up and about, or just the house making noises. If I'd been on my own I'd've called out his name, but I didn't want to wake Lucy, which was stupid because what I did instead was jog her to ask if she'd heard anything.

'What? Oh, God. What time is it? Kit, you frightened the life out of me. I'd just got to sleep then,' she said, dozing off almost instantly.

When I didn't hear a second knock I dropped off myself and didn't think any more about it. Was it Danny? Was he about to tell me something? Would it have made a difference if I had called out his name? Would this have stopped it happening? I don't know.

By Christmas morning I'd forgotten about the knock and we had our normal family Christmas. Sophie cooked us bacon and eggs for breakfast while we picked up Danny's car from the pub, and then for tradition's sake we opened our presents in Dad and Jane's bed in two shifts. We'd been doing this ever since we were kids. Sophie's kids – Harry, Rose and Ben – went first, and then Sophie, Tom, Lucy, Danny and me all in a row under the covers with Paul perched on the corner grinning, Jane taking pictures and Dad moving around making sarcastic jokes.

'We got you some soap, Kit, because we thought you needed it.'

'We got you a calculator, Tom. Works in a bank and still can't add up in his head.'

'Danny, that's called a tie. People wear them to look smart.'

'Lucy, that's a red ribbon. Tie it to your car keys. It will stop you losing them.'

Then we had the usual fight about church, Danny rowing with Dad that as a Christadelphian he didn't have to go; Dad making him go anyway by threatening to take his main present off the tree: 'So you don't want this large one at the back of the tree, Danny?'

The Christmas meal: me insisting on making the gravy because it has to be a certain colour and consistency like the way Mum used to make it when we were kids and messing it up and Jane having to intervene to sieve out the lumps. The main presents: all of us sat round the tree in the living room, always a real one despite Dad's rants about the pine needles; Danny sat by the fire without his shirt on; Dad on his knees at the base of the tree; Tom in Dad's armchair; Sophie with a pen and paper on the sofa next to me and Lucy with her list of who got what ('Don't go so quickly – I missed that one. Whose were the bath salts?'); Dad reading off the labels, flinging over the presents dismissively as if he doesn't really care what's in them, but always making sure we get them in strict rotation, always youngest to the eldest, just like when we were kids ('To Danny – my middle lad, the most infuriating child in the world, but who I love more than anything. You're finally a success. Well done, and I didn't even have to bribe you. Lots of love, Your Silly Old Man'); red soporific faces by the end because of the heat from the log fire and the draining excitement.

'That's your lot,' says Dad, and hands out the envelopes – always the highlight and always containing fifty pounds, except for that incredible year in 1986, when Dad was at his profligate height, when all that was in my and Danny's envelopes was the message 'My two youngest boys, go downstairs to your bedroom and see what you've got.' It was a six-by-three snooker table, the best present we ever had.

In the evening we had to watch what Sophie wanted because she'd ringed all the programmes in *TV Quick* a week beforehand so no-one else got a say.

'Get lost, Sophie – I'm not watching *While You Were Sleeping.*'

'You could've ringed what *you* wanted, but you didn't and it's too late now because if we don't watch it we're all out of kilter for Harry Enfield.'

'I've driven five hundred miles. I only got here yesterday.'

'Well, you should have got here earlier.'

Then, finally, round to the Rising Sun, the local pub across the road, for a lock-in with Dad's mates, Andy and Laura, who run the place, Dad taking the piss out of Danny, but still proud he's standing up at the bar with us, father and sons. 'A Stella for Tom, Paul and Kit. And Danny, oh, nothing for you, is it? You're a Christadelphian now. It's a Coke for this one, Andy.'

'Get lost, Dad – a Stella please, Andy.'

When Dad, Paul and Tom went home at closing time I stayed out with Danny. Andy had put on a compilation of Mexican music, which he'd got for Christmas because they were going there in the New Year, and they'd come round to the front of the bar to drink tequila, while Danny and I and a few other stragglers finished up.

'I think I'm paranoid I'm becoming boring,' Danny told me.

'You're never boring,' I said. 'You're the least boring person I've ever met. Don't be daft. That show from Bosnia was fucking excellent. I don't know what Hamlyn's going on about. What's up? You seem a bit down.'

Danny's mood darkened and as he got up for a piss he said, 'What would you think if I never came back, Kit? What if I disappeared and you never heard from me ever again? That would be so fucking cool.'

He returned a couple of minutes later and laughed, and we started imagining what it would be like if one of us disappeared, like the guy from the Manic Street Preachers, and started a new life somewhere under an assumed name. We were joking around and Danny felt like Danny again.

'I feel I am there,' I said. 'My face is all stubbly. I'm in Tijuana. This music is playing.'

' "They called him Menge and no-one knew where he came from, only that each day he sat in the taverna and drank a litre of Rombola in quiet reflection," ' said Danny.

'You'd go all quiet and occasionally your face would freeze over and you'd say,' I said.

' "That is something I never speak of," ' said Danny.

' "Everybody knew Menge. But nobody *knew* Menge," ' I said. ' "There were many stories – some said he used to be a journalist, others a lazy bastard who couldn't make gravy without lumps." '

'But nobody knew and nobody asked for there were some things Menge would never speak of,' said Danny.

'And gravy was one of these things.

'Danny, are you all right?' I asked just before we left. 'Work's all right and stuff – you're not still down about Wendy? That thing you started to tell me that time . . . All that Christadelphianism stuff.'

'I'm fine,' said Danny, cutting me off, but he didn't want to go straight home so we went for a walk after Andy and Laura closed up and ended up lying on the grass on a bank alongside the Grand Union Canal that snakes its way out of Aylesbury and on to London through Aston Clinton. I was on my back looking at the stars. Danny was, too, with his fleece over his head because it was cold. At one point we heard what sounded like a rumble of thunder. I said it must be a barge scraping against the canal bank when Danny sat up.

'I'm serious,' I continued. 'You've been a little odd lately. I know you're just winding us up, but sometimes I get worried.'

Danny lay back down and there was another loud rumble, which made him jump.

'Christ, it *is* thunder,' said Danny.

'Actually, it's the end of the world,' I said. 'You'll probably be whisked off on a cloud any minute to a new fucking Eden.'

Danny laughed. 'You really had me worried in Germany, you know,' I said and Danny laughed again.

It started to rain and we walked back to the house with our arms round each other.

Danny was never the most conscientious at phoning to let you know he was going to be late, had arrived safely, or whatever, so nobody worried when we didn't hear from him the next afternoon. He'd left on Boxing Day morning, two hours before Lucy, who was driving up to Birmingham to see her parents. I'd helped Danny pack his presents into the boot at 7 a.m. and everyone had got up to wave him off down the drive. The family tradition – wave all the way. He'd been quite emotional saying goodbye to everyone, I remember. Since Mum left us Dad's never been that great at showing affection, part of the reason Jane's never moved in with him before now, I think, but I remember Danny brushing this aside and giving Dad an incredibly big hug and still hugging for a long time after Dad had stopped hugging back. He kissed Sophie on the lips, something he hadn't done for years. He chatted to the kids, who he was usually so good with, in a very earnest way that slightly frightened them. He asked Lucy very sincerely
to take care of me. And after we'd hugged he gave me an incredibly long stare that brought tears to his eyes, and, because of this, to mine as well.

'Watch yourself, Kit-Kat,' was the last thing he said to me, using the nickname he'd used for me when we were kids.

'You watch yourself, too,' I said. I didn't know it then, but it was the last proper conversation I'd ever have with my brother.

Boxing Day was a big day in its own right. It was the day Sophie chose to tell us she was pregnant and expecting her fourth kid. Dad opened a bottle of champagne and we were still celebrating this when there was a knock at the door. Dad had recently become a part-time magistrate at Aylesbury Magistrates' Court. It's a warrant they're after, I thought when I saw the policeman at the door. It quite often happened at weekends. The policeman looked uncomfortable on the doorstep, I noticed through the window. Our drive at Beech Road is long and narrow and normally you have to reverse down it to get out because there's not much room to turn round, but the policeman had somehow slewed his squad car halfway round in front of our cars as if for a quick getaway. This seemed odd, too.

Dad went to the door, grumpy about the interruption, and I stood in the doorway that connects the living room to the dining room with a glass of champagne in my hand.

'Mr Farley?'

'Yes,' said Dad.

'I am very sorry, but do you have a son named Daniel Farley, a resident of Flat 56 2345 Salzufulerstrasse, Herford, Germany?'

'Yes,' said Dad less confidently.

'I have some bad news,' said the policeman. And then he took off his helmet.

7 December 2000

Amazing things happened last night, which now mean I'm not getting a Greyhound. The reason: Dominique talked me out of it. It happened in the Brown Bag Deli restaurant we drove to in El Paso after they got back from Lake Lea last night, and I'm still stunned.

'Have you told Dominique about the Greyhound?' I asked Carlos when we arrived at the restaurant, and he said yes, but that when he'd gone down to the lake to speak to her she'd said *she* was going to get a Greyhound. 'I don't want you both fucking off on Greyhounds,' he said.

For a while I couldn't work out what the fuck was going on, whether it meant I was going or not. 'I'll check out the

Greyhound times in Tucson in the morning, shall I, then?' I said in front of Dominique when we sat down.

Carlos pretended he hadn't heard me, but that's when Dominique surprised me. 'I don't think you should get a Greyhound,' she said. 'Do you?'

I said I thought it was for the best.

'Why, because I am such a moody scorpion-woman you cannot stand to be with?'

'I'm aware I'm getting on your nerves,' I said. 'I'm coming between you.'

'But you will miss the Grand Canyon and everything if you go. You do not want that.'

I should have said, 'I never wanted to see the Grand Canyon,' or, 'There'll always be another time.'

'You can bear to be with me for another two weeks,' she said. 'We have done the hard driving now. It is only a few days. We can stay a few days at places and I can have some room. I need some hours to be alone in each day. I do not know why I was like that with the cheese. Here: I give you my hand.'

I reached over and held Dominique's hand. It was bony and cold, but it felt nice. I looked across at Carlos. His eyes were inscrutable, but I felt a wave of emotion flood over me, fear and panic about the thought of travelling alone. I almost felt like bawling with relief that now I wasn't going to be.

'You would die on your own,' she said, and nodded seriously, and I laughed to try to hide the pathetic tears in my eyes that had come from nowhere.

'Yes, I think so. I would worry the whole time,' she said, still serious.

I had no idea what Carlos wanted me to do, because he changed the subject again and began discussing the American football on the telly, and I thought, Fuck you, you invited me, why should I wind up in a chest freezer just because you want to go for tasty meals?

'It was the peanuts that did it, wasn't it?' I said, just as the burritos arrived.

Dominique said yes, that and the mozzarella. And at that moment the nachos were brought over. The cheese was the same colour as the orange stuff I'd stopped Dominique buying earlier that day in the supermarket.

'I'm *not* fucking eating orange cheese,' I said, pushing my plate away, but then I laughed, and Dominique laughed, too.

After this the atmosphere was different. Dominique said I'd been up very late last night and wanted to know if I was scanning the campsite for bears. She'd seen my torch on past 2 a.m. and I found myself telling her I was writing a journal about Danny and everything that had happened. Carlos turned away. Dominique held my hand again.

After this we ended up reminiscing about Europe and everything Danny had made us do. It's the first time we've really discussed it this whole trip. At one point Dominique reminded me about the time we'd stolen the pedalo on Rimini beach, something I never normally feel comfortable bringing up when Carlos is around. I said I thought she'd changed a bit since then. She blamed it on her divorce and said I'd changed a bit too, but for the better.

'What sort of little things annoy you? Because I don't know I'm doing it,' I said. 'Maybe if you told me. I know I'm annoying. I'll try to be better.'

Dominique said, 'Nothing, silly things. The mosquitoes. Maybe I am used to them from Australia.'

Then Carlos butted in: 'It's other things, too, though,' he said. He looked at me as if he was unsure whether he should say anything. 'Like the way you always put your tent up right next to ours. Dominique always tries to put ours up last so we can get some privacy.'

Dominique claimed this wasn't true.

'You always seem to wait for us to do it first, Kit.' Carlos looked to Dominique for back-up. 'There's a whole campsite and he always puts it up *right* next to ours.'

'He is frightened of the animals,' said Dominique.

Carlos looked embarrassed. 'I just wondered why you were

doing it. I don't mind. I just couldn't work it out, that's all,' he said. 'Come on, Kit.' He put his arm round my neck. 'You can sleep *in* our tent if you get really scared about the mosquitoes.'

I felt I had to tell Dominique I wasn't really scared of mosquitoes, but what Carlos said next annoyed me: 'Kit, you're scared of *everything*. I don't know anybody more scared of things.' Then he added softly, in a way that seemed infinitely more patronizing: 'That's why you're here, mate.'

I think I was wrong about Dominique. I've misjudged her. She's very practical and sometimes I think this is why we've fallen out. I've misinterpreted it as rudeness or condescension. She *does* have a sense of humour, but she has to know it's a joke in advance or she doesn't get it. You can't say anything deadpan, but if you smile as you say a joke she understands. When she tries to make a joke herself it's hilarious. She sneaked up on me at the comfort station after we got back last night and made a growling noise pretending to be a bear, and when I jumped, she laughed her head off. 'It is a practice – play dead, remember.'

Today's news: we only drove 300 miles, north on I-25 to Les Cruces and then on I-10. I got stopped for speeding by a state trooper and we're about to camp in Rockhound State Park, near Deming, New Mexico.

> Subject: < nutter >
> To: Kit Farley Kitfarley@yahoo.com >
> From: Tom Farley Thomasfarley@hotmail.com >

Dear Kit, I've just got your messages. What's going on? Are you still speaking to Lucy, still with Dominique and Carlos? What's happening with Christmas? You keep changing your mind and sound . . . odd. Get your arse home. I want my turkey gravy lumpy this year.

Tom.

p.s. And make up with Lucy, you tit.

> Subject: Re: < nutter >
> To: Tom Farley Thomasfarley@hotmail.com >
> From: Kit Farley Kitfarley@yahoo.com >

Dear Tom, I'm writing this in a campsite in Deming, New Mexico, and I'm still with them because, amazingly, Dominique talked me out of going. I've got her all wrong and feel guilty about all the things I've said about her. She was really sweet last night and I know for sure now it's all Carlos's fault.

The atmosphere has definitely changed. This morning I was stopped for speeding, something Dominique's been warning would happen from day one. We had to drive to a courthouse in La Mesa and pay a $110 fine and Dominique paid her third without a murmur. She even took a picture of me handing the money over to the judge and started getting all chatty about when the Southwestern New Mexico State Fair was on so we could see a rodeo. She'd have gone mental a couple of days ago. In the end it was a complete role reversal because Carlos got into a strop.

Kit.

p.s. Serious younger brother stuff now. Do you ever think about Danny the way he used to be? I've started writing a journal about it, to work it all out, and I've found myself writing the odd email to him in my head. What's this all about? Am I in denial or just a nutty twat on the edge?

Journal Entry 12

The policeman on the doorstep hadn't been able to give us any details, just the name of the hospital, the Gilead in Bielefeld, which we discovered was a few miles from Herford when we looked on the atlas. One of the few things the policeman *did* say was: 'There's no need to hurry, Mr Farley.' No need to hurry. It's incredible how many nuances you can get out of this one phrase. No need to hurry. Did it mean it wasn't serious? That Danny had just broken an arm? But why would a policeman come to our door to say something as low-key as that? No need to hurry. Did it mean it was so serious Danny wouldn't be alive when we got there? No need to hurry. Or was the policeman just trying to make sure we didn't break our necks getting to the airport, the reason, possibly, he'd slewed his car across ours in the drive.

International directory enquiries could only give us a fax number for the hospital. We tried to speak to someone at BFBS Radio in Herford, but as it was Boxing Day there was nobody there, just a voicemail message with details about phone-in competitions. We tried BFBS in Chalfont but had no luck. So then we called international directory enquiries again and asked if there were any other hospitals in Bielefeld, thinking we might get the Gilead through them. The woman gave us a number for the Yohaaes Hospital, but when we explained what we wanted the receptionist, who didn't speak very good English, put us on hold and for ten minutes we just heard a robotic voice saying, '*Bitte varten, bitte varten.*'

In the end we gave up and Dad decided we should fly straight there and find out what was going on for ourselves.

We took off at about 9 p.m. and I can't recall much about the flight apart from every few minutes we were offered a drink, a hot towel, a magazine or something to eat. Dad kept checking his phone in the armrest, looking for a message from Paul; Sophie held Jane's hand because she couldn't stop crying; Tom stared out of the window; and I played little mental games with myself. If that door to the toilet opens in the next five seconds it's good news and he's all right. If the orange juice has pulp in it he's going to be all right. If I get out a hand of seven-line patience he'll be all right.

The other thing I did was try to think of Danny alive. This seemed important. Mind over matter. If I could picture Danny being Danny, if I could remember things about him, things we'd done together, he would somehow know I was doing this and would think about them too, and if it was very serious, if it was a matter of life and death, this would keep him going. Danny and I with cane swords in Vale Park with Zorro masks on; Danny and I on the wall in Heston; Danny and I stealing strawberries from the Rumbolds' back garden in Beaconsfield; the stupid little games Danny, Carlos and I became ridiculously competitive over in Tring Road; painful freekick, where we would take it in turns to volley the football as hard as we could at the other two standing six yards away on the sofa chairs with Ladybird books down their pants.

All the time I was going through it I couldn't believe the worst-case scenario that Danny was dead already, because I felt sure I would know if he was: something in my head would've told me. I would have sensed it. Whenever Danny rang me from Germany I was often able to predict it was him before I picked up the receiver. It seemed to ring differently, a Danny ring. It was the same when I opened my Yahoo account: I always knew a second before if there'd be a message from him. We could finish each other's sentences. We laughed the same. I was his brother and we'd collected fucking bears together – there'd have been some omen if he was dead. I was sure about this.

The hospital was about an hour from Hanover Airport, and when we got there the British Army liaison officer was paged – a woman called Mandy who spoke with a German accent. She took us to her office and contacted the senior consultant, Dr Schafe, from there. He arrived a few moments later. He told us to come with him and led us to a small waiting room outside the accident and emergency department. There was a nurse already in there. The room had pictures of swans on the wall, there was a box of tissues on a table and one book on the shelves, a German Bible.

The nurse had a plastic bag with her – it was a flimsy, unbranded blue bag, like the ones you get in cheap off-licences. She gave it to us. It contained Danny's clothes. This was the first terrible shock. The second was worse.

Mandy the liaison officer came into the room with a tray of tea she had fetched from the nurses' station. I started to brace myself. Until then we'd all assumed it was a car accident. Danny was travelling 500 miles, crossing four countries, he was in a new car, probably tired, driving too fast; Danny tended to drive too fast. Perhaps he was still slightly drunk from the night before, over the limit maybe. The policeman had even used the word accident, I think. We could imagine how it had happened, picture the collision. But Dr Schafe started talking about carbon monoxide, Danny's brain being starved of oxygen. He was in a coma, he had a blood clot they'd have to operate on. It wasn't looking hopeful. Hang on a second, there's been a mix-up, I started to think.

'My son is Daniel Farley,' said Dad, who was obviously thinking the same. 'We've flown in from England, we're hungry and tired, my daughter is pregnant and we just want to know what is going on. We were told to come to the Gilead. I think there's been—'

The doctor looked down at his polystyrene cup. He exchanged a look with Mandy and I twigged at the same moment as Tom. Oh my fucking God. Danny tried to top himself.

They let us see him briefly before the operation to relieve the blood clot. Dr Schafe explained they couldn't operate any earlier because of the carbon monoxide in his blood, which meant he'd had to be oxygenated first. We couldn't all go into the unit together because of the risk of infection. There was another patient with bad burns who was critical, so we went in shifts, Jane, Sophie and Tom first. They came out crying. Then it was Dad's and my turn.

I think I expected a scene out of *ER*, people haring around with crash trolleys barking out, 'BP 120 over 40, triple biectopy, give him the adrenalin now.' But the ward was incredibly quiet. In the nurses' station there was a radio on and we could even hear laughter. Danny was in a bed at the furthest end of the ward, in a two-man bay next to the guy with the burns. He was lying on his side with a sheet over his midriff. His hair had been combed into a side parting that made him look like a stranger and there were lots of tubes coming out of him: one in his nose that splayed his nostrils wide and connected him to the ventilator that was breathing for him; clear tubes in his arms that fed him fluid, medication and sedatives on remote-controlled drips; a catheter tube that led to a urine bag attached to the metal frame of the bed. A TV screen full of different-coloured squiggles was monitoring his blood pressure, heart rate, pulse, breaths per minute and the oxygenation of his blood.

But the main thing was his face. It was enormously swollen – the result of the steroids he'd been given to counteract the blood clot, the nurse told us. At Sophie's wedding Paul's best man made cardboard masks of Paul's head which everybody wore for the first dance. Except they were done on the 125 per cent setting on the photocopier. This is what Danny looked like. His head seemed out of proportion to the rest of his body.

There was a sickly sweet smell in the air, and the only sound in the room was from the plastic tube connected to the ventilator Danny was breathing through, which sounded like a straw sucking out the last drop from a milkshake. Dad went straight up to Danny and kissed him on the forehead. He did it like Danny was a kid being tucked into bed and it made me think Dad was assuming Danny was going to die.

'It's all right, everyone's here now, Danny – we're all here,' Dad whispered, and held Danny's limp hand that had the pulse monitor attached to his forefinger. 'Tom, Sophie and Jane have just been in and Kit's here. Kit's standing next to me.'

'I'm here, Danny,' I said, and I kissed him on the head, too.

Dad put his head very close to Danny's ear: 'You're going to have an operation and then you'll be better. I promise you that. Please be strong, my lovely lad. Be strong. We all love you and we're all here. You're going to have an operation, then you'll be better. Can you hear me? Please be strong, my lovely lad.'

After a couple of minutes a few nurses started gathering in the doorway. Then one of them came into the room and unclipped one of the drips. She reattached it to a portable trolley full of more apparatus.

Dad was still going on about Danny being strong as we were moved round to the foot of the bed to let the nurses unhook more tubes. Dad gripped one of Danny's feet. I held the other one. It was all we could reach of him now and it seemed to jog me back to reality. I started to panic.

'And if you don't make it I'm having your car, do you understand?' I found myself saying. 'Dad, he's got to wake up or I'll have his car, won't I?'

Dad looked at me as if I'd gone mad. 'We'd better go, Kit,' he said, and put his arm round my shoulder.

'Bribe him, Dad,' I said. 'You've got to bribe him.'

The head nurse said we could stay. 'One minute,' she said, looking at her watch.

'You've got to bribe him, Dad,' I said again. 'We have to do something. He thinks we're saying goodbye. We're not saying goodbye. You've got to bribe him.'

They were getting ready to wheel him out now.

'I'll leave chip wrappers in it, knacker the gears, stink it up and wrap it round a tree. Imagine what I'll do to that car. Danny, you've got be strong or I'll ruin your fucking car. He's got to be strong, Dad, hasn't he?'

Dad moved round the bed and leaned forward to kiss Danny again, and the tears were streaming down his face. I did the same and the tears were streaming down my face, too. Then Danny was off down the white corridor, my beautiful brother, still beautiful even with a head the size of a watermelon. 'And nobody knew Menge apart from his brother,' I shouted, trotting along the side of him just before he went through the double doors of the lift to theatre.

'Talk to me, boys,' said Dad very seriously as he almost collapsed into a chair in the waiting room beside Jane. Tom and Sophie instinctively looked at me, just like everyone always looked at me if it was anything to do with Danny; just like they looked at him if it was anything to do with me. And, of course, I said nothing about the knock on the door, and what I'd already started to suspect was the reason for Danny doing what he'd done. Because what would that show? The closest person to me in all the world had knocked on my bedroom door on Christmas Eve, two days before he tried to kill himself, probably looking to be talked out of it, and what had I done? Turned over and gone back to fucking sleep.

8 December 2000

We're still in Deming, New Mexico. The original plan today was for Carlos and Dominique to go over the Mexican border at Columbus and have a meal, but Dominique changed her mind at the last minute and didn't want to go, so we've done nothing all day but sit around in the sun. Carlos was pissed off because it was supposed to be his and Dominique's time alone together and they ended up having a row when we were sat around the campsite's hot spa and Carlos asked Dominique who she was writing postcards to. Without thinking, she said, 'Some of our friends in Perth.' Carlos wanted to know when she was going to stop referring to her and her ex-husband's friends as 'ours', as if they were still together.

In the middle of it all, just as I was about to leave and give them some space, three guys arrived in ten-gallon hats. It turned out they were bronco riders. I asked one of the guys when the next rodeo was. He said we'd just missed the New Mexico State Fair, it had been last night. I told him the judge in La Mesa mentioned it was actually tomorrow. The youngest bronco rider clearly didn't like being disagreed with and gave me a look that suggested he wanted to lasso me and drag me round the campsite, so I said, 'Not that it matters, hey – you're probably right.' Dominique overheard, lifted her sunglasses and couldn't suppress a laugh: 'Kit, are you being a coward again?' she said.

It was very bad timing. Carlos shouted: 'Fucking hell, our relationship's on the line, Dominique, and you're talking to Kit – what's the point?'

> Subject: < where are you? >
> To: Kit Farley Kitfarley@yahoo.com >
> From: Lucy Jones Lucyjones23@hotmail.com >

Kit, I have to know what to do about these tickets.
Shall I cancel them or what?
Lucy.

Subject: < Christmas >
> To: Kit Farley Kitfarley@yahoo.com >
> From: Jon Farley Jonathan_farleyRBS@aol.com >

Dear Kit, Any luck getting yourself measured up for the suit? I do need to have those measurements soon. Have you thought any more about Christmas? Tom said you might be coming back. Let me know what you plan to do because I'll have to sort out beds. Would you mind being in your old room in the basement? You do understand about the house, don't you? Tom says you're feeling a bit odd about it. I do, too. But I know it's the right decision.
Dad xx

It's later now, after midnight, and I had a long chat with Carlos by the side of the hot spa after Dominique went to bed. It was strained and at one point Carlos was so desperate for something to say that he started talking about the plot of his Frederick Forsyth book.

I smoked a cigarette and spoke to him in the same awkward way, mostly about Lucy. I said the pendulum had swung the other way and she was now missing me more than I was missing her.

Then Carlos made an apology of sorts: 'I'm sorry this is so shit,' he said. 'Perhaps you're happy now, though. It's not only shit for you, but for me, too.'

I watched a column of steam rise slowly from the hot spring and disappear into the dark like a piece of flicked elastic.

'It's weird, you know,' said Carlos. 'Sometimes I get the feeling it's all turning around. I think I know how you felt being a gooseberry. Sometimes, like today, I don't know.' He looked me so hard in the eye, I had to turn away. 'I've started to feel a bit like one myself.'

Journal Entry 13

At Heathrow I'd called Lucy to tell her what had happened, but she was out having a meal with her parents. She phoned the Gilead on the number we'd given Paul at about 1 a.m. Her call was put through to intensive care just after we'd been told more bad news by Dr Schafe. The operation to remove the brain clot had gone as well as could be expected but Danny's life signs were very weak and he wasn't expected to survive the night.

Again we had to see Danny in shifts: three hours each. Again it was difficult – were we saying goodbye, or were we giving Danny hope? You're meant to talk to coma victims because hearing is the last sense to go. This is what Dr Schafe told us and initially this is what Tom and I did.

We told him we loved him, that he was going to get better. We talked about mundane things, we told him how strong he was. Then, as the hours wore on and we took it in turns to take the seat nearest his head to rub Vaseline into his lips that were dry from the oxygen he was being given, we ran out of things to say directly to him and talked among ourselves as if we were sitting round the table at Sunday lunch. 'Shit, that duty nurse is pretty, don't you think, Danny?' 'That Mandy's been marvellous. I think she's a fan of the show. Did you hear that, Danny? Someone likes your show. Obviously not from Hamlyn.'

Eventually, at around 3 a.m., we ran out of things to say and went down to the cafeteria. We got the Turkish cleaner to let us in so we could raid the tables for English newspapers. To stay awake, we read them out loud on Danny's bed, then, as we grew more tired and our mouths started to dry, we just read to ourselves, until Dad took over at 4 a.m.

After a brief sleep fully clothed in two beds in one of the empty medical wards down the corridor we were woken by Sophie at about 11 a.m. We had to go to intensive care immediately.

Dr Schafe was at Danny's bedside when we got there. He explained the situation: Danny's blood pressure was slightly lower, his breaths per minute had improved, they wanted to reduce the amount of oxygen supplied by the ventilator to see if Danny could make up the shortfall himself. Dr Schafe asked Dad what the family wanted to do. He stood very close to Dad's face when he asked us, and searched our eyes for clues. I felt like we were somehow conspiring against Danny.

Dr Schafe said we would have to tell Danny to breathe. He would be used to the ventilator by now and might have forgotten how to breathe for himself.

'You've got to breathe, Danny,' Dad said, stroking Danny's head.

'Danny, breathe, man,' said Tom.

'Come on, you lazy bastard,' I said. 'They're pissing for you, shitting for you, you can at least breathe.'

'In, out,' said Sophie. 'That's all it is. In, then out.'

Dr Schafe left and came back with three male nurses. He said because they'd reduced the sedative level Danny might wake up and start grabbing at the tube in his nose. The nurses were there to restrain him. Sure enough, when Dr Schafe pressed a button on the ventilator Danny began to thrash around like a demon. 'It is normal,' said Dr Schafe. 'Please, you have to remind him to breathe.'

And so we chanted, 'In, out, Danny. In, out. Come on, Danny. In, out, in, out,' as if he was a woman in labour, taking big breaths ourselves to encourage him and demonstrate how easy it was. Danny's thrashing was so violent that he had to be held down not only by the three nurses, but by Dad, Tom and me, too. And then finally we saw Danny's chest inflate. 'In, out,' said Sophie and gripped my hand. 'He's doing it,' she said. 'In, out, in, out,' we kept saying, watching his chest anxiously between each breath.

When Danny had settled back into his coma and the doctors said he had stabilized we learned some more about what had happened from the welfare officer. Danny had been found unconscious in the underground car park of his block of flats and had been taken to the Gilead. He had something called UK BC status in Germany, which meant he was treated as a civilian member of the British Army, so the British liaison officer based in the hospital had been informed when he was brought in. She'd contacted GCHQ in Munchengladback, who'd in turn contacted Danny's radio station boss, Sam Smythe, in Herford. He'd then informed the Royal Military Police in Bielefeld, who'd informed the police in Aylesbury, who'd come and told us the news.

Dad, Jane, Sophie and Tom and I drove round to Danny's flat to find the *Hausmeister*, who'd found Danny.

Karl Kobel was a tall, shabby-looking man who didn't speak much English.

In the end we used his phone and, through Mandy translating at the hospital, passing the phone backwards and forwards, we managed to establish that Karl had only gone down to the car park to check the entrance barrier was working, and that he'd dragged Danny from the fume-filled car at about 3 p.m. on Boxing Day. Karl was about sixty-five and he hadn't been able to hold up Danny properly; that was how he'd got the blood clot – when Karl had opened the door

Danny had fallen to the ground head first. Karl then called an ambulance.

Later Karl took us up to Danny's flat and waited outside while we looked for a note. There was no sign of one, but, looking at Danny's roster on the noticeboard of the fridge, Tom discovered something: Danny had been lying about coming back to do a show on Boxing Day afternoon. He hadn't had to come back to Germany that day at all. He wasn't down to work again until the 27th. What's more he wasn't doing the breakfast show any more. The next month's roster had him down for a lunchtime slot, something he hadn't mentioned over Christmas.

That night, after our shift at Danny's bedside, sitting on the stone walls of the fort 500 feet above Bielefeld, looking down on the red-tiled roofs of the town, I told Tom about the knock on my bedroom door on Christmas Eve. I said I thought there was more to it than just the radio thing, that I should have done more. I didn't believe it was just a Danny freak-day, as Dad had started to refer to it. What about Christadelphianism, Wendy too? Tom became angry with me, repeated one of Dad's phrases, 'We've all got to sing from the same hymn book.' He said there was nothing anybody could do and, even though I didn't believe him, I felt better and closer to Tom for having told him.

Over the next couple of days Danny's condition improved slightly. The amount of oxygen the ventilator supplied was cut down again so Danny was breathing 50 per cent for himself. He had to wear plaster-cast boots to stop his feet going into the ballerina position; his left arm, which had already begun spasticating under his chin, was gradually plastered further and further down so it was by his side. We were taught how to operate the chest suction pump: because Danny wasn't breathing naturally, gunk collected in his lungs which had be sucked up with a hoover-type attachment that was fed into his lungs through his nose.

We made phone calls to our various places of work to let

them know what had happened, to say we wouldn't be back at our desks in the New Year. Dad tried unsuccessfully to track down Mum, relatives were informed and I called Wendy, who wanted to fly straight out to administer beans but whom I persuaded not to after explaining the circumstances. 'Oh my God. Oh my God' was basically her reaction, but she hadn't any clue about why he'd done it and said she hadn't heard from Danny for a few weeks.

'It's not your fault,' I had to keep telling her. 'It's all my fault,' I wanted to tell her.

We'd fallen into a routine. We stayed in the same three-hour shift sequence we'd had from the beginning: Sophie, Dad and Jane, if she was up to it, would see Danny in the morning, while Tom and I ate a buffet breakfast in the Catterick mess. Tom and I would visit in the afternoon while the others went to the restaurant a few hundred yards away from the hospital for lunch, because they couldn't stomach the food in the cafeteria. Sophie, Dad and Jane would then take over in the early evening while Tom and I went down the Bum, as we came to call the Bum Bethelerk restaurant. We'd then take over until 11 p.m., after which we'd walk up the hill to the fort overlooking Bielefeld to drink bottles of Veltins beer on the ramparts and discuss Danny's progress, always looking for hopeful signs. 'We'll his blood pressure's down' . . . 'His breaths per minute are better' . . . 'When do you think he's going to wake up?' These sessions would always end with me blaming myself, and Tom being reassuring and trying to switch the attention to Jane, who still didn't like going to the hospital, kept her coat on the whole time when she was there and preferred to deal with all the admin through the welfare office to keep busy. Finally, we'd all regroup at the hospital at about 1 a.m. to drive back to the barracks, where we'd drink in the Scuffs bar, praising Jane for what she'd managed to sort out and discussing what the doctors had said. It was exactly the same every day. 'The next day is crucial,' we'd be told. This would come and go and then it was the next day that was going to be crucial.

During our visits, occasionally Tom and I referred to what Danny had done and called him a berk, but usually not, and when we ran out of conversation we read to him: two Nick Hornbys, a Bill Bryson and his favourite book, *The Little Prince* by Antoine de Saint-Exupéry.

In the early evenings – never earlier than that, for some reason – we'd always switch on the telly and compete at *Wer Wird Millionar?* on RTL, the German version of *Who Wants to be a Millionaire?*

'*Was ist ein Abendsegler?*'

A *Scmetterling*
B *Fledermaus*
C *Vogel*
D *Stierkampf*

We'd shout out the answers even though we didn't have a clue: '*Fledermaus*' . . . 'Definitely *Scmetterling.*' Danny would occasionally make a moaning sound like someone stirring during a nightmare and every time he did this we'd pretend he was answering the questions. 'Fucking hell, Danny, did you just say *Vogel*? I thought you only knew how to order a beer in German.'

By the end of the third day the doctors stopped telling us he was going to die. They never said he was going to live either, but then when do doctors ever give you good news? This change of tack marked the start of the 'That boy is invincible, that boy is a fighter' phase, of Dad stalking round the bar in the evenings telling anyone who'd listen, 'My son came in the back door of the hospital, but, my God, he's walking out of the front one.'

Then on the fourth morning they lowered Danny's oxygen level to 20 per cent, but had to put it back up to 30 per cent when Danny's blood pressure shot up. The results from some neurology tests weren't encouraging.

Back in the Swan room that afternoon – a running joke between Tom and me by then ('Shit, not the fucking Swan room') – we were told it was a duse brain injury. Dr Schafe said the oxygen starvation was going to be general across all areas of Danny's brain which meant almost any function of Danny's brain could be affected and they wouldn't have a clue which ones until, and if, he woke up.

There are basically two crucial aspects to a coma: first, the longer you're in one the worse will be the brain damage when you wake up; second, the longer you're out the more likely it is your muscles will contract and waste away.

But even as the days went by Dad's optimism was infectious. When he spoke to his bank he told them Danny would be home in a few days. He never said Danny had tried to kill himself or mentioned brain damage and he referred to the accident as a nasty bump on the head. We were all swept along with this. We even joked about it. '*Das Kopf ist kaput*' ('The head is broken') was the closest translation we could find for Danny's condition in the German–English dictionary. 'Your *Kopf ist kaput*, Danny. So will our jobs be if you don't get off your arse, man.'

On New Year's Eve Paul flew out and we moved out of the barracks and into Danny's flat.

The burns victim was moved to a surgical ward that day and Danny had the bay to himself, so Dr Schafe allowed us all in at once and we had a little party around Danny's bed. We covered his tubes in paper streamers, listened to the sound of distant firecrackers coming from the town centre and counted down to the New Millennium with a few bottles of Veltins. '*Frohes neues Jahr*' the nurses taught us, and at midnight Dad rubbed beer on to Danny's lips with a cotton bud. 'Happy New Year, my son. And hang on in there. You're doing brilliantly, my lovely lad. We're all very proud of you.'

Occasional visitors had begun to arrive by then, too. Granny had flown in from Cornwall on the 30th, with, for some reason, a patchwork cushion she'd knitted for Danny to rest his head on that made us all laugh at its sheer uselessness. A few presenters from BFBS had stopped by, including his boss Sam Smythe, and through them we found out more about the mysterious roster. Danny had been switched from the breakfast to lunchtime slot a couple of weeks before Christmas, and although they never called it a demotion – he was simply being 'kept fresh' – it was clear something had happened. The station manager, Sam Smythe, got back from his holiday on New Year's Eve and dropped in to apologize for not being on the scene quicker. He told us Danny had changed the 7.20 a.m. 'Pause for Thought' feature on the Breakfast Show and instead of Padre Tim Phillips from Wentworth Barracks coming into the studio he'd given air-time to the leader of his local Christadelphian church. Symthe explained that squaddies took an oath of loyalty to the crown and the Church of England. On top of adding Christ-adelphian meetings to the what's on listings, it was deemed sufficiently serious to transfer Danny from the Breakfast Show as a punishment.

On 2 January the oxygen level from the ventilator was reduced to 20 per cent, then a day later to 10 and on 5 January it was switched off altogether.

But another week then passed with no change. Then another. Then, just as we were beginning to think Danny would never wake up, on 23 January Danny's eyes opened. It was an incredible moment – and I missed it. We all did. In a way it was typical Danny, to do it when nobody was there.

We were cautioned not to get carried away – the opening of the eyes in itself didn't mean much, it could be just a reflex. But it was the best news for a fortnight and we couldn't contain ourselves. Lucy, who'd just started her new job at *Insurance Monthly* and so hadn't been able to get away any earlier, hopped on a plane. Sophie, who'd been back home to see her kids, came back out. And once we were all together we didn't know quite what to do. So we had a party – a barbecue on Danny's balcony. A bottle of champagne was sent to Karl

Kobel, one to Mandy and another to Dr Schafe, and Sam Smythe gave out a dedication to Danny on the air at midnight. We were all very drunk by then. 'Good mornnnn-ning, Herford. This is for Danny Farley, who most of you will remember from the Breakfast Show, and who today woke up from a very long sleep.'

The next couple of days were thrilling: Danny spoke his first word in almost a month – 'Fuck.' Suddenly, it seemed my brother was coming alive.

9 December 2000

There doesn't seem to be any plan of action at the moment and we're still in Deming. Dominique and Carlos fought all morning, disappeared off in the car this afternoon and when they got back Carlos announced they were going to the New Mexico State Fair to see the rodeo. I think he expected me to say no when Dominique invited me, but I said yes, imagining they'd probably split from me once we were in there anyway. It turned out to be another strange evening, which I don't know what to make of now. The rodeo riders were on right at the end. It wasn't the state fair at all, but a junior rodeo. We took our seats around the dusty arena of the Coliseum Stadium expecting to see a Wild West show – lassooing, bucking broncos.

'And now, ladies and gentlemen, will the four- to six-year-olds take up their positions for the barrel run,' said the announcer.

A handful of tiny kids with huge Stetsons, making them look like carpet tacks, raced into the centre of the arena with wooden horses between their legs. We watched them run round three white barrels to commentary: 'That's a good run out of Andrew Grayson – fourteen point five with a five-second penalty for breaking the pattern.'

We watched the four–sixes, the six–eights and the eight–tens do the same thing and Carlos said it was shit and that we should have listened to the rodeo riders. 'It's just fucking kids – the only people in here are their parents. Look in the pens, there are no animals at all. Let's go.'

Dominique and I had got into it, though – we'd both burst out laughing when the kids had rushed into the arena – and we wanted to see an older kid, maybe a ten- to twelve-year-old, do a sub-ten-second round, but Carlos kept saying it was shit so we left and wandered round the fair, Carlos walking in the loose-limbed way he does when he feels put upon. He broke his diet with a double-sub burger with mayonnaise and proclaimed it gorgeous just to annoy Dominique, then refused to go on any rides, using the topsy-turvy logic that he was saving money to make up for the eight-dollar admission. When I said, 'Come on, Carlos – there's no point paying to come to a fair and then going on nothing,' he snapped at me: 'Dominique warned you about speeding, Kit. We could've spent that money on a meal or a night in a motel. Someone's got to save money.'

Just as we were about to leave we came across the bungee-jump. 'Fiona Tummit did one in Australia with roller-skates – come on. Let's die,' said Dominique.

Carlos said it was stupid: 'See what I mean, you have no idea about money, that's thirty dollars,' although he was probably just too heavy for the rope.

In the end I somehow found myself saying I'd do one with Dominique instead. We started queuing, but every time we got near the front Dominique had second thoughts. Then she'd get cocky and we'd rejoin the queue at the back before the same thing would happen: 'No. Definitely no. Come on, we do something else. This is crazy. What are you making me do?'

It was very funny. I could tell Carlos thought it was, too, but he had to pretend to be annoyed. He kept the mood up all the way back to the campsite, climbed into his tent complaining of a migraine and refused to go for a drink when Dominique suggested one, even when we tried to coax him out: 'They do food there, Carlos. Sticky buns?'

So, unheard of, Dominique and I went out together. Inside

Bill's Bar and Grill I told her Carlos's mood was all down to the fact that she was going early to Australia and that he was worried about her meeting John.

'I know this,' said Dominique vehemently, 'but he was my husband for one year. His family is part of my life now. I have a responsibility. Lying on some beach in San Diego when his mother is sick. It is unresponsible!'

She asked me about Lucy and I found myself telling her about my doubts about marriage and children after all that had happened, and she told me it was difficult to 'forget the souvenirs of the past' in a way that made it seem like she was commenting more on her own situation. She told me what a French writer said about love: that it was all a fallacy, just an outlet for your emotions. You needed to love just like you needed to eat, sleep and shit, and whom you loved wasn't nearly as important as there being *someone* around to love. She said love was like a form of emotional diarrhoea, and sometimes when you felt insecure and your confidence was low you got caught short and had to run for the nearest toilet, even if it wasn't a particularly nice one.

'You're comparing Carlos to an outside toilet?' I said.

Dominique laughed and said, 'No, I am talking about you going back with your girlfriend.'

Every now and again throughout the night Dominique would bring up the arguments she'd been having with Carlos: 'Of course, I have to speak with John' . . . 'I have tried to live in London, but I do not like. It is not reasonable that I have to choose – Perth or Carlos. I cannot choose.'

After the second drink I asked about John's mother. I did it because I wanted to discuss Danny. 'Let's not speak of these bad things,' said Dominique. Then she looked at me sadly and asked for a cigarette. Her top lip was moist with beer, and she sucked on the cigarette like it was a straw, the way inexperienced smokers do.

'You speak of your brother very much,' she said thoughtfully. 'It is good for you to speak of him. I like your brother, he was a nice man – wild, a bit like you. I think you feel bad for him, though, for what did happen. It is normal. For John and his mother it is the same. Things were not said. Regrets!'

Because I was so pleased about being considered wild the way Danny was I started telling her about some of the things Danny and I used to do deliberately to create memories, and then the mysterious virus we caught in Tring Road that made us lose control of our limbs. Carlos obviously had never told her these stories and when I got to the bit about thinking we had Parkinson's disease Dominique said, 'You thought you had a disease?' and then laughed more than I've seen her do before. It wasn't that funny, but she turned her head from me to wipe tears out of her eyes, and when she turned back I realized she was crying.

'Dominique!' I said.

She collapsed into my arms: 'I am scorpion-woman, who leaves when there is trouble.' She looked up from my chest, nodded emphatically before burying her head again. 'I have not been responsible for John.'

I said it wasn't true, she phoned John all the time. It wasn't her fault things hadn't worked out. She wasn't to know John's mum was going to get ill after she left him. I tried to think of more arguments: 'It was just bad timing,' I said, echoing one of the justifications Lucy had used to me.

'No,' said Dominique into my chest, 'I knew his mother was diseased . . . before I leave. See, I am scorpion-woman,' she said, getting up.

When she came out of the toilet she was dabbing her eyes with a tissue. Her mood seemed to have switched again. 'You thought you had a disease,' she said and punched me on the arm, laughed again, then finished her drink in one swig and told me with a forced happy smile, 'Ten-thirty. Ah, we go now. Carlos will be thinking things in his tent.' She moved her head from side to side comically. ' "Where is she? What is she doing? Are there men around to run away with? Is she calling her husband?" '

We walked back.

'I mean it – your brother was a nice man. Now I tell Carlos you made me cry,' she said outside the tents. Then, 'No. Now I *am* joking. Goodnight.'

> Subject: < Interpol >
> To: Kit Farley Kitfarley@yahoo.com >
> From: Tom Farley Thomasfarley@hotmail.com >

Kit, Where are you and what are you up to? Are you all right?
Tom.

It's around midnight now and about half an hour ago I heard a noise and the arc of my torchlight rested on Carlos and Dominique's tent. She shouted, 'What are you doing, Kit?'

I said I thought I'd heard something moving about and she said, 'It is rabbits, go to sleep,' and then in the new spirit of détente, 'If you get scared shout out – we are only over here.'

The way she said it made me really like her. It was absurd that she should be comforting me, and that she didn't think it was in any way absurd made it even more absurd.

Journal Entry 14

A few days after he'd woken up, Danny was moved out of intensive care and into a medical ward. The wards in Germany aren't the great long Nightingale wards you get in England: they are small private rooms containing a couple of beds each off a main corridor. Danny was put in one overlooking the car park. His speech and memory became the main focus then. Mrs Frare would come in and sit at the end of Danny's bed and hold up flashcards of everyday items – a house, a car, a kettle, – and Danny would try to remember them. His physio – Mr Brinkman – would then manipulate Danny's arms and legs to loosen the muscles.

We set Danny little targets – in a week's time he would not

only be able to name his whole family, youngest to eldest, but the England team, too. In two weeks' time he would walk unaided to the cafeteria to eat a hot meal.

But three weeks after he'd woken up Danny still didn't know who any of us were. Talking to him was still like speaking to someone on a transatlantic phone line twenty years ago. He'd look at you blankly for almost five seconds after you'd said something before he even tried to form a reply. Then, when he did talk, it was like he was drunk, most of his speech incoherent and lispy.

'I'm just . . . goingth to the . . . toiletsh to smokemyarm.'

'What are you saying, Danny?'

'I'm want to . . . goingth to the . . . toiletsh to smokemyarm.'

'What?'

'For fuck's sake. [A phrase he never had a problem with.] I'm want to . . . goingth to the . . . toiletsh to smokemyarm.'

There were some highs – the first time he said my name; the first time he ate a whole meal – but in the ninth week more tests were done and they weren't encouraging. Danny's left arm was confirmed as useless: it was always going to hang pathetically at his side. He was looked at by a neurologist. A British clinical psychologist from Vegberg Hospital near Düsseldorf was flown in. He spent a day with Danny and explained his findings to Tom and me in the welfare office. Damage to Danny's occipital lobe meant hemianopsia – basically blindness in the right side of both eyes. This explained why Danny didn't look anybody directly in the eye – the blind-spots meant he had to shift his gaze slightly, so it was like he was looking to the right of you. His temporal lobe was 'compromised' in the region of the hippocampi, the area responsible for memories. This meant he wouldn't be able to remember the accident itself, was always going to be incredibly forgetful and would have a problem laying down new memories. The brain is like a computer: most of what he had already filed away was safe, but he'd never be able to save anything new from his desktop to his long-term memory file.

Disinhibition – another word we learned – meant there was probably going to be no screening process in Danny's brain: he wouldn't ever stop and think before he said or did anything. Another related problem was the lack of what's called the executive function – damage to the frontal lobe caused this one. It meant Danny would probably be unable to plan anything. If he found himself in any new situation, even a very simple one, he wouldn't have a clue how to handle it. Basically we were being told he had brain damage.

Lucy's never been good in stressful situations. I suppose she imagined Danny would be up and about and back to his old self. What she saw that week was a shock.

She was with me at Danny's flat when I had my big row with the *Gazette*. I hadn't phoned in for a couple of weeks or given them a clue when I was coming back to work because I knew what they'd say. Lucy persuaded me to make the call, though.

Steve Pandy: 'The death of a loved one, by that meaning an immediate family member, spouse or child, the member of staff shall be permitted one week. Other compassionate leave, and that's what this is, three days. You've been away over two months, Kit. I appreciate what you're going through. But it's not fair on the rest of them.' He suggested he write off the week of holiday I hadn't taken the year before and my whole five weeks' holiday for the year we were in, and I retaliated by suggesting I quit instead.

After a series of increasingly angry phone calls this is what happened, although after a telling-off from Lucy I rang back and they agreed that I could carry on TV reviewing on a freelance basis when I got home.

Danny showed occasional signs of improvement: recognizing Boots our old cat from the family photo albums Dad brought in; the day he took his first steps with the Zimmer frame. But the breakthroughs then came fewer and far between and the strain began to show on all of us: Dad had to go to see the doctor for chest pains; back in England Jane was prescribed sleeping pills; and I started rowing with Lucy.

We had been going out about a year by then. She'd become the practical one in the relationship and in Germany our arguments were initially over money. She thought I'd been hasty quitting my job. I was angry she didn't seem to understand the importance of my being there. Typical conversation during her visit:

'I spoke to Andrew the other day. They need someone to write a backlog of ad features – what about flying home and doing that for a couple of days? Get a few quid.'

'My brother's recovering from a coma, Lucy, in a foreign hospital. I'm staying here until he's better.'

'I only meant it as a break. You heard what the doctors said – it could be weeks. Don't bite my head off, I'm only trying to help. And everyone else keeps flying home, why can't you? You've got to stop this guilt. It's not your fault.'

The best people to talk to when you feel shit aren't people who sympathize, I think now. When someone sympathizes it's like they're saying, 'Yes, I understand how upset you are. It's awful, isn't it?' In a way you feel worse. This is how Lucy made me feel then. She had a there-there-put-a-plaster-on-it tone that just seemed to wind me up. When she was upbeat I thought she was being naïve and thoughtless for not studying the facts. When she was downbeat I was angry that she expected me, who it was worse for, to pick her up.

On her final night in Germany she told me, 'Kit, I was supposed to go on a press trip to Turin. I didn't tell you because I knew I wasn't going to go. It's somewhere I've always wanted to go. And if I'd written up the article I could have flogged it on to the *Mail*, but I decided to be with you because I love you. I've been here a week and you've given me no credit.'

'We're as poor as church mice,' was another phrase she'd come out with. 'We'll manage somehow, although God knows how,' she said in front of my dad when he asked about my job. Then she put her arm round me, and I'd wanted to shake her off and say, 'For fuck's sake, we're all right – stop feeling sorry for yourself: at least you're not lying in bed with one useless arm, with your fucking memory gone.'

What you want in this situation is somebody to take a problem apart and put it together in a totally different way so it doesn't seem like a problem any more. Or you need somebody to laugh about it with you, someone who cares about you, and who you trust and know with 100 per cent certainty is laughing in exactly the same way, about exactly the same thing, as you are. Basically a true friend, like Tom. It's what I'd thought Lucy was before and Carlos too. But they didn't feel like true friends at the time and that hurt for a while. But it's strange because eventually I realized what I was missing, and it wasn't them. I realized the person I most wanted to console me about Danny was Danny himself.

10 December 2000

The drive west to Casa Grande today took us through the Santia Mountains. It was beautiful. To start with it was scrubland and roads straight as arrows with nothing on either side for miles except a railroad, telegraph poles, spiky plants and brown earth. Then, suddenly, it was mountains and lush scenery. Dominique sat up front today, something she still refuses to do when Carlos is at the wheel, and we played pulling-the-face-that-best-represents-the-song to KAHM Radio, an easy-listening station. She was appalling, pulling the same face each time – eyebrows raised and mouth open at the side like Woody Woodpecker.

'No, it's hope-is-dashed-but-look-at-me-I'm-bearing-up. You're doing Woody Woodpecker again. Watch me biting my lip at the side. That's the bearing up. You've got to be more subtle.'

'Funny Girl' by Barbra Streisand: 'OK,' says Dominique and

hides behind her fingers. 'Right, what about' – she withdraws her fingers – 'this!'

'It isn't a cheeky song. Look!'

'What is that?'

'It's happiness but with a tinge of regret. See the way my eyes are a little bit closed? That's the regret.'

I made her laugh at the Arizona Welcome Center this afternoon, showing her a brochure which informed us about etiquette in the Indian reservation we were about to drive through. It told us not to bring in alcohol and drugs and not to clap if we saw Indians dancing because it was a religious festival not a theme park. Then it added, 'If you are invited into a Native American's home, don't pick up things and take them away with you, even if they seem very interesting.'

The laughter was soured by a run-in with Carlos. I asked the woman behind the desk if there was anything deadly we should be wary of in Arizona, my standard procedure at every new State Welcome center. 'We've got black bears. Smokey the bear is the national symbol for fire safety. But they don't come down to the road much, only to state parks when they smell food.'

I was quite concerned: 'How do you keep them away from state parks?' I asked, and later in the car Carlos told me, 'You do ask some stupid questions. "How do you keep them away from state parks?" ' He said it was obvious, you just didn't leave food lying around, everyone knew that, and we weren't even sleeping in a state park, we were staying at a Kampground of America.

'Right, and the bears read, "Kampground of America" and think, Shit, we can't go in there,' I replied.

The mood continued all day. We had problems finding a decent campsite. The first one we tried was overrun with strange black-and-white insects copulating in mid-air. I went on a killing spree with Dominique's Lornett Elle hairspray canister, stiffening their wings and watching them sink to the ground. But even more appeared. Then Carlos nearly banged one of his tent pegs through a natural-gas pipeline that ran through the campsite. And when a genuine drifter called Dave from Cali-forn-I-A came up to us and started eyeing up our bumbags, telling us he was having to lie low for a while because of a little bit of trouble downtown, it was the final straw and we decided to leave. 'Lovebugs – they mate once a year and then they die. Should be the same for humans, hey,' he said as we pulled away in such a hurry that Carlos left his torch behind on the picnic table.

As soon as we arrived here I put up my tent and immediately it was covered in another pest – tiny ants marching in diagonal lines across the canvas. Dominique demonstrated her amazing practicality again: she poured talcum powder over the apex of the tent. 'It disturbs their route. Their foots get stuck and they do not like the smell so they fuck off,' she said, and, sure enough, they did.

Carlos was still moaning about his torch, though, blaming me because I'd been using it to squash lovebugs, and for a joke I asked Dominique if she'd pour some talc round Carlos to get him to fuck off, too, and she laughed: 'I understand your jokes now. I think they are good jokes. Really.' Then she threw talc at Carlos.

> Subject: < Where are you? >
> To: Kit Farley Kitfarley@yahoo.com >
> From: Tom Farley Thomasfarley@hotmail.com >

Dear Kit, I haven't upset you, have I? This is unlike you. Where are my moaning emails? What's going on, little brother? It's not the Beech Road thing still, is it?

Tom.

Journal Entry 15

The day Danny finally came home was another special occasion, although we'd learned our lesson by then. It was now late February. Dad was right, Danny did walk out of the front door. The nurses cheered him out, there were tears from Mandy, the liaison officer. We took Danny round to see the *Hausmeister* and they shook hands. Dad put £200 in the nurses' kitty.

The builders had been in and refitted Beech Road, something Jane had arranged under the guidance of Danny's occupational therapist from Germany. There were rails up the stairs, metal sides to Danny's bed to stop him falling out because he was still having problems walking and a special bath was put in because Danny found it hard levering himself in and out with only one good arm.

That first night home was fairly low key. We were all there, but there were no dedications this time, no big party. We wanted everything to seem as normal as possible. Jane cooked what had been Danny's favourite dinner (chicken Kiev), we opened a bottle of wine, but when we raised a toast – an omen of things to come – Danny spilt his drink down his front. When his meal arrived it followed suit. And the evening ended in Danny having a temper tantrum. These had become increasingly common in the weeks leading up to Danny's discharge. Danny had never been a violent person before, but all of a sudden there was this incredibly aggressive person to deal with. And a strong one, too. Anything could trigger it off – if you failed to understand him, if he didn't get exactly what he wanted, if he couldn't find something, if there was any tiny break in his routine like his breakfast not arriving on the dot of 8 a.m.

Through Stoke Mandeville Hospital, where Danny went for physio while Bucks County Social Services tried to locate a live-in rehabilitation centre, we found out about Headway. This was a charity that looked after brain-injury victims and we took him to a few of their drop-in sessions in the first couple of weeks. But he didn't like being left alone there, and when he hit one of the organizers and tried to stick his hand up the skirt of another client, we thought it best to stop the visits.

We'd been warned to expect this sort of behaviour, of course, but it was still a shock. We took him on outings and he'd go up to people in shops and hug them. He got called a spaz by some kids on Aston Clinton recreational ground when he tried to join in a game of football.

It was suggested we give Danny a diary to help his short-term memory. Jane used to write what had happened to him at the end of each day so he'd have some record of his life to boost his memory, and there was something very sad about the way she wrote it in the first person for him. 'Today I went to Tesco and bought after-shave and deodorant' . . . 'Today I went to Vale Park and fed the ducks.' It was like the way parents write cards as if they're from their three-year-old kids to thank you for a present you've given them.

The one breakthrough was the discovery that it wasn't Danny's memory that meant he still had problems recognizing us. He was suffering from a separate brain dysfunction – prosopagnosia. Faces were too complicated for Danny, but if they were reduced to simple symbols it helped him. The trick was to reduce the detail of our faces to their most distinctive feature, like a nose or a high forehead, which Danny could then home in on to tell us apart. This was the occupational therapist at Stoke Mandeville's great masterstroke. Initially she drew caricatures of us all to emphasize these features, but in the end, through sheer fluke, it was discovered that the numbers on playing cards worked even better. Dad has a low forehead, for instance, and not much of a chin. If you look at him in profile and fuzz out the rest of his face, he looks like the number 2. Jane has a slightly flat face with a sort of quiff hairstyle at the front – in profile vaguely like the number 1.

Danny would carry a pack around with him permanently with our names written over the top of our appropriate cards. Our way of dealing with him began to change subtly. On top of the violent outbursts, Danny developed this really annoying habit of saying, 'Ready, willing and disabled, dude,' a phrase he'd picked up from the lance corporal in hospital. Whenever anything was suggested he'd say it. It had been funny the first time, but later – 4,000 times later – it got on your nerves.

There were other things too: because he'd been praised for recognizing Boots in a photo, he kept saying, 'Boots,' in expectation of a similar response. None of us really knew how to deal with him. Treat him like a kid, or as a mate who was drunk and would not remember any of it in the morning? If you praised him, it was patronizing. If you told him to shut it, it seemed insensitive.

In the month Danny was at home I found myself becoming quite angry with him, and also with Dad, who was always fussing around him. I stopped wanting to be around the house and visited less. Why couldn't he put his jumper on the right way round when you'd showed him a dozen times? I got sick and depressed at cheering him because he'd learned how to make a cup of tea.

Whenever he was reasonably lucid he seemed to prefer to live in the past, which you couldn't blame him for, because with his short-term memory gone he never really had a present. Old Danny had been such a live wire. He'd been so warm and affectionate, so funny, active and creative, it was difficult not to resent this other person, this twenty-seven-year-old child, who seemed to be masquerading in Danny's body. It was a terrible irony, too, that he'd wanted to kill himself before for no good reason, yet now here he was 1,000 times worse off and the thought never crossed his mind.

Things slowly worsened with Lucy, too. I was still doing the TV reviews for the *Gazette*, but hadn't applied for a new job, and she started resenting the fact that I was around the cottage all day doing nothing. Especially as I wasn't even seeing Danny so much any more. But I resented her, too. A brain injury can completely invert the personality of the victim. In a funny way that's exactly what happened to me, too. All the things about Lucy that had once endeared her to me started repelling me: her nagging and cajoling that had seemed well meant before were just annoying and coercive and made me feel as if she was getting at me for not having a full-time job. Her impressionable nature irritated me – Why doesn't she have her own opinions? I thought. When we argued about what somebody had said about me at her work, Lucy always seemed to have swallowed it whole: 'Simon's right – you're in a rut. You've got to get yourself out of it, and the only way is for to me to force you out to work again and stop you wallowing. It's what Danny would want you to do.'

'I'm not fucking wallowing. And since when was Simon such an expert?'

Her flippant outlook and readiness to make light of everything stopped being funny, too, and just seemed shallow. I suddenly felt like I'd grown up. I found myself becoming angry with Lucy's perspective on life, the fuck-it attitude that had initially attracted me to her. I was an adult now, I thought; she still behaved like a child. I didn't feel we were equals any more. I saw her as someone I was expected to protect from the outside world and was annoyed that she couldn't do the same for me. She even seemed to play up her inability to cope: every time she cried about a bill or a bad day at work I found myself wishing misfortune on her so the equilibrium could be restored to teach her some perspective. Her granddad had a bad back around this time, he started walking like an old man, his face went sallow and he lost weight. Cancer, I thought, even though it turned out to be a trapped nerve. Her mother's headaches caused by wearing the wrong prescription spectacles: Brain tumour, I thought. I once hinted to Lucy that her dad's effusive goodbye when we visited her parents in Birmingham one weekend might have a hidden explanation – was it the final goodbye from a man too proud to tell his daughter he was dying? She went crazy: 'What are you saying? What are you saying? It's not true. You liar. Stop scaring me. You want him to be ill, don't you? Don't you?'

Yes, I did. I wanted Lucy to understand so that when I rolled over to her in the night and said, 'Luce, put your head on my shoulder,' she did this automatically, without saying, 'Kit, it's two o'clock. Please.' Please! What does this say? It says, 'I know you're suffering, but I am becoming bored and tired of this so please look elsewhere for it.' Which is, of course, what I did.

Dad had been fourteen stones at Christmas; by the end of March he was down to eleven and after just a month of Danny living back at home the original plan of waiting for a rehabilitation unit closer to home was abandoned. Danny was to be placed in a centre called The Claymore in the north-east.

The Claymore was an assessment point, an entrepôt for people with brain injuries. They did cognitive and all sorts of other tests, and there were three choices afterwards, dependent on the results. The best option was a centre for the less severely brain damaged: somewhere with learning facilities and work experience. Then there was another Claymore-style place for more tests. Finally there was the mental institution, in all but name. The day we were dreading, but half expecting, came out of the blue. Dad had been in the north-east for a rare and uneventful weekend during which Danny seemed to be better. He'd just got back home when he received the call. Danny had groped a nurse and he was going to be moved to a special unit for the mentally ill. That's where he is now. Grange Grove, it's called. It's a few miles from Whitchurch, but I've only been there once.

My single visit, his birthday, I drove down telling myself it wasn't going to be as bad as I imagined. I was encouraged when I was buzzed into the unit by the fact that I was immediately surrounded by wheelchairs. I thought this was good – they all seemed welcoming. Then one of the clients, as they're called, introduced himself robotically. He told me the date of his arrival and his name, like a captured airman informing the enemy of his rank and serial number. Then one of the women in the wheelchairs asked if I was there to put the Christmas tree up. They were so pleased to see me because they were just so bored.

Beverly, the unit manager, had a poster on her wall of Dr Evil from the *Austin Powers* film holding his little finger thoughtfully up to his lips. The caption read: 'I make the declarations here – I demand a little respect.' After she'd fetched Danny, who didn't recognize me, she left us in the day room. I gave him his birthday present – a new pair of trainers, which he didn't seem interested in – and then I had lunch with him in the school-canteen-style dining room. On one table a man in a wheelchair was being fed with a spoon. There was another group playing snap on the table behind us and two women with grubby faces were moving draughts randomly around a board on the table opposite. We fetched our sausages and chips from the service hatch, sat down, and Danny ate by moving the spoon to his mouth very slowly. He was very abrupt with me and spoke as if I was a stranger. He didn't seem aware it was his birthday, either, even though he had a badge on the lapel of his shirt saying, '28', and wouldn't reply to any of my questions about other presents he'd received. Then he told me why he was there, something I never realized he knew, because, of course, nobody had told him and we assumed he couldn't remember.

'Have you guessed yet?' he said. 'My dad . . . was . . . furioursh.'

'Our dad,' I said. 'He's our dad, Danny. It's Kit. I've come to see you. Where are your cards? What have they done with your playing cards?'

'Carbon mon-oxide,' he said triumphantly. 'It wash a . . . very . . . stupid thing,' said Danny. 'I re-mem-ber lying there . . . and hearing some-one say . . . to my dad, "I'm afraid . . . your son is dead" . . . and then . . . bam . . .' Danny opened his eyes wide, ' . . . I wash back.

'Bam,' he repeated. 'I . . . wash back. I op-ened my eyesh . . . and I could re-mem-ber . . . everything. Noth-ing . . . wrong with me . . . now. I wash lucky . . . I'm normal. For the firsht . . . few daysh . . . I couldn't . . . get dressed. In-shide out . . . and every-thing. Now,' he opened his jacket to show his shirt on the right way round, 'I am . . . totally normal. I should be dead . . . but I'm perfectly normal.'

I didn't know what to say. He was causing a bit of a scene and Beverly came over to check we were all right. When she'd gone Danny started slagging off some other clients from one of the bungalows who occasionally came over to the main block for their dinner. 'They come in . . . and queue up . . . for their dinner,' he said.

I didn't understand and asked if they were staff.

'No,' he said angrily, 'clientsh.'

I asked what they did and Danny said they sat down and had lunch. I thought maybe they were problematic clients. He'd already complained about a guy called Andrew who slept across the corridor and kept him up all night banging doors and breaking things in his room. 'What do they do?' I asked.

Danny repeated that they came in and sat down to have their lunch. This was clearly their only crime, so I didn't say any more.

I went back to his room after lunch. Jane and Dad had decorated it for him when he'd first arrived: on the wall were some of his old posters of Leeds players from when he was a kid. There were three birthday cards: one from Sophie and Paul, one from Dad and Jane and another from Tom. The room was a tip, but he shouted at me when I tried to tidy up his clothes on the floor. He started going on about dinner again and all these people in wheelchairs who the company were subsidizing and could walk really but were just being lazy. When I asked him which company, he became angry again.

Before I left I tried again to get through to him. To tell him who I was, I showed him my card, the six of spades, which I'd brought with me, but each time he just changed the subject. And it wasn't until I spoke to Beverly on the way out that I realized what he was going on about. Danny thought he was a member of staff. The problematic client who Danny claimed kept smashing up his room was Danny smashing up his own room.

I kept meaning to go back, but I never did. I told myself it was better, let him live in his own world, that it was better than his real one, but I feel like shit. We promised we'd always be there for each other and I'm not there, but I can't be, because he's not really there any more, either.

11 December 2000

The countryside changed again today and we saw our first cacti. We crossed another time zone, passed through Phoenix on I-10 and then headed through the Mingus Mountains. We've just checked into a campsite in Sedona, Arizona, and Carlos was instantly worried about a concert here tomorrow. Apparently, some tribute hippie band that used to be something to do with the Grateful Dead are playing. 'Let's go somewhere else. It'll be really grungy and there'll be loads of drifters and students puking on our tents, throwing beer cans and pissing everywhere and our stuff'll get fucking nicked,' he said, looking on the bright side.

But Dominique wanted to stay so he descended into another childish strop. They're still at the campsite and are planning to see the Grand Canyon tomorrow, but I've taken the car and I'm writing this sitting on the wall at Mather's Point. In front of me is the Grand Canyon, 10 miles wide, 1 mile deep, 277 miles long. The red rocks are turning black as the sun goes down. To my left, a fat woman in loose-fitting shorts with elaborately coiffed hair and, to my right, a thin American man in slacks with poofy shoes and gold spectacles feeding Big Macs to the rock squirrels you can catch bubonic plague from.

It's a chasm so large it doesn't seem real, more like a child's pop-up book or a 3-D picture. If you stare for long enough it doesn't seem to be a hollow but a mountain, like those white masks that could be convex or concave. The rocks are a billion years old at the bottom where the thin Colorado River snakes in and out like the diamond-headed rattlesnakes in the Joshua trees all around. The cicadas are sounding, bluebirds are swooping and I wish someone was here to see this with me. The beauty of it hurts because I can't reflect it off anyone. It's like a trick with parabolic mirrors: it's there, but it isn't. I thought the canyon would move me, I wanted to feel goosebumps, for it to make me feel intense, inspired and reckless, but all it's been is a fleeting stimulus: 'Oh, so that's the canyon then.' I've been trying to imagine Lucy here with me, but I can't. It's like the time difference has created two different worlds.

I've thrown a few stones over the edge: the canyon is so deep you can't hear them land. I'm trying to imagine what it would be like to free-fall to the bottom.

> Subject: < alive or dead? >
> To: Kit Farley Kitfarley@yahoo.com >
> From: Lucy Jones Lucyjones23@hotmail.com >

Dear Kit, No email for a while. Have you been eaten by grizzlies? It's too late to change the tickets now. It's your own fault. I'm coming out. You should have emailed.

Lucy x

> Subject: < presents >
> To: Kit Farley Kitfarley@yahoo.com >
> From: Tom Farley Thomasfarley@hotmail.com >

Kit, If you want a Christmas present contact me immediately.
Tom.

Journal Entry 16

Before Danny's accident I thought a head injury was like any other injury. You went into a coma and when you woke up you were treated in hospital for a little while, and then you just carried on with your life. It's what you see on films, it's what you read about in the papers. I've done stories about it myself – as soon as somebody wakes up that's it, end of story, a happy ending, send round the snapper. Miracle escape. Nobody tells you what really happens because it's just so fucking grisly.

Head injuries are totally different. Your brain isn't like a leg or an arm, once it's damaged that's it – it doesn't really get any better. Since Danny's accident I've bumped into dozens of people who haven't seemed all there, a bit simple, people in shops, on buses. You see them everywhere and I always wonder what happened to them. Before I would have assumed they'd had breakdowns: Poor bastard, that'll never happen to me, I've thought. Now I bet half of them are head-injury victims and it *can* happen to anyone at any time. I think that's why it's such a taboo. That's why everyone's so queasy about it. It's too scary to think about. Something falls on your head on a building site and your life's fucked. You go through a car windscreen, your life's fucked. Brain haemorrhage: fucked. Carbon monoxide poisoning: fucked. Nobody knows this, though – we certainly didn't – because you can't make a film about it, because there is no happy ending. If you're a relative, a friend, a wife or a husband of someone who gets brain damage you can't come to terms with it because it's not over when they wake up from their coma. They've died and been replaced by someone else, somebody who's often not that nice any more, who doesn't possess any of the things that you used to like, but does have hundreds of things you can't stand. And how does that make you feel? Suddenly you don't really like this person you once loved and it's nobody's fault and there's nobody to blame.

By July, Lucy was really starting to get on to me about finding a new job, but for some reason reporting, what I'd enjoyed so much before, suddenly seemed utterly pointless. I'd gone into it thinking it was glamorous. But in a year and a half on the *Bucks Gazette* what was the most glamorous thing I'd done? Interviewed the Mayor about the Aylesbury gyratory system. And the only worthwhile project I covered was the reforestation campaign for Vale Park, marred by the fact – the huge fucking fact – I had to attend the launch ceremony dressed as Woody Tree. John Thaw is a local celebrity. He was there: my only brush with fame, interviewing Inspector Morse, dressed in an inflatable rubber suit made to look like a horse-chestnut tree, staring through the hole in the latex, trying to bend the rubber arms back to make shorthand notes.

'So how important is it that there are still green areas in Bucks, Mr Thaw? Mr Thaw? Over here. I'm in this. Mr Thaw, could you hold this flap of rubber back for me while I ask you some questions? I can't hold it back and write at the same time. Do you mind?'

Without Danny, my whole life seemed aimless and instead of pulling myself out of the spiral I sat at home and rented videos, and got addicted to computer games. I inhabited Internet chat-rooms. I asked myself questions and cut my pack of playing cards and imagined Danny was helping me make decisions by influencing which card I picked.

I played 3,000 games of FreeCell during those weeks before Lucy left. It said so on my statistics box. I became obsessed with it. It became like my job. What do you do for a living? I play FreeCell. If I played well it was a good day, if I didn't it was a shit day. I just didn't want to think.

When Lucy uninstalled the game from my computer ('I'm sorry, Kit, but this has got to stop') I played Minesweeper, Hearts and Solitaire instead until she uninstalled them, too. Cutting the pack was part and parcel of this lifestyle. The cards were the only reason I got out of bed in the morning. I used them to make all my major decisions. 'OK, Danny, if I cut a five I'll get up, if I don't, you want me to lie in some more.' The cards became a way of motivating myself. They took Danny's place. Shall I have lunch now? Should I phone someone? Get the pack out.

When Lucy got home at 9 p.m. after her marathon commute home from London to Whitchurch I felt so pleased to see another human being I'd almost cry with relief, yet within a few minutes she'd be shouting at me for not having done the washing-up. We'd then have an argument about dinner, Lucy claiming she was tired and I should make it for her because she'd been to work. There were other rows about the fact I hadn't bathed and stank, about the state of the cottage, about the fact I never wanted to go out with friends any more because I never had anything to say for myself and hated the uncomfortable atmosphere I sensed because of what had happened to my brother.

And then right in the middle of this I got fired from the TV reviewing. Thirty letters of complaint for stating at the bottom of a harmless review of the *Antiques Roadshow* that there should be themed TV for old people on Sunday nights – OAP TV; a whole night of pensioner-specific programmes. All the programmes starring Thora Hird, Judi Dench and Hugh Scully, get them out of the way in one go, intersperse them with ads for hernia safety pants and orthopaedic mattresses. They could even have an anthem: not 'Three Lions on a Shirt', 'Three Eccles Cakes on a Doily'. Three Eccles Cakes on a doily, never stopped dreaming.

Of course, I wasn't quite myself at the time, but you'd have thought they'd have given me a bit of leeway. The hernia joke and one about liver-spotted hands reaching for the remote were the two main bones of contention. Some of the letters were virulent. Mixed in with the usual you'll-be-old-one-day jibes were some saying they were sick of my smart-Alec arrogance, my stream of sneering obscenities. Some even hoped I would not make it to old age.

Alex Hammond, the chief sub, phoned me up to say there'd been a bit of an outcry, that the deputy editor wanted a humorous but sincere apology in the next column. I wrote it based on me being a marked man like Salman Rushdie, living in fear of pensioners. My gran had made me watch *Animal Hospital* with her as a punishment and I admitted I'd once worn hernia pants after a football injury.

I showed Alex Hammond the copy the next morning and he said it seemed OK. But the next week was worse: dozens of pensioners on the phone, not satisfied with the apology.

Every time I walked around the Market Square I half expected to be struck down by a knobbly stick. My pace instinctively sped up as I passed a post office, a bus queue or a Cancer Research charity shop. They became an amorphous entity, one great second-hand duffel coat of hate slinking after me like a hungry wild animal. It was all I needed at the time.

Steve Pandy called me eventually. 'Is there anything you think with hindsight that you did wrong?'

I said perhaps the liver-spotted hands had been misjudged.

He seemed fairly good-natured. The complaints showed how many people read the column. Then a week later the cunt sacked me for spelling Sooty's name wrong during a review of the *Sooty and Sweep Roadshow*. I'd spelled it with an 'ie' instead of a 'y'. They were looking for an excuse. It wasn't the pensioner thing, either. They just wanted me out after all the compassionate-leave business.

'Who cares? So I spelled Sooty's name wrong. What's he

going to do? Write in? I feel there's a hidden agenda here. You're using Sooty, Steve. Is it because John Townsend [the MD] is a director of Aylesbury Age Concern?'

'It's not so much the spelling as the subject matter. Kit, why didn't you review the new *Ivanhoe* series? How many of our readers watch the *Sooty and Sweep Show?* And you did *Sesame Street* last week.'

It was while flicking through the *Independent* on one of those despair-filled summer afternoons after my sacking that her name leapt out at me. My heart literally skipped a beat. It was underneath a review of a new revolutionary car seat for the disabled: 'By Nikki Aldridge'. When Granny Cornwall lost it before she had her breakdown she started seeing coincidences everywhere. I think you do this when your world disintegrates, you cling to things. It's a way of putting the world back together, making some order of the chaos. But it's like an under-five trying to do a fiddly 10,000-piece jigsaw puzzle – cramming the pieces into spaces where they don't fit. She was a journalist, I was a journalist. She was writing an article about the disabled, Danny was disabled. Because I'd known Nikki had become a reporter after school, I felt sure it had to be her.

If Lucy and I had been getting on better, I doubt I would have done anything. But then we had our big row about marriage and babies at just the wrong time.

'Will we ever get married and have children?' she said dramatically one night on the walk home from the Cherry Tree. I'd been talking to her about Danny all evening. It made it seem as if she hadn't been listening to a word I'd been saying.

I didn't respond, but I must have closed my eyes for a second.

'I'm not nagging you. Don't say I am nagging you. I just want to know', she said, 'whether I am being a *total* fool.'

We had a huge argument that resulted in her accusing me of treating her like shit, of being totally self-indulgent.

'I want you to make up your mind if you're going to marry me,' she said the next morning when we were making up. 'I'm nearly thirty. I'm not giving you a deadline. I'm giving myself one. We've got to start thinking about the future. This can't go on. I am as upset as you about Danny, but we've got to get on with things. Why can't you try to get yourself a job in London? I can't go on commuting from the sticks every night. There's nothing tying us to here any more except money. Please, Kit.'

Bollocks you're as upset as me, I thought. That was the night I wrote to Nikki care of the *Independent*, leaving my email address and setting off the chain reaction that I'm still living with.

12 December 2000

This morning Carlos woke me up. He crouched down at the side of my tent and said, 'What we gonna do, then? I don't want to have another couple of weeks like these.'

I said fine, if he could drive me to Las Vegas after the concert I'd take off on a Greyhound to LA airport.

At the supermarket afterwards I did my own food shopping and bought Dominique some sunscreen to make up for what I've used of hers. And while Carlos was paying for their food, Dominique asked when I was going to Australia and which hostel I was staying at in Sydney. When I told her I'd read good things about Eva's in the *Lonely Planet* she said, 'Perhaps we will see you there. I am not happy with Carlos. Thank you for the sun cream.'

Carlos and Dominique must've had another big row this afternoon too because Dominique was still up when I got back tonight. She was sitting alone in the car reading the Australian *Lonely Planet*, using the interior light. 'Did you have a good time with your hippie?' she said. I'd been to the campsite's Hungry Wolf Café with a women called Allban I met yesterday at the canyon. She'd seemed fine then but she'd tried to relay all sorts of psychic messages to me in the bar and had gone on about coming out of an abusive relationship, so I told Dominique she'd turned out to be a bit of a New Age nutter. 'She has this boyfriend, well it's sort of a threesome, and he wants her to listen to dolphin music and have orgies.'

'Uhm,' said Dominique, marking her page, 'a sexual sandwich.'

I was still thinking about this comment after I'd had my shower. Dominique said something I didn't catch as I was saying goodnight so I walked to the driver's door and leant down.

'I ask you – do you think Carlos and me have a good relationship?' she said.

I didn't know what to say, so I said yes, I thought so, then changed my mind slightly and said I didn't know, what did she think?

She shrugged her shoulders and I climbed in the car beside her.

'Why, don't you think you have?' I said.

She put her book on the dashboard and scrunched her hair up in frustration and said, 'Carlos is such a teenager. So jealous. Maybe I go even earlier to Australia. Isolation. Time to think. Stay with my friend in Noosa. I have been reading about it. They have bears – but they are koalas and kill nobody.' There was a pause, and she smiled. 'And what about you? When do you go to Australia? Is it the same? Will you be pleased to be out of this jail?' She indicated the inside of the car.

I told her about Lucy flying to Thailand and how I'd have to catch a Greyhound to LA from Vegas and probably would need to get an even earlier flight out to get there in time.

'Ah, we go together,' she said, as if I'd engineered this deliberately to be with her, but added, 'No, me and you, we are too different.'

I was surprised she thought I'd been thinking about this, but she didn't seem too shocked, so I said, 'We are not so different, and anyway, I thought I was like Carlos.'

'Noooo,' she said, 'please, not another Carlos. We have another bad fight. Always arguing. Why do I discuss Australia so much? Well, because it was my home. Why do I mention John? Because he was my husband.'

We climbed out of the car and sat down beside each other at the picnic table because I wanted a cigarette and she didn't like me smoking in the car. I told her I felt very bad about Danny. I'd been writing about him again and I had to go and see him more. Dominique's eyes looked at me dopily for a second and then, without saying anything, she burrowed her head into my shoulder. 'You are a nice man,' she said into my chest.

I said I wasn't, I was a scorpion-man. I started telling her about the knock on my door on Christmas Eve and how I hadn't called Danny's name out and how I was sure now he'd wanted to tell me something. It was the first time I'd told anybody apart from Tom and Lucy this.

'We're *all* scorpions,' she said, and reached up and put her hand over my face like a claw. Her head was still resting on my chest and I reached underneath and did the same thing to her face with my hand. She laughed and popped her head up and asked for a cigarette.

The end of her cigarette glowed orange after I'd lit it and the situation suddenly reminded me of Europe; for some reason I found myself bringing up the pedalo again. Dominique laughed throatily, making my shoulder vibrate. 'You are obsessed with this pedalo,' she said.

'I wanted to paddle to Morocco, do you remember? But every time we tried to paddle away we just came back to the beach. I thought you weren't paddling hard enough and you thought I wasn't paddling hard enough, then you said it was the current so we swapped places. We moved along the beach in semicircles for half a mile before I noticed . . .'

'There was a lock on one of the paddles,' said Dominique, stubbing out her half-smoked cigarette. 'Yes, I think you are obsessed with this pedalo. It was very different in those times. We are all very different now.'

We didn't say anything for a moment. She leaned closer and her heart was beating fast. I felt mine speed up to match hers.

'All holiday you tried to persuade,' she said, rising to get her fleece. 'Not this holiday: we just fight about the petrol. You have changed. You have been kidnapped by these aliens.

'Body heat better than a jumper,' she said, coming back to sit next to me. Then she started telling me about the row with Carlos over Australia. She said she no longer wanted him to go to Perth with her. He would only complicate things; she needed time to herself. I didn't really know what to say, so I started stroking her forearm, telling her everything would work out for both of us. Then my hand brushed her leg.

'No,' she said quietly, even though it was accidental – I'd been scratching a mosquito bite on my own leg. For some reason I didn't tell her I hadn't meant it and looked at her sorrowfully. 'Carlos?' I said.

'Carlos', she said and shook her head again before edging away from me, 'is a teenager.' She moved round the other side of the table. 'And what about you?' she said. 'You will be happy to see Lucy?'

I can't have looked very happy because her hand snaked across the table towards mine. 'Come on,' she said.

I squeezed her knuckles like they were bubble-wrap and looked her in the eye. Her fingers were tiny, like baby carrots.

Then she told me about John, who she loved as a friend but had never felt passionately for, who made her feel safe and whom she'd enjoyed sharing her life with in Perth.

I told her my theory: the only reason you go travelling is to discover why you went travelling in the first place. She said there was always one 'practical' reason and one 'emotional' reason: 'I go travelling to go back to Perth to see my friends. Carlos goes because I tell him to. You go because you want to think about things. But emotional reason – I go on this trip to distance myself from John and the bad situation of his mother, and for you it is the same.'

'Lucy,' I said.

'Ah,' she said, as if I was a bright pupil she was teaching, 'and your brother,' and she got up with a happy bob to drag the roll-mat out of my tent. 'I want to see the stars. They are different from Australia. Do you know these stars?'

I suggested we go up to the café by the main block because the ground was a bit dirty round the tent. But she saw through me.

'Now you persuade me,' she said teasingly, 'now I know this behaviour.'

I carried the mat up to the café. We sat down on a grassy patch.

'I'm sorry I hurt you,' she said, touching my arm, 'before, on this trip. I think it was the pills. They are not the secret of my equilibrium. I have stopped them.' She looked up at the stars and traced patterns in them with her finger.

Then I asked her to play the mangle game: the army has a gun to her head and she has to mangle someone in her life that we both know.

'Oh no, I cannot play. It is an awful game.' But then she said maybe Lucy because she was unkind to me. She whispered it as if someone might overhear, and then laughed when I did, and her face showed two vertical lines from the corners of her mouth to her cheeks. After that, it was Carlos's mum, who didn't approve of divorced women. 'But I cannot play any more. It is an awful game.'

She told me why she really split with John. Their sex life wasn't good and she couldn't stop thinking about Carlos. But now she was with Carlos she couldn't stop thinking about John and all the things she liked about him that were missing from Carlos. She said she thought it might be a mistake to go back. I told her about Lucy and how I used to fantasize about her and Nikki Aldridge becoming combined in a science-fiction experiment like in *The Fly* so I could have the best parts of each of them.

'Yes, but in the film they have the bad parts of everyone, and anyway, your girlfriend left you for another man from a . . .' Dominique spat the words out contemptuously '. . . pet shop.'

'I think we should cuddle,' I said.

'Yes, OK,' she said, and we did this for a while.

I tried to get her to mangle the remaining five people in her life: her mum and dad, John, Carlos and me. I think she was stalling because I was next.

'Yes, but what are the criteria?' she kept saying.

I replied that it was personal, the criteria were whatever she wanted them to be.

She did her dad next, then her mum. She lay back with her head tucked into my armpit and I put my arm around her. But then I tried to kiss her. Every time I moved down Dominique avoided me. I was scared if a minute passed without conversation that she'd fall asleep so I suggested she come up with a game.

'OK, I have one, have you some paper?'

I tore a page out of a notebook from my bumbag and she made me write down twelve words that came into my head in a line across the page. I then had to link them. The connections build to a pyramid so there are two final words to link. These were 'sex' and 'nose' and as Dominique has a fairly big nose, it was like someone saying, 'You want to have sex with that girl with the big nose.'

When we finished the game she turned over as if to go to sleep and I said, 'Goodnight kiss?' She didn't poke her head up, though, so I kissed her on the side of her face, which was very cold and powdery-soft like a pillow. I fell asleep and at dawn woke up to find myself only half on the mattress. I'd shuffled down to follow Dominique so much I was up to my waist in mud.

Dominique had gone.

Journal Entry 17

Nikki didn't reply to my email straight away but her first message was very funny and she seemed as pleased to hear from me as I was to hear from her. She remembered as much about me from school as I remembered about her, too – who my friends were, what subjects I did, even old jokes we'd shared: 'Ask your brother, has he hidden in many trees lately?'

I'd never have written a letter, wouldn't have had the guts to call. Email, somewhere between the two, just seemed easier. Over the first couple of weeks the messages were joky, résumés of what had become of our colleagues from geography and what we'd been up to job-wise. But soon we were talking about day-to-day things. She asked me about my family early on, not knowing anything about Danny, and tellingly I found myself lying, and saying they were all fine. It should have been the first clue it was all unreal, but at the time I made the excuse to myself that I didn't want to bring down the atmosphere. It wasn't something you could just introduce into the conversation. It might put her off: 'Oh, I see, that's why you contacted me – you're a bit of a fuck-up.'

Lucy and I were getting on worse and worse, too. Her best friend Zoë got engaged to her boyfriend Pete, whom she'd known for less time than Lucy and I had been going out, and everyone on the subs' desk at *Insurance Monthly* was married. She'd turned twenty-nine that month, too, and all this combined with the fact that I didn't have a full-time job made Lucy think more and more about the future, just when I was thinking more and more about the past. Everything suddenly became make or break between us. Dominique being back on the scene probably added to it all, too. Carlos, who'd always been so anti-marriage, was suddenly talking about it after his reunification with Dominique. It was coming from all sides. People started referring to Lucy as 'Poor Lucy' around this time: Poor Lucy, who wasn't loved enough by her boyfriend for him to propose. I got a new name as well: 'Oh Dear Kit', who was being left behind because he hadn't got a pension or even a job.

After the marriage row the subject wasn't talked about openly. It became like some underground terrorist movement, inspiring arguments but never officially claiming responsibility. We started having rows about things we weren't really arguing about: Lucy's stealth arguments. They wore both of us down. One moment she could be shouting at me for leaving Marmitey knives on the throw in the living room, and the next she could be using this tiny oversight to question the whole basis of our relationship, and my love for her, without being in the slightest bit aware of the ridiculousness of the link. 'You don't love me. You can't. You never do anything for me. You never help around the house. I do everything. Do you love me? Answer me honestly. Tell me now, please, before it goes any further. Have some decency – if you have any respect for me, if I'm making a fool of myself, you must tell me now. Do you love me? I know you don't, but I want you to tell me.'

'Lucy, all I did was leave out a fucking Marmitey knife.'

Everybody was suddenly full of advice. 'You just know when it's right' was a phrase of Carlos's I grew sick of hearing. He made it sound like some sixth sense. And what made it right? 'When you find your soul-mate, Kit. I lost mine but now she's back. You have to find out if Lucy is your soul-mate.' But what's a soul-mate? His definitions were never precise. They were the person you shared everything with, but I'd shared everything with Danny, so it couldn't just be that. I certainly didn't share everything with Lucy. I rarely spoke about Danny to her. I couldn't because, 'I'm sorry, Kit – it just upsets me too much.'

When you boiled it down, it always came back to Dominique's definition, the one Carlos repeated as if it had been his, the reason why she claimed to have left her Aussie husband: your soul-mate was the person you wanted to have children with. Like a salmon returning to its mating grounds, she'd flown halfway round the world because she'd woken up one day and realized she didn't want to have children with John but with Carlos, she said.

Emailing Nikki became a haven from all this. From one every couple of days, the emails became once a day, then several a day. Pretty soon they were the focus of my day: addictions require constant reinforcement and instant rewards. Her emails provided that. They saved me from daytime telly, from thinking about Danny and Lucy. I was composing emails, thinking about what to reply in emails, cutting the pack to let fate decide whether I should be sending emails or laughing at her emails.

When I was about fifteen Danny and I used to keep a diary in which we logged how many miniature cans of Dad's Heineken we'd stolen that day from the garage fridge in Beech Road. It was how we judged the day's success: 'Half a can today – bad day. Two cans – good day.' My day's success was now based on how many messages Nikki sent. To begin with it didn't feel like I was doing anything underhand, either. I was in the cottage when Lucy left for work, there when she got back. Nikki and I were just old friends catching up.

When Nikki revealed she was married – although she didn't say it like a revelation – even this made no difference. She never referred to her husband by name or in any other way. It was always *I'm* doing this, *I'm* doing that, never *we're* doing this, *we're* doing that. I assumed they were virtually estranged. But I still didn't really think anything was going to happen. I wasn't even sure I wanted it to. Half the time I felt I was still in love with Lucy, but every now and again, after a bad row, Nikki would nag at the back of my mind. She became like a third person in the room. Nikki wouldn't go on about dirt round the bath rim, I'd think. Nikki wouldn't care that I hadn't applied for any jobs and that she'd caught me watching *Brambly Hedge* in my dressing-gown. Sometimes I'd be chatting with Lucy and I'd imagine how Nikki would respond to a particular question.

'Do you want parsnips with the roast?' Lucy would ask and I'd reply as if I was writing a joky email to Nikki: 'No, I think parsnips are Satan's own vegetable.'

'But you like them.'

'No, I don't like the way they impersonate floorboard nails. I hate their shape.'

'I'll get a cauli then, shall I? Are you OK?'

I started counting the kisses she put on the end of messages as if I was a teenager. I studied how many Ks the message was before I opened it to prepare myself for the disappointment if it was only a one-sentence reply. The fact that she never seemed free to meet up for a drink didn't concern me. I assumed she must be as nervous as I was about this prospect. It also, of course, allowed her to continue existing in a bubble of unreality.

I used to look forward to Lucy coming home. Then I started dreading it – it meant I had to stop emailing, it meant I had to wear my mask.

'You haven't done the washing-up. Can't you bring in the post instead of leaving it on the mat for me to tread on? Hang your coat up. Put those in the washing basket, you're not wearing those shorts again – you stink. Arghh, a Marmitey knife – you know how that annoys me. Put it in the sink. Please empty the bins when I ask, you don't do much. What is the matter with you? How does that poo get there? You're sitting too far back on the seat. You're not an emperor, it's not a throne – you've got to stop eating so many peanuts.'

Lucy and Nikki became like mental scales in my mind. Nikki was like some weight that I used to measure dollops of Lucy against. Nikki was *my* British Standards Approved girlfriend. How would she react in this situation? How did Lucy react? Which was better?

And then Nikki revealed she had a baby. Again it wasn't

like a revelation: she mentioned it in passing as if I already knew. It helped complete the jigsaw puzzle if nothing else. This was why she was freelancing from home – she was on maternity leave. Alarm bells should've rung. She was as bored as I was. For a week I felt let down, but at the same time there was a delicious delight in the disappointment. It fitted my new ordering of the world. I could remonstrate about the vagaries of fate. 'If only I'd contacted her sooner. Perhaps it just wasn't meant to be. Maybe we'll meet up in another twenty years.' I could stay up late and listen to Leonard Cohen while shaking my head ruefully about life, cut the pack and picture Danny's face and ask for guidance, create some drama in my life.

But then slowly, over time, it mattered less. It added to the infatuation. That I was still thinking about her even though she had a kid surely showed how much I cared for her. By Carlos's definition, she was my soul-mate.

And it was Carlos who I turned to for advice about all this. Feeling guilty about his reaction to Danny, he was eager to give it. But it turned out to be crap advice: 'Go for it' was basically the gist of it. Carlos, of course, was used to two-timing; his theory was 'I treat my girlfriend better when I'm seeing someone else, too.' I wasn't used to it, though, and it fucked me up.

I picked over every email like an encrypter desperate to give Nikki the best possible interpretation. In one she told me her favourite book was *Love in the Time of Cholera* by Gabriel García Márquez. I read it in a day. The story's about a couple who have a fling in their youth but are separated by fate, only to be reunited in old age to experience the love they were denied fifty years earlier. I took this to be a coded signal – one day we'd be together, too. I'd never understood stalking until then. Now I can see how it happens: you just shuffle the whole world behind one fact which you must believe in absolutely.

Every now and again reality would puncture the bubble –

she wouldn't reply for a couple of days, would make up an excuse why we couldn't meet, or a mildly flirtatious remark would simply not be referred to in her reply. I accepted this as part of the long game. Carlos advised me, too: 'She's married with a kid, Kit. Of course she's going to be careful. There's definitely something there, though. I can't believe you might end up with Nikki Aldridge – *imagine* what Danny would say.'

A pattern emerged: I would up the ante slightly, she would down the ante slightly, things would return to the joky beginnings and then I'd misread a cue and up the ante again, always a little bit more than the time before. In one drunken email I admitted I *might have* fancied her at school. She pretended I was lying. I told her I'd dreamed about her. 'A nightmare, was it?' she said. The more I revealed about my feelings, and the more she dismissed them, the greater I felt the need to reveal more.

It was a dam slowly bursting and it was three days before Lucy and I went to Greece last August I sent the killer message. We still hadn't met up. We'd been emailing for about a month and being away for a fortnight seemed a good enough time for her to digest my bombshell, and it would give me something to look forward to when I got home. I felt a tremendous relief when I went to bed that night that my feelings were finally off my chest, and a tremendous panic in the morning about what I might have set in motion.

13 December 2000

A girl woke up this morning in a camper van on the next pitch to ours. It was one of those with the elevated roofs. She stood up and shouted through it, 'Good mornin' world.'

Instead of ignoring her, about a dozen people shouted, 'Good mornin'' back, including the old couple in the VW next door who woke me up chopping wood to make their fire.

The atmosphere here for the concert is peace-loving, laid-back and friendly. Guys with goatees in their mid-thirties rattle round the campsite on skateboards. There are lots of loved-up couples: men with long dreadlocks, nose piercings and psychedelic shirts; women in long floral skirts, bikini tops and bare feet.

The concert started this afternoon and goes on until this evening. We wandered up to it. People sat on tiny-legged chairs or lay on Indian hand-woven rugs and rocked their heads or massaged each other. Everyone had ponytails, rat's-tails, baggy, pyjama-like trousers, combat pants, and rose tattoos, ankle bracelets and sandals so I felt out of place in my Gap shirt and Tom's boots, even more so because of my bumbag bulging at my side screaming out: 'He's coveting his possessions, he's not a hippie.' I spoke to a few people, mainly those who wanted to sell bong pipes, ganja biscuits or raffle tickets, and they all spoke in the same slow way, calling me dude. 'You like Sedona so far? Dude, it's like this every fuckin' day. Every fuckin' day.'

Peaches in the spring, apples in the fall, the words to the Grateful Dead song I can hear from the tents behind me now. It was pointed out to me by Damien, the Deadhead on the other side of the fence. He has wispy grey hair all over his leathery face. He's just been telling me about the Deads. He spoke of it as a spiritual thing. 'Jerry always says go forth, that was his big thing, go forth. If the authorities tell you not to go to a concert you go forth, but be careful. They told me I couldn't pitch my tent by the park – it's an Arizonian ordinance – but you guys have, and I guess I should have. I should have gone forth, yer see.'

He and his wife Marion, who teaches elementary school kids, live on a ranch in the Mingus Mountains. He said he'd followed the Deads for years, living in car lots. 'That's where it all happened. It was a family, there were about thirty thousand of us. Then they introduced some ordinance to break up the peace movement and you couldn't sleep in the lots. Helicopters an' shit overhead.'

I pretended I knew about the Grateful Dead, but slowly revealed I didn't. I asked why they'd stopped touring and Damien said, 'Jerry died,' as if I should know the significance of this. When I said I was a journalist he gave me a big stare with his small eyes and said that's what he wanted to do – write. 'I used to write quite a bit. *Misdemeanors, Maladjustment, Misappropriation and Misery*, volumes one and two. I was on speed a lot then.'

They've disappeared with a basket of purple sage to sell. Marion gave me one just now, tying it to my tent. 'The Indians here used to use it – you can smooch with it, use it for tea and it cures aches. Good aphrodisiac, too. Powerful stuff, purple sage.' She also told me about a concert twenty years ago where the vibe was so strong everyone was at one and it brought on lightning. 'I'm telling you, it's weird. It's true but it's weird,' she said. 'Other times we'd get the birds to fly in one direction overhead. All those people concentrating on one thing. You wait for tonight. Something's bound to go off.'

Midnight. Listening to Steely Damned and the Dave Nelson Band at the concert. The girl half dancing, half skipping, bending her leg in weird places like a BSE cow. The guy who twirled, a blissful expression on his face, Jesus locks on his head. Two friends in their floral print skirts and cow-hide waistcoats swinging a young girl of seven or eight round off the ground, giggling. Signing the marriage book to show we are here today, taken round by the tanned woman with the frank stare and a daisy-chain in her hair. The women clapping to the music, their hands in flip-flops for extra volume. The mandolin music strong and twangy and getting you in the stomach in that area sensitive to high pitch. Dogs being rotated round on their leads to the sounds, tongues hanging out from thirst. Fathers with babies high in their arms. The drug dealer with his ponytail high on his head, stroking his ginger beard at the picnic table, slowly arranging his bulge of dollars on to a clip, his plastic earring nodding as he moves his head to count. Carlos looking disdainfully on at the hippies: 'Look at that one there – God, what a state. I knew we should have camped somewhere else.'

I bought two chocolate-chip cookies laced with pot and ate them at the front with Dominique. Carlos didn't want anything to do with it. 'The first biscuit'll give you a buzz. The second – you're stoned. You'll be under a tree. *Enjoooy.*'

Carlos went to bed at 11 p.m. to read his book after another row with Dominique, who's now arranged to stay with her friend in Noosa after Sydney. When almost everybody had left after the concert Dominique and I sat on a grassy knoll at the edge of the campsite. There was just the sweet smell of herb and joss stick and stifled giggles from a group in a camper van playing instrumental music. The ganja biscuits had kicked in and the bottom half of my body felt disconnected and numbed.

Dominique asked whether I was 'drugged'. I said yes and she taught me French words – 'vous' and 'tu' – and the difference between them. Then she lay in the crook of my elbow. The contact felt good but I wanted to kiss her. Then suddenly we kissed, with alcohol dehydration, a caress from one lip to the next. I kissed her neck and she retreated.

'Are you hiding?' I asked.

She said she didn't know, then admitted she was. When I asked why she said with indignation, 'Because you are crazy.'

But I had the serenity of booze to brush it aside and we kissed again. I rubbed my face into her cheek and she said, 'No, I do not want.' I laughed and asked why and she said we were behaving like teenagers. I said, 'It is good to be teenagers.' I've started to talk like her: 'it is' for 'it's'.

She said it isn't and I laughed again and stroked the back of her neck. As we looked at each other I saw her deep-set eyes in her paper-white face and knew it was a flashbulb picture I would never forget. She said she knew nothing about me, really.

We walked back to the tents relaxed and under no pressure

to hold hands. She gave me a 'vous' kiss on the cheek before we turned the corner by the comfort station: 'Now we go to bed, separately, I think.'

Now I can see the stars as I lie in my tent, with my head outside, the purple sage is tickling my face. The clouds are speeding past like birds.

> Subject: < FBI >
> To: Kit Farley Kitfarley@yahoo.com >
> From: Tom Farley Thomasfarley@hotmail.com >

Dear Kit, Have Dominique and Carlos murdered you for your fussy cheese-eating ways? Should I be contacting the FBI?

Tom.

> Subject: < annoyed, but worried >
> To: Kit Farley Kitfarley@yahoo.com >
> From: Lucy Jones Lucyjones23@hotmail.com >

Dear Kit, Are you all right? I'm getting worried now. Tom hasn't heard from you either.

Lucy xx

Journal Entry 18

The holiday in Greece with Lucy was a nightmare. We'd been looking forward to it for weeks. It was supposed to be a new start, but I couldn't stop thinking about Nikki. One night on the island of Antiparos I spent forty-five minutes cutting the pack picturing Danny's face, telling myself if I got Nikki's card then it was meant to be.

Moths had become a symbol of the end of Lucy and me. The day after I first emailed Nikki there was one in the toilet at home, and on the day of Danny's accident a giant one had surprised and frightened me in my basement bedroom when I'd packed for the hospital. The theme was more vivid on holiday. We went to a butterfly valley on the island of Paros. There were millions of tiger moths, there for the cooling springs. The moths were resting, waiting for the mating season, and their furled black-and-white wings were hard to spot because they blended into the undergrowth. I noticed them on branches and leaves but when I pointed them out to Lucy she couldn't see them, even when there were dozens on one leaf.

When I got home after the holiday there was no message from Nikki. I waited another day. Nothing. Then another day. Nothing. I was going out of my mind by the time I emailed and asked if she'd received my dot, dot, dot message. She said it had shocked her. She really had no idea: 'You're right, I am happily married and couldn't possibly run away with a man who only eats cheese. If you'd said something ten years ago it might all have been very different. Now it's going to be awkward between us. I'm sorry for being so flippant. I'm always like this when I'm nervous. What should we do?'

At first I was pleased she'd replied. Anything was better than nothing. Then I was angry at her flippancy. And finally, as time went on and things began to improve with Lucy and the frequency of the emails decreased, I was almost relieved. But by then I'd already missed the warning signs with Lucy and the bolt out of the blue happened just a week later.

14 December 2000

Carlos wasn't around and Dominique was leafing through my Australia *Lonely Planet* on the picnic table when I woke up. We didn't speak about last night, but when Carlos was in the shower she said Eva's, the Sydney hostel I was heading for, sounded good and we chatted for a while about Perth, where I have to catch the plane to Thailand.

'Ah, when you are there you must go to North Bridge and you must eat marron – it is like a lobster and it is very nice. If you want to drink there you must go to the Brass Monkey Bar – it has comedy people and the food is cheap. Rottnest Island – it is close by and you could hire a boat and go dolphin spying, but be careful because they have animals, Kit. You will be scared of them, but they are not dangerous.'

Carlos and I hardly spoke all day, but Dominique and I followed each other's movements, and when in the evening Carlos went into town to watch the local baseball game it felt like a great weight had been lifted. Dominique and I went to the café again and talked about literature – Cohen and Stendhal, her favourite writers. She told me about Stendhal's seven stages of love: it was a metaphor about a branch which I didn't understand. I told her Danny's and my ridiculous theory that everything should be funny in the perfect world – disease, famine, war; that the world's problems were all down to people without a sense of humour; that as long as you could laugh at everything you'd always be all right.

'Ah, so you would be Prime Minister in this world?' said Dominique and I said no because I didn't believe in the humour theory any more. Dominique said love was like comedy and that you couldn't analyse it or else it died.

'But you always analyse,' I told her.

'Yes, of course,' she said.

I asked her to analyse the situation between us, but she said she didn't want to because it would stress her out.

She is starting to have an allergic reaction and soon will need cortisone which is too powerful to obtain over the counter to fight it. Her mossie bites look like squashed tomatoes and she's worried the reaction will spread to her neck and face. 'I know it will do this,' she said. She cannot solve problems, she must just create more to distract herself, that's her theory. I don't know if I am a problem. I want to be one; I think I am growing into one.

She is a bit of a hypochondriac, like me, I think, and we spoke about this for a while. Her best illness was a general infection that required three months of hospitalization, she said, laughing. When she laughs her head bobs up and down and her teeth go on display and she always ends it by sweeping her black hair back over her head and eye-balling you charmingly.

She's still saying America is another world and that is why 'nothing more can happen'.

On the way back to the tents tonight, in the same spot as before, she kissed me on the cheek. I asked for a proper one and she leant forward. We had to be quiet because I could see the shadow of Carlos sleeping. When she kisses only her mouth moves, the rest of her face is placid and her eyes look dopey. There's something very sexy about this.

Dominique whispered that she doesn't want the situation to get complicated. 'It is not logical,' she said. But I persuaded her to stay another hour. We walked aimlessly round the campsite and stopped to talk to a hippie with Tarot cards laid out on a milk crate outside the camp entrance; he's one of the handful who've remained after the concert. Dominique wanted a go and I translated during the reading because the man talked very quickly and she couldn't understand him. Apparently, she will have a period of loss soon. That loss will come from a relationship which doesn't suit her. I only marginally changed the facts to suit me and the hippie didn't contradict me because I paid for the reading. Then the hippie picked up a crystal and a box of matches. 'This is you,' he said, banging down the white crystal. He picked up the matches and threw them on the ground. 'This is not you,' he said.

Dominique, sitting on a milk crate opposite him, had her chin on her hand and looked across at me. It made me tingle the way she smiled, slanting her brown eyes at me then back to the cards. 'The future is favourable,' said the hippie, 'she has drawn a powerful card.'

We went down to our dirt patch by the café with my roll-mat to discuss it. She made a joke about last night: 'It is too dirty, we must go to the café – I know what you do.'

I'd brought my pack of playing cards along and told her I was her powerful card, and then about Danny recognizing people through his own pack of cards. I told her she was the seven of clubs because of her nose and hair colour, and tried to get her to pick a card for me. She said I am a nine (for no good reason) and I got her to try to cut this, but after three attempts she gave up.

I asked if I was now an obstacle. She said no, because 'we are not having a relationship'.

'In that case,' I said, 'I want to be an obstacle.'

She laughed. 'You want to be an obstacle now?'

I said the logical thing to do at this point is something irrational because she is at a crossroads and has no idea where the various roads lead. She looked at me very seriously and told me I was 'awful'. Lying back, I asked her to put her head on my shoulder, which she did. Nothing is impossible in this position and I felt I could persuade her to do anything so long as we remained like this. After I stroked her bony head and caressed her fingers we kissed, more passionately than before and she didn't say, 'No I do not want.' The dirt between our faces grated round our lips, round our cheeks and necks and we gripped each other close and I could hear desire in her throat, but in the end she pulled back.

Later she said she thought it best if she went to Australia without me or Carlos. She wants to 'recreate herself' and she's worried about me – I have lost all rationality. I pleaded as the forked lightning sliced through the 1 a.m. darkness, the sky tinged blue, the trees waving in the wind before the rumble and thunderclap.

'I can't believe,' she said.

'I will persuade you. I just need more time.'

I stayed at the picnic table while she prepared for bed and now I'm wondering if it's all become a game that's got out of control. I can't work out what I really think or even what I want.

'I can't leave you here to think alone,' she whispered.

I told her I was watching the storm. A part of me wanted her to go so I could feel the moment – nature and emotions both letting rip. Plus I wanted to smoke a butt from the ashtray on the picnic table, which I knew she'd be appalled at.

I kissed her on the lips then went to bed to think and mull and wonder how it has got like this so quickly. The kissing and hugging seem real in the dark but during the day the screen comes down, she puts on her sunglasses and it makes me wonder if it's the alcohol or just a holiday or the situation or something I don't know about because it's better expressed in French.

Journal Entry 19

Lucy didn't come into the bathroom to talk to me – that was the first odd thing. She shouted in to me instead: 'I'm the one who commutes two hours to work and yet I do *everything.* I make the bed. I pay the bills. I empty the bins. I cook tea, tidy the bathroom. I spend half an hour clearing up every time I get in. I'm sick of it. You haven't even done the washing-up. Your one job.'

I was out of the bath watching telly when she came and stood in front of me on the sofa. 'How can you sit there and not care? Look at it! And don't give me that shit again about men don't see dirt. You can see it as well as I can.'

Lucy picked up a dirty plate. She held it out for me to inspect. I couldn't help smiling at the absurdity of this.

'Now you're fucking smiling,' said Lucy.

I looked away.

'Now you're watching telly!' said Lucy. 'Fucking hell, it's like talking to Jack Duckworth. I can't believe you're watching fucking *University Challenge.*' She flounced out of the room.

'I wasn't watching *fucking University Challenge,*' I shouted after her. 'I haven't heard a single question. I don't even know which universities they're from. You haven't been looking me in the eye the whole time. But when you look away there's a blank wall behind you. It just so happens that behind you there was a telly. It's not my fault what's behind you. I'm not watching fucking telly.'

Lucy came back into the living room. She sighed and said with great seriousness, 'Great! You've left newsprint all round the bath as well, and have you been eating peanuts in there again? You have, haven't you? The plug's all blocked and the water's not going down. Who's going to clear that up? Me, *again.*'

I should have remembered – Lucy never argues about what she seems to be arguing about. I have to stop and look beyond whatever it is she seems to be in a mood about and try to hunt for the real reason. It's difficult and sometimes in the heat of a row when you're sticking up for yourself about peanuts down plug-holes you forget to do it. At the back of my mind I knew she wasn't really arguing about all the housey things. She was arguing about the big things: the fact we hadn't bought a house, were still living in Whitchurch, that all her friends were married and had babies and she didn't, that I had no job, that we weren't getting on.

Having an argument with Lucy its like playing a game of three-dimensional Connect Four. But it's a game she doesn't even know she's playing because she's not employing a clever debating strategy: at the time she really does think she's annoyed about what she seems to be arguing about. And the stupid thing is, if you bring up what she's really annoyed about and imply she's not really concerned about what she seems to be arguing about she goes fucking ballistic and accuses you of being even more insensitive than she thought you were in the first place. You can't win, so you respond to the minutiae.

When I turned off the telly half an hour later, above the portable stereo Lucy had on in the bathroom I heard her sobbing. I went in to speak to her. She was crying over the sink, holding on to it to support herself. My first thought was that she was crying about Danny. That week we'd received the report from Grange Grove that his physiotherapy was going to stop. It was the final acceptance that there was nothing more they could do. Both of us had been in tears earlier in the week about this. I went up to Lucy and put my arms on the back of her shoulders and said, 'I know, I know. Come on, Luce – let's not fight. It's not going to help.'

And that's when it all came out.

'Don't touch me,' she said. 'Don't call me that.'

I backed away and she needn't have told me the rest because somehow I'd already guessed. She'd met someone, she said: Sam. Her face imploded. It had happened last weekend when I'd been at Dad's, and she'd seen him again on Tuesday night when she'd told me she was seeing her friend Zoë. She hadn't slept with him, but he'd made her feel attractive, and she'd had a good time. She starting slagging me off: I was selfish, irresponsible with her money, never helped round the house, smelled, hardly got out of bed, didn't have a proper job, wouldn't stop wallowing, didn't laugh any more. I walked into the living room and sat on a chair, reading things on the wall – the framed front page when Lucy'd left the *Bucks Gazette* for her new job at *Insurance Monthly*: 'Luscious Lucy Waves Goodbye'.

Lucy was crying continuously, complaining her head was pounding, saying she was having a breakdown. Then she started pitying me. She said she was sorry, couldn't go, wouldn't leave me, was worried what I might do. She said she hadn't the energy to pack a bag and went to lie down on the sofa.

I drove to the offy in a daze and Lucy was in the High Street waiting for me when I got back. She looked insane. All the lights were on in the cottage and she was at the car window in her dressing-gown before I'd switched the engine off. She thought I'd 'done something stupid' I'd taken so long. She shook in my arms. We went inside and she said, 'I've had an epiphany – I realized when you'd gone how much you mean to me. I was running up and down the street. Oh, Kit, let me make it up to you. Let me build you up again. I'm so sorry, I had to tell you. I know the timing's shit. I wanted to wait, but I had to be honest.' She started to cry again. Her eyes were red, her bottom lip puffy. She kissed me on the mouth with passion. We French-kissed, but because we didn't normally do this, I thought to myself, She's comparing this with Sam's technique.

'We'll go on holiday. I'll pay for us to go on holiday,' I said. She held her head and looked out of the window. 'What's the matter?' I said.

'*I'll pay.*'

'What?'

'There you go again about money.'

'What? I said I'll pay.'

'Why do you have to say it like that? *I'll pay.* And the last holiday wasn't much good, was it?'

'Because I will. Tom will lend it to me. It won't be like last time. Come on, what's happened? Have you had another epiphany? A negative one?'

'I don't know. Kit, this just isn't working. I don't know any more. It's not just Danny, it's everything.'

'If we stay together we'll move,' I said. 'This place is jinxed. It's shit. It's been nothing but bad luck: Danny, now this. We'll move to London to cut down your commute.'

Lucy slept on the sofa and in the morning she packed an overnight bag and left. I heard her car engine start from the bedroom – the distinctive sound of her Polo misfiring and then revving wildly. For the whole of the next week I waited to hear that sound again, but she didn't come back.

15 December 2000

I'm sitting in the Horse-Around Bar in Circus Circus on the Strip in Las Vegas with a triple-in-one can of Bud Light, chain-smoking, speaking to the barman about the wealthy people who come to the casino and own Lear jets. The ringing sounds, chut-chut-chut of a quarter coin win on the Red Hot Seven slot machine, the do-dah, do-dah of the Wild Cherry one-armed bandit. Neon flickering, cocktail waitresses with blue shiny skirts that ruck up at the thigh tops, walking round with coiffed hair and bored stares offering free drinks to players.

The gamblers here are mostly middle aged or elderly and walk around with giant tubs full of quarters, their expressions not changing whether they win or lose. They just feed the slot and stare at the triple bars and plug the hole until the money's gone.

Along the Strip there are coin news-stand dispensers, except they aren't filled with *USA Today* like normal, but adult entertainment guides – *Red Hot*, *Nude News*: scraggy pictures of semi-naked women in stilettos and high hair next to 1–800 phone-sex numbers. At one point they were two inches thick on the ground and I shuffled through them like fallen leaves.

Carlos has affected an aloof sort of indifference to me. He won't talk to me unless I ask him a direct question, which he then answers very politely. It's like he's made a resolution. I know it's freaking out Dominique. She's hardly looked or said anything to me all day. They've been gone four hours and I've just wasted $200 on the roulette wheel at Caesar's Palace – black seven: Dominique's card; then red eight: Lucy's.

I'm in my hotel room at Circus Circus now. Carlos and Dominique didn't get back until 10 p.m. tonight. Dominique knocked on my door eventually. Carlos kept up his indifference and I was monosyllabic with Dominique for not saying goodbye to me properly. I was expecting more from my last night with them.

'We saw *The Truman Show*,' she said.

'Uhm.'

'It took one hour to get back. All the bus drivers were watching the football game.'

No reply.

'Are you going to sleep?'

'Yes.'

'I am sorry we are so late. Did you win any money?'

'No.'

> Subject: where are you? >
> To: Kit Farley Kitfarley@yahoo.com >
> From: Lucy Jones Lucyjones23@hotmail.com >

Kit, Now I'm worried. Your Dad hasn't heard from you either. He wants his measurements, by the way.

Lucy x

Journal Entry 20

It was three days later that I went round to Nikki Aldridge's house. It was the first and last time I've seen her since school. She kissed me on the cheek on the doorstep. Her hair was long, just like it used to be in geography, but for some reason, even though it was a moment I'd been looking forward to for months, I didn't feel the same attraction and I couldn't work out why. The floor of the kitchen was scattered with bright plastic toys. On the walls were three pictures – one of a baby wrapped in a blanket, another of the same baby with a beach ball, and one more of the baby in hospital.

Nikki's daughter Jennifer was writhing on the sofa in the living room. She had blond hair and green eyes and pointed a chubby finger at me. I sat in the armchair by the telly while Nikki sprawled across the sofa, picking up Jennifer every now and again and swishing her through the air making *weeee* noises. At one point Jennifer broke away from Nikki and took a few tentative steps before collapsing slowly to the floor like a well-oiled hinge. 'She's only ever taken three steps before – that was five,' said Nikki. I wondered if this was a good omen, but I couldn't help feeling slightly irritated that Nikki wasn't giving me her full attention. We'd waited months for this yet in the middle of a conversation she'd say, 'No, don't put your hand in that,' or 'Jennifer come away from the stairs.'

'You're not used to being around children, are you?' Nikki said on the way to Toys Я Us half an hour later. 'I thought you'd be better from your emails.' It made me so self-conscious about being bad with children in the shop that everything I said to Jennifer sounded ridiculously formal. 'What do you think of this slide, Jennifer? It has a lovely glossy sheen. Little Tikes is a good company, too – my nephews use them a lot – and it's snap-together and should be easy to assemble.'

Nikki moved around picking up toys for the under-twos, giving me wry looks, and I tried to summon up some enthusiasm. In the buggies aisle I managed to convince Nikki to buy Jennifer a red fire-engine, which had a door she liked to open and shut. 'What a great car – and look at its manoeuvrability. I like the front-wheel drive and, look, it's got a realistic petrol cap. Is it Little Tikes as well?'

Nikki gave me a sidelong glance. 'Don't pretend you're enjoying yourself,' she said. 'You wish you'd never come, don't you?'

After a few purchases and a tantrum from Jennifer, which resulted in tears and her snotty nose being wiped on a cuddly Tweenie, Nikki paid at the tills, leaving me alone with her daughter. We were about twenty yards away and I couldn't help thinking it was a test. When Nikki had said I was bad with children in the car I'd made a big deal about people who only played with children to show off to other people about how great they were with children. OK, so he is no good with children when anyone else is around – what about when he's on his own? It seemed like a test. Jennifer was tired, Nikki had said so, but when, right at the end, she slid off a rocking-horse and banged her head ever so slightly on a replica Strimming attachment and started crying, I knew Nikki thought it was my fault.

'Bring her to me,' she shouted when Jennifer erupted into tears. It was like the way people with dangerous dogs make you feel inferior by calling them off when they're jumping up at you.

'She just slipped off,' I said as Nikki scooped up Jennifer. 'She didn't bang her head.'

I got us some Chinese food when we got back and Jennifer went to bed. I meant to tell Nikki that Lucy had left me, but it felt all wrong. I tried to get into our normal email joky groove but we just couldn't capture the fluency. She didn't seem like the same person and nor did I.

'Email me,' she said on the doorstep.

A week earlier this prospect would have thrilled me, but I knew she knew I wouldn't and she knew I knew she didn't really want me to anyway.

Back home from Nikki's it hit me so hard as I opened the front door that I had to sit down on the sofa and stare blankly ahead for a full ten minutes: the house looked as if it had been vandalized. Lucy had moved her stuff out while I'd been at Nikki's. There wasn't a single view inside the house that wasn't blighted by the absence of an item of hers. Every single thing somehow managed to represent an element of the relationship that was now over: the little plant pot on the shelf by the sofa we'd bought at B&Q the week after I got back from the hospital in Germany; the gaping hole where her television had sat; the bath mat her mum gave us for Christmas; her electric toothbrush; her underwear from the drawers; her dresses from the hangers; the plates. And, for some reason worse than anything else, the fucking bread knife, the absence of which meant I had to tear off chunks of bread for my tea.

I rang Lucy at Zoë's that night. Half of me felt like

proposing as soon as I heard the phone being lifted. I realized at that moment I'd known what I wanted all along. But Lucy wasn't there and it was Zoë who answered. I tried again at 11.15 p.m. and then at 1 a.m. Each time there was no reply and a panic started rising in me.

I slept for half an hour, then something woke me – a terror gripped me, a bright flash across my mind of something irrevocably sad. I don't know how, but I knew at that second that Lucy had gone to see Sam. That she was with him at that moment; that things were happening I wouldn't be able to undo.

At 7.10 a.m., having had no sleep, I phoned the house again. Lucy should've been getting ready for work, but there was no reply. I phoned ten more times – each time no reply.

I called Zoë at the *Richmond and Twickenham Times.* She'd worked with us at the *Bucks Gazette* and was my friend, too. I left a message on her voicemail to call me and then phoned Lucy at *Insurance Monthly.* She was subdued. Unhappy. Barely talked. No warmth. It wasn't like the previous calls that week when things still seemed to be up in the air. I said I just wanted to speak to her – tell her I was still around, that I was thinking about her, that I had something important to say.

'Right,' she said, 'I'm thinking about you, too.'

I asked where she'd been the night before.

She was out with work, she said.

I said I'd called very late and very early and there'd still not been anybody around. 'If you went to see Sam – and I thought you might have done – I wouldn't mind,' I said. 'I'd understand. I think you should be honest with me.'

'I went out in Teddington and stayed over at Jess's,' she said.

I asked once more about Sam. I thought if she hadn't seen him she'd get angry. She didn't.

'I'm not ready for any of that yet,' she said.

I put the phone down and called Zoë again and left another message for her to ring me the moment she got in. Then when I called her yet again at 9.05 her phone was engaged. I immediately rang Lucy, just to see if I was right – sure enough, her phone was engaged, too. They were getting the story straight.

At 9.30 a.m. Zoë called. 'Sorry, I couldn't get back to you. I had a few calls to deal with.'

I said, 'Zoë, don't lie to me. I know you've cooked up a story together. Lucy's left me, I haven't slept all night, my brother's in a mental institution – I just want the truth. I had a funny feeling last night that she was with him and I was right, wasn't I?'

Zoë didn't say anything.

'I'll say I tricked you. I won't say you told me,' I said, tricking her.

'OK.'

The OK sealed it. Then I called Lucy.

'I can't believe you think I'll fall for this double bluff,' she said. 'If you think I am going to say anything . . .'

'I know you went down to see him,' I said. 'And it doesn't matter who told me, I knew anyway. I suspected last night. I had a dream . . .'

'You're such a know-all. I hate you. You reckon you know everything about me – you reckon you know everything I do, everything I say, before it's even out of my mouth. You promised me you'd give me two weeks to think about it and here you are in my face.'

I told her about reapplying for full-time jobs. I mentioned getting married.

Lucy just said, 'I can't bear this – not here at work.'

Then I said I was going now but that I just wanted to say one final thing: that I wanted her back, that I loved her.

'Right,' she said.

I said I'd never ring again if that's what she wanted, that I just wanted her to know all this. But, of course, I phoned one more time. 'I have just one more thing to say. I phoned Hamways and the earliest we can move out is 11 November. I might need your signature' (I knew I didn't, I just wanted an excuse to call to say what I'd done). I wanted her to change her mind, I thought if I took it to the brink she would, but she didn't say anything. Not a word. Just a deep silence, a black hole of silence through which our whole relationship seemed to disappear, strung out like infinitely thin spaghetti down a crack in the conversation which she could have plugged with something, anything.

16 December 2000

Dominique woke me up this morning. I hadn't locked the door, ever hopeful. And she slid into my room and put her hands on my face. She'd just had a shower. Her hair was wet and shiny and smelled of apples. Her face glistened. I didn't kiss her because I hadn't brushed my teeth, but I held her chin, which was cold and angular like a polished stone.

Carlos never bothered to get up to see me off this morning. But I said goodbye to Dominique at the Greyhound depot. Her eyes were uncertain, her eyelids flickered from the concentration when we kissed. I took off her sunglasses and she cried. If I hadn't pressured her she might have come, she said.

'You're blaming me?'

'Yes,' she said and laughed. 'I always reproach you.'

She wouldn't wait for my bus. She was worried about falling unconscious from her spreading allergy. She said she'd miss me, but only after I'd gone. Then, just before she went, she said, 'I start to believe now.' When she turned to go I felt incredibly alone.

Now I'm outside LA airport after the Greyhound ride. The zip on my rucksack – when I opened it to take out my laptop to write this – said DOM–in–IQUE, it sounded like. I phoned her just now. She was out. I left a message with Circus Circus reception: 'Kit called and wanted to know what your latest infection was.' The receptionist said he'd give her the message, but I think he thought I was implying something rude related to herpes, so I doubt he'll bother.

Journal Entry 21

Suicide. I remember the first time it crossed my mind. It was October by then. I was sitting in the living room watching *Countdown*. One minute I was pleased because I'd defeated Rick Wakeman in dictionary corner with a seven-worder on the letters round. The next second it popped into my head: I wonder if I should kill myself. It wasn't the way you think about it as a teenager – this will show them, they'll be sorry. It was just a mundane, totally practical thought and the only shocking thing about it was that it was the first time it had occurred to me. What shall I do, thought? Read the *Guardian* in the bath, watch *15 to 1*, go into Aylesbury and have a shish with extra cheese or top myself?

Once you recognize suicide as a possibility it becomes a face on the dice you roll every time you feel down. From a random thought that had entered my head it became something I started thinking about more and more. In a way it gave me a sense of freedom, too. When you're happy you spend half your time shitting yourself: you worry about locking the front door in case a burglar gets in, about catching fatal diseases, eating properly, being in a car accident, your career. When you're unhappy you don't give a shit. You welcome it. Come on in, burglars; come on, gang across the street – try to mug me; fuck you on the blind bend coming the other way, I don't care.

I started having little fantasies about it. I began to think old Danny, the way he used to be, was out there somewhere on the other side looking down on me. I went through what I'd say to him when we met up in this other dimension. I imagined we'd both be incredibly casual about it all in an ironic-cool sort of way. 'Now look what you made me do,' I'd say, and old Danny would raise his eyebrows: 'You tit,' he'd say. But then we'd hang around together creating memories and having a laugh like it always used to be.

Lucy and I had two bogus reconciliations before the final one a couple of weeks before my flight. In a way these were more humiliating than the original betrayal. They followed the same pattern each time: we would ring each other a few times, meet up, have a good night, I'd become optimistic and then something would go wrong. Normally this would be the result of us arguing about why we'd split up in the first place. I was so desperate to get her back, initially I accepted all the blame.

'It had nothing to do with Danny, you do realize that, don't you?' she'd say. 'That was just bad timing.'

And I'd nod. But deep down just when things started to get better I'd begin to doubt this and occasionally I wouldn't be able to contain myself. I always tried to couch it in diplomatic terms. 'We weren't getting along, I had other things on my mind, it wore us down and you got sick of me being miserable,' I'd say, and Lucy would jump down my throat.

'No. You were just incredibly selfish. I wouldn't leave you just because you were miserable. I left you because I felt like you didn't give a shit about me. You've changed – that's what's different.'

The first reconciliation ended when she slept with one of Zoë's friends, Pete. She never told me this – I guessed it and she didn't deny it. Her excuse was we still weren't officially back together, that she was still unsure I really had changed. For two weeks I didn't answer her messages and then in a weak moment I called her. It had ended with Pete, she said. It wasn't about him: it was about her and me. She'd finished with him because he wasn't a patch on me. She'd realized this when he'd brought her breakfast in bed. 'I wanted it to be you bringing me breakfast,' she said. That was supposed to make me feel better. Funnily enough, it actually did.

When I was with Lucy I always imagined there were lots of girls out there who'd be after me if I was single. I didn't think I'd struggle. The reality was different. Tragedy seems to give off a bad smell. I tried it on with everyone: old friends from work, old girlfriends, women in bars Carlos and I went to. I even got back in touch with Nikki Aldridge. I emailed her in a frenzy one night – five or six messages telling her everything, the truth about Lucy and Danny. I called her twice, left a message on her mobile and finally one at her parents' house. Her email the next day said simply, 'Please stay away from my family.' So I'd become a stalker.

I called Lucy. In my head I made out I was being magnanimous – looking back I was just desperate. And, of course, the same thing happened again. This time it was someone from her work. I went a month without speaking to her. I tried to rebuild my life: I stopped smoking and drinking, and I started going to the gym.

In a way it was getting myself sorted that was to blame. The final reconciliation started because I wanted to speak to Lucy to prove how much I was over her. I can still remember the call. I'd had a good day: I'd got my travelling jabs at Trailfinders in Kensington with Carlos and Dominique. Another reason for calling – 'I'm going round the world for a year. You see – I no longer need you.' But I must have had an inkling of doubt because I cut the pack of cards to decide if it was a good idea. I got Lucy's card. Coincidence? So I cut again. I got it again. Before the third cut, I said to myself, 'Danny, if I get her card again then Lucy and I will end up back together. This is what you think is best.' I got it. The odds against this is 52 × 52 × 52 – over one in 100,000. Never mind that her card was slightly bent and therefore more likely to be chosen: it had to be an omen from Danny. Nobody would've ignored this. This time we stopped arguing about whose fault it was. There was no point any more because I was going away for a year.

Lucy didn't think I'd go. I didn't think I'd go. Somehow I did but I still don't know exactly why.

And writing this journal hasn't given me any answers. I think I'm going to stop now.

17 December 2000

I met a girl called Karina from Surrey on the plane with a figure-eight-shaped head. She was backpacking, too, and I spoke to her for about three hours and let her tell me how amazing Australia was. I had verbal diarrhoea, too. I told her about Carlos and Dominique and she listened. I think she thought I was coming on to her because at around midnight she took a sleeping pill and offered me one, too. She said on her flight to LA from London she'd sat next to a guy who'd got drunk and kept waking her up to talk. I told her I was going to Australia to do an article on the Oz Experience bus and maybe to write novel about opal mining because I thought it sounded cool, but she was more enthralled with a guy she'd met in the airport bar who'd just been in Bhutan, where they only let in 5,000 tourists a year.

It was a bit embarrassing when we woke up next to each other, because it implied some intimacy and it was difficult to capture the fluent conversation of before. I kept saying I couldn't believe we couldn't smoke on the plane and gave her ten reasons for why I liked cigarettes, and I realized I was being boring, but couldn't stop myself. She had pale skin, and when she became excited – normally about the Bhutan guy – her top lip protruded more and enveloped her teeth like a sheet covers a mattress.

We landed this morning, shared a cab from the airport, and we're both staying in King's Cross, the Sydney red-light district. It is Soho condensed into one street. Every second door is a live show or adult bookshop, and haggard, stoned-looking hookers stalk the streets. They look soiled, like cardboard that's been left out in the rain.

Eva's Backpackers on Orvell Street is painted in pastel colours with pictures of footprints walking up the walls and adverts for the Oz Experience bus that Carlos and I were supposed to take, and adventure sports like kayaking, rap-jumping, zorbing, tandem sky-diving and bungee-jumping.

The woman on reception gave us bed linen and pillows and then had second thoughts and asked us if we wanted a double, assuming we were together, and Karina said quite emphatically, 'I would like a same-sex dorm, please.'

Afterwards she said to me, 'It's easier getting changed without blokes around.'

From then on it was like we were a couple who'd had a row. 'See you – I'll probably be kicking around down here later,' she said, indicating the communal kitchen area.

I said, 'Yeah, see you,' knowing she was snubbing me.

There were five bunk-beds in my mixed dorm. Everyone was asleep and it felt quite intimidating and I didn't feel safe leaving my laptop there and didn't know whether it was cool to say, 'Hi, I'm Kit from England,' or simply act self-sufficient and unpack my rucksack and look busy reading the *Lonely Planet*. It was around 11 a.m. and everyone was obviously sleeping off hang-overs and therefore had had a night out with mates they'd made or travelled with, and on top of the Karina blow-out it made me lonesome so I tried to go to sleep. But even though I was tired I couldn't because Eva's voice kept booming over the Tannoy – 'Sarah in room 23, are you checking out?' . . . 'Paul in 17 – there's a phone call from your brother downstairs.'

I listened intently to each one, hoping there'd be one from Dominique, responding to my hypochondriac joke, but there wasn't.

I'm at O'Malleys pub now on William Street. It's the main pub in the Cross area and I've made my first attempt at mingling with backpackers. It was quite difficult. There was an Irish band playing 'Dirty Ol' Town', and the weekend English Premiership highlights were on the mute overhead TV screens and nobody seemed interested in chatting. It's 7 p.m. and I've been here for three hours drinking black & tans and I'm quite pissed and getting stared at for writing on a laptop.

I did meet three proud-to-be-traveller types earlier: Sonia, the personal trainer, with the exuberance of a star-jump; Steve, her boyfriend, who stared intelligently, sizing everything up; and Vim, the Norman Lamont-lookalike Dutchman, who worked for Amsterdam Radio and said, 'Yeah thatsh good' after what everybody had recommended I should do in Australia. They'd been in Sydney for six months and had a cool-box with them, fresh from a picnic overlooking the harbour in the Botanical Gardens. They were delighted I'd just arrived and rubbed in my ignorance of the city: 'Oh, Steve, this one's just arrived – *just* arrived. Vim, he's a Sydney virgin.' They reeled off a list of things to do, I nodded, didn't listen to a word of it, and then quickly moved away to this corner. I told them I'd meet them in Coogee in a couple of days, which is a much better backpacker area, according to the *Lonely Planet*, but I have no intention of speaking to them again.

I'm on the rooftop terrace of Eva's now. Three people are passing a joint round on a table next to me, several people are writing their journals and there's a B52-drinking contest going on at another table. I have to keep permanently on the move so I don't look lonely and it's getting on my nerves. I've just emailed Dominique to table the idea of me coming to visit over Christmas in Noosa. I had a backlog of messages from Dad and Tom, and one from Lucy counting the days down to Thailand which I didn't have the heart to reply to.

I'm going to bed now and setting my alarm for 8 a.m. so I can watch all the girls in the mixed dorm who work in Sydney getting changed.

> Subject: < Crocs >
> To: Kit Farley Kitfarley@yahoo.com >
> From: Lucy Jones Lucyjones23@hotmail.com >

Dear Kit, I'm getting really worried now. Where are you? I emailed Carlos yesterday and he said you'd left for Australia. He wasn't very chatty. Have you two fallen out again? Are you there yet? I've been reading about Thailand – there's loads to do: crocodile wrestling, elephant trekking. Just email me, will you?

Lucy xx

> Subject: < Christmas >
> To: Kit Farley Kitfarley@yahoo.com >
> From: Jon Farley Jonathan_farleyRBS@aol:com >

Dear Kit, I am now assuming you won't be home for Christmas. A week with no contact – too long. I am also assuming you've left America. Again, can we be informed, please? I am going to give you Aunty Ange's address in Perth. It's 2034 Cann Street. The number is 546 345232. This might be a good place to stay before seeing Lucy – if this is what you are going to do. Lucy seems to think this is what you're planning. The girl is worried sick. She's phoned here twice. What's going on?

Your father.

p.s. You haven't given that fitting for your suit yet. I need it ASAP.

> Subject: < Ring Dad >
> To: Kit Farley Kitfarley@yahoo.com >
> From: Tom Farley Thomasfarley@hotmail.com >

Kit, You're probably having a fantastic time and have forgotten all about us. But Dad's worried. He's panicking about the bloody suits. Give him a ring.

Tom.

18 December 2000

I slept in until 1 p.m. partly because I was tired and partly to be cool. There is cachet here on being the last up in the dorm because it implies you had a heavy night. I'm watching the Test match in the TV area. Hanging around the TV area is also considered cool. It's even cooler if you do this without shoes and socks on to show how casual you are. Next time I must remember this. To show I'm not bored, which I am (I hate cricket), I crane my head round every time someone walks in front of the screen as if I'm annoyed and anxious not to miss a single ball. I am desperate not to look lost and lonely. Being lost and lonely is one thing, being seen to look lost and lonely is quite another.

I've got about three weeks to get to Thailand and meet Lucy, if that's what I end up doing, and I've started to get depressed about Christmas and being stuck in Australia on my own. They played 'Bring Us Some Figgy Pudding' over the Tannoy earlier, and I felt incredibly homesick – it reminded me of standing in school assembly beside Danny in Aston Clinton County Combined – but apart from this there doesn't seem to be anything Christmassy about Sydney at all. It's almost like it's not happening. It's boiling hot (which is making my verruca itch again), there aren't any Christmas lights and I suppose it would be slightly anomalous for the pimps and prostitutes to put tinsel in their hair and fake-snow the windows of the strip clubs.

I saw Karina earlier on in the kitchen area and said hi. She said hi back as if she'd never spoken to me before. *It's easier changing without blokes around* – don't flatter yourself. I wouldn't want to watch you get changed, dear – your back is too long for your legs and you look like a prehistoric horse.

I don't know why I haven't heard from Dominique and I can't help wondering what she's up to. I miss her. I miss talking to someone who cocks their head ironically and laughs and holds my hand. I miss Dominique's blank face, eyes wide when she doesn't understand, forcing you to clarify before she admits the words have jumbled and made no sense. Dominique's boobs were the size of mince pies, long nipples like detonation fuses. In her XL bed-shirt she looked like a piece of spaghetti in a hanky. I still fancied her, though. They should be in LA any day now.

I'm having to fight off the guilt, too, on so many fronts it's disorientating me. I feel bad about Carlos, but not as bad as I would have thought. Mostly I feel sad. Let's work it out – no, don't let's.

This hostel is cliquey and full of wankers. The atmosphere's like university with people desperately trying to demonstrate kudos through knowing a lot of people to say hi to and through chatting to them about nothing in particular in loud, designed-to-be-overheard voices. 'Yeah, might see you there Tudgy, Mudgy and Smudger' . . . 'No, I'm going to Oxford Street with Shazza, Bazza and Dazza.'

I've left the TV room and I'm alone in a corner at the Café in the Cross. For some reason I was ostracized even when I took my shoes and socks off – possibly the verruca. The TV room filled up with English people for *Neighbours* and somebody switched off the cricket without even asking me. After that it was *Home and Away* and everyone pretending, like at university, to be massively hooked on the soaps; all the time showing off about how they'd found work in Sydney or how they'd partied all night and would now die for a café latte.

I hate the way long-stayers tramp around the hostel in bare feet deliberately not catching eyes or returning smiles to demonstrate they've been there longer and that in the end it doesn't pay to socialize because – stern look here – it gets harder and harder to say goodbye. What shit! And why can't I even find anyone to say hello to? And what am I going to do about Lucy? It's D-day minus twenty. I'm thinking about Carlos, too. This is how he started. He would half fall in love with whoever it was he'd cheated on Dominique with. He'd agonize about leaving her but wouldn't have the courage and his life would chug along until the next infidelity. Then, after a while, he stopped feeling like this and just did it anyway minus the guilt. 'It was just sex. She smelled of Johnson's and Johnson's baby oil and she was fucking gorgeous, I'm not joking.'

I hope I'm not doing the same thing. I hate to think I've become Carlos. I don't think I have, although I would like to know why this keeps happening to me. Nikki, Dominique: is it the thrill of the chase? What chase? I hunt down the prey and when it is in my sights I lower the rifle and wander home to eat vegetarian.

It's 2 a.m. and I'm back in the hostel kitchen area. In O'Malleys tonight I got talking to a couple of Essex lads from Basildon. They'd rented a flat that day for $380 a week on Victoria Street and were looking for people to fill it and make money on the sublet. I pretended to be interested to get a latch. They bragged about a barwoman from Bailiees they'd taken out for the night and were aloof in a casually unpleasant way because I'd not been to Circular Quay yet. They recommended Coogee as well, because of the Coogee Bay Hotel that has the biggest bar in the Southern Hemisphere. 'It's just like being back at home. It's nice and that but every now and again, like, the fuckin' glasses.' He lowered his head as if ducking. 'Fuckin' 'ell. Yeah.'

New Zealand, they concluded, was 'fuckin' beautiful'. Australia, they concluded, was 'fuckin' big'. I concluded they were fuckin' thick and left and moved off further down Darlinghurst Avenue past the neon Coca-Cola sign, the gateway to the Cross, and on to Darlo's bar after a bag of chips and tartare sauce at the trendy Fish Face restaurant. Darlo's was done up like a seventies flat with orange settees and elaborate but cheap-looking wicker lamps. It was full of ostentatious gay guys holding their elbows in when they smoked. I got quite drunk on Tooheys and walked back to the hostel via the main drag. The pimps sat on the doorsteps with Sporty Spice tattoos on their upper arms and I asked how much it was for sex. I was offered two girls for $100 a piece. Then two girls agreed to give me a full-body massage for $50. They would bring me off by writhing over me. I said thank you, I would think about it, and came back here to the hostel feeling randy.

> Subject: < flight details – don't lose >
> To: Kit Farley Kitfarley@yahoo.com >
> From: Lucy Jones Lucyjones23@hotmail.com >

Kit, I arrive on 7 January at Bangkok airport. BA Flight 751. Do you want me to bring you anything? Some peanuts?
Lucy.

> Subject: < Suits >
> To: Kit Farley Kitfarley@yahoo.com >
> From: Jon Farley Jonathan_farleyRBS@aol.com >

Suits??????

> Subject: < info >
> To: Kit Farley Kitfarley@yahoo.com >
> From: Lucy Jones Lucyjones23@hotmail.com >

Dear Kit, Did you get those details? I've sent them again as an attachment just to be sure. What do you want for Christmas?

You haven't given me a clue. What about some cool pyjamas? If you like I can bring out presents from your family.

Lucy.

> Subject: < the latest please >
> To: Dominique de Cabissole Dominiquede@yahoo.com >
> From: Kit Farley Kitfarley@yahoo.com >

Dear Dominique, In Sydney having a shit time. Where are you? Are you still going straight to Noosa after Sydney? Shall I wait for you here? Email me if you want to meet up. I'm at Eva's Backpackers. How is your allergy? I miss you.

Kit xx

19 December 2000

I've checked out of Eva's – I've been seen on my own too much. I'm damaged goods. I need to try a new place where my lonesome ways are not known. Plus, I got caught ogling a Norwegian girl getting dressed this morning. I've always thought if you closed your eyes almost completely and just squinted out of the bottom bit nobody could tell you were awake. 'I go to bed at one a.m. if you want to stay up for that, too,' she said, turning her back on me to slip her bra on, and a couple of people looked up and I couldn't turn my watch alarm off so they knew it was me she was talking about.

I took the train to Bondi Junction, caught a number 314 bus and I've checked into Beachside Backpackers on Book Street, Coogee. The hostel is pretty cliquey here as well, though. I spoke to a Canadian in my dorm earlier while we watched the cricket highlights on the TV in the room, but he only replied and never initiated a conversation. He's in the other camp – the people who work in Sydney, who feel they're magically elevated above normal backpackers just because they pull pints of Tooheys seven hours a night in some bar.

It's evening now and I went with some Jap to the CBH (what everyone calls the Coogee Bay Hotel) tonight. It had about seven bars and was full of aggressive English blokes. Big groups arrived in Scouser wigs with luminous test-tubes attached to their chests. The girls were all in DJs and dark glasses. It was an Oz Experience forfeit party complete with eighteen-year-old bra-less girls in micro-skirts deep-throating boomerang-sized bananas to the psycho-scene music from *Reservoir Dogs* – 'Stuck in the Middle with You'.

The Jap left after one drink because he said he had to get up early for a surfing lesson (I think he was slightly appalled), and I tried to speak to a couple of backpackerish people, but as soon as I said I'd just arrived in Sydney they backed away from me like I had a disease. In the end I decided to fit in I'd have to lie. I decided to say I'd worked as a diving instructor in Shark Bay but had come to Sydney because I was mauled by a great white when the owner of the boat company forgot to secure the metal doors of the underwater cage: 'Fucking bastard, I'm suing his arse,' then I'd point to the scar on my forehead. But by the time I'd figured all this out there was nobody left to tell the story to, so I came back here to the kitchen area to write this. The other thing I may do to fit in is maybe sit in the kitchenette at about 8.30 a.m. in my smartest clothes studying the employment section of the *Sydney Morning Herald*, tutting at the few opportunities for trained clerics. That's another thing the people who think they're cool do.

This country is weird – everyone seems addicted to adrenalin sports. All the talk is of surfing, jet-boating, bungee-jumping and sky-diving and I can't get a foothold in any conversation.

I am starting to hate backpackers, too, I think. All the time in America I craved their company, now I can't stand them. One of the reasons you go travelling is to escape the pecking order of the world of work, and, lo-and-behold, you just enter a completely new one, except now it's not based on how much you earn, what car you drive, what your salary is. It's all about have you swum with dolphins, bungee-jumped, smoked opium with the Burmese hill tribes, how long have you 'been out', what do you mean you never stroked a dingo on Fraser Island? How many email addresses have you got? Why haven't you seen the Botanical Gardens?

Nineteen days to go until I meet Lucy. I keep hoping if I don't email she'll change her mind about coming out and then I can go home. All I want to do is go home. But it's not working. And where is Dominique? She should be in Sydney by now. Do I hang around and wait for her or start making my way up the east coast? I have an internal flight from Cairns to Perth, but Cairns is at least 2,000 miles away and I might miss it if I stay here too long. I keep checking at Eva's to see if Dominique's left a message, but she hasn't. I also feel incredibly randy. How on earth do you wank in a mixed dorm?

I'm lying in my bed now writing this. It's 1 a.m. and everyone else in my dorm is still out partying and I'm thinking about Danny and what I almost did just now.

In a drunken haze I left the hostel after writing my last entry and took the 373 back to King's Cross, but all the pubs were shut so in the end walked up one of the sleazy stairwells advertising 'models'. I knocked on two doors before a maid answered. The girl was busy, she said, and led me into a kitchen area where I sat with her watching *Brookside*, which I didn't know they got in Australia. Sinbad was knocking about the close, the maid smoked a Peter Jackson and just as I decided I wasn't going through with it, the girl popped her head round the door, and, not wanting to disappoint the maid after having debated the Max Jordacre situation with her, I followed her into a small room.

There was a bed, a sink and a small wastepaper basket. The prostitute told me to strip off. She looked old, about forty-five, and had a distended white belly that was streaked with blue veins so she looked like a lump of Gorgonzola. She put a condom on me, even though my knob was about the size of a seahorse, and put her lips over me.

She said, 'Let's get this cock nice and hard,' and it sounded strange and out of place, as if it was Delia Smith giving out cooking instructions. Nothing happened.

Continuing her Delia commentary, very matter-of-factly she said, 'Let's see it all spurting out.' *Roast until golden brown then serve with vegetables.*

Finally she asked if I wanted to pay another ten dollars for penetration. I said no and started to get dressed. She said I was probably nervous. 'When I feel frustrated I just want to do it,' she said. To make her feel better about being haggard I told her it wasn't anything to do with her and that I found her very attractive.

Outside, I thought, She probably thinks I'm gay. She probably thinks I've been building up to this moment for years. I started to think of Danny, and what it must have been like for him.

20 December 2000

I was up early enough to justify going down to the city today. Koalas are active on average for just four minutes a day, I've learned. It's the same with backpackers.

In Hyde Park I won a game of chess on the giant board against an inscrutable East European. He had a shaggy beard and played in a cycle helmet with a rucksack on his back. He had no conversation. He just stroked his chin with a hairy hand throughout and tried to psyche me out by stamping his foot whenever I took too long over a move. His Aboriginal friend didn't help either. He muttered throughout, 'Hurry up, mate,' and kept saying, 'Oh no,' whenever I made a risky move with my queen.

Two pawns down, I offered to resign, but Mr Inscrutable fucked up badly and I got four back and he gave me the signal it was over before I got my queen's pawn to the back line. He didn't want to shake my hand but when he saw me coming towards him he had to. 'Good strategy – too warm,' said his Aboriginal side-kick and I couldn't work out whether this meant I was too hot for his friend or that the midday temperature had upset his friend's game because he was from a cold country like Romania. So I said, 'Me too,' and walked away feeling jittery.

New fact about myself: I get more of a buzz from mental challenges than I do from physical ones. Maybe there should be a country geared up for these recreations the way Australia is for risky activities. I would fit in better in a place where travellers wore T-shirts depicting images of the verbal reasoning tests they've done particularly well at, instead of the usual bungee shirts. 'You did the analogies in the Whitsundays? Me too. I don't think it was as hard as the what-comes-next-in-the-series at Byron Bay: that was awesome.' It would be great, people debating their brain-teasers and talking about people who choked: 'There she is, the girl who bottled the anagrams three days in a row in Cairns.'

Afterwards I took a ferry to Manly. It passed the Opera House and the Harbour Bridge, which respectively looked like turtles fucking and an old coat hanger, and I saw an English couple who had obviously been away too long. They'd lost all self-awareness and were taking it in turns to pluck nits out of the back of each other's head. At Manly, the jewel of the North Shore, I had a McDonald's and went to Oceanworld, where I learned puffer fish contain a deadly poison called TTX, which is more lethal than cyanide and one drop can kill up to thirty people. Also, if you stand on the estuarine stonefish the sharp tendrils puncture your feet and paralyse you, resulting in drowning. The manta eel has a vicious bite and crocodiles and sharks claim three lives a year. I've decided not to swim.

> Subject: < losing patience >
> To: Kit Farley Kitfarley@yahoo.com >
> From: Lucy Jones Lucyjones23hotmail.com >

Dear Kit, Hellllllllllloooooooooooo.
Lucy x

It's early evening now in the dorm. I'm in my top bunk preparing to go out to meet backpackers and I'm thinking about Danny again, racking my brains, while worrying about this fan because it's only a few inches from my head and if I sit up straight too fast it will slice off the top of my head like a boiled egg.

Just before Danny left for Germany he fell out with Carlos. Why on earth didn't I pick up on that? It was around the time when Carlos was perfecting a new pulling strategy – comparing hand sizes. It went like this: Carlos would get talking to a girl and halfway through the conversation he'd tell her she had tiny hands. He would say this even if she didn't have tiny hands. Even if she had hands the size of frying pans he'd say it. He'd make out he'd just noticed this fact and use it as an excuse to press one of his hands next to hers to compare their sizes. Then, suddenly, he'd change his demeanour and, pretending to be overcome by the electricity of her touch, he'd bend his fingers over hers, stare into her eyes and say in a carefully mesmerized voice: 'I bet you've got smaller lips than me, too.'

The incident happened right at the end of the night just before we came home from the Gate. Carlos had just trawled the pub with his 'magic hand' and had got a couple of snogs from some drunken admin clerks from Equitable Life out on a hen night, and we were at the bar listening to him relaying his most recent triumph at work, another secretary. Then Danny butted in. Trying to sound casual, he asked Carlos how he was getting on with Dominique. This is always how Danny voiced his disdain for Carlos's antics. Carlos replied that they were getting on fine. Then, a few moments later, seemingly out of nothing, Danny put his beer down heavily on the bar. 'What?' said Danny, acting all innocent, although it was obvious he was annoyed.

A little later he leant across me, stared at Carlos, and said, 'Do you know something, Carlos? You really *are* a disgusting lech.'

'Am I?' said Carlos, smiling, as if he was pleased, although I could tell he was upset.

That was the night Carlos first talked about Danny's sexuality, just a passing comment: 'What was that all about, Kit? Why is he so worried about what I get up to? You don't think he's . . . do you?'

'Fuck off,' I said. 'He was making a valid point. You *are* a disgusting lech. Sometimes I can hardly bear you myself.'

'Yeah, maybe,' said Carlos and that was that.

I probably made it worse for Danny, which is what gets me now, and maybe why Danny never told me. While he was openly disdainful of Carlos playing around, I used to pretend to Carlos that I was the same as him. I'd find myself talking up my encounters with women when I was with Carlos. He would tell me about a girl he'd slept with and even when I was seeing Lucy I'd try to match him with my own pale experiences: 'Yeah, I know what you mean. It's so hard to resist, isn't it?'

This is how I pitched myself. I wanted Carlos to think I had just as many opportunities as him, but that the only difference between us was that I had more qualms about cheating on my girlfriend than he had. We got into a mutual back-slapping performance where I'd claim to admire him for the balls he had to go for it, and he'd claim to admire me for having the self-discipline to resist the temptation. In this there came to be a condemnation of Danny: he's not like us, he doesn't understand. Danny was aware of this and I know it used to bother him. I hate myself for this now and I hate Carlos for it, too.

21 December 2000

I'm in the kitchenette at Beachside now. I got talking to an Oz Experience bus driver last tonight, part of the crowd who were at the Palace bar the other night, and when I lied and told him I was a journalist from *19* magazine here to do a feature on his bus company, he introduced me to their Oz Experience marketing man called Chubbs.

Chubbs was a fat Aussie who looked like Robbie Coltrane. 'Come to write about all the sex, have you, Journo?' he said. I thought I'd schmooze him, half hoping for a free lift on one of the Oz Experience buses up the east coast to Cairns as I'm running out of money. He was with a few other drivers. They were all called TJ, AJ or JT or something like that, so I didn't know who anybody was after they were introduced. 'He's a legend,' Chubbs said after I'd shaken each one of their hands. 'He zorbed the fackin' Opera House . . . He bungeed naked off the Hackett Bridge in Kiwi Land . . . He rafted the Clarence with just a fackin' cheese slice.'

One of the AJs or TJs or JTs bought me a pitcher of Matteson's Loopy Juice, because it was named after him. 'Greatest compliment in the world that. Get a beer named after you,' he said, nodding towards the pitcher. 'He climbed Ayres Rock in a pair of fackin' wellies,' said Chubbs when he'd gone, pointing at the gumboots logo on the bar tap. 'He's a fackin' legend.'

I thought it might be good to speak to a few of the girls on the bus. They were mostly Bunac-types but I got off on the wrong foot by asking too many questions about the shagging that went on between passengers. I was trying to sound like an authentic sleazy magazine reporter. 'It's more about the culture here than shagging,' said one of them, when I asked how many people she'd slept with so far, but they became increasingly open when they were drunk and I half fell in love with a nineteen-year-old Danish girl called Anne Hensen, who spoke faultless posh English and kept saying, 'I am not going to talk to you any more because you will put it in your magazine.' She had the smallest mouth I'd ever seen, great wide blue eyes, blond straight hair and a tattoo on her belly, which you could see under her crop-top. 'Do you like my tattoo, magazine-man?' she asked. I said I did and kept positioning myself in the middle of the bar so I'd bump into her when she went to the toilet. But we had less and less to say and I found my role as journalist restrictive because what I really wanted to do was be honest with her, and in the end she went off with an Aussie who was a foot taller than me and a rap-jumping instructor.

I'm writing this at the McWhippy ice-cream parlour in Clovelly car park a few miles from the hostel, trying to look preoccupied and thus self-assured and confident and definitely not lonely. I thought travelling would make everything clearer, that it would give me a kick up the arse and I'd return to England and hit the ground running and suddenly know what to do about everything. I'd apply for jobs, marry Lucy or break up with her, get myself sorted. But I can't see that happening any more. I am having dark thoughts about my future. And Dominique, what's she playing at? I've had three cuts of the pack today but the results have been inconclusive.

> Subject: < Ring me now >
> To: Kit Farley Kitfarley@yahoo.com >
> From: Jon Farley Jonathan_farleyRBS@aol.com >

Kit, I would like you to phone me, please.
Dad.

> Subject: < lump >
> To: Kit Farley Kitfarley@yahoo.com >
> From: Dominique de Cabissole Dominiquede@yahoo.com >

Dear Kit, When you left I developed a large red lump on my forehead. I am very allergic currently. The result of unfulfilled desires, possibly? I don't think it is a good idea to see you, however. It is too complicated. But you ask me what I feel and it is enough for you if I tell you I have been looking for you in crowds. But I need some time for myself. I have realized Carlos is far away from me. He is gone off by himself and not to see him again is for now the best thing. It could be the key to my equilibrium. I arrive Sydney one day from now. Then go to see my friend in Noosa, who I have found out is away for Christmas and back for New Year. So to be on my own to think is good.

Dominique.

> Subject: < Phone call >
> To: Dominique de Cabissole Dominiquede@yahoo.com >
> From: Kit Farley Kitfarley@yahoo.com >

Dear Dominique, I hope the bump on your head grows so huge you resemble a unicorn. Come on, let's meet up in Sydney. I'm in Beachside Backpackers in Coogee. The number here is 345 678. Please call me and tell me what you think about everything.

Kit.

It's the evening now and I'm in the Café Blah Blah on Coogee Bay getting drunk on Carlton Colds to try to stop my stomach churning because this afternoon I did a tandem sky-dive a few miles south of Sydney. I had no plan to do this and took myself by surprise. An Aussie from the Truly Awesome Bushsports Action Club simply announced over the Tannoy there was a place going spare in the bus for 'a real hardcase adrenalin seeker to leap out of a plane over Wollongong beach'.

One moment I was thinking, What twat is going to volunteer for that? and the next I was handing over $275 and climbing aboard.

It was a 10,000-foot jump from the back of a small aircraft that sounded as rickety and noisy as an old washing-machine. I didn't think about what I was about to do the whole way there. During the ten-minute briefing about going into the banana position all the jokes about parachutes not opening didn't affect me, and even in the plane with my Ray-Banned instructor strapped to my back I couldn't understand what all the fuss was about. Why was everyone else biting their nails? We climbed for several minutes over the coast and out we went one by one, me last. At one point I was dragging the instructor to the edge, but then sitting with my feet out of the plane, staring down, the survival instinct kicked in. I leaned backwards, while the instructor leaned forwards, and suddenly we were in the air, turning in a circle – sky, ground, sky, ground, water, sky, ground – the wind billowing through my frozen cheeks as we fell for several seconds at terminal velocity. As I fell I thought, I wonder if the parachute will open, and then I realized I didn't care, because I had no choice and, anyway, it might solve a few problems.

The instructor whooped when the parachute opened and said, 'Fackin' awesome,' and I replied very politely, 'So how fast are we going now?' to sound interested, but really I was more concerned about my balls, which were being crushed by the straps. On the ground everyone was talking really fast – 'Would you do another one?' . . . 'Did you hear me shout?' – because it had given them a buzz. A couple of Americans were giving each other high fives. But I felt no adrenalin rush at all, except for an hour later I did notice I ate my McChicken Combo a bit faster than normal.

22 December 2000

I'm still in Coogee and I went for a surfing lesson this morning to see what that was all about.

The surf dude was a *Beavis and Butt-head* character with New Age okey-dokiness – 'It's all about lifestyle, man, you know. No worries, argh, *yeah!*' He'd moved out of Bondi because of the V8 temperament, the designer swimsuits and the fuck-you style. He had the bum wig, long blond hair, goatee, a cattle-grid chest, and spoke with that croaky-smoky, weed-addled voice that comes from the throat not the mouth. His eyes looked like vegetables frying: green, steamy and unaware.

We lay on our Malibu MacB longboards on the sand and practised catching waves, but in the water the board smacked me on the head the only time I tried to stand up because I panicked when I thought I saw a puffer fish.

I rang Dad afterwards to shit him up that I was risking my life plummeting from aeroplanes, and he said everyone was worried about me. I told him I was fine, we had a few jokes about Christmas and the fact that I wouldn't be there to fuck up the gravy, and then he became serious. He said it would all be clear when I met Lucy, all I had to do was make sure I didn't do anything daft in the meantime. 'Forget Christmas – it's a write-off. We'll have a few drinks in the New Year in the Rising Sun and laugh at this, Kit. I promise you that.'

Then, for no apparent reason, he started to tell me about number-one calls. 'This is something that happens in life,' he said. 'At one point you are number one on a lot of people's lists. You are a lot of people's first call – when they have good news and when they have bad news. That changes, however. When your mother and I were together I was number one on her list. Then she left. Sophie's got children, so I see less of her. I'm further down that list. That's understandable. Tom is married: down his list I go. You are – I hope you are – about to propose to Lucy. It means I'll go further down that list, too. I've got Jane now. She is who's important to me. Danny is . . .' his voice went funny, 'Danny,' he said.

'I am worried about you. I'm not talking about my mortality here. But I'm fifty-five. I don't want me to be gone and you to be on your own. You're not good on your own. You wither, Kit. You're like me: you need people around. Marry Lucy. I don't know what you're up to. I don't pretend to understand what you're going through. He was your brother and your best friend, but I know a lovely girl when I see one. She made a mistake; we all make mistakes. Make sure you look up Aunty Ange in Perth. I would feel much better knowing where you are over Christmas.'

I told Dad about Dominique and what's been going on and he wants me to ring him on Christmas morning (Christmas night here) when Sophie and the kids will be opening their presents in his and Jane's bed.

I'm thinking about this number-one call business now. Danny and Lucy were always my first calls and now it does feel like I haven't got anyone. Even my third-placer, Carlos, is gone. There honestly isn't anybody in the world I feel like speaking to right now, apart from Dominique, and I'm starting to doubt I'll ever hear from her again. 'I start to believe now,' she said in Vegas. I thought it meant I was beginning to convince her. I've been living off this, but it could mean anything.

> Subject: < Danny >
> To: Tom Farley Thomasfarley@hotmail.com >
> From: Kit Farley Kitfarley@yahoo.com >

Dear Tom, Sorry I haven't been emailing. I'm in Sydney. I'm fine, although quite a lot has happened. Dad's probably told you so I won't go into details of my heinous crimes. Tell him I'll try to email the measurements when I can.

Tom, do you ever wonder if it would've been better if Danny hadn't woken up? Do you know what I mean? I know we're not supposed to say this: 'It's not Danny any more, but someone else and we love him just the same,' and all that. But do we? Do you? I still love Danny the way he was. Do you know what I mean?

p.s. Tom, I am fucking confused.

> Subject: < Frogs and herrings >
> To: Kit Farley Kitfarley@yahoo.com >
> From: Tom Farley Thomasfarley@hotmail.com >

Dear Kit, Yes, Dad's told me what you've been up to and what the hell are you doing sky-diving? This from the man who's scared of golden retrievers. At least it explains your email blackout. To be honest, I am astounded. You total berk! Dominique is a fucking nightmare – you know she is. She leaves her husband for Carlos, then she has a thing with you and all the time she's still not sure about her husband. Come on! And of course I've thought about what it would have been like if Danny hadn't survived. The fact is he did and we've just got to make the best of it. It'll take time. I've never said this to you before, but the way to make it better is to see Danny more. I'm not having a go at you. Don't forget what he was like before, I'm not saying that, but the more you see him the more you get used to it. I thought the same as you to begin with. He is a new person, but he's still our brother, isn't he?

There's no point feeling guilty, either. I've tried that and it just screws you up. You know what Danny was like once he'd made up his mind: there's no way you could have done anything. None of us could. I've been thinking about it all and I reckon Danny could be a bit of a fat red herring, actually. I think it's why you're confused. A little bit of what you're doing is running away from getting married. It's obvious. You've got the jitters after everything that happened. But you can't see the wood for the trees any more, Kit. Think about it. Remember what it used to be like between you two. And you had that crush on Nikki Aldridge, too. You weren't an angel.

Anyway, what's wrong with getting married? A big party, me as best man telling the world what a selfish, poncey git you are. I got the wobbles, myself – remember that girl I fancied at work? I was almost (but not quite) as nutty as you are now. It probably shows you are more ready for marriage than you think.

I know you think I'm a bit of a steady-Eddie but I've thought about this quite a lot since I got married and I've come to the conclusion that it's Hollywood which is to blame – watching Billy Crystal and Meg Ryan in action. That's why men get the jitters. You were always a bit of a sucker for those films. I think you've got some romantic idea about what it's like being 'in lurve'. You've been hanging around your mate Carlos too long. Those films always make you unhappy about who you're with because your own relationship never seems to match up. It's true. In the movies couples who're in love never have rows about the washing-up. They never stay in and watch TV on separate sofas and go to bed at different times and complain that each other's breath stinks of Silk Cut. They only ever row about serious stuff and when that's sorted out they're happy and you know that they're going to be happy for ever. Except it's bollocks. Take it from me. Same in the adverts. That Bounty ad when the guy walks past the beautifully tanned woman under the palm tree sucking suggestively on the chocolate bar – what happened next? I'll tell you. The guy went back to his apartment and had a wank. I used to watch those films and think my relationship was shit, now I watch them and realize it's the films which are shit. You've got to do the same.

Suzie will probably ask for a divorce tomorrow, then I'll look like a tit! Give Lucy a ring, you berk, and make up. Or see Dominique one more time and get her out of your system.

Tom the guru.

p.s. You'd better meet Lucy. I've given her your present and it cost me twenty quid.

p.p.s. I swear, Kit – there was nothing you could do.

23 December 2000

Ostracism in the morning. Everyone stayed in bed until midday and chatted about why some bloke called Pierre hadn't come back to the hostel and I sat on my bed and typed and looked at leaflets of things I wasn't interested in, pretending to plan something significant.

I went back to the Palace this evening and Chubbs gave me some scenic stills of Ayres Rock he'd got from the Australian Tourist Board. He asked me how the article was coming on and what angle I was taking – he hoped I wasn't just going to stress the sex angle. I told him I hadn't decided what tack I was taking, but I'd call it as I saw it.

'No worries, you know what you're doing, Journo,' he said.

Later, for extra authenticity, I borrowed his camera and took pictures of the Oz Experience bus people. I asked a girl whose dad was a journalist on the *Daily Express* if she could identify the girl who was the biggest slapper on the bus so I could take her picture, but she was very annoying and said I should say it was more about meeting people. Yet when they left a few minutes later she was the one sinking Red Bull and leading the conga singing, 'We're horny, horny, horny,' at the top of her voice.

I was about to leave myself when I bumped into Danish Anne again. She was sitting with another Danish girl at the bar. Using my journalist licence to badger people I started talking to her and after a few schooners of VB she reverted to the girl of the other night – the one who stared at me, whose mouth became Quaver-crisp-shaped when she made a sarcastic remark and who overstated opinions for effect. I asked her what the most famous things were about Denmark. She said, 'Lego,' then couldn't think of anything else. 'They have rollercoaster rides you can go on at Lego-land. Have you heard of it? And there is the bacon.'

I told her to think of other good reasons to visit Denmark. She said her parents were nice, and I said I didn't think that would make a good brochure: 'Things to do in Denmark – bacon, Lego and Anne's parents.' I asked her again what was famous and Anne said: 'We don't like to promote ourselves. Come if you want to. Don't come if you don't.'

When her friend left – bored of being excluded – we played categories. Her most frightening moment was her bungee-jump. Her proudest moment was yesterday when her parents emailed to tell her how wonderful she was for sending so many postcards home. 'I don't know, I really liked that,' she said, and stuck her chin out and looked emotional. The next category was the worst time ever. She told me she'd had a blazing row once with her mum about going to stage school. Her mum wanted her to be a primary school teacher. I found myself telling her about Danny and last Christmas and Grange Grove and all kinds of things about Lucy and Dominique. Anne was staring at me afterwards. 'Sorry,' I said. 'I'm a bit home-sick.'

After an awkward silence she said, 'Mine is not like yours,' and patted me on the shoulder. Then she taught me '*Tobsay de u smoken owsoh*,' which means, 'You are beautiful and nice.' She would say it, I would repeat it back to her and she would say thank you. I would forget it, she would say it again, I would parrot it back and she would say thank you again.

She left half an hour later and I hugged her and told her she had a real spark and should try to become an actress. I think she expected me to try to snog her. As she left she held my shoulder, then her hand slipped down my arm and into and out of my hand. I've decided to email her and try to become the most inspirational person in her life. On that category she said it was her father, who was funny and sarcastic like all Danish people 'and nothing like *Keeping up Appearances*,

English humour, which is no good'. She was intelligent, naïve and beautiful, and I could have fallen in love with her if I wasn't in love with two people already.

Some Oz Experience bus people turned up after she'd left. They'd been on a pub-crawl and were wearing T-shirts signed by a member of staff in all the pubs they'd visited. They didn't look pleased to see me. The passengers have obviously been talking about me asking about sex because another Danish girl called Lima punched me on the arm and called me a '*slicken licker*', which I don't think is very good.

> Subject: < Phone call >
> To: Dominique de Cabissole Dominiquede@yahoo.com >
> From: Kit Farley Kitfarley@yahoo.com >

Dear Dominique, Where are you? Have you arrived yet? What harm can it do if we meet up? Come on.

Kit.

> Subject: Re: < Phone call >
> To: Kit Farley Kitfarley@yahoo.com >
> From: Dominique de Cabissole Dominiquede@yahoo.com >

Dear Kit, I arrive Sydney yesterday and have a hard time there so I have gone straight to Noosa. Fiona arrives in three days so you can see it is really not possible to see you.

You explain to me that you want to know my feelings. So then I have to start with the past, because it explains a lot of my current behaviours. When I left John I gave him continuously the hope that we might go together again, but when I was confronted to the situation, I have never done it. I don't know whether this was because of my feelings for him, which might have disappeared, or because of Carlos who I didn't want to abuse again.

Anyway, I did give hope to John. The problem is that he was believing in it. He was very hurt because of my behaviours. Then I was less sure about Carlos and thought I wanted to go back with John, and this feeling was growing in me. I started to tell John in America by email and phone and to promise him that I was really meaning it this time.

I cannot forget such a promise. The thing is that I don't want to have given him hope and to refuse again, even if my feelings tell me to go away and dig the tomb of my past love.

I was really thinking anyway that these things were quite clear for you.

I know you are going to say this is stupid. So why didn't you tell your girlfriend about this story? I think you might also not be sure about the situation either (mistrust once again?).

I don't want to see you as a victim, and me as a dirty awful scorpion playing with everyone as it suits. Have a good Christmas.

p.s. The heat rash I had on the arm disappeared, but I have still marks on the face: that's disgusting . . . I am still very allergic currently.

24 December 2000

There are two other English guys here in the hostel who have befriended me because of my 'I Jumped the Wollongong Beach' T-shirt or because there is no-one else around, I'm not sure which. The hostel is virtually deserted because everyone else has gone home for Christmas or they're on Bondi beach for the big party. Mark and Ade know each other from home and keep making out I'm from Eton because I've got a Home Counties accent. They ask where my porter is who carries my rucksack, and talk in put-on Dutch accents. 'Right, gentlemensh. Timesh for a Jim Beansh.'

I'm thinking of hiring a car and driving to Noosa to be with Dominique on Christmas Day even though she's told me not to come. Noosa is over 1,000 kilometres away but I feel I need to do something. Anyway, it is in the right direction for Cairns and, besides, Chubbs is getting suspicious of me. He's been asking for his camera back via notes to reception and when I saw him briefly this morning leaving the Congo Café he asked me again which magazine I wrote for.

I'm sitting in the Coogee Bay Hotel writing this. It's very quiet on the beach and even McDonald's is shut. Christmas Eve in the Palace, sipping Tooheys New, adding *sh* to the end of words. Then, the Orphan's Christmas Meal at Beachside Backpackers, and the horizontal bungy on stage at the CBH.

'Kitsh, have you decidedsh to go to Noosa or notsh? Ade and me would liksh to knowsh.'

The Sydney Discount Car and Truck Rental shop at Bondi Junction closes in an hour so I have to make up my mind. Rationality doesn't exist any more: my brain is hibernating away from the heat, my heart; some arse-crazy baby-sitter is minding the cottage and taking monstrous decisions that I will be brought to book for. 'Dig the tomb of my past love.' What the fuck was she on about? I've brought the playing cards with me and will try to cut Dominique's card in a minute. Instinctively, I feel Danny would be in favour of the risk. Come on – one cut!

25 December 2000

Australia is a spread-out, dusty, hot, inhospitable shit-hole full of fifth-generation convicts masquerading as a civilized society under the cloak of cricket and the Waugh twins' batting ability. There are too many creatures that can kill, maim or hurt you here for it to be classed as civilized – everything has sharp teeth or a sting: green ants, jumping ants, box jellyfish, bats, hornets, funnel webs, redbacks, taipans, possums, even the grass can fucking sting. Heart-shaped lime-green leaves on the elephant plant with harpoon tendrils that snare your legs and arms up to 1,000 times per square inch and double you up in agony then expand and contract excruciatingly depending on the weather.

There is always something crawling up your leg in Australia. You only have to stand still for a nanosecond in this infested country and something with more legs than you is trying to suck your blood, drink your sweat, sting you, bite you or send you into anaphylactic shock. The funnel web spider, for instance: seven reported deaths last year; ten near fatalities. They're no ordinary spider even by the mutated standards of this country. They can leap three feet and, what's more, they want to attack. None of this 'they're more scared of you than you are of them'. They're not scared of anything. They actually want to attack. It's their aim.

Hardly any of the country is populated. It's like the Wild West. A strip of settlement up the coast geared exclusively for tourism, a few industries in half a dozen cities, then nothing but desert and gap-toothed rednecks digging for precious metals.

It's difficult to see why people come here. Suckered into the drudgery by Peter Lik panoscapes of the Great Barrier Reef shot through light blue filters at early morning before the place is invaded with pissed-up backpackers. I asked at the news-agency bookshop at McCafferty's Travel Centre the other day if they had a book on Australian history. The woman looked at me as if I'd just asked for a tube of anti-matter.

I'm on a downer. Christmas Day in Noosa and I feel stupid for having come. I'm sitting on the top bunk in the sleep room at the Dolphin Lodge hostel in the Noosa Heads Resort on the Sunshine Coast – behind me twelve hours of driving through the night like a deranged idiot at 170 k.p.h. up the Bruce Highway in a hired Toyota Camry, the radio turned up to maximum, the window open to stay awake. Creek after creek, the only landmarks in this place – five Six Mile creeks, two

Eight Mile creeks, three Alligator creeks. I overtook 98 cars and 26 juggernauts, lit up in the night like fairground rides and I wasn't passed once. Three times I nearly fell asleep and began careering into the bush. Another time I nearly swerved into oncoming traffic after a huge spider bigger than a dinner plate that had been hiding behind the sun visor fell into my lap. But it felt good to be doing something, going somewhere.

My eyes are tired now, my throat's sore from Marlboro Lights, but the 1,021-kilometre journey has ended and I got a hug for a greeting and a Christmas present from Dominique: *Emily L.* by Marguerite Duras ('Because you always come back').

During the call last night that made up my mind Dominique said I was 'completely crazy, not rational', but that she would like to see me very much. Fiona was still at her parents' and wouldn't be there until the 28th, Carlos is in Sydney, and I think she felt as lonely as I was.

'I'm coming tonight. See you tomorrow,' I said.

Maybe I expected too much. I hugged her when she showed me the dorm but it was awkward. It was a goodbye-in-Vegas hug instead of a hello-in-Noosa hug. I may go early. Stock up on sleep, bomb to Cairns, another 1,000 miles. I'm now virtually broke, as well – $150 a day for the car, $120 on petrol.

> Subject: < losing patience >
> To: Kit Farley Kitfarley@yahoo.com >
> From: Lucy Jones Lucyjones23@hotmail.com >

Kit, Look, if it's anything to do with Danny can we talk about it, please? I'm sorry I said that about Christmas. Of course, I realize how you must be feeling. But I have got feelings, too. You know I am always there to talk to about it. Stop shutting me out. You know I am coming out whatever. So we may as well speak before we meet. Tom's told me you did a sky-dive. Please don't risk your life again. Do you want me to put some money in your account? You must be getting skint by now. Let me know.

Lucy xx

> Subject: < Frog lover >
> To: Kit Farley Kitfarley@yahoo.com >
> From: Tom Farley Thomasfarley@hotmail.com >

Dear Kit, I'm at Dad's, he's looking over my shoulder muttering about suits and you being a moron. Everyone says Happy Christmas for tomorrow.

Love, Tom xxx

p.s. You will feel differently when you meet Lucy. I know you will, you big berk.

p.p.s. Dad has paid £200 into your account for your present. Don't spend it on an adrenalin sport.

26 December 2000

Boxing Day and I'm tired of feeling toyed with. Dominique can't have a meaningful conversation before 7 p.m. We had a Christmas meal at a bistro in Noosa last night after visiting the national park to see the koalas. I told her I felt stupid for coming and she said, 'I would not be with you now if you were being stupid. Here, I give you my hand.' So I travel 1,000 kilometres and she agrees to catch the courtesy bus to town to give me her hand.

She's still staying it is 'not possible'. I am the bolt-hole she's used to escape from Carlos and John. What is she my bolt-hole from? 'It's all part of the play' is another of her phrases. It's a typically French way to look at life and I don't like it because it implies nothing is real.

On the hostel sunloungers afterwards: 'What is this? A friendship degraded into a couple of kisses,' she said when I pestered her to tell me more about her feelings. I told her she must think me stupid, persisting like this in the face of apparent indifference. Then I said, because I knew I wasn't stupid, that must mean there was something there, she was just denying it to herself. But when I said it, it just felt like going through the motions.

'People do stupid things when they are in love,' said Dominique, and this angered me, because, of course, it's obvious – I'm not in love with her at all, I just can't help myself. She continues to try to hew me into the shape she wants – the forlorn lover. She said in a couple of days alone with her I'd discover she was empty. I said I didn't think so, although I suspect she's right.

'Maybe *you* are empty,' she said.

I said maybe and started resenting becoming a character in one of her fucking Marguerite Duras novels – the future is the present of the past, etc.

I've forgotten how to sleep at the moment as well. The night drive has fucked up my body clock and I'm very tired. I lie down, my pulse races, and my head thumps like an old radiator and all I want to do is get back in the car and drive as fast as I can somewhere that's so far away I couldn't possibly get there in one stint without falling asleep at the wheel and careering off the road.

I've sneaked off to write this at the Sunshine Beach deli down the road from the hostel. Dominique's at the pool showing off the dress her mother and father sent her for Christmas to the two French cleaners. I'm going to wait a while before I go back so she knows I'm unhappy with her and that she has to make it up to me.

Past midnight. I spoke to Dad, Tom and Sophie just now from a call box in reception. All the kids were on Dad's bed opening their Christmas stockings – Harry, Rose, Ben and Emma. 'Just like you four, all those years ago,' said Dad and I felt a lump in my throat and Tom came on the phone and was serious with me. 'Just be careful and make sure you see Lucy before you make any decisions. Dominique's a fucking nutter, and you're just lonely – remember that.'

'I think we have chimie,' I said to Dominique this afternoon by the pool when I got back from the deli. Chimie is Dominique's word for sexual chemistry, what she's already told me exists between her and Carlos.

'Stop it,' she said.

Conversation tires her out – it makes her think and she doesn't want that. I feel the opposite – a lack of conversation tires me out.

'How can you know we have chimie until afterwards?' said Dominique, staring wistfully into the palm trees. 'It happens at the same time and then you know.'

I felt like telling her an experienced man could time it so it always happened together, that I could do this, but in the end I said nothing.

She chatted with the two French cleaners afterwards, laughing and joking in French as if she hadn't got a care in the world, and there I was again, the fool with the hire car.

Later she told me what she was laughing about: she'd told Sabrine, when she'd asked if there was something between us, that her problem was she couldn't trust men any more. Sabrine apparently said to this: 'Oh, you can trust him. Some men will come back with another woman, this one will come back with a flower for you.'

Dominique thought this was very funny. I was worried, though.

Another conversation they'd had was about nice and nasty men, and how they'd both mistreated nice men, because they took them for granted. I reminded Dominique I had once attempted to steal a car to make it clear I wasn't the sort to be walked over. 'I wasn't talking about you,' she said.

I phoned home again just now. Tom answered. 'Dad's down the bottom of the garden having a cry,' he said. Danny had been asking after me, said Tom. 'He seems a lot better. I told him you were in Australia and you'd bring him back a boomerang. No temper tantrums at all thanks to that new drugs cocktail. You know what Dad's like for anniversaries, though?' One message from Lucy, which made me feel guilty.

> Subject: < losing even more patience >
> To: Kit Farley Kitfarley@yahoo.com >
> From: Lucy Jones Lucyjones23@hotmail.com >

Dear Kit, If you're still reading these emails I know today is the anniversary and I just want you to know I've been thinking about you a lot, and Danny, too. I've been thinking a lot about us, all the good times and how it went so wrong. I was sitting outside on the doorstep and I just thought, For God's sake, what are we doing? How did this war start? Who cares whose fault it was? About getting married, having bloody kids, you were selfish. Actually, you were unbearable. But I admit I was pretty crap, too, if that's what you want to hear. I was talking to Lorraine about it and I don't know why I was like that. It's not because I didn't love you. You know I did and still do. I just didn't know what to say to you. Everything I said seemed wrong, so in the end I stopped saying anything. You're right, too: that's even worse and I'm sorry.

Nothing bad has ever happened to me. Lucy Jones living in la-la-land. I didn't know what it was like. You were behaving so differently that after a while I couldn't work out why you seemed to be taking it all out on me. I thought it meant you'd gone off me and then we both dug in. Please let's try to dig our way out.

I haven't told you this before, but I've been going to counselling. It's really helped. I told the counsellor about your diet the other day and she said you sounded like a real one-off.

Kit, please email and say you'll be at the airport. I've put £100 in your account.

27 December 2000

I kissed Dominique good morning today as an experiment more than anything else and with the look on her face you'd have thought I'd drawn a knife. 'You like physical contact *too* much. It is disturbing.' Then: 'You want some breakfast?' trying to stifle and forget the tiny peck. She keeps wanting to read this journal and pretends she plans to steal my laptop. I will let her read it this evening if there's an opportunity.

Tonight everyone from the hostel is going to Koala's, the bierkeller-style backpackers' bar, a bus ride away in town. Fiona arrives tomorrow and I would've preferred Dominique and me to be alone on my last night. It's only when she feels she's hurt me that she shows any feelings, something else that annoys me. She suddenly doesn't like kissing (too wet), would never spontaneously offer up an emotion, talks continuously about John and Carlos, and still I'm here scratching about like a chicken in the dirt, hooked on setbacks.

A theory of love someone told me once: love turns an extrovert into an introvert and an introvert into an extrovert. I have become introverted. I don't know whether it's because of Dominique or whether it's because I'm tired of the backpacker mentality: Benidorm with dirtier clothes, everyone believing they're soaking up culture and broadening their minds through getting drunk in less warm clothes. *Cuddle a koala and boogie board – yeah, I know Australia.* Maybe Tom was right: I was just lonely. Maybe Dominique was right, too: loving someone is not really as important as there being someone around *to* love.

I am tired of persuading now, and am starting to think she's right. She is a fucking scorpion.

28 December 2000

In McDonald's, Airlie Beach, resting after another 200-mile belt further up the east coast on the Bruce Highway. The car is smeared in so many dead bugs it looks like an exhibit in the Natural History Insects and Arachnids section.

We sat on the balcony in Noosaville Yacht Club last night after leaving Koala's. She's going back to her old job in Perth, she's decided, has phoned John and can sleep on the floor of their old flat, although she says nothing will happen because John 'doesn't want. I have hurt him too much. I told you, I am scorpion-woman,' she said and started to wonder if I ever wanted her to be anything else.

A storm brewed up and flocks of rainbow lorikeets skirled through the air, like blown cigarette ash, screeching like a million electric wires. On the way back to the hostel we talked about sex. When I said I preferred to be on the bottom she said she liked to be dominated in bed and that her men had to work. 'You are lazy,' she said, bringing it up again on the beach by the marina. We lay down on the sand and I snuggled up face to face with her and pressed my body into hers and we started to kiss. Her back was hard like wood and her face looked sexy in a sleepy, expressionless kind of way.

'Do you want to make love?' she asked.

'Yes.'

'I know. I feel it. That is why I am over here,' she said, disengaging and sitting on the bench behind us, but to demonstrate I am dominant I pressed on, told her I'd move to Perth to be with her, that we'll get married and have bilingual children as I took off her jumper and T-shirt, then her trousers, even though she protested throughout that I like 'physical contact too much'.

'I do not want to hurt anybody,' she whispered to me in the middle of it. We were sitting on the bench, her in my lap, gripping the bench slats behind me, me half sitting, half standing, grinding into her, watching the new funny expression on her face, worried that in my attempt to be dominant I was going to ping a thigh muscle.

On sunloungers by the pool outside the hostel I showed her this journal. She gripped my hand when it was funny, stroked my forearm when it was sad, stared into space and put it down when it was too much. Three-quarters of the way through she gave it back.

'The play is over,' she said and I nodded.

Before I left Dominique this morning she made me a lime-cordial drink for the journey, packed my things and walked me to the car. I didn't think I was going to cry. I squeezed her back and rocked from foot to foot and saw her eyes go moist and her chin cave in, but I didn't feel anything, only tiredness.

Then she said she'd better go and it hit me and my eyes went, too. I didn't rub the tears away on her dress. I let them fall on to her neck so she'd know how I was feeling. She had hair in her mouth, tired, sullen and gamin-like, and we both stared at each other's saddened face. I was disappointed her crying made no noise and stroked her face. It was blighted only by the red lump in the middle of her forehead, the result of her hormone rush. Her wrists had small spots all round them as well, like a heat rash; another stress reaction, she said.

She kissed me on tip-toes to apply more pressure, and I hugged her very tightly. Then she said she had to go because it was too painful and I got in the car and she kissed me through the window. I turned the car round, opened the window, kissed her again and she laughed that I'd return: 'You always come back.'

Then I drove away, waved twice, and it hasn't been until now I realized why I was crying. It was because I knew I wasn't ever going back.

I've just dropped the car off at the Economy Car and Truck Rental franchise here and had to pay a huge one-way drop fee of $300. I'm in Magnums Backpackers now in a stilted hut that looks like something out of the *Deer Hunter*. It's eleven days before I meet Lucy and I'm not sure how I am going to make my way further north or how long it will take. I've only met one other guy from the hut: he asked to score a bag of weed off me and said he had just changed rooms because they were animals in number 14. They'd stolen his food and a couple had been rutting on the floor one night. 'Still, eh, it's not bad here, plenty of pussy. Argh, yeah. Lots in Perth, too, but more slots here, I reckon.'

The reasons why I am sick of backpackers: the way they hang around in big groups and all look and act the same – the obligatory tattoos, floral beach shorts, same short hair, same cargo shorts; the mind-blowing tedium of listening to their bus timetable plans and their regurgitated insights from the *Lonely Planet* ('Byron's very hippie' . . . 'Hervey Bay is a bit spread out' . . . 'Only spend a day in Brisbane').

I am sick of backpackers because what's worse than anything else is that it's better to be with them than alone. Conversation, however dull, is better than no conversation and a pitcher of VB alone at a corner table in Magnums.

It's later and I've got a latch – Pete. I met him in the laundry area just now. We had a laugh about the Oz Experience bus – the 'green fuck bus', he called it – and we chatted on a wall overlooking the beach where he revealed he suffered from periodic depression and said his energy levels had been low for a while. He got sapped from laughing, and being cynical and had gone through a bad time since parting company from an organized Dutch girl called Sada whose positive energy he fed off, he said. He had a big thing about weak and strong people and wanted to be more strong.

'I have to listen to my inner voice more and stop being a sheep. I sheeped down the east coast for too long on the fuck bus. I need space to be myself.' He wanted to go for a swim in the sea to invigorate himself, but changed his mind after I told him about the deadly puffer fish.

He has a good sense of despairing humour. 'When I laugh it's almost hysterical. It's nervous laughter and it tires me out. I must try not to watch so many funny films or satirical comedy – they tire me out and are no good.'

I've moved out of the hut and into a double room with him and I read his journal just now when he went for a shower. In it he said he was depressed and isolated and struggling to come to terms with the death of his dad. Everyone's a fuck-up.

> Subject: < still losing patience >
> To: Kit Farley Kitfarley@yahoo.com >
> From: Lucy Jones Lucyjones23@hotmail.com >

Dear Kit, Another email down your bottomless well. More thoughts: If you really want to know the truth, I was always slightly jealous of you and Danny. You always seemed so close and I felt left out when you two started joking around because I couldn't keep up. It made me feel a bit of a fool. It wasn't that I didn't like him, something I know you think. I thought he was a top fella. I really did. Thinking about it now, I should have been better about the hospital and I should have bullied you into going to see him more in Grange Grove. You don't know, but your dad and Tom tried to persuade me to do this. I should have made you come with me. But I knew how hard it was for you. It wasn't that I couldn't be bothered and had better things to do. I was only thinking of you.

I realize now I picked the wrong time to bring up marriage and babies, but I couldn't help myself. I only did that because I loved you. I still don't know whether you're reading this or what you're up to. You could have run off with someone, for all I know, and not be thinking about me at all. Please email, Kit.

Love Lucy xx

I'm thinking about Lucy and things I miss now. And I miss a lot of things. Lucy getting angry with the cats who split the bin bags we left out for the binmen; the way she gripped my forehead when I was ill and bought me mini-sausage rolls because she knew they were what I wanted when I had a temperature; the way she was always late for everything; the way her bottom tingled when she got excited; the way her small hands fold into her lap when she's asleep; seeing toast crumbs round her mouth; Saturday mornings lying in bed watching Ant and Dec on *CD:TV* and *Rugrats*; Sunday evening blues during *Frost* and the *Antiques Roadshow*; hunting for her keys each morning before she left for work; going to the cinema and debating the films afterwards; her shouting at me for leaving Marmite stains on the throw and the white duvet; closing my eyes and sleeping soundly with our bottoms touching lightly; having to explain science and war shows on the telly to her; the fights over *University Challenge*; her tips on shopping ('When you buy a melon you have to squeeze it to see if it's ripe' . . . 'Tesco's Finest isn't as good as regular Marks & Spencer's, but it's better than Asda. And Asda is better than Somerfield. Never go to Somerfield!').

We had so many running jokes in those days. There was one that her life was like her Risborough page because she was always so gossipy, and in a good mood she'd always come in and talk to me in the bath. I wouldn't ask how her day was. Instead she'd plonk herself down on the toilet seat and I'd ask if her lead was still the same, had anything happened that day to knock yesterday's news off the front page. And she'd say through gritted teeth, her eyes darting about like an animal's in our special voice, 'Kit, no news – the splash is still the same,' or 'I've cleared page three, Kit – the man at the BP garage shouted at me when I asked him to come out of the booth and open the bonnet for me to check the water.'

I miss sitting on the sofa and the familiarity, her Plasticine-soft skin, and her eyes behind her little round glasses with love in them. The way she twiddles her hair on the sofa and knocking her hand to make her stop. Our cosy life and planning ahead for weekends, which I don't have to worry about and fill. Her tiny hands and the right-angle she makes at her elbow when she bends her arm that I like to feel. Her soft neck and her long hair that smells of something out of a bottle. And, most of all, the little jokes we had when we were getting on that were more important than the bills, our jobs or the fact that we didn't have any money.

29 December 2000

Pete and I went to KC's Char and Grill last night. We met a guy called Dave from the Oz Experience bus and Pete was uncomfortable immediately. Dave started bragging he'd been pissed every night for a month and had done six bungee-jumps, including the one in Queenstown, New Zealand, called the Elevator, where you remain vertical when you jump backwards from the ledge holding your neck. 'You see the sky for the whole fucking free-fall until you're suddenly jerked down to see the Stopover River. It was fucking awesome,' said Dave, and Pete gave me a funny look and later said: 'Your typical fuck bus.'

We had a couple of VB pitchers and Dave told us he was heading for Cambodia where for fifty dollars you could hire a military rocket left over from the Vietnam War. For another ten they threw in a cow for you to fire at. 'Only they fuck the sights up, don't they. They're not stupid. They want you to miss so they can buy the fuckin' cow back off you. You don't get ten dollars for it, neither. More like five. I mean, what you gonna do with a fuckin' cow? Stick it in your backpack? You got no choice. Aim at their fuckin' hooves, that's what I'm gonna do.'

When Dave had gone, promising to email if he got a shag between here and Cairns, Pete said his negativity had sapped him. I said never mind him, what about the Israelis, the father and daughter Tal and Danni, whom we'd met at the hostel bar earlier, and who said they'd be following us down in a few moments.

We'd sat at the kitchen table earlier and Tal, an El Al pilot, had gone through who gave way to the right and left in the all the countries he'd flown to, using a packet of Pall Mall cigarettes to demonstrate: 'And in Johannesburg they even give way at roundabouts to oncoming traffic.'

We'd biked it down to the pub to get away from him. Danni, his daughter, had shaved off her hair. She was on a year out before joining the Israeli Army and when she walked through the pub door at that moment with Tal, we both said, simultaneously, 'She'd be very attractive if she had long hair.' Pete laughed too much in his dysfunctional frenzied way and then said we should all play pool so we didn't have to speak to Tal. I put our names up on the chalk board, but when it was my turn to play Pete asked if he could go first. 'I am very, very good at pool,' he said.

I said I was quite good, too. Pete said very seriously, 'I don't know anybody who is better at pool than me, and I know club players.'

He started getting on my nerves. He'd already bummed half a pack of cigarettes from me and said his budget had run out when I asked if he was getting the next round in. I got him another drink anyway and then he took a dollar off me to have his game of pool. He played very intensely with a vertical thumb grip and was no good at all.

'It's the pressure. If it wasn't for the pressure no game with me involved would last more than two minutes,' he said.

He lost the game and then when it was my turn he took another dollar off me to play doubles with Danni, and I was stuck with Tal discussing the relative highway benefits of nations of the world. Danni walked back to the hostel with her dad, and Pete and I cycled back without lights.

'You do realize we're breaking the law,' Pete said seriously, and I really started to dislike him.

After Tal and I turned in Pete stayed up until about 4 a.m.

'mucking about with Danni on the beach', and this morning he took off with them for Byron Bay.

'What a lad. I should be on the green fuck bus' was the last thing he said to me. Later I noticed he'd stolen Chubbs's camera as well, the twat.

'You can't run away from your problems.' You can if you run fast enough. I got a lift with Heddee and two other Japanese, Chio and Emiko, from the hostel this afternoon and I'm in Mackay, 140 kilometres further north on the Whitsunday coast.

They tried to teach me Japanese on the way and I learned the words for mountain, tree and car, and a phrase popular with young Japanese – *cho-my.* It means double, as in double-delicious, and we had a laugh adding *cho* to words. When a car overtook us on a dangerous coast road Heddee said, '*Cho* fast,' and cracked up laughing. He handed me a mint after learning the phrase 'You want some?' and I said, '*Cho-my*,' and he laughed hysterically again.

The conversation on the differences between Japan and England and adding *cho* to words became a bit boring after a while so this evening I went to Sam's Bar with an Irish girl called Follet I met at the Larrikin Lodge on Peel Street I've checked into. Follet told me she worked in PR but wanted to do a doctorate in conflict-resolution focusing on the troubles in Northern Ireland because she lived in Belfast. She told me about her boyfriend, a bond dealer who considered her his emotional investment, and I was honest about the Lucy situation. She said I should talk to her about it and it wasn't fair stringing her along if I wasn't going to propose. I had to accept women did change when they approached thirty: they needed to feel secure because they had biological clocks ticking.

I said, 'Typical PR woman, trying to run my life,' and as we walked back to the hostel Follet pointed out the Milky Way and we agreed to have a stroll along Town Beach because we weren't tired yet.

At the hostel I had a massive shit which lasted twelve minutes and when I came back out she'd gone to bed, the sweater she'd borrowed from me for the walk folded on the kitchen table. Why was she travelling? 'Escape,' she said. She wanted to get out of PR 'I spent ten thousand pounds and four days getting someone to paint a Marks & Spencer logo on a butter model of a cow for a dairy promotion and thought, What am I doing with my life?'

What am I doing with *my* life? Why is it everyone I meet travelling is fucked up in some way? There's definitely a pattern to it – the hippie in Sedona, Follet, me, Pete and Dominique. I was reading about Captain Cook in the *Lonely Planet* today and all I could think was: I wonder if he had one emotional and one practical reason to go travelling. Maybe he'd recently split up with his girlfriend, too. Was Vasco da Gama really just coming out of an abusive relationship? Travellers should have T-shirts made to cut out all the bollocks – 'Brother brain damaged' . . . 'Abusive relationship' . . . 'Failed career' . . . 'Dead Dad.' It's a fact – you don't meet many enormously successful people who've decided to put their Palm Beach mansions into rental to come to Australia with a Millets fifty-litre rucksack.

I've emailed Chubbs to say sorry about not saying goodbye and not returning his camera. I said I'd been called away on an important assignment covering the Sydney–Hobart yacht race. Then I thought about calling Lucy to talk to her, like Follet had recommended, but I'd only have felt guilty and wouldn't have been able to sleep, so I emailed her instead.

> Subject: Re: < still losing patience >
> To: Lucy Jones Lucyjones23@hotmail.com >
> From: Kit Farley Kitfarley@yahoo.com >

Dear Lucy, I will be there.
Kit.

2 January 2001

It's a few days since my last entry. I've been killing time before I meet Lucy. Three days at Platypus Bushcamp in Finch Hatton Gorge behind me. The place is a few miles from Mackay and I got here on a McCafferty's bus. The bush retreat is in the middle of a rainforest. I slept in a Thai-style stilted hut with a roof but no walls. Skink lizards in your bedroom, golden orb spiders bigger than your head, a scorpion I crushed with my shoe, jumping ants, flying ants, green ants the size of grapes, Christmas bugs as loud as Spitfires. The flash flood, the creek flowing so loudly outside it feels like it's in your hut.

Wozza is the foul-mouthed host, a ZZ Top lookalike with a bald parrot which sings, 'Der-der-der derderder-de der der der der der der der Tequila'. He wouldn't let anyone turn on the radio in the living room he'd created outdoors from pine trees and corrugated iron even on New Year's Eve. 'No, mate, the music of nature. It's fackin' paradise 'ere, mate. Away from the rat-race in Airlie Beach. No listening to your neighbour getting his rocks off with his missus, no kids with syringes 'anging out of their arms. Some of the cleanest fackin' water in the world. Look at it – crystal clear. Better than the bottled shit you get in Mackay. My, that place is a fackin' hole. It's got the personality of a wet bag of cement. Who's been dropping cigarette butts on the floor? Throw them in the fackin' fire, Kit, or I'll step on your toes.'

Ian is a beatnik hippie strumming Bob Marley songs. He came to Australia four years ago on the run from the social over a £7,000 fine for working while on the dole. He lives in a cave at the base of a hill up the road. I went there last night. His cave smelled damp, there were hundreds of huntsman spiders on the walls, frogs everywhere, but 200 bottles of home-brew beer and a banana tree on the roof.

'It's fuckin' great – I can 'ave banana whenever I want,' he said and I had to laugh.

I'm at the Lyon Hotel, Cairns, now. It's the best accommodation I've stayed in and I'm about to have my first bath in a month. I did try a hostel earlier, the Caravella, but the receptionist was a wizened old crow who called the backpackers her children ('One more child to check in'), and was by turns helpful, scolding and unnerving. 'Put your full name and address in the registration book, my child. If you died over here in a car accident I don't think "England" would be enough to get your body shipped home and how would your parents feel about that?'

I got freaked out by all the backpackers striding about purposefully, checked out immediately and moved into this hotel so I could be by myself. I've been in my room all day watching TV.

A telephone call for me at reception just now. It was Lucy.

'I got the number from your dad. How are you?'

'Lucy, I feel terrible.'

'Me too.'

'Lucy?'

'What?'

'Nothing.'

'I've got to go, Kit. I'm just checking you'll be at the airport. I didn't want just to turn up.'

'I will be. Lucy?'

'What?'

'Nothing. Lucy?'

'What?'

'I've been very stupid.'

'We both have.'

'No, I mean I've been really stupid.'

'I don't think I want to hear this, Kit.'

'OK. Lucy?'

'What?'

'Nothing.'

'Let's talk when we meet up. I've got to go.'

I dropped Dad a line just now, as well.

'I feel so guilty,' I said in a pathetic moment.

'So you should,' said Dad. 'Make sure you pop in and see Aunty Ange in Perth.'

Little Harry was in the background asking where Uncle Kit was at Christmas and I heard him demanding: 'I want to speak to Kit-boy.'

Sophie came on: 'God, Kit, are you finally seeing sense? What's got into you? Did Tom tell you about Christmas and Danny's new cocktail? He's a lot better. Don't expect miracles but they're talking of allowing him out to the drop-in centre.'

> Subject: < flight details again >
> To: Kit Farley Kitfarley@yahoo.com >
> From: Lucy Jones Lucyjones23@hotmail.com >

Kit, I got your message. Thank God, you're all right. I'm giving you the details again because I know what you're like. I arrive on 7 January at Bangkok airport BA Flight 751. Kit, I am not expecting anything, by the way. You know what I mean. Love. Lucy xxxx

3 January 2001

I flew across Australia this morning, saw Ayres Rock from the air, and I'm at Aunty Ange's now in Perth. It's a home carefully maintained by pensioner hands, cream-brown doors, floral wallpaper, burglar-proof window locks. The female mynah bird never speaks, the opposite of Aunty Ange and Uncle Tom. They're yin and yang: yang, yang, yang. Aunty Ange is neurotic, warm, batty and bulldozerish, and has started wheezing because of my cigarette smoke. 'Oh, darling – I worked on a lung cancer ward. No, I'm not going to say anything – your chest, oh, darling. I'm sorry. *Those things.*'

I used a call box to phone Dominique in Noosa this evening. Fiona answered.

'Can I speak to Dominique, please?'

Dominique came on surprised and told me facts: what she'd been doing, how John's mum is. What will she tell everyone now that I've phoned? I told her I think things will work out in the end, but she thought I was talking about her.

'You're very positive today,' she said in her mocking voice, 'but you know me, always negative,' and I laughed falsely and told her I was sorry, that it wasn't about her, that it was about Lucy and me. I said I felt very bad for Carlos. Then the money ran out and I hadn't said everything, so felt terrible.

I wanted to ring Lucy, too, and tell her I was missing her, looking forward to seeing her and watching the crocodile wrestling.

Sitting upstairs in the spare room at Aunty Ange's. It's peaceful here in this retirement house and being polite in their company has saved me from the ravages of brooding alone. I'm saying no to a tin of peaches, or another sliver of Tasmanian cheddar instead of agonizing over what I've done, how I could have been so stupid and what might happen if it all comes out. Should I tell Lucy about Dominique before she flies out? But then she wouldn't come. If I tell her afterwards I'll only ruin her holiday and all our plans: 'Lucy, I have to say something . . . I was selfish before you left me, but I wasn't selfish because I'm naturally this way . . . it was because . . .' What came first? The chicken or the egg or the row about the egg?

Pensioners always say at golden weddings, 'You have to work at a marriage, it's all about give and take.' I never knew what this meant before. I think I do now. All the time I thought the reason I was attracted to Nikki was because Lucy and I weren't getting on. But was it the attraction to Nikki that *stopped* us getting on? As for Dominique. God, I still can't explain that one.

We had lunch at Cousin Jane's earlier and I met some second cousins once removed. They lived in a Spanish-style villa overlooking an artificial lake that had once been a quarry and talked about how I was six when they last saw me, being tucked into bed with Danny in Leicester. Then it was a tour of the family's polyurethane factory and I was shown a cyclone centrifugal machine and bits of plastic moulding. I said it was very interesting and asked questions about their suppliers while maintaining eye-contact from behind my safety glasses.

Aunty Ange has just come into my room in the middle of writing this to ask if I'm all right. Uncle Tom popped his head round the door, too, and the light glinted off his glasses and he smiled at me and said he'd take me to the Perth mint tomorrow. Then I stunned him slightly by asking what he thought the secret of a happy marriage was. He didn't say, 'Compromise,' like the normal diamond wedding couple, though. In fact, he didn't say anything. He said he'd met Aunty Ange at a church dance when they were fourteen and they'd been together ever since. 'Fifty years,' he said, looking at the ceiling. 'Things were much simpler in those days.' He seemed almost apologetic, stroked the back of his head and smiled at me.

I thought about him collecting railway memorabilia in his garden, Aunty Ange worrying about the dryness of the lawn and having enough of his favourite cheddar in the fridge.

'I don't think I'd want to be a young man these days.' He sighed. 'So many choices.'

I loved Uncle Tom then and wanted to be like him.

He said night-night to me like I was a kid, told me I could open the window if it got hot but not to tell Aunty Ange because she worried about intruders, and I tried to picture myself fifty years down the line with Lucy, shuffling around the house in a cardigan, discussing day trips to model railways.

Uncle Tom closed my door quietly.

'Uncle Tom?' I said.

He popped his head back round the door.

'Thanks,' I said.

'They've got a gold bar at the mint. You can put your hand through a slot and touch it,' he said.

4 January 2001

I'm in Singapore. A five-hour flight across Indonesia and the Indian Ocean sitting next to a man who sucked up his in-flight noodles meal so fast he kept splashing black-bean sauce in my face. I took an airbus from Changi Airport to Bencoolen Street and I've checked into Lee's Boarding House. I had a Singapore sling in Raffles and I've just walked into St Andrews Cathedral, a huge white building, the colour of icing sugar. A pock-marked Chinese woman handed me a leaflet about the cathedral and its history: site chosen by Raffles, twice struck by lightning and rebuilt, south transept completed whenever – and an order of service, and a few paragraphs from the Dean Trevor story about how many people had found God beneath this ceiling.

I sat in the back pew. A guy on the dais was strumming the guitar melodically and I started imagining how everyone would react at home if I returned with a beatific smile to tell them I'd found God and now realized I had neglected my own vineyard and was opening my heart to Jesus.

A couple in the pew in front of me were hugging – I wondered if it was love for each other, love for God, or some sort of prism effect love triangle – God's love triggering their own. It made me think of Carlos, Dominique and me and I tried to imagine being struck by faith and love, but my arse still felt flaccid after the chicken noodles on the plane and I needed to fart and couldn't concentrate properly.

Then the pock-marked Chinese woman came up to me and told me to move down to the front of the transept because I couldn't hear anything. I said I could hear everything and then the guitar-man switched on an overhead projector and the words to 'Strangers in the Night' beamed on to the screen in different coloured inks.

'Come on – let's all move down the front – make sure you're sitting next to someone and introduce yourselves,' he said.

I got up and walked out, hoping the woman, whom I gave the leaflet back to, felt guilty for chasing someone away from God by forcing group interaction on them.

Outside the church I felt guilty for leaving, though. Fruit bats flew over my head as I walked down Northbridge and I started picturing what it would be like if I proposed to Lucy. I thought if I did, I'd buy a copy of her favourite book, *Jane Eyre*, and cut out a hole in the middle and place a ring in there. Either that or do it in the middle of the crocodile wrestling. That way every time we did our hugging and rolling thing at bedtime we'd remember it. I catch the train to Kuala Lumpur tomorrow. I've bought myself a first-class ticket.

5 January 2001

I checked out of my hotel room at Lee's this morning and I'm on the Malaysian Express heading north. The train left two hours ago and within a few minutes someone had already brought me an orange juice, a bottle of water, a clean towel, told me to have a good trip and two Malaysian stewardesses when they came in to give me the menu closed the door behind them, drew the curtain and asked if I was travelling alone. 'No garlfen'?'

'Yes,' I said. 'I'm meeting her tomorrow.'

The younger stewardess has just come back and picked up my packet of cards. I've been cutting them trying to get Lucy's card.

'You play?' The girl sat next to me and I tried to teach her knockout whist and the concept of trumps. 'How ol' you?'

'Twenty-six.'

'Ahhhhh!' she said like she'd seen a puppy. 'You alone?'

'Not for long.'

'Ahhh!' she said again.

I'm meeting Lucy the day after tomorrow. She's booked us into a five-star hotel in central Bangkok. She sent a page from their website yesterday. She's got to interview the manager of an insurance company in the city, then she wants us to go and watch the crocodiles the day after.

Just in case I feel like doing something rash I bought a copy of *Jane Eyre* at the MPH bookstore yesterday in Stamford Road, but I am having a job trying to hollow it out with my Swiss Army knife.

I tried to ring Lucy's dad earlier from an international telephone exchange booth when the train stopped at Seremban. It didn't go very well and I hope it's not an omen. You had to ring a number and they were supposed to put you through, only the man on the other end of the line didn't understand a word I was saying.

'I want to make a call to England. How do I do it?'

'Orrrr.'

'I want to call England. Do you have the code?'

'Orrrrr.'

'What about the operator? How do you call the operator?'

'Ah operator. Hang up, please?'

I hung up. The phone rang three minutes later.

'What your name?'

'Kit Farley.'

'No, what *your* name?'

'It's Kit Farley. I wanted to make an international call. I phoned a minute ago.'

'Orrrr!'

'You were going to—'

'Hang up, please.'

I hung up. The phone rang a minute later.

'What your name?'

'It's Kit Farley. I told you.'

'Your name?'

'Kit Farley. I just said it.'

'Sorry, I mean who you call?'

'I'm calling Peter Jones.'

'Pepper?'

'No, Peter?'

'Deter?

'No, Peter. Peter Jones. My girlfriend's dad. Peter Jones. The number's 0121 345 7765. It's an English number.'

'Orrrr. Peter, hang up, please.'

The phone rang a few seconds later.

'Who that?'

'It's me. Kit Farley. Have you got through?'

'One moment.'

The operator came back on.

'Who that?'

'It's me again. Kit fucking Farley.'

'Sorry, the phone you want to call is on a machine. Hang up, please.'

6 January 2001

Yesterday I stayed the night in Kuala Lumpur and caught a bus to the Batu Caves. It was 272 steps to the Hindu temple and I almost fainted on the way up. At the top were gaudy images of gods, dripping limestone rocks and monkeys chewing plastic bags.

I'm now on the terrace of the Twin Pines Hotel in the Cameron Highlands, Malaysia, after catching the KTM Express north. A chill from the 4,500 feet altitude is penetrating my fleece and the cicadas sound like bad radio reception. In the evening I met two English lads at the Hard Rock Café, conspicuous among the lady-boys. One was doing media studies at De Montfort University and was thinking of going into PR afterwards and I found myself telling him, 'No, become a journalist. It's the best job in the world.' I got quite drunk and found I couldn't stop going on about how great it was – all the weird people you met, seeing all sides of life, and I probably bored them.

'Fucking mad. You invented a panther, man.' They asked me why I wasn't a reporter any more if it was so fantastic and I couldn't think of a good reason, because there is no good reason.

In less than twenty-four hours I'll be with Lucy.

8 January 2001

Lucy and I are just about to go to the Jarong Reptile Park, thirty miles east of Bangkok. She's in the shower and I'm writing this at the window of our five-star hotel, overlooking the city. There is a haze of smog in the sky and I can still hear the crazy tuk-tuks revving their engines below.

Last night we went to a sex show and saw women pulling razor blades from their fannies. It was Lucy's idea. Then we had a Thai meal. The atmosphere is slightly odd and has been from the moment she arrived. We're being almost too polite with each other. The conversation is being crowded out with all the things we can't talk about.

'Look at all the fat old English men with beautiful Thai girls,' I said at one point. 'That one must only be seventeen.'

'There were dozens of them on the plane. Bald and desperate. No prizes for guessing what they're here for. Men,' she said and looked sharply at me. It was the closest she came to challenging me about my lack of contact.

Back in the hotel room wondering about things. The crocodile wrestling performance kicked off with 'The Final Countdown' blaring out. Then three Indians bowed deeply on the concrete island, which was surrounded by a moat full of huge crocodiles. Raj introduced himself and splashed water on to the island to make it slippery and then dragged a crocodile on to it by the tail. Sandy, the chief performer, stroked its head with a red wooden stick, soothing its jaws open. The third performer then wedged his head between its teeth. 'Now you will see Musa's throat is completely exposed. Raj has to be careful Pinocchio doesn't whip round and bite off his legs,' said the man brightly over the Tannoy. There were only six people in the audience besides Lucy and me so the applause was muted, but Musa looked like he'd had a hit of adrenalin from the experience and grabbed the wooden stick from Sandy and poked the crocodile in the neck, causing it to snap wildly at him. Then Sandy rolled up a banknote and, using his teeth, placed the money in the crocodile's mouth. He then retrieved it with his teeth before kissing Pinocchio on the snout to the accompaniment of a kissing sound effect.

I tried to phrase the question in my head: 'Lucy, I have something to ask you' . . .'Lucy, I tried to phone your dad and do the old-fashioned thing, but . . .'

Raj approached the crocodile from behind, lifted up his head and went chin to chin with him. Pinocchio lashed out with its tail, catching Sandy on the ankle.

'Ouch!' said the man on the Tannoy. 'The tail of the crocodile is enormously powerful. Sandy will have quite a bruise in the morning.'

'Lucy,' I said, 'I've got something to tell you.'

'I can't believe they risk their lives between two o'clock and four o'clock every day for just eight people,' said Lucy without looking at me.

Again Musa put his head in the crocodile's jaws. 'One thousand pounds per square inch of pressure the jaws of a crocodile exert. If Pinocchio decided it was lunchtime now, girls and boys, Musa's head would be bitten off.'

'Lucy,' I said.

She didn't turn to look at me and we watched a king cobra being released from the basket it had been curled up in. Sandy held it by the tail as it flattened and curved its neck into the S position. It tried to turn round and strike him.

'Sandy has to be very careful with this snake – the venom of the king cobra, boys and girls, is strong enough to kill an elephant. One mistake and Sandy would be dead within just one hour.'

'Lucy,' I said again, and she turned her head and looked at me very closely, searching for something which she obviously found, because in that moment I knew she knew.

Raj mesmerized the snake by prancing in front of it. Sandy held the rear of the snake as it lunged at Raj, who was forced to dive off the concrete island into the crocodile moat to avoid being struck. 'That was close, Raj,' said the Tannoy.

'I knew the moment I saw you. We're quits,' said Lucy, turning away from me again.

'But where's Pinocchio, boys and girls?'

'Let's not talk about it again,' she said.

'Into the frying pan and into the fire, Raj. But there's Musa on hand to palm him off. Dinner time isn't until later, Pinocchio, you know that.'

'It's not what you—' I started to say.

'Ever,' said Lucy. 'But don't ever test me again, Kit.'

30 January 2001

The day after my dad's wedding, two and a half weeks after we got back and a week after we moved into this new flat in Ealing, I'd lain on the sofa all day with a hangover. When Lucy came back from the shops she had a stomach ache, too, and claimed to have nearly passed out buying our dinner in Waitrose.

We had already acquired set positions in the new living room, just like we'd picked different sides of the bed. Lucy sat in the armchair and I lay on the sofa. The advantage of the sofa is you can stretch out. The advantage of the armchair is its proximity to the radiator. For the rest of the day and night we did nothing. Lucy slept in the bedroom for a while after dinner, unable to finish the *Observer Life* magazine, demonstrating how poorly she was, and I got sucked into the World Darts Championships.

Eventually we got a video from Blockbuster. It was very cold and the pavement was icy and we walked back to the flat hand in hand so slowly that at the same moment we both had a thought about what it would be like to grow old together. 'It's quite nice,' I said.

'There's no hurrying,' said Lucy, 'you look around, watch your step. You look forward to returning home to put the fire on.'

I invited Lucy over to the sofa when we got back so I could hug her. 'Would you like to come and sit next to me?' Lucy said she would and for the rest of the night we fought each other for leg room, me every now and again commanding her to do things for me in the voice I use when we're getting on and know she isn't going to shout at me. She had done my ironing, toasted me three crumpets and brought me in two cups of tea. On these sorts of days I become schoolboyish and childishly excited about these little treats, overpraising Lucy for her effort initially, but then immediately afterwards, when I have softened her up and she has told me just how good she is to me, ordering her to do other tasks. When she'd finished the ironing and was flushed red from the steam she came and lay on top of me. We hugged each other and then she said, 'You're the luckiest man in Ealing. I bet nobody else gets their shirts ironed for them.' I said I knew that, and then, 'Thank you, whore.'

Lucy pulled away laughing, then scolded me. 'I want you to stop that,' she said. It was our first new running joke that I was attempting to persuade her to allow me to call her a whore by overusing the word and slotting it into conversations at inappropriate moments. We pretended that we hoped we'd get so used to the word as a term of endearment that it would lead to an embarrassing social occasion when I called her a whore off-handedly and she responded to it so blithely everybody would look at us shocked and we'd both feel ashamed at how they perceived our relationship and my obvious mistreatment of her.

Lucy didn't scold me much, though, and I loved her a lot that day. Not just because she'd done lots of things for me and allowed me to call her a whore. She was wearing my white fleece with the blue arm stripe that was much too big for her. She had her glasses on, which I always prefer to her contacts. I like her face when she's in a happy mood: it's very expressive. Lucy's grin is huge and cheeky and her laugh jerks her blond hair back.

Later we watched the video, *Casino*. Lucy's head was on my shoulder and I played an unspoken game of putting my finger in the corner of her mouth. To stop me Lucy would purse her lips, holding them tightly shut. Then I lay on her rounded shoulder and we teased each other about who was the most ill. 'Admit it,' Lucy said after I made a joke, 'you're feeling better. I'm more ill than you.'

'Maybe the Nurofen's kicked in,' I said. 'My head's still pounding, though. I'm not better.'

About an hour later Lucy tried to tickle me. 'Admit it,' I said, 'you're better.'

She started laughing.

'That's the price you pay for having a good time,' I said.

At midnight we moved the video into the bedroom to watch the final hour of the film. When I locked the front door I felt a strange satisfaction and Lucy felt it too. 'That's it, no more callers,' she said.

I got into the trendy pyjamas she'd bought me as a Christmas present in Thailand, and Lucy changed into hers and we hugged periodically during the non-violent sections and told each other to be careful. This phrase more than anything is always what's represented the pinnacle of our love. We never really say, 'I love you.' What we say is, 'Please, *please* be careful.' The phrase is really saying 'I couldn't manage without you.'

I pretended to be Joe Pesci for a little while during the film, calling Lucy a motherfucker and accusing her of showing me no respect because my pyjama top hadn't been under my pillow like normal. Then, after a little hugging and rolling, we held hands across the bed, and almost simultaneously started laughing. It struck us at the same moment how ridiculous it was that we lived together. How criminal it was that Lucy and I, obviously two children, could have been left for so long to fend for ourselves. It felt like some great Social Services story – 'Their parents left them and they fed and clothed themselves for years before anybody knew.'

Sitting under the three duvets that Lucy always insists we have because the weight of them makes her feel safe, with one of her feet poking out on top, acting as a sort of snorkel to the cooler air, I leaned over and asked her to play the S and C game with me. This is word association with the twist that you're not allowed to say any words that start with S or C. The secret is speed of thought and being able to trap the other person. I thought I could remember all the prepared traps, but I couldn't.

'Epsom.'

'Er . . . salts. Shit, I should have said Downs. I forgot that one.' Then the hair on the back of my neck stood up as I started it. 'Will,' I said.

'Inheritance,' she said.

'You,' I said.

'Ram,' she said.

'Marry me,' I said.

There was a tremendous pause.

'Yes,' said Lucy.

And we both started to cry.

6 April 2001

It was a week after I'd proposed. I phoned Dad to double-check that the completion date for the sale of Beech Road was still the day after next. Then I arranged my cuttings into a file for my interview at the Brighton *Argus* the next day and at around midday the garage phoned to say I could pick up Danny's car – they'd fixed the exhaust. The original plan had been to go to Beech Road the next day, the last day before completion. On the bus to the garage I decided with the car fixed I might as well go that day.

On the way I fiddled with the radio, trying to find the Donna Lewis song that reminds me of Danny to get me in the mood, but I couldn't. Then, checking to see who'd hooted me from behind on the Chiswick roundabout, I noticed Danny's old brown leather glove on the back seat. It gave me quite a shock – I'd been driving the car for a while and hadn't seen it before. It must have worked its way to the surface during our move to Ealing. I reached round and put it on. Danny's hands are very small and it was very tight, so I couldn't bend my fingers properly round the wheel. But I thought, This is like holding Danny's hand.

Beech Road didn't look any different, but I tried to make everything register to make it feel like a real goodbye to the house. There was the noise of the drainage gutter down the centre of the drive when the wheel caught it, which sounds like a train going slowly over a sleeper. I found the old spare front-door key hanging up by the hosepipe stand next to the water barrel. It was black and rusted but still turned in the door. On the mat there was a phone bill addressed to the Mackenzies, a connection fee for the family moving in. I stepped over this and closed the front door behind me and that was another noise: the slam sound and then the echo afterwards of the pendulous horseshoe metal door-knocker hitting the wood of the door.

The house itself was almost totally bare except for a few

framed pictures on the walls – two of them Picassos, the artist Dad used to be very superstitious about, always having to see one of his paintings before he left for work to prevent bad things happening.

There was nothing in the living room at all. And then in the kitchen I looked at the cork board attached to the side of the freezer with all the numbers of local handymen Dad was leaving for the Mackenzies. I looked under one or two of the larger business cards without really thinking about what I was doing. Underneath one for a plumber were two recipes in Mum's writing, for stew and fishpie. For some reason, seeing Mum's writing about pouring water into a saucepan upset me. The kitchen clock was still up on the wall over the breakfast table and I took this down because it was so synonymous with the kitchen, and anyway we needed a clock for the kitchen in Ealing. The Mackenzies wouldn't miss it, I thought.

I went upstairs. In Dad's old room there was nothing. In the bathroom it was the same. The last room I looked through was Danny's and my old bedroom in the basement. Again I felt like I was looking for something without really knowing exactly what. I looked through the wardrobes, and then on top of them. I checked all the drawers in the bedside table that Dad had left behind because it wasn't a genuine antique. Then, at the last moment, as an afterthought, I swept my hand behind the built-in wardrobe mirror and my fingers touched something. My heart started beating fast and I squeezed my thumb and forefinger further down the back and managed to tease out a folded piece of paper. My hands were shaking now. It was folded twice. I opened it to see a list of four questions in Dad's writing and four answers in Sophie's, and at the top it said 'Christmas Quiz 1999, round one: popular culture'.

- Q 1. Why did David Hasselhoff have such a falling out with his father on *Baywatch*?

- A. Because Mitch wanted to pursue a career as a full-time lifeguard and his dad wanted him to be an architect.
- Q 2. Name the fifth Banana Split.
- A. Grober.
- Q 3. Why is Mike Baldwin's dad upset with his son?
- A. Because he had an affair with his girlfriend.
- Q 4. Who runs the coffee shop on *Neighbours* with Harold?
- A. Madge.

I sat down on the floor and pictured Sophie doing the quiz while Danny and I were at the pub that Christmas Eve night and it felt like the proper goodbye to the house I'd been looking for. I decided to take it away with me as a memento and then just as I was leaving the room a ray of sunlight came through the bedroom window and caught the piece of paper. For a second the paper was transparent: I saw writing on the other side and something went very cold in my stomach as I turned the paper over. It was Danny's suicide note.

> Dear Kit,
> We've left a few notes for each other behind this mirror down the years and it feels a bit weird this will be the last. I'm not going to give a great long explanation. If I could explain it, I don't think I'd be doing it. I don't know whether you know this, but I'm gay. It seems strange writing that down at last. I'm sick of trying to be somebody I'm not and am too exhausted to become someone else.
>
> Look after yourself, Kit-Kat. You always were my family.

I read it five more times, tears streaming down my face. I tried to imagine Danny that night after I'd gone to bed creeping into the room while Lucy and I were asleep. Not a knock then; the sound of the bedroom door closing behind him as he left. I wasn't angry. I didn't swear at him and call him a bastard.

The sun was shining brightly outside in the garden and I could hear the horses behind the back fence munching the grass that the farmer's tractor could never reach. I sat down in the Dad-trap by one of the rose bushes on the garden bench on which we'd once laid out all the animals. A wind came up from the bottom field and ruffled my hair and I felt Danny all around me. Out loud I said that I wouldn't be able to come again because the house was being sold. I told Danny I'd asked Lucy to marry me and that she'd accepted. I told him I would watch myself. I told him to watch himself, too. Then I took out my pack of playing cards from my jeans pocket. In doing this Danny's letter fell out. It looked strange lying in the earth among the roots of the rose bushes, like a little shrine almost, so I left it there. I shuffled the deck, closed my eyes and told Danny whatever card I pulled out and dropped into the soil would be my future. I said I would never cut the pack again. From now on I'd take my own decisions. I concentrated hard on Danny's face: on his wet brown eyes, his mouth turned down at the sides. I imagined him gripping my shoulders tightly to prove he could still have me in a fight, then I felt for the right card and dropped it. It fell face up and shocked me. The card that fell and lay side by side with the letter was Danny's card, the five of clubs. It hadn't crossed my mind that this would happen. I'd been expecting Lucy's.

I grabbed Sophie's Wellington boots that she'd asked me to collect for her from the cellar, and then I had a thought about uprooting one of the rose bushes to replant in our tiny garden in Ealing. It would be a little bit of the old house and of Danny and me in the old days. I touched the base of one root with my right hand. I felt the thorns and realized there was no way I'd be able to pull it out without cutting my hand to ribbons. Then suddenly I noticed: I still had Danny's old driving glove on my left hand. It made me laugh and I imagined Danny banging his forehead and saying, 'Doh,' as if he'd arranged all this and I'd been slow on the uptake. I grabbed the stem of a bush with my gloved hand and wrenched it free in one go.

*

Grange Grove isn't far from Beech Road – about five miles down the Aylesbury Road. I decided I may as well go there as I'd come this far. It was the first time I'd been back to Aylesbury since we'd moved house and even though that was only a couple of weeks ago, already it felt like the past. Every building and road triggered a memory of the *Bucks Gazette*, Lucy or Danny. There was the kebab van we used to go to that I once did a story about because the owner claimed he'd invented Britain's first vertical kebab and where we were for ever after given free food and wonderful bottles of Turkish lager. The Plough where we used to play the memory-master game, the Bell where we celebrated my twenty-fourth birthday, the blue-glass rhombus-shaped Equitable Life Building Danny was sacked from for stealing stationery, the railway station Danny cycled to on his bike with no brakes to commute to Chalfont, the multistorey we threw eggs at people from, the Lobster Pot where Lucy and I had first admitted we made up quotes. And, of course, the house itself on Tring Road I had to pass, which still looked exactly the same: the same black door, the same net curtains, the bin at the end of the front garden with the number 76 on it. I slowed down briefly, but didn't stop.

The front door of the unit was locked and I pressed the buzzer. One of the volunteers fetched Beverly, the unit manager, but when she arrived she told me that Danny wasn't in the unit that afternoon – he was at the Headway group a few miles up the road. 'He's been going for two weeks,' she said. 'Didn't you know?'

I said I'd been away and she clocked my fading tan, nodded and gave me directions.

It wasn't an easy place to spot. It didn't look anything like a mental institution or even a hospital, just a very bog-standard house in a very ordinary cul-de-sac. There was no big sign outside saying what it was – just a discreet notice above the door the size of a car number plate that said, 'Headway', in black on yellow. I pulled up and parked by a row of garages and saw three people smoking outside. Their frank stares showed me I'd got the right place.

Taylor was the first person with a brain injury I spoke to. Paul, a volunteer, let me in and suddenly Taylor was in front of me in his wheelchair. The wheelchair was matt black all over with a joystick on one arm that Taylor used to manipulate the chair like a helicopter pilot with one finger. On one side of the chair there was a yellow sign fastened to the seat with string which read: 'My other vehicle's a Porsche.' I laughed at this.

There was a large tea machine in the corner of the first room you entered from the front door and lots of people were milling about it. I could hear a game of pool going on in the room that led off to the right. Another group sat round a large school dinner-table eating their packed lunches in front of me, and through a glass partition at the back I could see two men painting a rocking horse in a workshop. It looked like a youth club.

Taylor wanted to know where I was from, what I was doing there, and when I told him I was there to see Danny, my brother, he smiled and wheeled away shouting, 'Goldfish – your brother's here.'

Danny was in the pool room waiting his turn. Two other clients called Luke and Jim were at the table. Danny didn't recognize me right away and Taylor helped him out: 'Goldfish – it's your brother,' he said, and Danny looked to the side of me with his skewed eyes, half smiled and came towards me. He held out his hand uncertainly and I shook it. In the next moment I was hugging his head. Danny held my head with his one good arm. 'Grip me harder. Dig those fingers in,' I said, and he did.

'It's Goldfish's brother,' I heard Taylor say to Paul, who'd followed us into the room.

Danny pulled away and asked if I wanted a game of pool in his stop–start voice. During the game Danny talked to me and I listened. He was still surprisingly good at pool for someone who couldn't even look directly at the cueball and only had one good arm, and I let him beat me three times. Every time he came to the table I had to remind him what colour he was.

'Goldfish . . . that's what every-one . . . calls me – I can't re-mem-ber nothing,' he said.

Once I'd played him the best of five, he made it best of seven, then nine and finally eleven. He was goading me about how bad I was and in the end I started playing properly. The better I got the more he wanted me to carry on playing. 'I'm better . . . than every-one else . . . here – it's good . . . to have a proper game,' he said.

After a while, when he felt more comfortable, he started talking about us being kids again. 'This is my brother . . . we stole a car once together . . . in France,' he said to Luke and giggled. 'When we lived together . . . we were animals. Slugs . . . and mice . . . every-where.'

He had a new theory about why he was there, too. It was complete bollocks, of course, but in a way it felt like a bit of old Danny. He said he'd been injured in a car accident, and then became cagey, and whispered, 'It was . . . a stolen car.' His mate had been driving and had run away from the scene, leaving him there. 'That's why . . . I'm different – has that changed your mind . . . about Goldfish now?' he said. I said it hadn't.

Round the walls there were photographs of Headway clients in canoes and at parties, and joky speech bubbles were coming from the mouths of some of them, worse off than Danny, who couldn't talk: 'What's Jim up to?' . . . 'Don't bother with the solar eclipse, just look at Taylor's head' . . . 'Someone remind Danny whose turn it is to make the tea'.

Later Paul told me that Danny had been very aggressive at first. 'He was ready to explode. One day his voice started getting louder and louder as he was talking and by the afternoon he was calling everyone a twat and I thought he was about to hit someone. But he didn't and afterwards he apologized: "I normally only shout at my friends and family," he said. I could see the cogs turning in his mind, and then he said, "Which must mean you're my friends now." He's a special lad, that one.'

For some reason that made me feel incredibly proud, and when I left I asked Paul if I could come back and maybe help a little from time to time. 'Of course,' he said.

'I'll come next week, then, shall I?' I said.

'We're going away to Anglesey in the summer,' Paul said, as an afterthought just as I was getting into the car. 'Good to have someone to share the driving with.'

This was a few weeks ago now and I've seen Danny several times since. It's not like it was. It's never going to be, but I'm starting to think I can get used to it. Danny still spends most of his time going over old memories – it is amazing how much he remembers of when we were kids. But this doesn't make me sad any more. I don't know why – maybe it's the irony that's been there all the time but which I'm only just starting to appreciate. Now I know you can think a lot of bollocks in these sorts of situations – I've done my fair share of that over the last year and a half – but I can't help wondering about the symmetry of it all. Danny, who spent most of his early life creating memories, at the age twenty-seven is told he's never going to form any new ones. Is that a coincidence? I don't know, probably. But then again perhaps Danny always knew. Maybe that's why he lived his life the way he did: as a mad rush. Maybe he had a subconscious eye on the clock the whole time. Memories were going to be Danny's pension when he was old. In the end he just took early retirement.

As I said, it's bollocks, of course, but it's my bollocks and I'm sticking with it.

Danny was always my driving force. In a way he still is. Because I think I've got one eye on the clock now, too. You can wait around for life to happen to you, or you can make it happen yourself. You might not know if you're making the right decision, but that doesn't really matter because, right or wrong, what's the end result? Another memory.

As for Carlos. He *was* the best traveller, after all. He's still out there now. I occasionally get a reply-all email from him telling a hundred or so of what sound like his traveller friends where there's a cheap Internet place for under 100 baht or where to go for the next full-moon party. He sent me a photo last month from Koh Samui. He was outside a beach hut with a girl on his arm. He'd dyed his hair blond, had lost about two stones and looked like a member of a boy band. I had to laugh because I counted almost a dozen friendship bracelets up his arm.

Dominique, as far as I know, is still in Australia. She sent me back the Marguerite Duras book I left in Noosa. Inside the cover was a message: 'I'm still not sure.' I don't think she ever will be. I am, though.

And Tom's wrong about movies and adverts. They're not all shit. I watched one the other day for Sunny Delight. For the first time in my life it made me broody. The hassled father was telling his son off for not drinking enough milk. It gave me a pang, just a little one: Yes, I thought, one day I'd like to tell my children off for drinking something innutrious.